M.R. Mackenzie is the aut
crime fiction novels set ma
an ongoing series of mysteries featuring criminology lecturer
Anna Scavolini.

The first book in the series, *In the Silence*, was shortlisted for
the Bloody Scotland Scottish Crime Debut of the Year and
longlisted for the McIlvanney Prize for Scottish Crime Book
of the Year 2019.

Praise for M.R. Mackenzie

'One of the most consistently accomplished writers on the
current scene.' FINANCIAL TIMES

'Brings a fresh new voice to the field of Tartan Noir.'
JAMES OSWALD

'Writes with precision and passion.' CARO RAMSAY

'An immersive slow burn of a tale, peppered with
disquieting fire-crackers of revelation.' MORGAN CRY

'Mackenzie has come up with something that defies easy
definition and is truly original.' NB MAGAZINE

'Up there with the best contemporary authors working today.'
DAVID B. LYONS

Also by M.R. Mackenzie

The Anna Scavolini series
In the Silence
Cruel Summer
The Shadow Men
Women Who Kill
The Reckoning

Other novels
The Library Murders
Bury Your Secrets

Box sets
The Anna Scavolini Mysteries – Volume One

M.R. MACKENZIE

THE RECKONING

AN **ANNA SCAVOLINI** MYSTERY

Cover design by
Tim Barber / Dissect Designs

Typeset in 10pt Minion Pro

First published in 2024 by Mad House

ISBN: 978-1-9160948-7-1

Text version 1.0

mrmackenzieauthor.com
facebook.com/MRMackenzieAuthor
author.to/mrmackenzie

Cast of Characters

University staff

Professor **Anna Scavolini** (38) – Professor of Criminology; Course Director, Criminology MA, Kelvingrove University

Professor **Robert Leopold** (53) – Professor of Social Anthropology; Course Director, Social Anthropology MA, Kelvingrove University

Dr **Farah Hadid** (27) – Teaching Associate in Criminology, Kelvingrove University

Dr **Fraser Taggart** (45) – Head of School of Social and Political Sciences; Senior Lecturer in Political Theory, Kelvingrove University

Professor **Hugh MacLeish** (64) – Professor of Sociology; former Head of Department of Law and Social Sciences, Kelvingrove University

Dr **Marion Angus** (31) – Lecturer in Criminology, Glasgow Caledonian University; Anna's former student

Others

Zoe Callahan (37) – Anna's best friend and housemate

Jack Scavolini (3) – Anna's son

Paul Vasilico (41) – Detective Chief Inspector, Specialist Crime Unit; previously worked with Anna on the 'Shadow Men' case

Sal Brinkley (29) – Zoe's girlfriend

Ruby Burns (9) – Zoe's niece

Mandy Burns (27) – Former sex worker; Ruby's mother

You thought you were a mind, but you're a body, you thought you could have a public life, but your private life is here to sabotage you, you thought you had power so let us destroy you.

Rebecca Solnit

Prologue

'The problem with most people,' said Narinder, 'is, at their heart, they're fundamentally opposed to any sort of meaningful change, even when it would demonstrably improve their material circumstances.'

She spoke earnestly, emboldened by a combination of the alcohol in her bloodstream and a certain innate self-assuredness that one of her former schoolteachers had once remarked to another would *either take her far in life or bring her to a sharp and sticky end*. To date, it certainly hadn't held her back.

Judging by their expressions, her three friends were less than convinced, though not exactly surprised to be treated to such an impassioned declaration. They were perched on tall stools, clustered around a small, circular table a convenient stone's throw from the bar. Taken together, the low mood lighting and tasteful R&B music on the speaker system suggested a far mellower ambience than the one Narinder seemed intent on engendering.

'So you win them round gradually,' said Eva, her perfectly manicured fingers toying with her straw. 'You introduce reforms bit by bit, instead of spooking the horses by trying to introduce anarcho-communism overnight.'

Narinder gave a dismissive *pfff*. 'Gradualism's a total cul-de-sac. It's just a way for the establishment to keep us lefties in our place. And why do they keep getting away with it?'

'I've a feeling you're going to tell us,' said Soledad.

'Because we're too damn nice for our own good.'

The others shared surreptitious glances. Evidently, they weren't buying it.

'We always end up compromising,' Narinder went on, undeterred, 'while *they* never budge an inch. They keep telling us, "What you're asking for is too radical. Let's meet in the middle instead." And we go along with it like suckers, while the so-called middle shifts further and further to the right.'

'All right then, Miss "I've got a PhD in rabble-rousing".' Camille leaned her folded arms on the sliver of space on the table that wasn't crowded with empty and half-empty glasses. 'What's your solution?'

Narinder shrugged, as if the answer was obvious. 'We've gotta stop playing their game. Stop trying to achieve our aims through the systems they built with the express purpose of keeping us in our place.' She snorted. 'What, you think the Yanks or the Irish would've gotten their independence if they'd just kept asking nicely?'

Camille regarded Narinder with a look of incredulity. 'So you're saying . . . what? That we ought to abandon the ballot box and take up arms instead?'

Narinder shrugged. 'No pain, no gain.'

'But who gets to decide when violent action is justified?' insisted Eva, adamant that she wasn't going to let such an incendiary remark pass unchallenged. 'Certainly not the ones advocating for it. I reckon they might be just a *teeny* bit biased. You've got to have some sort of system that acts as a neutral arbiter – some way of laying down rules everyone respects.'

Narinder snorted. 'You think the ethno-nationalists and neo-fascists have any respect for the rules? That's half our problem. The other side are busy tearing up the rulebook while we cling to it out of desperation, kidding ourselves it still means anything.' She picked up her glass and gesticulated with it animatedly, as if to reinforce her point. 'Besides, there's such a thing as *moral* justice, even if it conflicts with the law.'

'But that's my point. *Everyone* thinks their cause is morally just. So did Pinochet. So did Hitler.'

'Well, if you have to invoke your actual *Hitler*, you've lost the argument before you've even started.'

Narinder fortified herself by downing the rest of her drink in a oner.

'I'm telling you,' she continued, setting her glass down with a thump, 'it's the radicals and extremists who see the world as it really is – *far* more clearly and accurately than the supposed moderates, most of whom are actually just fascists without the courage of their convictions. It's your so-called fanatics who actually understand what needs to change and have a plan for achieving it. Everything else is just waffle.'

This time, judging by the eye-rolls and groans of incredulity, there could be no doubting she'd comprehensively lost her audience.

'I think someone's had a few too many margaritas,' Eva muttered to Soledad.

'Hey,' said Narinder, 'I can't help it if I'm full of piss and vinegar.'

'But mostly piss,' said Soledad.

Eva and Camille both laughed uproariously. Even Narinder joined in somewhat sheepishly, recognising that she'd pushed her rhetoric to the point of absurdity.

'All right, all right.' She raised both hands in a plea for truce. 'Maybe I *am* getting just a tad carried away. But I'll tell you *one* thing for certain: the four of us'll be dead from old age before the politicians and armchair experts get off their arses and lift a finger to make this world a better place.'

This earned her a rousing chorus of agreement. On this, at least, they were on the same page.

'Well,' said Camille, folding her hands primly in her lap, 'at any rate, we've established one thing beyond a shadow of a doubt: when the revolution comes, it'll begin in the wine bars of the West End.'

The others whooped uproariously in agreement and clinked glasses, their earlier ructions forgotten.

They spilled out into the street in the wee hours, bundled up in their winter coats, their continuing sounds of merriment carrying in the still night air till Narinder's taxi pulled up. Following multiple rounds of full-bodied hugs and boozy kisses, accompanied by earnest pledges to get in at least one more night out before the year's end, Narinder tumbled into the back seat, serenaded on her way by a chorus of farewells.

As the cab pulled away, Eva snapped a photo of the departing licence plate and texted it to the rest of the group. An excessive precaution, perhaps – but then, no one ever came to regret being too careful.

* * *

Less than half an hour later, Narinder let herself into the communal hallway of the converted sandstone townhouse in Shawlands where she and her flatmate lived. There, she got out her phone, opened the WhatsApp group she shared with her three friends, and tapped out a message:

Home safe and unmolested. Sweet dreams my gorgeous bitches XOXO

She headed up to the third floor and let herself into the small, cluttered flat. She locked the door behind her, then hung up her coat, kicked off her heels and once more inspected her phone. The lock screen informed her that it was 2.38 a.m. She groaned inwardly, before setting her alarm for 7.30. She had a supervision meeting at 9 a.m. sharp. Who in their right mind scheduled a meeting for nine o'clock on a Monday morning? A sadist, that's who.

Barefoot, she sloped through to the kitchen, grabbed a bottle of mineral water from the fridge and headed through to her bedroom, necking from the open bottle. Having drunk enough to quell her raging thirst, she set it down on the nightstand and began to get ready for bed.

As she struggled with the zip at the back of her sequin top, she failed to notice the lithe figure dressed from head to foot in black slipping out from behind the open door and making his silent way across the floor towards her.

'Fucksake,' she muttered, her fingers once again failing to make purchase on the pesky zip.

Behind her, a floorboard creaked.

Spinning around, she found herself staring into two piercing eyes, drilling into her through the narrow slit of a balaclava. She only managed to let out a brief, frightened squeak before a hand clamped over her mouth.

The figure flung her backwards onto the bed, straddling her before she had time to recover. With his weight bearing down on her midriff, he continued to cover her mouth, the force of his hand pressing the inside of her upper lip into her teeth. Her nostrils flared. She tasted the metallic tang of blood. He leaned in close, their noses almost touching, his eyes glinting in the half-light from the bedside lamp.

A powerless scream rose up from her diaphragm and escaped through her nose in a near-silent exhalation of air.

Seconds later, his fist connected with the side of her head, and her vision exploded in a kaleidoscope of stars.

PART ONE

A STORM IS COMING

1

Monday 28 October

'This is Farah Hadid. Unfortunately, I'm unavailable right now. Please leave a message and I'll respond when I am able.'

Anna, standing in the corridor with her phone clamped to her ear, waited for the sharp beep before speaking.

'Farah, it's me again, still wondering where you've got to.'

She glanced over her shoulder as the door to the meeting room opened and her boss, Fraser Taggart, leaned out, shooting her a questioning look. She nodded an acknowledgement, raising an index finger to signify 'one minute'.

'Look,' she went on, as Fraser ducked back inside, 'they're ready to get started. I'm going to have to go in. If you get this . . . I don't know, just get here as soon as you can. I'll stall them for as long as possible. I . . .' She hesitated. 'I hope everything's OK.'

She ended the call, took a deep breath, steeling herself, then headed in to join the others.

In total, there were fifteen women and men already seated at the long conference table that took up the bulk of the small, airless room – all senior figures within the School of Social and Political Sciences. Fraser had already assumed his position at the head of the table. Lanky, sandy-haired and dressed in an overly tight shirt with rolled-up sleeves, he was forty-five but seemingly determined to pass for at least a decade younger. On a good day, he was just about able to pull it off. He biked

9

everywhere and was frequently to be seen power-walking along the corridor to his office first thing in the morning, clad from head to toe in Lycra. To Anna, he gave off the whiff of someone who was trying overly hard to impress someone – though who that might be was anyone's guess.

In stark contrast, the occupant of the seat nearest the door was making no effort to project an air of anything other than disdain for the whole enterprise. Sporting a thick shock of black, oily hair and dressed in a sports jacket and an unironed, open-neck shirt that struggled to restrain his bulging belly, Robert Leopold, the recently appointed Professor of Social Anthropology, sat with one short, stubby leg folded over the other, scrolling on his phone with a pudgy index finger. He briefly glanced up at Anna before returning his attention to the glowing screen.

'Good of you to join us, Anna,' said Fraser. 'Everything all right?'

It was possible he was being sarcastic, but Anna couldn't detect any hint of it in either his voice or his expression of mild curiosity.

She nodded tightly. 'All good.'

There was, she noticed, an empty chair next to Leopold – in fact, the only remaining one at the table. She glanced at Fraser, politely waiting for her to take a seat, and for a brief moment came very close to doing so. Then, as Leopold absentmindedly tucked his finger behind his ear and began to scratch, her resolve strengthened.

Pointedly ignoring the empty seat, she instead crossed to the other side of the room and lifted a chair from the pile of spares stacked in the corner. An awkward silence ensued, punctuated by the occasional cough, as two of Anna's colleagues shifted sideways to make room for her. If Leopold felt in any way snubbed, he gave no sign, continuing to scroll contentedly while Anna slid into her seat and shrugged off her coat.

'Sorry,' she muttered, not sure who she was actually apologising to – Fraser, the two colleagues she'd displaced, or the room in general.

Fraser cleared his throat. 'Right. Well, let's make some progress, shall we? First item on the agenda: the upcoming industrial action by the university's teaching associates. Obviously, minimising disruption as much as possible is paramount, so I trust you're all putting contingency plans in place to ensure the delivery of teaching is unaffected.'

'Do we have any feel for what proportion of the TAs will be taking part?'

asked Craig Eckhart, course director of the Economic and Social History MA.

'The vote in favour was sixty-eight percent,' replied Fraser, 'and I imagine we should be anticipating a participation rate closer to one hundred. The idea of a strike may not be a universally popular one, but that doesn't mean those who voted "No" won't support it now that a democratic decision has been reached. The important thing is that, as far as possible, we maintain continuity of delivery . . .'

And on he continued to drone, a past master in the art of talking a great deal while saying very little. These meetings, held at 10 a.m. every Monday, had been his brainwave, initiated shortly after he assumed the vaunted position of Head of School. Intended to foster greater communication and cooperation between the different disciplines that had been unceremoniously folded into the umbrella of Social and Political Sciences, in reality they simply succeeded in sucking up valuable time that would have been better devoted to more productive matters, such as tackling the reams of additional admin they all seemed to have accrued ever since the 'Great Restructuring'.

As Fraser continued to pontificate, seemingly inexhaustible in his drive to find new ways to reiterate the same stultifyingly obvious talking points, Anna chanced a glance in Leopold's direction. He continued to pay more attention to his phone than to Fraser, occasionally pausing from scrolling to tap out a message, his thick fingers moving with surprising dexterity. She wondered that he dared be so blatant about his disinterest – but then, past experience had taught her that he was capable of getting away with just about everything short of murder.

'. . . and hope for a speedy resolution that satisfies both sides in this dispute,' concluded Fraser, having, it seemed, finally run out of banalities.

'It seems to me,' declared Leopold, without looking up, 'that someone should consider calling their bluff.'

And now, all of a sudden, everyone was looking at him. He'd always, to Anna's mind, had an infuriating ability to effortlessly command attention without so much as lifting a pinkie – of which she was more than slightly envious.

'Call whose bluff?' said Laura Pickering, the softly spoken Reader in Public Policy.

'The TAs,' said Leopold, as if it was obvious.

Everyone waited for him to elaborate.

'The university,' he continued in his languid, RP-inflected drawl, 'should refuse to give them any quarter. It's not as if they're irreplaceable.' He shrugged serenely. 'If they were at all concerned about providing their students with a decent standard of education, they'd soon put down their placards and get back to work.'

'So you think the university should blackmail them by appealing to their better nature?' said Anna icily, even as the voice at the back of her head screamed at her not to take the bait.

Leopold chuckled softly. He put down his phone and looked directly at Anna for the first time. 'I *think*,' he said, 'that the university should use whatever means are at its disposal to ensure it isn't held to ransom by a gaggle of far-left malcontents who don't know how good they've got it. It's time they learned there's a price to irresponsible agitation.'

'And what precisely about their "agitation" is irresponsible?'

An awkward silence ensued. Everyone, it seemed, was waiting to see how this would play out. At the head of the table, Fraser shifted uncomfortably but made no move to intervene.

Leopold treated Anna to a long, hard look – less one of contempt than of weary forbearance. 'The average salary for a full-time TA is – what? £26,000 a year? That might sound like chickenfeed to the people in this room, but tell some impoverished labourer toiling in a field in Somalia that a bunch of pampered academics in Northern Europe think earning above the national median wage constitutes unacceptable exploitation and prepare to watch their brains spontaneously combust. Come to that, tell it to the average refuse collector or supermarket worker right here in bonnie Glasgow.'

'I think—' Laura began.

'That is a *fatuous* argument,' snapped Anna, her voice cutting off Laura's tentative interjection.

She knew she shouldn't get involved in this exchange. Knew, too, that hers was precisely the response Leopold had been hoping to provoke – if not from her then from one of their other colleagues, outraged by his willingness to say the unsayable; his blatant disregard for the mores of the company in which he found himself. But she couldn't help herself. *If no one stands up to him,* she thought, *he'll think he can browbeat us into accepting his way of thinking on this and every other subject under the sun.*

'In fact,' she went on, as Leopold folded his arms and tilted his head sideways, regarding her with a look of wry amusement that she knew was deliberately designed to goad her, 'it's not even an argument. It's whataboutery. It's a ploy to shut down any form of rational discussion. It basically says no one has a right to object to their circumstances, *ever*, because someone, somewhere, has it worse. You might as well say, "You can't complain about having been assaulted as long as other people are still being murdered."'

Leopold gave a barely perceptible smirk but made no attempt to interrupt. The more rational part of Anna's mind knew he was leaving her enough rope to hang herself. But, at that moment, the part that was spoiling for a full-blown brawl simply didn't care.

'It *is* possible to care about more than one thing at a time,' she said, practically spitting the words out in her disdain. 'Just because something doesn't happen to be as bad as the worst thing you can possibly imagine doesn't mean we shouldn't still try to do something about it.'

And it's not just about the pay, she thought. The TAs' grievances were wide-ranging and varied, encompassing everything from an increasingly unrealistic workload to the fact that most of them were on term-time-only contracts, renewed on a yearly basis, to the chronic lack of opportunities to contribute to research or get onto the lecturer scale. The current dispute had been simmering for a long time, and she had nothing but sympathy for them and their cause.

But she felt she'd given him more than enough to chew over. She fell silent, quietly fuming – partly at him, and partly at herself for having allowed herself to get so riled up. Leopold said nothing, but his almost imperceptible eyebrow-raise served as an acknowledgement that her message had been received, if not accepted. He seemed almost impressed.

Fraser cleared his throat again, a wincing smile contorting his features. 'Ahem! Far be it from me to stymie a spirited airing of views, but might I suggest that this isn't, perhaps, the optimal venue for a debate on the rights and wrongs of industrial action? Provided everyone's amenable, I'd like to make a little progress, if I may . . . ?'

Anna muttered something that fell just short of actually being identifiable as an apology. Leopold shrugged amiably, as if the matter was neither here nor there to him.

Fraser beamed. 'Excellent. In that case, I suggest we park this matter for now and move to the next item on the agenda.' He paused to consult his notes. 'Anna, I promised we'd find time to hear your proposal for . . .' – he read from the page – '. . . "a qualitative study of the gendered outcomes for victims of crime in the West of Scotland". Well, I'm sure we're all looking forward to hearing what you have to say. The floor's yours.'

All eyes in the room were now on Anna. Something shifted in the pit of her stomach. She felt her cheeks flushing.

'Well . . .' She cleared her throat awkwardly. 'That is to say . . . I'm afraid there's a slight hitch.'

'Hitch?' Fraser appeared confused.

'Dr Hadid took the notes home with her at the weekend to prepare the slides for the presentation and . . . unfortunately, she appears to be indisposed.'

'Indisposed?' Leopold sounded incredulous. 'You mean she hasn't shown up?' He gave a gleeful smirk, playing to the gallery. 'Perhaps she's decided to go on strike ahead of schedule.'

No one laughed.

'I'm sure Dr Hadid has an entirely valid reason for her absence,' said Anna stiffly.

'And therein lies the danger in palming your responsibilities off on your skivvies. They invariably let you down at the most inopportune moments.'

With a monumental effort, Anna succeeded in ignoring this jibe. 'I can do the pitch from memory,' she told Fraser, failing to keep the faint ring of desperation from her voice. 'But without the slides or access to our notes . . .'

'No, no.' Fraser shook his head. 'It's unreasonable to expect you to recite the entire thing without a crib sheet. We'll park this for now, I think, and reschedule somewhere down the line.' He looked around at his assembled colleagues, his expression infuriatingly jovial. 'Well, it seems we have an opening in our itinerary. Anyone have any pressing business they'd like to discuss?'

Leopold, who'd resumed scrolling on his phone, glanced up. 'Actually, I'd like to float a proposition I've been mulling over for a while.'

Fraser shrugged. 'Does anyone have any objections?'

No one did, though Anna was sorely tempted.

Fraser gestured to Leopold. 'Floor's all yours, Robert.'

The others watched as, with the air of someone with all the time in the world, Leopold slid his phone into the inside pocket of his jacket and got to his feet.

'Ladies and gentlemen,' he announced, in his rich, sonorous baritone, 'it strikes me that there is a significant gap in our curriculum. Namely, the conspicuous absence of a Men's Studies course.'

Anna, who'd taken the opportunity to get out her own phone to check for missed calls from Farah, fumbled and dropped it. It hit the table with a thud, causing everyone to look in her direction.

'At the risk of sounding presumptuous,' said Leopold, with a note of amusement, 'I'm going to assume that wasn't an attempt by Professor Scavolini to signal her enthusiasm.'

'Not in so many words, no,' said Anna, her tone decidedly chilly.

'Then perhaps, before I lay out my arguments in *favour* of a Men's Studies programme, you might care to explain your objections.'

'Are you sure we have *time* for them all?'

It was her attempt at a joke, but she saw, from the strained expressions of her colleagues, that no one had taken it in that spirit. On the contrary, the overriding mood in the room seemed to be one of quiet dread, as they all braced for a showdown to which they'd prefer not to have to bear witness.

Leopold gestured to her, a picture of magnanimity. 'Please.'

She hadn't expected to be put on the spot like this. She was even less prepared for this than she had been for the now aborted research proposal, and she felt the heat of mortification spreading throughout her entire body.

'Well, I mean,' she began, desperately hoping it wasn't obvious to all and sundry just how unbelievably flustered she was, 'for a start, it would put a serious strain on severely limited resources. Surely I don't need to remind you that we already *have* a Gender Studies course?'

'One which singularly fails to acknowledge the unique disadvantages men face in today's society.'

'Disadvantages? You mean like not knowing what to do with all the power they hold?'

'I mean disadvantages such as the long-term psychological effects of a generation of boys being taught that they're guilty of original sin purely by virtue of having been born male in an increasingly gynocentric world.'

'You actually think that? You think the world is built to favour women? That's your *genuine* belief?'

She already knew it was, but she wanted to hear him state it unequivocally. To actively own it. But, rather than oblige her, he merely smiled at her placidly, as if the two of them were both in possession of some intimate knowledge to which the others weren't party.

She looked around, appealing to the gallery. 'Can someone explain to me why it is that those in positions of power always imagine themselves to be the victims, despite all evidence to the contrary?'

But before anyone had the opportunity to respond, Fraser was on his feet, hands raised placatingly. 'All right, all right. I'm not sure this is the most appropriate venue for a philosophical debate on the nature of systemic oppression.'

'Quite right.' Leopold dipped his head obsequiously. 'It was naïve of me to attempt to advance a proposition I knew would prove contentious for certain colleagues without expecting a certain amount of pushback. I'll submit my plan in writing through the usual channels, where it can be subjected to the usual levels of rigorous scrutiny.' He settled in his chair once more.

'Excellent.' Fraser smiled, relief practically radiating from him. Returning to his seat, he consulted his notes again. 'In that case, moving on to the next item on the agenda . . .'

The meeting adjourned shortly after eleven, having – as per usual – accomplished the square root of nothing. The moment Fraser called time, there was an immediate rush towards the door, as colleagues gathered their things and beat a hasty retreat, relieved to have completed their penance for another week.

Among the last to leave, Anna was on her feet and in the process of zipping up her bag when she sensed a presence by her side. She knew, even before she turned to face him, that it was Leopold.

'I enjoyed our little sparring match there,' he said, flashing a grin that showed off twin rows of veneers. 'A shame it was cut prematurely short.'

'I'm glad,' said Anna, not returning the smile.

'Yes.' Leopold chuckled softly, then glanced around, as if what he was about to say was unfit for modest ears. 'You know, if you ever fancy picking up from where we left off, there's an open invitation to come onto my podcast to debate the matter in greater depth. I'm sure my listeners would welcome such an exchange.'

Anna laughed dryly. 'I don't think so.' She shouldered her bag and turned to go.

'Why is that, out of curiosity?' Leopold's tone was one of bemusement, tinged with what sounded almost like regret.

She turned to face him again. 'Because I know how these "debates" usually go. You invite someone on with an opposing viewpoint, then proceed to caricature them and talk over them . . .' She shook her head defiantly. 'No thank you.'

'Well, if you're worried your views won't stand up to scrutiny . . .'

It was all Anna could do to stop herself from rolling her eyes in contempt. 'Please. If you think goading me is going to get you anywhere—'

'Perish the thought! I'm merely suggesting that someone who's secure in her opinions – as you most assuredly are – has nothing to fear from a rigorous exchange of ideas.'

'Except it won't *be* an exchange, will it?' said Anna, sticking her chin forward to accentuate her point. 'It'll be the usual circus, where your interviewees don't get a word in edgeways, and anything they *do* manage to say gets edited and clipped out of context.'

Leopold shook his head softly. 'You don't like me very much, do you?' He sounded more amused than hurt.

'I don't like what you stand for,' said Anna, which was also true.

'Regardless, I see no reason why we can't explore our differences of opinion through civil conversation.'

Anna straightened her spine, standing up to her full height as she met Leopold's gaze. He wasn't an especially tall man, but at five foot two, even people of average height towered over her, and the effect was amplified significantly if they stood uncomfortably close to her, as he was.

'Well, that's the difference between you and me, isn't it?' she said coolly. 'You've got nothing to lose. But, for some of us, your ideas are dangerous provocations masquerading as innocent questions, and I'll be damned if

17

I'm going to lend them credibility by "debating" them with you.' She shook her head. 'Find yourself another patsy, Professor Leopold. I'm not interested.'

With that, she turned and strode out.

Anna wound her way through the network of dimly lit, linoleum-floored corridors inside the Hutcheson Building, which, ever since the Great Restructuring, had been home to her and the other refugees from the former Department of Law and Social Sciences. But, of course, there were no longer any departments, only semi-autonomous 'subject areas', each falling under the broad umbrella of one of the university's twenty Schools, the groupings of which often seemed completely arbitrary, as if those calling the shots had had their hearts set on having exactly twenty, then shoehorned every subject into one of them, regardless of how unnatural a fit it proved.

For Anna, the building – a stark, brutalist monstrosity from the 1960s – served as an apt metaphor for the changing fortunes of her former department. Once housed in the grandeur of the university's historic main building, it now felt as if she and her colleagues had been put out to pasture – exiled to a concrete high-rise on the north-western outskirts of the campus that bore more than a passing resemblance to the social housing commonly found in the former Eastern Bloc.

She wondered if that made her an insufferable snob. *Someone* had to be based out here, and she and her colleagues could hardly profess to hold a greater claim to their former, considerably more ostentatious lodgings than any other department . . . sorry, *School*. Still, the optics were difficult to ignore – to say nothing of the myriad inconveniences that accompanied the move, including a pronounced lack of office space and a heating system that was perpetually malfunctioning, meaning the place was invariably either unbearably hot or cold enough to freeze the very blood in your veins.

As she turned onto the corridor leading to her own cramped office, she fished out her phone and rang Farah's number again. She wasn't really expecting a response, and was therefore unprepared for the click, followed by the husky voice of her star TA and de facto second-in-command.

'Hello? Anna?'

'Farah? Are you OK?' Anna came to a halt, pressing herself against the wall to make room for a couple of colleagues as they passed her in the narrow walkway. 'I've been trying to get you for nearly two hours. The meeting—'

'The presentation! Oh, *putain de merde . . .*'

'What's wrong? Where are you?'

'One moment.'

There was a burst of incomprehensible speech on what sounded like a loudspeaker at the other end of the line, which, after a moment, became more muffled as Farah presumably covered the mouthpiece. Anna heard footsteps, followed by the voice on the speaker growing more distant. When Farah spoke again, there was a tremor in her voice which Anna hadn't noticed before.

'Anna, I'm so sorry. I completely forgot. I'm at the hospital. It's . . . Oh God . . .'

As, bit by halting bit, she explained the situation, Anna felt the muscles in her jaw growing increasingly tight.

2

Anna hurried into the crowded reception area of the Accident & Emergency department at the imaginatively named Queen Elizabeth University Hospital, eyes skimming over the various signs with their directions to different departments. The bold, white text; the harsh, fluorescent lighting; the tumult of voices – it all amounted to sensory overload, multiple stimuli competing for her attention.

As she continued to cast around, the door at the end the corridor opened and a woman in her mid-twenties emerged, nose buried in her phone. With her short, dark curls and round, wire rim glasses, plus her ubiquitous black polo neck sweater and high-waisted slacks, Farah Hadid had an unassuming quality, but her distinctive fashion sense nonetheless made her easy to spot in a crowd. Looking up from her phone, she noticed Anna and greeted her with a distracted half-wave. Quickening her pace, Anna hurried towards her.

They met in the middle of the corridor, Anna instinctively offering up her cheek for the French-style kiss that was Farah's default method of greeting. The resulting double-cheeked peck had more than an air of going through the motions about it, Farah's mind clearly on other matters.

'They took her upstairs to X-ray her face,' Farah explained, once they'd dispensed with the formalities. 'Oh, Anna, it's so horrible. I spent the night with Émile and only went back to the flat in the morning to pick up some essays I'd been marking . . .' Her hand hovered in front of her nose in anticipation of tears. 'And when I got there she was just . . .'

That was as far as she got. Covering her mouth with her hand, she began to sob. Anna automatically folded her into her arms. She continued to hold Farah until her sobs subsided, before releasing her.

Straightening up, Farah gave a rueful grimace. 'Look at me, behaving as if it was me it happened to.'

Anna shook her head, dismissing this as an irrelevance. She looked Farah up and down.

'You going to be OK?' she said gently.

Farah nodded tightly, eyes still glistening.

Anna led her over to a relatively quiet corner next to a vending machine sporting an 'OUT OF ORDER' notice.

'You feel up to talking about it?' she asked, as Farah, her glasses in one hand, dabbed a tissue at her eyes with the other.

'I think so.'

'What exactly *happened*?'

But before Farah could respond, they heard heavy footsteps striding towards them. Anna turned to see a large, red-faced man in a Celtic T-shirt heading their way. He came to a halt facing them and ran a hand through his hair, the agitation coming off him in waves.

'Can you believe this fucking place?' he asked, of no one in particular. 'Gotta walk half a mile just to find a fucking toilet.'

Farah turned to Anna. 'You know Callum? Narinder's boyfriend?'

Anna nodded distantly. She knew Callum to look at, but would hardly describe them as acquaintances, let alone friends. Privately, she'd always viewed him and Narinder as the most mismatched couple she'd ever met. She couldn't think of a single thing they had in common. She recognised that this was hardly the time and place for such thoughts, and yet she found it impossible to shake the feeling that Callum's presence was unlikely to have a positive impact on the situation.

'She not back yet?' Callum directed this particular question at Farah. 'Fuck they doing with her?'

'I'm sure you'd prefer them to be thorough,' said Anna levelly.

'Dunno what the fuck they're playing at, more like. Fucking doctors, think they know everything.'

He began to pace back and forth, swinging his arms like a pair of thick, meaty flails. Anna and Farah both watched him warily.

After a few seconds, he stopped abruptly and swung round to face them. 'D'yous know they haven't even let me see her?'

'They'll let us *all* see her as soon as she gets back from X-ray,' said Farah soothingly.

'And when the fuck's that gonna be, huh? Doesnae take a half a fucking hour to take some pictures.'

'Perhaps you'd like to get something to eat,' Anna suggested, 'or something to drink?' She gestured to the vending machine, then remembered it was out of order. 'Something to take your mind off it while you wait.'

'I don't *want* something to fucking eat!' Callum bellowed.

He slammed the machine with his fist, causing both Anna and Farah to flinch involuntarily. Anna took a precautionary step backwards. She was fairly sure he didn't pose a threat to them, but all the same, it was obvious he was in an unpredictable frame of mind, and hardly predisposed towards behaving rationally.

'All right, all right.' With what was clearly considerable effort, Callum succeeded in moderating his tone. 'I'm sorry, yeah? It's just . . .' He waved his hand helplessly. 'This fucking place, yeah?'

Anna smiled and nodded sympathetically, though she drew the line at hugging *him*.

At that moment, she once again heard the sound of approaching footsteps. As one, they turned to see a woman in her early thirties approaching. She wore green scrubs and had dark bags under her eyes that bore more than a passing resemblance to bruises.

'Doctor,' said Farah. They'd evidently met already. 'How is she?'

The woman, whose name badge identified her as Martha Keller, ran a hand through her lank hair. 'Narinder's doing OK, on balance. She has various fractures to her cheekbones and upper jaw, and we're a bit concerned about the reduced vision in her right eye, but we'll continue to monitor that over the next twenty-four hours to see if it improves.' She lowered her voice. 'There's also the matter of the, um, intimate injuries she suffered. There was some tearing, as well as a small amount of internal bleeding.'

Anna and Farah glanced at one another. Both of them implicitly understood what they were being told.

'On a more positive note, there doesn't appear to be any bleeding on the brain,' said the doctor, her voice returning to its normal volume. 'I don't, for a second, wish to downplay the severity of the ordeal she experienced, but, all things considered, things could have been considerably worse.' She gave them a tight, but encouraging, smile.

Callum, who gave the impression of not having taken any of this in, nodded impatiently. 'Right. So when can I see her?'

Dr Keller turned to him. 'You'll be Callum, then? She's been asking after you. Saying, "Is Callum here yet?" every five minutes.' She smiled. 'I can take you through to her now if you like. This way.'

She led them through two sets of double doors to the main treatment area, then past a long row of cubicles until they came to one with its curtains closed. Gesturing for them to wait, she opened the curtain a crack and poked her head in.

'Narinder, got some people here to see you,' she said brightly.

She withdrew her head and pulled back the curtain to reveal Narinder, sitting upright on a trolley in a hospital gown. Her face was awash with livid bruises, both eyes swollen almost completely shut. She blinked painfully, clearly struggling to see.

'Rindy?' said Callum. The word came out as barely a whisper.

'Callum?' said Narinder. 'Is that you?'

'Jesus Christ,' Callum murmured.

Dr Keller shot a warning look in his direction. 'Mr Finnie . . .'

'What the fuck did they *do* to her?' he bellowed, somewhere between anger and disbelief.

'Cal?' Narinder's voice was a frightened whimper.

Dr Keller glared daggers at Callum. 'What's the matter with you?' she hissed.

'What's the matter with *me*?' Callum stared at her in disbelief. He gesticulated towards Narinder with his entire arm. 'LOOK AT THE FUCKING STATE OF HER!'

This was too much for Narinder. She began to cry, her hands hovering in front of her swollen face, unable to bury it in them.

'*Mister* Finnie!' exclaimed Dr Keller, unable to hide her fury. Placing herself in front of Narinder like a human shield, she brought her face close to Callum's. 'You're of no use to anyone in this state. If you can't keep your emotions in check, I'm going to have to ask you to leave.'

For a moment, Callum just stared at her, as if he couldn't believe what he was hearing. Then his expression hardened. His fists tightened.

'I'm gonnae kill 'em,' he muttered. 'I'm gonnae kill those fucking bastards. They're not gonnae get away with this.' He raised his voice, directing his words at no one in particular. 'Y'hear me? I'm gonnae sort this!'

With that, he turned on his heel and stormed out, the cubicle curtains billowing behind him.

'Cal!' Narinder wailed, tears streaming down her cheeks.

But it was no use. Callum continued down the corridor, slammed through the double doors and was lost from view.

As Narinder sobbed uncontrollably, Farah snapped into action. Brushing past Dr Keller, she hurried into the cubicle and enveloped Narinder in her arms, whispering soft reassurances. Anna and Dr Keller remained side by side, watching them – both, Anna sensed, feeling somewhat surplus to requirements.

Slowly, Narinder's sobs subsided. She lifted her head from Farah's shoulder, her puckered eyelids blinking in confusion as her gaze fell on Anna.

'Anna.' Her tone was one of surprise. 'You came.'

'Yes,' agreed Anna, somewhat helplessly. She fancied now wasn't the time to clarify that she'd come primarily for Farah's sake.

Narinder gestured to her face. 'I apologise for the state of this old thing,' she said, halfheartedly attempting to inject some levity. 'If I'd known I'd be receiving visitors, I'd've put on my war paint.'

Anna smiled dutifully. 'That's all right.'

As Farah remained by Narinder's side, an arm wrapped protectively around her shoulders, Dr Keller drew Anna to one side and addressed her in a low voice.

'We'll be moving Narinder upstairs as soon as a bed's available. She'll be with us for at least twenty-four hours, so she'll need some things from home – pyjamas, toiletries and whatnot. Is that something you can arrange?'

'Um . . .' Farah relinquished her hold on Narinder and took a step forward. 'It would make more sense if I went, perhaps? I know what to look for, and . . .' She shrugged. 'Well, I expect the police will more likely let me in.'

Anna nodded. Farah's proposal made a great deal of sense . . . though she sensed what was coming next.

'Though I don't like the thought of leaving her on her own,' Farah admitted, nodding surreptitiously in Narinder's direction.

'In that case,' said Anna, 'you go and I'll stay.'

Farah looked at her, relief vying with uncertainty. 'You're sure?'

In truth, Anna *wasn't* sure – not really. She was acutely aware that she'd run out of work on what was invariably the busiest day of the week, leaving behind a mountain of emails that had come in over the weekend, to say nothing of the teaching commitments she had to prepare for. But she could hardly say any of this – not when weighed against what Narinder was going through.

'Of course,' she said firmly. 'Go. The sooner you're out of here, the sooner you'll be back.' She fished her car keys out of her bag. 'Here. Take the Skoda. It's in the short stay car park.'

Farah accepted the keys with a smile of thanks, then turned to Narinder and, in a soft voice, explained where she was going. Narinder nodded stoically. For now, at any rate, she was succeeding in keeping the tears at bay. Farah leaned over to give her hand a brief squeeze, then headed off, flashing Anna a last look of gratitude as she went.

Dr Keller jerked a thumb over her shoulder. 'I'll just go and see how that bed's coming along.' Then she too vacated the cubicle, leaving Anna and Narinder alone together.

An awkward silence unfolded. Anna had met Narinder on roughly half a dozen previous occasions, but, all told, she knew next to nothing about her, other than that she was Farah's flatmate and was studying for a Masters in one of the social science fields. Until today, they'd never had cause to be alone together for more than a few minutes, and Anna now found herself at a loss for words. She wasn't great at making small talk at the best of times, and the current situation was about as far from normal as it was possible to get.

'So tell me,' Narinder broke the silence, 'do I really look as bad as all that?' She managed a small smile. 'You can be honest with me.'

Anna looked at her helplessly, not knowing what to say.

Narinder laughed humourlessly. 'I knew it. Well, least I've got my winning personality to fall back on, huh?'

Anna smiled out of obligation.

Narinder sighed, folding her hands in her lap. 'Sorry about Cal. His heart's in the right place, but he's never been good at dealing with stress.'

'I'm sure he'll be back once he's calmed down a bit.'

'I just hope he doesn't do something stupid.'

'It'll be fine,' said Anna, without much confidence.

The curtain opened a crack and a young, gawky-looking nurse with thick glasses poked her head in. 'Hi, Narinder,' she said, with a bright smile. 'How're you feeling? Um, there's a couple of police officers here to see you if you're up to it.'

Narinder looked confused. 'I already *gave* a statement to the police.'

'Oh, right.' The nurse was evidently thrown by this. 'Well, I, um, think these ones are specialists or something? One's a *Detective Chief Inspector*,' she added, as if the very words were supposed to inspire awe.

Narinder shrugged wearily, as if she didn't care either way. 'All right. Send 'em in.'

The nurse pulled back the curtain and stepped aside as a woman and man in plain clothes entered.

The woman, who looked to be barely in her twenties, had a slight, androgynous build and was clearly aiming for 'Alternative' with a capital 'A': bleached fohawk hair; denim jacket; black skinny jeans, ripped at the knees; Converse shoes.

The man was her polar opposite in every respect. Around forty years old, he was tall, clean-cut and classically handsome – a Greco-Roman statue in a fitted suit.

'Hello, Narinder,' he said, giving her a friendly nod. 'Sorry to hear you've been in the wars.'

He turned to Anna, who, since the moment he'd walked in, had been staring at him with a mixture of horror, disbelief and no small amount of righteous outrage. He dipped his head in acknowledgement, a small smile on his flawless lips.

'Hello, Anna,' said Detective Chief Inspector Paul Vasilico.

3

Anna watched, still stunned into silence, as Vasilico produced his police ID and showed it to Narinder.

'I'm DCI Vasilico. This is my colleague, DS Kirk.'

Kirk flashed her own ID, along with a smile. 'Alex,' she clarified.

'We're both with the Specialist Crime Unit,' Vasilico went on, addressing Narinder as if Anna wasn't there. 'We deal with the cases that require just a bit more TLC than your average, run-of-the-mill investigation. If it's all right with you, we'd like to ask you some questions about what happened to you last night.'

Anna saw, from the tensing of Narinder's shoulders, just how she felt about the prospect of reliving the whole ordeal yet again.

Kirk took a couple of steps towards her, wincing sympathetically. 'We know it sucks, and we know you already spoke to the plods, but it'd be *really* helpful if you could take us through everything just once more. The sooner you talk about it, the better your recall's gonna be – and if we do this now, it means we'll be outta your hair lickety-split and then you can get some shut-eye. Whaddaya say?'

Narinder exhaled heavily and nodded. 'OK.'

Kirk smiled encouragingly. 'OK.' She nodded towards the trolley. 'Mind if I perch there?'

Narinder shook her head and drew her legs up, making room.

Kirk clambered onto the bottom end of the trolley and sat cross-legged, facing Narinder. It was an oddly intimate arrangement and one Anna suspected she wouldn't have been entirely comfortable with had she been in Narinder's shoes. But Narinder didn't seem to mind – or, if she did, was too polite to say so. She waited patiently as Kirk produced a small notebook and pen from the inner pocket of her denim jacket and began to flick through it, searching for a blank page.

'I'll give you some space,' said Anna, and made to leave.

Narinder's hand shot out, grabbing her arm. Anna turned as the other woman gazed up at her through her swollen eyelids.

'No,' she said. 'Stay. Please.'

There was a pleading note in her voice.

For a moment, Anna hesitated, torn, before her sense of duty won out.

'Of course,' she said, as if there had never been any doubt in the matter.

She moved to Narinder's side – partly as a show of solidarity, partly to put some distance between herself and Vasilico. Vasilico, who remained standing by the curtain, arms folded behind his back, gave no indication of having noticed – or, if he had, of being in any way bothered.

Kirk smiled encouragingly at Narinder again. 'Why don't you tell me a bit about yourself, Narinder? What is it you do?'

Narinder, somewhat thrown by the question, gave the closest thing she could currently manage to a frown. 'I'm a student.'

'Oh yeah? Whatcha studying?'

'I'm doing a Masters in Global Health Policy.'

'Global Health Policy. Nice.' Kirk nodded approvingly. 'That's a good, solid, proper degree, not like Harry Potter Studies or whatever.' She made a show of looking suddenly worried. 'No one here's doing Harry Potter Studies, are they?'

Anna forced a smile and shook her head. In the process, she inadvertently met Vasilico's eye. As he began to smile at her, she quickly looked away.

'Whew!' Kirk mimed mopping her brow. 'Thought for a minute there I'd gone and put my size sixes in it.' She focused her attention on Narinder once more. 'Okey-dokey, so talk me through your movements last night. You went out to meet up with some of your pals, right?'

Narinder nodded. 'That's right. Um, three old friends from way back. We all went our separate ways after we finished school, had our own lives, but, uh, we've stayed in touch. Get together once in a while for drinks and whatnot.'

'Uh-huh.' Kirk wrote this in her notebook. 'Where'd you go?'

'Well, we started out with dinner at the Wee Curry Shop on Ashton Lane. Then we moved on to The Mix on Byres Road for drinks.'

Kirk nodded approvingly. 'Nice. I've been there. Bit outta my normal price range, mind.'

Narinder grimaced. 'Mine too. But we don't see each other often, so . . .'

'Right. Once in a blue moon typa thing. So, you were there from . . . ?'

Narinder considered the question carefully. 'Um, we got there about nine, nine-thirty? And we were there till just before two a.m. A couple of the others wanted to stay on till closing time, but . . .'

'I get ya,' said Kirk. 'School night. So you live at . . .' She checked her notes. '84 Syracuse Road, right?'

'Uh-huh. Flat 3/2.'

'That's Shawlands, yeah? Nice area.'

Narinder nodded slowly. 'It is, yeah. It's quiet. Safe.'

An awkward silence fell. The irony of this statement was evidently lost on none of them, least of all her.

'How long ya lived there?' asked Kirk, once more moving things forward with a deft touch.

'Just over eight months, I think? Me and Farah decided to pool our resources. It meant a longer commute for both of us, but it's a bigger place than either of us would've been able to afford in the West End.'

Kirk consulted her notes. 'That's Farah Hadid, am I right?'

Narinder nodded.

'I'm guessing you got a taxi home?'

'That's right.'

'And was that a black cab or . . . ?'

Narinder shook her head. 'No, it was a local firm. One I've used before.' She paused for a moment, then added, 'I got my friend Eva to take a photo of the licence plate.'

It seemed to Anna that she felt it was important they know this – as if it was somehow a point in her defence that she'd taken this precaution.

Kirk grimaced. 'God, yeah. I do the exact same whenever I'm out with my gal pals. It's a faff, but . . .' She shrugged. 'Ya gotta do what ya gotta do. So you got home when . . . ?'

Once more, Narinder considered the question carefully before replying.

'Well, when I set my alarm for the morning, it was two thirty-eight, so I guess, like, two thirty, two thirty-five?'

'And Farah wasn't in?'

'No, she was spending the night at her boyfriend's. He stays over in Mount Florida. I knew she'd be out. That's why I wasn't worried about waking her when I got in.'

Kirk's pen danced across the page as she scribbled this down, before lifting her head and meeting Narinder's eyes once again.

'And your own boyfriend is Callum Finnie, right?'

'It wasn't him.' Narinder's response was instant and unequivocal.

Kirk raised both hands in a placatory gesture. 'Never said it was.'

'I'd *know*,' Narinder insisted.

'OK. I hear you.'

This time, Kirk wrote carefully and deliberately in her notebook as opposed to her usual rapid scrawl. Watching her, Anna strongly suspected this was more to convey to Narinder that she'd got the message loud and clear than because she was in any danger of forgetting it.

Narinder watched her in silence until she'd finished writing, then continued, unprompted. 'I WhatsApped the others to let them know I was home safe, let myself into the flat, got a drink of water . . . No, wait, I set my alarm for the morning, *then* got a drink. I went through to the bedroom and I was just starting to get undressed when . . .'

She shut her eyes. Inhaled a deep, shuddering breath. Kirk said nothing but watched her intently, waiting for her to recover.

At length, Narinder exhaled heavily and reopened her eyes – at least, as much as she *could* open them.

'I heard a creak behind me, but I think . . .' She trailed off, her expression almost sheepish. 'I know this is going to sound silly, but I knew something was off before that. I can't explain it, just this . . . feeling. But I heard this creak, and I turned, and there was this . . . this *shape* standing there.'

She shut her eyes again. Another shuddering breath escaped from her. 'I got as far as trying to scream, but I couldn't get anything out. And then his hand was on my mouth, and he pushed me backwards onto the bed, and he was on top of me. I couldn't move. I couldn't shout. I couldn't *do* anything.'

She sounded almost angry with herself.

'And then, he started on me. He kept punching me in the face, over and over. And then, just when I felt like I couldn't take any more, he stopped. Then he got out the . . . *thing*.'

She paused, grimacing, as if embarrassed by what she was about to say. 'It's OK,' said Kirk softly.

Narinder gave a small nod of gratitude. 'It was like, um, a sex toy, y'know? One of those hard plastic things that I've always thought must be too, well, *big* to actually be practical. And he . . . he stuck it up me. Just rammed it right in up my . . . up my back passage. The pain . . . it was like nothing I could've ever imagined. I thought he was going to tear me in two. And he kept jamming it back in, over and over again. And, when he got bored of that, he'd go back to punching me. And I kept thinking to myself, *If I just lie still and don't fight, it'll be over soon. He'll get bored or tired and he'll stop.*' A beat. 'A-and sometimes he did. He'd stop for a few minutes. You know, take a breather. But then he'd start up again.'

She choked back a sob. Anna, who rarely went in for physical intimacy, especially with people she barely knew, laid a hand on her shoulder and squeezed it gently. She felt utterly useless, standing there like a spare part, not knowing what to say or do.

Kirk waited patiently until Narinder pulled herself together enough to continue.

'A couple of times I think I blacked out for a bit . . . and then, at the end, I must've lost consciousness for real. I don't know how long it went on, or how long I was out for, but eventually I came round and realised he wasn't there anymore.' She paused. 'I wanted to move. I thought he could be back any minute. I really *tried*.'

Again, it was clear she felt it important that the detectives knew she'd made every effort.

Her shoulders slumped. 'But I couldn't. It was like my muscles didn't want to obey me.'

'Sometimes,' said Kirk, selecting her words carefully, 'when the nervous system's overloaded, the body shuts down as a protection mechanism. People talk about fight or flight, but there's another "F" as well: freeze.'

Narinder nodded indifferently, as if she didn't really believe Kirk but nonetheless felt the need to humour her.

'And that was it until Farah got in at . . . I guess it must have been around seven, seven-thirty. I don't know. I'd lost track of the time. And she found me and then . . .' She shrugged. 'She phoned you guys. And that's it, basically.'

She watched intently as Kirk scribbled another note in her book, as if waiting for feedback on how she'd done.

Kirk finished writing and lifted her head. 'That's good, Narinder,' she smiled, seemingly sensing her need for validation. 'That's really, really good. Just a couple more questions and we'll be all done.' She turned to a fresh page. 'This intruder . . . can you describe him at all? He was definitely male?'

Narinder's nod was emphatic. 'Definitely. He was . . .'

She shut her eyes. Whether to help her remember or because she wanted to forget was unclear.

'He was about medium height, I think. I mean, I'm five nine, and he was a bit shorter than me.'

'What was his build? Slight, heavy, average?'

'He was . . . um . . . I think . . .'

'Take your time. No rush.'

Narinder thought for a moment. Then, with some certainty:

'I'd say he was compact. I mean, he wasn't like a bodybuilder or anything, but he *was* strong.'

'How was he dressed?' said Kirk.

'Black trousers, black pullover, black balaclava. With, y'know, a slit for the eyes.'

At the mention of the balaclava, Anna, surreptitiously watching Vasilico out of the corner of her eye, saw his jaw momentarily tensing, though he said nothing.

Kirk finished writing the description in her notebook. 'What colour eyes?'

'Grey,' said Narinder promptly. 'Grey with little flecks of brown.'

'And was he wearing anything on his hands?'

'Yes. Gloves. He was wearing gloves.'

'You're positive about that?'

'Uh-huh. I felt the fabric.' Narinder hesitated. 'That's bad, isn't it? For fingerprints and DNA and whatnot?'

Kirk gave her a reassuring smile. 'Not necessarily. We've got some real whiz kids working for us in Forensics. Never ceases to amaze us what they can magic outta thin air.'

Anna wasn't sure she believed her, but had no intention of voicing her thoughts.

'Any feel for his age?' said Kirk.

Narinder shook her head. 'No. Uh, I mean,' she clarified, 'I couldn't say for sure, but I'd say he was young. Like, my age or younger. That was the vibe I got.'

'What about his ethnicity?'

'White. He was white.' Once more, Narinder's response was emphatic. 'He was wearing black from head to foot, but I was able to see through the slit in his mask that he was white.'

'And, at any point, did he either speak to you – or say anything, even if it wasn't directly addressed to you?'

'No. Not once. But his eyes said it all.'

Kirk frowned. 'What did they say?'

Narinder drew her arms about herself and inhaled heavily through her nostrils. 'Just pure hatred.'

It hung in the air like a lead weight. Anna was acutely conscious of the effort it took for her to swallow.

'And other than the assault with the sex toy,' said Kirk, 'did he do anything else to you that was sexual in nature?'

'He touched my breasts a few times,' said Narinder. 'Like, over my clothes. But it felt like . . . I dunno, almost an afterthought, y'know? Like that wasn't what he was really interested in. But throughout the whole thing, while he was on top of me, I could feel that he was . . . you know, erect.'

Kirk gave her a small, sympathetic smile. As she wrote this down, Narinder spoke up once again, her tone hesitant.

'I haven't . . .'

She trailed off. Kirk looked up.

'Haven't what?'

'Told anyone. I mean, apart from you lot . . .' She nodded to Kirk and Vasilico. 'And you.' She gestured to Anna. 'And Callum and Farah, obviously. I mean, you all know already. I mean like my parents.' She hesitated, then added, in a small voice, 'Is that bad? I mean, I don't wanna lay this at their door. They worry about me enough as it is. But it feels dishonest.'

Kirk reached across and squeezed Narinder's hand. 'That's entirely your decision. No one else can make it for you. And whatever you decide, know that it'll be the right one.'

She closed her notebook, then met Narinder's eyes, her expression one of utter sincerity. 'You've done amazing, Narinder. Remembering all these details. It's a huge help to us. Thank you so much.'

The corner of Narinder's lips flickered in a momentary attempt at a smile. 'Just . . . you know, promise you'll get him. Don't let him do this to anyone else.'

Kirk continued to meet Narinder's gaze, making no attempt to hide from her scrutiny. 'I promise we'll do everything we can to make sure he doesn't.'

She pocketed her notebook, then swung her legs off the bed and climbed down.

'We'll be in touch again soon. Until then, I want you to do something for us. I want you to get some rest, OK? You'll do that?'

Narinder nodded.

Kirk smiled. 'OK.'

She reached across, gave Narinder's hand one last squeeze, then turned to go.

'I can only echo DS Kirk's words,' said Vasilico, speaking for the first time since introducing himself. 'You've given us a lot to work with. Thank you.' Stepping forward, he produced a business card. 'This is my number. If you remember anything else, or if you just want to talk to one of us, please don't hesitate to call.'

Narinder gave a small nod. She took the card mechanically, evidently more out of obligation than because she particularly wanted it.

Vasilico glanced in Anna's direction. For a couple of seconds, it seemed as if one of them or the other was going to say something. Then the moment passed. He nodded to her.

'Anna.'

'Detective,' she said, every muscle in her body tensed.

Vasilico gave a flicker of a smile, then turned and followed Kirk out of the cubicle. Anna remained by Narinder's side, listening to their footsteps receding down the linoleum corridor.

For several seconds, neither Anna nor Narinder moved or spoke. Then, as if exhausted from the effort of having successfully kept it together for so long, Narinder's shoulders sagged, a great, heavy breath escaping from her body.

'Tell me something,' she said, as Anna once again laid a reassuring hand on her shoulder.

'What?' said Anna.

'Why did this happen?' She looked up at Anna beseechingly, the inflamed skin around her eyes glistening with fresh tears. 'I mean, I never left my glass unattended. I didn't accept any drinks from strangers. I got my friends to note down the taxi's licence plate. I messaged them to let them know I was home safe. I did all the things you're supposed to do. And then *this* happens. Is there something else I should have done?'

Anna knew what she was really asking. It was the same question all victims of sexual assault inevitably asked themselves at one point or another.

Am I to blame for this?

She shook her head firmly. 'This is not on you, all right? You didn't do anything wrong. Remember that.'

The words sounded unbearably hollow in her own ears. It was, after all, what you were *supposed* to say in these situations – a mantra drilled into you and repeated so many times it had ultimately lost all semblance of meaning. These were the same words women repeated to one another time and again when they, or someone they knew, fell victim to this sort of violence. Words which, no matter how well-intentioned, no matter how truthful, invariably fell on deaf ears, because they'd been conditioned so comprehensively to believe the opposite.

Narinder gave an insincere flicker of a smile and nodded softly. She'd probably heard it before. Hell, she'd probably *said* it herself, or some variation of it, to at least one of the women in her life when they'd asked the same question of *her*.

Anna was still racking her brains, trying desperately to come up with something with which to fill the silence, when the curtains parted and the gawky nurse from before returned, a couple of porters behind her.

'Good news, Narinder,' she beamed. 'We're on the move. Your room's ready for you.'

4

By the time Farah made it back from the flat, lugging a sports bag crammed full of clothes and other assorted items, Narinder had already been installed in her room on the fifth floor, which had a toilet door that didn't close properly but boasted an impressive view of the hospital's helipad – a perk which the nurse had eagerly pointed out upon their arrival.

Farah was, if anything, in even more of a flap than she'd been previously. She kept apologising profusely to all and sundry, including the nurses, who looked at her like she'd just crash landed from a distant planet. The flat was still full of police and people in boiler suits, she explained, and they'd insisted she had an escort at all times, and once she got back to the hospital, Narinder wasn't in her cubicle and no one could tell her where they'd taken her—

'Well, you're here now,' said Anna firmly, stopping Farah's increasingly frantic babbling in its tracks. 'That's the important thing.'

She recognised that, of all of them, she was the least directly affected by what had happened, and was determined to continue to play the role of 'responsible grown-up' for as long as was necessary, though she remained acutely conscious both of the ticking clock and of her no doubt overflowing email inbox. She stuck around for another twenty minutes or so, making sure Narinder was settled and had everything she needed within easy reach, before wishing her a speedy recovery and finally taking her leave.

Farah, who intended to stay with Narinder till they turfed her out, walked Anna to the lift. As they waited for it to arrive, Farah turned to her, her face ashen and drained.

'I feel awful,' she said, her voice thick with emotion. 'I should have been there. If I hadn't spent the night at Émile's—'

'Hey.' Anna laid a hand on her arm. 'Stop that. Right now. I said this to Narinder and I'll say it again to you: none of this is your fault. You understand that, don't you?'

'But—'

'But nothing. The person responsible is the man who did this. No one else.'

And the fact that women still doubt this simple, incontestable fact is why I'm going to continue to say it till I'm blue in the face, she thought.

Farah offered up no further objections, but her continuing glum expression told Anna she was far from convinced.

Just then, her eyes widened as something occurred to her.

'Oh, *putain.*' She slapped her forehead. 'I have a tutorial at two I'm supposed to be teaching. My first-year group.'

'Don't worry about it,' said Anna. 'I'll ask Simon or Agnieszka to take it. And if neither of them is free, I'll cover it myself.' She saw Farah's look of uncertainty. 'I mean it. Focus on Narinder. Right now, she needs you more than they do.'

She knew, as she spoke, that the likelihood of her leaving work while it was still light was close to nil.

She made her way back through reception and headed out into the open air. As she emerged from under the awning, she half-noticed a shape on the periphery of her vision, leaning against the wall by the door. Even as she quickened her pace, it straightened up and began to follow her. A second later, she heard Vasilico's voice.

'Anna.'

'Detective. We really must stop meeting like this.'

She continued towards the car park, not looking back. Vasilico hurried to her side and fell into step with her.

'Can we talk?'

She glanced briefly in his direction. 'Don't you have a violent offender to catch?'

He winced. 'Don't do that.'

'What?'

'Use the job as a deflection. Come on, it's been . . .'

'Three years?' Anna suggested.

Coming to an abrupt halt, she turned to him with an expectant glare, silently challenging him to either deny it or attempt some sort of mealy-mouthed explanation. He gave one of his trademark disarming smiles, but it felt forced – a half-hearted attempt to turn on the old Vasilico charm.

'Come on, Anna. Five minutes. That's all I'm asking for. Surely we owe each other that much.'

Anna treated him to a long, hard stare. 'We owe each other nothing, Detective.'

He smiled again, but it came off looking more like a painful grimace. 'You know, I liked it better when you called me Paul.'

'And I liked it better when you returned my phone calls.'

Any trace of a smile promptly faded from Vasilico's lips. If he'd been putting on a passable act until now, the mask had well and truly slipped. He could no longer brazen it out by pretending not to know why she was so utterly pissed off with him.

'But that's you in a nutshell, isn't it?' she went on, gazing up at him defiantly, hands on her hips. 'You were all over me just as long as I was useful to you. But the moment I turned down that job offer, you dropped me like a stone . . .'

Even as she spoke, she realised the implication of what she was saying.

'. . . meaning you wouldn't be talking to me right now if you didn't have some ulterior motive.'

Vasilico scoffed automatically. 'Don't be ridiculous.'

Anna folded her arms. 'What's going on, Vasilico? A DCI from the Specialist Crime Unit personally attending an interview with the victim of a random assault? There's more to this than meets the eye, isn't there?'

For the briefest moment, Vasilico looked to be on the verge of denying it. But then, as Anna continued to give him dagger eyes, he sighed heavily and relented.

'All right. I'll tell you everything. Lay all my cards on the table, just for you. After all,' he added, in a somewhat uneasy undertone, 'in a manner of speaking, this *does* involve you.'

5

'The first attack took place back in mid-June,' said Vasilico. 'A woman in her early twenties, living in a flat in Cessnock, woke to find a masked intruder in her bedroom. He groped her breasts and private parts and brutally assaulted her, leaving her with a fractured zygoma and various other facial injuries.'

They were seated at a table in the food court on the first floor of the hospital's main building. A handful of other tables were occupied, the bright lighting and hubbub of cheerful conversation carrying on around them in stark contrast to the subject matter under discussion. Vasilico kept his voice low, forcing Anna to have to lean towards him to hear properly.

'About a month later, another, similar incident took place in Scotstoun-hill. Again, the victim was a young woman in her early twenties. Again, the attacker was a masked intruder who broke into her flat in the middle of the night. No threats. No demands. Just aggressive sexual touching, accompanied by a sustained and brutal physical assault, focused almost exclusively on her face.

'All told, there have been seven similar incidents in the last four months, spread across the length and breadth of the city. The pattern is the same each time. The assailant breaks into the victim's home, either by forcing a window or picking the door lock, usually between one and three a.m. The target is always a woman in her twenties who either lives alone or is the only person home on that particular night – though one woman who lives with her parents *was* attacked while they were sleeping just down the hallway.'

He paused momentarily, as if uncertain as to whether to add this next detail. 'That case was a particularly upsetting one. It was the first one to involve repeated anal penetration with a dildo. Also, the woman in question was pregnant at the time. The experience caused her to miscarry.'

Feeling the need to put on a show of bravado, Anna took a sip of coffee. It required all her effort to force the mouthful down.

'You said earlier that this concerns me,' she said eventually. 'How?'

At first, Vasilico remained silent. Then, after a few seconds, he seemed to make his peace with what he was about to say.

'We've yet to establish why these individuals, specifically, are being chosen as victims, but, besides their gender and general age range, there *is* one other detail which links them. All seven were students at Kelvingrove University, and five – including Narinder Khatri – were enrolled in the School of Social and Political Sciences.' He paused. 'That's your domain, I gather.'

Anna nodded blankly. She didn't know what to say. Of all the turns this conversation could have taken, this was positively the last one she'd expected.

'We believe there are at least two perpetrators,' Vasilico continued, his tone brisk and businesslike. 'Four of the victims, including Narinder, described their attacker as slim but well-muscled and white. Another two say they were assaulted by an Asian male with a heavier build. The remaining victim blanked out the details of the assault and has been unable to provide us with a description. From her point of view, that's probably something of a mercy.'

'Is there any chance we could be looking at two separate, unconnected attackers?' asked Anna, forcing herself to think matter-of-factly. She noticed, as soon as she'd spoken, that she'd automatically used the word 'we'. *Just like old times.*

Vasilico shook his head. 'We're fairly confident that's not the case. The incidents are too similar in nature for two people to be working independently without referencing the same instruction manual, so to speak. There's also another reason.'

'What?' Anna asked.

For reasons she couldn't have articulated, she felt a powerful sense of foreboding, which was only strengthened as Vasilico reached inside his jacket and drew out a folded sheet of paper.

'A few hours after the first assault, this was posted to several well-known message boards and Reddit groups with an emphasis on what I gather are known in the trade as "men's rights". Shortly after the second assault, the same message was posted again. And again after the third, and so on. In each case, the message was posted by a brand new account created specifically for that purpose and tied to what was clearly a burner email account. It was posted again just before eight o'clock this morning, while Narinder Khatri was in an ambulance en route to A&E.'

He passed the sheet to Anna. With the blood pounding in her eardrums, she unfolded it and read the words printed on it in stark black-on-white Helvetica.

We, **The Reckoning**, hereby assert our rightful place in the social hierarchy and declare war on the Genocide of Men.

For too long, men have been cowed by the evils of radical feminism, anti-Westernism and postmodern Cultural Marxism. We have been conditioned to deny our natural impulses and to be ashamed of our innate, biologically determined superiority. It is time for men to stop apologising for themselves. The hour has come for a rebalancing of the scales.

Let it be known that the deviant females who flaunt their sexuality while simultaneously denying it to their male superiors are no longer free to revel in their hypocrisy. We assert our inalienable right to take what we want, when we want it, where we want it.

We call on men everywhere to draw courage from our actions and rise up to reclaim what is rightfully theirs from the scourge of gynocratic oppression.

A storm is coming.

Anna read the treatise in silence, the aching horror in the pit of her stomach growing with each passing word. When she'd finished, she slowly lowered the page and stared at Vasilico in disbelief.

'Jesus Christ,' she said.

Vasilico gave a grimace of agreement. 'You understand now why a DCI from the Specialist Crime Unit is involved.'

She nodded numbly.

'We've managed to keep the existence of this manifesto from the press so far. And we've been working proactively with the various platforms to get these posts taken down as quickly as possible. For the most part, they've been obliging. But we're fighting a losing battle. You know what the internet is like. Stuff like this spreads like wildfire.'

He gently extracted the page from Anna's hands and slipped it back inside his jacket. She barely noticed.

'Quite apart from the potential this has to create mass panic, we want to avoid the possibility of this little treatise inspiring any budding copycats. Having read it, I think you'll agree it amounts to rather more than the deluded ramblings of some aggrieved basement dweller who believes he's entitled to more nookie than he's getting. It's a full-blown call to arms.'

'And what about the women?' said Anna, finding her voice at last. 'How much do *they* know about what's going on?' A thought occurred to her. 'Is Narinder aware that she's the subject of a . . . a *manifesto*?'

'We haven't raised it with her yet,' said Vasilico. 'I think we can agree she's got enough on her plate right now.' He caught Anna's look of disapproval before she even had a chance to respond. 'But if what you're asking is, do the victims realise they've been targeted by the same self-styled group of woman-hating fanatics, then no, they don't. As far as they're concerned, they're each the victim of a brutal but isolated assault.

'And that's the way it's going to stay,' he added firmly, once again pre-empting Anna as she opened her mouth to speak. 'At least until we've got a firm grip on the situation.'

'I think that's up to them, don't you?' said Anna, her tone unmistakably frosty.

'No.' Vasilico's response was immediate and unequivocal. 'I have a duty to maintain public order that overrides any right for them – or indeed anyone *else* – to know more than they absolutely have to. Think about it:

if every woman in Glasgow believes she's a potential target, we'll have utter chaos on our hands.

'Don't give me that look,' he went on, before Anna had even registered that she was giving him *any* sort of look. 'You know it's the right thing to do. Tell me, what good would it do them if they knew? What could they actually *do* with that information, besides worry?'

'They could take steps to guard against the same thing happening to them,' said Anna. To her, that point seemed obvious.

'More than they do already?' Vasilico's expression was sympathetic. 'I'm not completely gauche, Anna. I may not be one myself, but I've investigated enough crimes of opportunity to know *something* about what it means to be a young woman in the twenty-first century. I know the sort of precautions they take – precautions they consider so routine as to barely give them a second thought. Look at Narinder. She did everything by the book and she still ended up in the Queen Elizabeth with internal bleeding and her face beaten to a pulp.'

He leaned towards Anna, fixing her with a look as determined as it was earnest. 'I'm going to get these fuckers, Anna. I'm not going to rest till I've nailed them to the wall. So, for now, please just trust me, OK?'

For a long time, Anna said nothing. It wasn't that she doubted his sincerity. Rather, she remained far from convinced that keeping this secret was morally right. At some length, she resolved – for now, at any rate – to swallow her reservations and give him the chance to prove himself. It wasn't like she had much other choice.

'All right,' she said, without a great deal of enthusiasm.

'Thank you,' said Vasilico, his tone sincere.

They sat in silence for a moment, each preoccupied by their own thoughts. Eventually, Anna spoke again.

'So what can *I* do?'

'You?' Vasilico looked at her in mild surprise.

'How can I make myself useful?' She gave a small scoff. 'You're not going to pretend you told me all this without the express purpose of seeking out my help, are you?'

Besides, she thought, it wasn't as if she could have just sat this one out, knowing what she now knew. It wasn't in her nature. And Vasilico would certainly be well aware of that.

Vasilico shook his head ruefully. 'No, I suppose not,' he said, with the ghost of a smile.

Anna said nothing. She continued to gaze at him expectantly, refusing to bow to the implicit pressure to fill the silence. After several awkward seconds, Vasilico sighed and spread his arms in a defeated shrug.

'All right – you got me. I was planning to ask you to lend us your expertise in establishing how the victims are being chosen and, perhaps more pertinently, who's doing the choosing. Actually, I'd have asked you even if you weren't tangentially connected to the case already. After all,' he finished, with a chivvying smile, 'you *are* the foremost authority I know in the field of criminology.'

Anna rolled her eyes. 'I don't need you blowing smoke up my arse,' she said – then immediately regretted mentioning her arse.

But if it had crossed Vasilico's mind to respond with some sort of innuendo, he managed to resist the urge. 'Nothing of the sort, I assure you.' He looked and sounded positively wounded by the very suggestion. 'I would genuinely value your input, and that's God's honest truth. Of course, if you'd rather not, I completely understand . . .'

'Now hold on. I didn't say that.'

Vasilico's expression brightened instantly. 'Excellent! So it's agreed, then? You'll come down to HQ and I'll show you everything we have on the attacks? Shall we say eight a.m. tomorrow?'

At this, Anna's jaw practically dropped open – though she wasn't sure why she was in any way surprised by his brazenness. Expecting him to have changed at all in the intervening three years was like expecting a leopard to change its spots.

She considered pushing back – perhaps quibbling over the hour, so as not to let him think he could get things *entirely* his own way. But she quickly disabused herself of that idea. However much his presumptuousness rankled, there was far more at stake here than her feelings regarding their personal history.

'All right,' she said. 'Eight a.m. tomorrow.'

'Marvellous.' He flashed that disarming smile she remembered so well. 'I need to get back to the crime scene,' he continued briskly as he swung out of his chair. 'See how the tech boffins are getting on without me. I'll see you tomorrow. It's the old schoolhouse on Napiershall Street. I'll make sure someone's there to meet you at the door.'

She nodded, committing this to memory.

He towered over her, a dry, self-deprecating smile on his lips. 'Be just like old times.'

'In a manner of speaking,' she agreed.

For a moment, he hesitated.

'Anna.'

She gazed up at him, her expression neutral.

'I *did* actually just want to talk to you, you know. No ulterior motive.'

She continued to stare up at him, refusing to let her expression soften.

'I'll see you tomorrow, Detective.'

Returning her gaze, Vasilico nodded softly to himself, accompanied by a small but audible expulsion of air from his nostrils. It was as if she'd passed some sort of test – lived up to his expectations; acted in some way that was in keeping with his perception of her character.

'I'll look forward to it,' he said, then dipped his head in farewell and, turning, strode off across the food court towards the escalator.

Anna waited till he'd disappeared from view before letting the tension in her shoulders subside. Despite telling herself he was no longer a part of her life – that he held no sway over her, for good or ill – she couldn't deny that seeing him again had rekindled feelings in her that she'd long suppressed. As she sat there, surrounded by the clinking of crockery and the babel of voices, she felt all the old familiar stirrings – of infuriation, of grudging respect . . . and, she hated to admit it, of something far more intimate.

6

Anna headed back to the university, where she spent the rest of the day frantically making up for lost time. As it turned out, neither Simon nor Agnieszka were available to take Farah's tutorial that afternoon, so Anna ended up doing it herself, which had the predictable knock-on effect on her already overflowing in-tray. She also took the pre-emptive step of reallocating Farah's Tuesday morning lecture and cancelling her afternoon tutorial group for the same day, on the grounds that, assuming Narinder was discharged from hospital in the morning, Farah would undoubtedly want to be on hand to support her.

Returning to her office post-tutorial, already feeling somewhat frazzled, Anna rang Zoe to give her the heads-up that she'd be home late, then knuckled down to dealing with the mountain of admin that, as she'd anticipated, was awaiting her attention. There was no question that the amount of bureaucracy she had to deal with had increased dramatically since the Great Restructuring – much of it coming directly from Fraser, who demanded constant written reports and updates, at least half of which she was convinced he didn't read. A significant amount of it boiled down to her having to explain to him, in layman's terms, what it was she actually *did*. Fraser's own field was political theory, and his understanding of criminology was rudimentary at best – yet another reason why mashing so many disciplines together under the auspices of a single School amounted to an act of wilful sabotage.

The bulk of the changes had taken place earlier in the year, while she was on her nine-month sabbatical, writing her book on women's experiences of the prison system. Not, she suspected, that her objections would have counted for anything even if she *had* been there to voice them. On the contrary, she knew that nothing she or any of her colleagues – many of whom had voiced the same concerns she harboured, either publicly or in private – had to say on the matter stood a chance in hell of halting the relentless march towards what the Principal varyingly referred to as 'modernisation' and 'securing a sustainable future for the university'. Still, it almost felt as if they'd deliberately waited till she was out of the way before ploughing ahead.

She'd come back to a workplace she barely recognised, with Hugh MacLeish – her former head of department and the closest thing she had there to a mentor figure – still employed but stripped of all authority and influence, like a ghost cursed to haunt the corridors in perpetuity. These days, whenever she ran into him, he always looked forlorn and vaguely lost, like someone who'd woken up one morning to find that new tenants had moved into his home without his prior knowledge or consent. The new occupants hadn't kicked him out, but had made it abundantly clear to him that they were calling the shots now, and because he had nowhere else to go, he'd meekly acquiesced and was now simply biding his time, a greatly diminished figure who was little more than a relic from a bygone era. There was, it seemed, no room for old-timers like him in this brave new world – nor, she was increasingly coming to believe, even people like her, still on the right side of forty but very much associated with the *ancien régime*.

Worst of all to her mind, though, was the hiring of Robert Leopold – a move so crass and craven she could scarcely believe the supposedly prudent doyens of the university had agreed to it. At the time, he'd been a faculty member at the University of Southend, with a twice-weekly podcast that was just beginning to take off in the charts. In what had clearly been a bid to ride that wave of notoriety, the university had offered Leopold an eye-watering sum to relocate to Glasgow, bringing with him his personal brand of populist rabble-rousing. It had generated considerable outrage at the time from the expected quarters, but the powers that be had evidently made the calculation that this would be more than offset by the kudos associated with being able to boast having the host of *Hard Truth: The Podcast for Men* on staff. So far, it seemed to be paying dividends. He'd already secured multiple externally funded research grants, application rates for the Social Anthropology programme were up that year by over sixty percent, and the university had recently been the subject of a fawning profile in the *Spectator*, lauding its management for its bold decision to hire, in the face of much liberal hand-wringing, 'that rare example of an academic who isn't afraid to speak a few inconvenient truths'.

The size of Leopold's paycheque would not, perhaps, have rankled quite so much were it not for the fact that, shortly before she went on sabbatical, Anna had been told categorically that there was simply no money in the kitty to offer Farah – on whose behalf she'd privately lobbied unsuccessfully for years – a permanent position as a lecturer. The stench of double standards was so strong you could smell it from the other side of campus. Farah, of course, refused to complain. She merely kept her head down and got on with the job – partly because that was simply who she was, and partly, Anna knew, because she was only too aware that to do anything else would be to risk labelling herself as an ingrate, a troublemaker, and thus put paid to any prospect of a faculty position in the future.

It was after nine by the time Anna wearily climbed the steps to the door of the townhouse on Clarence Drive she called home. As she stepped into the hallway, she heard a burst of canned laughter coming from the living room, followed by the equally canned voice of a male game show host announcing, with exaggerated bombast, that *'one of you is going home tonight'*.

She pushed on into the living room, in time to see Zoe and her girlfriend, Sal, sprawled side by side on the sofa, hastily separating. The room was in semi-darkness, the light mostly coming from the TV, but that wasn't enough to hide the flushed faces of both women, or the fact that Sal's trousers were unbuttoned.

Zoe raised a hand, the very picture of innocence. 'Oh, hey, doll. What's the craic?'

Anna gave a weary smile. 'Hey.' She nodded in Sal's direction. 'Hey, Sal.'

Sal gave a nonchalant salute of greeting, evidently not trusting herself to speak.

'Was beginning tae wonder if ye were gonnae show at *all* the night,' said Zoe.

Anna grimaced. 'Sorry. Been one of those days.' She paused. 'Jack get off to sleep OK?'

'Aye, it's all good. Wanted tae wait up for his mammy, so he did, but I put my foot down. Said ye'd look in on him when ye got in.'

'I'll do that now.'

'And I'd better be offski,' said Sal. She got to her feet, almost succeeding in concealing the act of buttoning her trousers as she did so.

'Don't go on my account,' said Anna. 'I'll be out of your hair in a moment.'

Sal gave a dismissive wave. 'Nah, it's cool. Jen's got an early start tomorrow, so I'm on munchkin duty in the morning.'

Sal lived near Dowanhill Park with her sister, who did some sort of high-flying and apparently deeply secretive job in IT security. She had an infant son and daughter, and she and Sal shared childcare duties. As for what Sal did for a living, she'd once described herself to Anna as a 'content creator'. Anna wasn't sure what that entailed, but hadn't thought to ask at the time, and felt the moment had now passed.

She remained, in many respects, something of a mystery to Anna. At twenty-nine, she was several years younger than both Zoe and Anna, but while the age difference didn't seem particularly pronounced when you looked at her next to Zoe, the gulf between her and Anna felt positively chasmic. Indeed, in both her mannerisms and her way of speaking, she reminded Anna a lot of some of her undergraduate students, still inhabiting that fugue state between adolescence and adulthood. This extended to her fashion sense; she was usually to be found in cargo pants or ripped jeans, and she had a seemingly endless repertoire of baggy, brightly coloured T-shirts, most of them emblazoned with one ironic or provocative slogan or another. And then there was her hair, which changed colour every few weeks. Right now, it was bright blue.

Zoe, too, was now on her feet. 'I'll see ye out,' she said, heading over to join Sal and snaking an arm round her waist.

Leaving them to it, Anna made her way up to the first floor, where she opened Jack's bedroom door a few centimetres and peered in through the gap. Light from the landing fell on Jack's pillow and on his shock of dark hair, his head turned away from her. For a few seconds, she remained there, watching him. Then, just when she was on the verge of shutting the door again, he stirred and rolled over to face her. Smiling fondly, she headed in.

'Hey, Trouble.' She knelt by the bed, running a hand through his hair.

'Where were you?' Jack sounded groggy, still half-asleep.

Anna winced apologetically. 'Oh, I'm sorry, darling. I had to work late. But I'm here now.'

'You said we'd build my Lego.'

Doing Lego with Jack was one of the few areas of childcare in which Anna had the undisputed upper hand. Zoe hadn't the patience for it, and seemed to regard the act of having to follow the instructions as a personal affront.

'I know,' said Anna, inwardly cringing with guilt. 'I'm sorry. We'll do it another night – promise.'

'You always say that,' growled Jack.

With that, he rolled onto his other side, pointedly turning his back on her.

His words, and the accompanying action, hit Anna like a blow to the stomach. For several moments, she remained kneeling beside the bed, gazing down at her son in a mixture of anguish and helplessness. She waited, but Jack neither moved nor spoke again. As far as he was concerned, this exchange was clearly over.

Admitting defeat, she got to her feet and slipped away. In the doorway, she hesitated, turning once more to look at him, but he remained with his back to her, unmoving, the blankets twisted around his hard little body. After a few more seconds, she stepped out, shutting the door behind her.

Anna sloped back downstairs to the living room, where she found Zoe stretched out on the sofa, channel-surfing.

'Sorry about that,' said Anna, grimacing ruefully. 'I get the feeling my sense of timing could use some improvement.'

Zoe shrugged. ''S no biggie. Hey, want me tae fix ye a sammidge or something?'

Anna shook her head. 'Nah, you're good. I grabbed something earlier.'

A bag of crisps and a bar of Dairy Milk from the vending machine.

She sunk into the vacant armchair, a heavy sigh escaping from her.

Zoe glanced across at her with a look of mild concern. 'Tough day?'

'You could say that.'

Zoe switched off the TV. 'Right, then.'

All business, she set the remote aside, got to her feet and made her way over. Perching on the arm of the chair, she began to massage Anna's shoulders.

'You just tell Agony Aunt Zoe *aaaall* about it,' she purred, digging into the taut muscles at the base of Anna's neck.

Anna smiled up at her wearily. 'What would I do without you, huh?'

Zoe grinned. 'You know it.'

And Anna began to tell her.

7

El Duce invites GodsGift2Women and LifeIsPain to a new chat channel.

LifeIsPain joins the chat.

LifeIsPain: Well?
LifeIsPain: Howd it go
LifeIsPain: I need DETAILS

El Duce: Wait til GodsGift gets here.

LifeIsPain: Were is he any way
LifeIsPain: *where
LifeIsPain: U said 10 sharp

El Duce: That's his business, not yours. He'll be here when he's good and ready.

LifeIsPain: Sorry
LifeIsPain: I jsut cant help it, im too excited

El Duce: If you need to relieve the tension, go rub one out. I gather that's your forte. Either way, stop being a pissant.

LifeIsPain: :(

* * *

El Duce opens a separate chat channel with GodsGift2Women.

El Duce: Where the fuck are you?
El Duce: ???

Three minutes pass.

GodsGift2Women joins the chat.

El Duce: What the fuck sort of time do you call this?

GodsGift2Women: Calm your tits amigo. Wheres the fire?

El Duce: I seem to remember us agreeing to be ready at ten on the dot.

GodsGift2Women: No u ORDERED us to be ready at 10
GodsGift2Women: Anyway Im here now. What do u care?

El Duce: I care when it affects my ability to start our meetings in a timely fashion. Plus, any display of insubordination sets a bad example to the junior partner in this endeavour.

GodsGift2Women: LOL
GodsGift2Women: Insubordination
GodsGift2Women: Im creaming my keks
GodsGift2Women: What u gunna do big man

El Duce: Keep testing me and you'll find out.

GodsGift2Women: ahahahahaha :D :D

GodsGift2Women: Seriously Im just fucking with you dude. You do you

El Duce: Just remember who you're talking to. Now get your arse into the main chat.

El Duce closes the channel.

* * *

GodsGift2Women joins the main chat channel.

El Duce: Good. We're all here. We can get underway.

LifeIsPain: Spill spill spill

El Duce: No one needs to know about your premature ejaculation, dicksprout.

GodsGift2Women: LOL
GodsGift2Women: But seriously whats the score
GodsGift2Women: Seen on the news there was breakin in Shawlands

El Duce: It was
El Duce: In a word
El Duce: Masterful.
El Duce: If I may be permitted to say so, some of my best work yet.

LifeIsPain: FUCK YES
LifeIsPain: Did it scream?
LifeIsPain: Did it cry like a bitch?

GodsGift2Women: Something ud know all about amirite?

LifeIsPain: Fuck off
LifeIsPain: Well El Duce?? Did it????

El Duce: No screaming. Didn't give her the opportunity.
El Duce: But she did piss her pants.

LifeIsPain: LOL!!!!
LifeIsPain: Filthy fucking whore

GodsGift2Women: BWAHAHAHA
GodsGift2Women: Golden shower for El Duce
GodsGift2Women: U do much damage to her?

El Duce: Between you and me, boys, I reckon she won't be sitting down without a donut cushion for a week or two.

LifeIsPain: HAHAHAHAHA
LifeIsPain: Serve it right
LifeIsPain: Dirty tramp putting it about every where
LifeIsPain: Flounceing around in those low rise jeans, thong sticking outfor the world 2 see
LifeIsPain: And did u mark it s smug whore face

El Duce: Let's just say by the time I was done, she looked more like a Picasso than an Old Master.
El Duce: (Waits patiently while you both Google "Picasso".)

GodsGift2Women posts a picture of Picasso's Weeping Woman.

El Duce: Perfect likeness.

GodsGift2Women: Shell not be showing her face again in a hurry I bet
GodsGift2Women: Mind you
GodsGift2Women: Feels kind of a waste
GodsGift2Women: She was a bit of a looker

LifeIsPain: Only if ur despirate
LifeIsPain: 5/10 at most imo
LifeIsPain: Any way it s damaged goods

GodsGift2Women: LOL. Like u d kick her out of bed if u ever got close enough

El Duce: Well, I doubt she'll find she's got many takers after today. Won't be at all surprised if that oaf boyfriend kicks her to the kerb.

GodsGift2Women: Never know, perhaps he can still fuck her if he puts a paper bag over her head first

LifeIsPain: Or may be it get so depressd looking at itself in the mirror it ll kill itself lol
LifeIsPain: 1 less foid slut in the world

El Duce: At any rate, it'll be a while before she so much as thinks about another night out with the girls.

GodsGift2Women: So whens the next hit?

El Duce: Soon. I need to work out a couple of details.

GodsGift2Women: This ones mine right?

El Duce: That remains to be seen.

GodGift2Women: Fucksake I sat out the last one too
GodGift2Women: Your worse then a fucking pricktease

El Duce: Time you learned some self-discipline then.

GodGift2Women: Is this about me being 5 mins late
GodGift2Women: Seriously dude this is bullshit

El Duce: If you don't like it, you know where the door is.

LifeIsPain: When do I get to do one

GodGift2Women: LOL not til ur balls have dropped

El Duce: Hahaha

LifeIsPain: Fuck off Gods Gift

GodGift2Women: Cry more incel

El Duce: All right all right. Enough fuckery for tonight. Next meeting: Wednesday night at 10. Don't be late.

GodGift2Women: Yes me lord

El Duce closes the channel.

PART TWO

THE PIPER'S SONG

8

At five minutes to eight the following morning, while the streets were still bathed in that hazy, late autumn, post-sunrise glow, Anna parked outside the grounds of the three-storey sandstone building on Napiershall Street, a couple of miles from her house on the other side of the West End, which served as the headquarters of the Specialist Crime Unit. She pushed open the wrought iron gate and crossed the grounds to the front entrance, where DS Alex Kirk was leaning against the wall, texting on her phone. She looked up, hearing Anna's approach.

'You again? Thought you'd've had your fill yesterday. Talk about your glutton for punishment!' She grinned. 'He's waiting for you up the stairs. C'mon.'

She pocketed her phone and headed inside, holding the door open for Anna.

Anna had never set foot in the building before and was surprised to discover that, in contrast to its relatively nondescript outer façade, its interior was, in fact, rather ornate, with high ceilings, swooping arches and wood flooring, scuffed by the passage of countless pairs of feet over the course of more than a century. It had obviously seen better days, but the lack of recent TLC could not hide the fact that it had once been a seriously impressive piece of real estate.

'So you and the gaffer go back a ways?' Kirk asked, as she led the way up a flight of stairs.

'We worked together on a case a few years ago,' said Anna, choosing to leave it at that.

'That the Shadow Men business? I'd've given my ovaries to work on *that* one. 'Course, I was just a whippersnapper barely out of probation back then.'

She looked back over her shoulder at Anna, clearly angling for some juicy gossip – either about the case itself, or the precise nature of Anna's previous dealings with her boss. When Anna's expression remained resolutely blank, her grin promptly faded and she turned away again.

'Wow, tough crowd,' she muttered, just loud enough for Anna to hear.

She quickened her pace, bouncing up the steps two at a time. Anna hurried to keep up.

They alighted on the first-floor landing. A middle-aged man with a lanyard round his neck nodded to them as he passed, prompting Anna to realise that, besides Kirk, he was the first person she'd encountered since crossing the threshold. Most of the morning shift evidently hadn't arrived yet.

They made their way down a corridor, at the end of which Kirk rapped briskly on a door, then opened it without waiting to be invited.

'That's your lady-friend here for you, boss,' she said, leaning in.

Anna felt her cheeks colouring as she stepped past Kirk and into a large, airy room with tall sash windows and several desks pushed together in the centre, on the nearest of which Vasilico was perched in rolled-up shirtsleeves, brows furrowed in obvious disapproval at Kirk's choice of introduction. As Anna entered, he rose to his feet and moved towards her, his frown quickly giving way to a smile.

'Anna. Wonderful to see you. Well rested, I trust?'

'I can't complain,' said Anna, choosing not to mention that her leaving the house an hour earlier than normal had prompted a mini-tantrum from Jack which had only been neutralised by bribing him with chocolate. *Quality parenting there, Anna.*

'Ready to get stuck in?'

'Positively raring.'

Vasilico turned to look at Kirk, still standing in the doorway, a look of earnest anticipation on her features.

'Will there be anything else, Sergeant?'

Kirk's face promptly fell. 'No, but—'

'Off you trot, then.'

With a barely disguised scowl and a sullen 'Yessir', she ducked out, shutting the door behind her.

Vasilico turned to Anna with a wince. 'Sorry about that.'

'Don't be,' said Anna, not quite masking her amusement. 'She's a breath of fresh air.'

'That's one way of putting it. She's a tad impetuous, but I'm slowly but surely breaking her in.'

'You make her sound like a horse.'

Their eyes met. Vasilico gave a smile. Anna found herself returning it, then remembered she was still angry with him and swiftly straightened her expression.

Vasilico cleared his throat awkwardly. 'By the way, I ought to make you aware – Callum Finnie was arrested yesterday evening in the city centre.'

'What happened?'

'Got into a brawl with a couple of randos fresh out of the boozer. It's about fifty-fifty as to which party came off worse. After the medics patched him up, the local bobbies gave him a night in the slammer to cool off.'

Anna felt her heart sink. 'That's all Narinder needs.'

'Not that it's any consolation, but he appears, in a wholly irrational sort of way, to have been attempting to avenge her honour.'

'By getting into fights with random men?'

'Hence the emphasis on "irrational".'

Anna didn't press the matter, though she privately suspected Callum's actions had rather more to do with avenging his *own* honour than that of his girlfriend.

Vasilico cleared his throat again, breaking the silence that Anna belatedly noticed had fallen on the room.

'Right, then. I know your time is precious, so we'd best press on. This is where we are with what we've dubbed Operation Penny Farthing.'

He gestured to the wall behind Anna. Turning, she now saw that two large cork boards hung on either side of the door, each festooned with various materials relating to the investigation: photographs of the crime scenes, of the victims, a map of Glasgow with several different coloured pins stuck into it . . . She made her way over to it, arms folded, slowly taking in the spread.

'I'm not sure where to start,' she admitted.

'Well, let's begin with the victims.'

Drawing alongside her, Vasilico pointed to a blurry, A3-sized photo of a short-haired, smiling young white woman in her early twenties, presumably blown up from an ID card of some variety.

'First victim: Chloe Mazzaro, age 21. At the time, had just completed her third year of Sociology. Attacked in the wee hours of Tuesday 18 June in her first-floor flat in Cessnock. Described her attacker as a white male of slim, muscular build.'

He pointed to another photo, showing another woman of similar age, this time of South East Asian origin, her dark hair neatly plaited.

'Victim number two: Jing-Mei Zhao, a.k.a. Lucy. Age 22, fourth-year Psychology student, originally from Beijing. Attacked Saturday 13 July in the flat in Scotstounhill she shared with three fellow exchange students from China, who all happened to be out on the razzle-dazzle at the time. Described her attacker as a heavyset Indian or Pakistani male.'

He pointed to another picture. This woman was slightly older than the previous two, and of Afro-Caribbean extraction.

'Tuesday 6 August, victim number three: Gloria Owusu. Age 26, in her second year of a PhD in Biomedical Engineering. Assaulted in her flat in Royston by a white male.'

Vasilico moved on to the next victim, but before he'd even said her name, Anna experienced a sudden pang in her chest as she realised she recognised the woman in the picture.

'Fourth victim: Grace Dunphy, 22. Attacked—'

'Grace,' Anna murmured to herself.

Vasilico looked at her in surprise. 'You know her?' Then he shut his eyes, groaning. 'Of course you do. She was studying Criminology.'

'She was one of my third-years,' said Anna, the words coming out in a strained mumble as she gazed at the image of Grace, with her loose blonde bob, round face and impish smile. 'She didn't come back after the summer holidays. She keeps submitting doctor's notes, citing personal issues. I thought . . .' She shook her head. 'I don't know *what* I thought. I suppose I assumed there must have been a bereavement in the family or something.'

'In a sense, there was,' said Vasilico quietly. 'Grace was the one who suffered a miscarriage.'

'Oh God,' Anna whispered.

Horror quickly gave way to self-recrimination. Why hadn't she pursued the matter? Why hadn't she reached out to Grace personally to find out what was wrong? She'd kept meaning to, each time another week passed and a fresh letter arrived from her GP, informing the university that Grace remained unable to take up her studies. It was just, she'd been so busy with other things, it kept getting pushed to the back of the queue . . .

'The attack took place in her parents' home in Kelvindale on the night of Friday 30 August,' Vasilico went on. 'She describes her attacker as white and small but muscular. As I mentioned previously, her parents were asleep at the other end of the hallway, but they didn't hear anything.' He gestured to his ear. 'Earplugs.'

Anna cringed inwardly. What must it be like for them to have *that* on their consciences?

'As I intimated yesterday, Grace was the first victim to be violated with a sex toy – an element that, since then, has been a standard part of the attackers' modus operandi. To date, the sexual assaults have all been anal rather than vaginal, and all four women have been left with non-trivial injuries as a result.'

Vasilico exhaled a heavy breath and moved on to the next image.

'Victim five: Kimberly Napier, age 23. She'd just started her fourth year in Sociology and was attacked by an Asian male in the house she shares with two fellow students in Dennistoun on the morning of Sunday 22 September.'

And now the next one, barely pausing for breath.

'Sixth victim: Amber Maguire, 19. The youngest to date. Second-year English Literature. Attack took place on Friday 11 October in her flat in Finnieston. She'd just moved into it in the last two weeks. Her parents bought it for her so she wouldn't have to commute from Kilmarnock every day. She doesn't remember anything about her attacker's appearance.'

For a moment, he seemed to falter, as if he'd lost his train of thought. Glancing sidelong at him, Anna saw the taut expression on his face, the twitching of the muscle in his lower jaw, and realised that this was the one that had hit him the hardest.

The moment passed. He stirred and gestured to one last photograph, added so recently that the tape holding it in place hadn't yet started to yellow.

'And finally, Narinder Khatri. You already know her story.'

Anna drank in the image of Narinder gazing back at her, her bright smile and flawless skin a world away from the battered, misshapen mess to which she'd borne witness at the hospital the previous day.

She took a step back, taking in the sight of all seven victims at once. Seven different women, all seemingly targeted by the same men, all subjected to the same vicious ordeal, and no doubt each damaged on the inside every bit as much as on the outside.

'Any initial observations?' Vasilico's voice interrupted her thoughts.

Anna continued to gaze at the spread in front of her for another minute or so before speaking.

'The attacks are becoming more frequent.'

'I was wondering if you'd notice,' said Vasilico quietly.

Anna turned to look at him. 'The first few were almost four weeks apart each,' she said. 'But then, after Grace, they start to accelerate.'

Vasilico nodded. 'Twenty-three days between Grace and Kimberly. Nineteen between Kimberly and Amber. Seventeen between Amber and Narinder. They're escalating big time.' He was silent for a moment before speaking again. 'What else? What does the nature of the attacks say to you about the perpetrators?'

'Well,' said Anna, choosing her words carefully, 'the first thing I'd emphasise is that I'm not a forensic psychologist by trade. Actually, if I may be so bold as to say it, I view that sort of top-down profiling as seriously reductive. Some studies suggest it's no more effective at identifying the culprit than a coin toss.'

'In that case,' said Vasilico, 'I promise to take your observations with a grain of salt.'

Anna let out a heavy breath. She still wasn't entirely comfortable with this line of questioning. Weighing heavily on her was the fear that Vasilico would, in spite of his reassurances, take whatever she said as the gospel truth and use it to construct a profile that would be ineffective at best, and, at worst, divert attention away from the true guilty party.

With a considerable effort, she forced her reservations to the back of her mind.

'For starters,' she said, 'the entire scenario is highly unusual. These sort of home invasion attacks on women are usually carried out by lone wolves.

The manifesto, the fact we have at least two men working in tandem . . . I'm not sure there's any precedent for this – at least not in *this* country. They're not crimes of opportunity committed to satisfy a physical urge – they're designed to make a statement. In a sense, everything we know – or *think* we know – is irrelevant. We're dealing with a total unknown.'

Vasilico said nothing, but it was clear from his expression that this was not what he'd hoped to hear.

Anna continued to study the wall of evidence. 'There's been no variation in modus operandi between the two attackers? No particular calling card that's unique to one versus the other?'

'Other than in the sense that the Caucasian one appears to be the more vicious of the two, then no. They always set out to do maximum damage to the victims' faces. A couple of the women ended up with broken ribs. Another had a sprained wrist. But those injuries were all inflicted in the process of subduing the victims rather than being part of the main assault. In effect, any damage sustained to a part of the body other than the face or, latterly, the anus, appears to have been incidental.'

'Injuries to the face are typically associated with efforts to destroy the victim's individuality,' said Anna. 'To erase their very humanity. It's a way of branding them – of marking them for all to see, and potentially of making them undesirable to others. Spoiled goods, if you like. The anal rapes play into the dehumanisation angle as well. Assuming the attackers are both straight men, they very likely see these as a more humiliating, more degrading form of violation than quote-unquote "normal" intercourse.'

She'd begun to pace up and down, increasingly using her hands for emphasis as she lost herself in the act of working through her thoughts.

'And the ferocity of the violence – there's real, unbridled rage there. Like I said, this isn't some opportunistic thing for them. They're not doing this just because they feel like it, or because they can. These attacks – they represent something existential for these men. If disfiguring the victims' faces is about denying them their sense of self, then the whole act of selecting a target; presumably watching them for an extended period; choosing the precise moment to strike; injuring them in such a specific manner – it's . . . well, it's almost a ritual. A performance of masculinity, or what they perceive masculinity to be.'

'Which brings us to the manifesto,' said Vasilico.

Anna recited from memory, '"We call on men everywhere to draw courage from our actions and rise up to reclaim what is rightfully theirs from the scourge of gynocratic oppression".'

'We're continuing to monitor the social media sites. So far, this . . . call to arms has only ever surfaced to coincide with a fresh attack, and, in each instance, we've succeeded in getting it taken down more or less immediately. But I fear it's only a matter of time before some beetle-browed little creep with a grievance against women sees it and decides to respond to the clarion call.'

They stood side by side, each contemplating the wall of evidence, as if hoping some sort of breakthrough would reveal itself to them unbidden.

After some time, Vasilico broke the silence again.

'Any further thoughts?'

Anna forced herself to think. 'Well, there doesn't appear to be any racial component to the victim selection. They represent a cross-section of ethnicities, and there's no suggestion that either attacker favours a particular group.'

'Correct. Besides, we have the perpetrators' manifesto, in which they're not exactly shy about stating that their beef is with womankind as a whole, not with any particular racial or ethnic subset.'

'But they're choosing their victims somehow. And their beef, as you put it, might be with women in general, but they're not going after just *any* woman.' She rested her chin on her clenched fist, racking her brains. 'The manifesto makes reference to "deviant" women flaunting their sexuality. How many of the victims were sexually active?'

'All but one. But then, that's hardly unusual for a bunch of university students.'

'No,' Anna admitted, 'but there are degrees of "sexually active". I guess what I'm getting at is, could any of them have been regarded as particularly promiscuous? Could they have distinguished themselves from their peers in *that* way?'

Vasilico frowned. 'Not that I'm aware of – or at least, none of them volunteered to me that they were. By the sounds of it, Narinder certainly enjoys a night out tripping the light fantastic, but as far as we're aware she's never been anything less than completely faithful to her boyfriend. That goes for the rest of them as well – those with a long-term partner, at any rate.'

Anna continued to think. 'Well, if they're not being targeted for their sexual activity, what about their ideological views?'

Vasilico looked at her, intrigued. 'Go on.'

'These women are all students at the same university, and are predominantly studying subjects that fall under the auspices of the School of Social and Political Sciences – right?'

'Right.'

'In that case, could it be the old "social sciences equals feminist indoctrination" canard? Like, to these people, *all* women are the enemy, but clearly *some* women are more active in this so-called "Genocide of Men" than others.'

Vasilico rubbed his chin, considering this. 'Hmm. Maybe. But then, how many women are studying one of those subjects? I'm guessing it must be well into the hundreds. Doesn't exactly narrow it down, does it?'

'No,' Anna agreed reluctantly. 'Plus, you've got one doing a PhD in Biomedical Engineering and another studying English Lit. These don't exactly scream "rad fem" – especially the former.' She looked again at the array of faces pinned to the cork board. 'They're not working through the alphabet, they're not targeting a particular subject area, *or* a particular ethnicity or age . . .' She turned to Vasilico with a despairing look. 'Perhaps the selection process really is just random?'

Vasilico said nothing, but the look on his face told her that he didn't like the thought of this any more than she did.

'The other possibility,' Anna said, after a moment, 'is that the attackers – or at least one of them – are Social and Political Sciences students themselves, and that they're targeting women they already know.'

Vasilico glanced sidelong at her. 'Can you think of anyone who'd fit the bill?'

Anna looked at him in surprise. 'What?'

'I'm serious. Have any of your male students recently expressed strong anti-woman sentiments?'

Anna half-laughed. 'It's a university. Everyone there is in the process of finding out how they see the world for the first time. You have a whole bunch of extreme ideologies vying for dominance. Plus, we've got Mr Men's Rights himself on the faculty now.'

Vasilico gave her a quizzical look.

Anna rolled her eyes. 'The one and only Professor Leopold.'

'I think I've heard of him. Doesn't he do that podcast?'

Anna nodded. 'Ever since he showed up, he's been a lightning rod for reactionary thought. We've had a big influx of male students this semester, all wanting to take his Social Anthropology course. Their views tend to be firmly in line with the ones he espouses.'

She sighed and shook her head. 'But if you're asking me to name names, then no, I can't think of anyone in particular. In Criminology, we get almost three times as many female students as we do male . . . and the men we *do* get tend to be at the more socially progressive end of the spectrum.'

Plus, she thought, it would be grossly unfair to point the finger at someone without good cause. The old adage of 'if you've done nothing wrong, you've got nothing to fear' was cold comfort when your entire life was being turned upside down by a police force hellbent on finding something, *anything* to pin on you.

Again, she forced herself to apply her mind to the matter at hand.

'Just to clarify, all four rapes were carried out using an implement? No penile penetration whatsoever?'

'Correct,' said Vasilico. 'Which, technically, makes them sexual assaults rather than rapes – which, I hasten to add, in no way diminishes their horror. Though, besides Narinder, two of the other victims mentioned noticing that their attacker was aroused during at least part of the assault.'

'In that case, we can assume it's not a question of impotence.'

'What's your take on it, then?'

'Well, it could be said to represent a further level of dehumanisation – or to indicate that these women are in some way "tainted" or unclean. It's the old "fallen women" trope – you never know what they might be carrying.'

'Interesting.'

'And then there's the practical angle, which I assume you've already considered. Using an object means they avoid the risk of leaving any DNA.'

'In that regard,' said Vasilico, 'they've been maddeningly successful. To date, the forensics mob haven't been able to turn up so much as an eyelash.'

Anna nodded, somewhat distractedly. Her mind was still whirring.

'And the break-in angle – that would take planning. Making sure the location is accessible, that the victim is going to be home alone at the time . . . That too points to patience; a willingness not to move until all the pieces are in place.'

'I wondered about that myself,' said Vasilico. 'What I keep coming back to is that there must be easier ways to get at someone – ways that don't involve gaining access to a third-floor apartment or a house where only a set of earplugs means the difference between success and discovery. Why not just jump them in the stairwell, for example?'

Anna, however, didn't find this odd at all. 'It's the same story with abusers the world over. A closed door gives them both the time and the privacy to carry out their "work" in peace. It also makes a statement. It says, "You're not safe anywhere. Not even in your own home. We can come for you whenever and *wherever* we want."'

As she spoke, a shudder coursed through her. She was suddenly reminded, with acute immediacy, of her own vulnerability as a woman – not to mention as a mother. Until relatively recently, she'd allowed herself to believe that society was slowly but surely moving in the right direction with regard to women's rights – perhaps not as fast as she'd have liked, but, generally speaking, the momentum seemed to be on their side. The last few years, however, had heralded setback after setback, from the increasing attacks on women's reproductive rights to the election, in the United States, of a president with a string of sexual assault allegations to his name and who proudly boasted of 'grabbing women by the pussy' . . . and now this latest horror, perpetrated right in her own backyard. Whether, taken together, they amounted to a last, violent gasp from a patriarchy whose time was almost up or the first stirrings of a successful counteroffensive against the long march towards equity remained to be seen, but she feared it was the latter.

As she and Vasilico stood there in silence, a door slammed somewhere in the building, which only served to hammer home the eerie stillness that enveloped this austere room with its grim tableau.

Anna and Vasilico remained cloistered in there for a little over ninety minutes, batting ideas back and forth without reaching any definitive conclusions. Once they had, by mutual agreement, concluded that they weren't getting anywhere, Vasilico walked Anna back down to the foyer. Along the way, they passed a handful of other men and women in plain clothes heading about their business, while sounds of footsteps and conversation emanated from elsewhere in the building. The place was certainly beginning to liven up.

'I'll keep in touch,' said Anna, as they reached the ground floor. 'If I have any other bright ideas, I'll let you know.'

'I appreciate it.'

'And I really think you need to reconsider your decision to keep the manifesto and the linked nature of these attacks under wraps. The women of this city have a right to know what they're up against.'

'Even if it inadvertently puts them at greater risk?'

'They'll put two and two together before long, you know. Some of them probably know one another. You really think they're not going to trade notes?'

'In which case, we'll cross that bridge when we come to it.'

Halting in her tracks, Anna turned to face Vasilico. She considered her response carefully before giving it.

'You know,' she said, 'misogyny comes in many forms. You have your violent, woman-hating fanatics like the men responsible for these attacks. But wrapping women in cotton wool, unilaterally deciding what they do and don't need to know out of some benevolent conviction that it's for their own good – that you have a right to make those decisions on their behalf . . . That's misogyny too.'

Vasilico didn't reply, but from the tightening of his jaw, it seemed to Anna that either he'd taken serious umbrage at her implied accusation, or else her words had succeeded in striking a chord.

If he was planning to respond, he never got the opportunity. At that moment, a young man in a rumpled suit, who Anna now realised had been hovering uncertainly on the stairs above them for a good couple of minutes, stepped forward tentatively.

'Sorry, sir. I've got the Chief Super on the line for you.'

Anna saw Vasilico's features contort in an involuntary grimace. 'Tell her five minutes,' he said, half-turning.

The young man looked uncertain. Anna, suspecting that he'd probably been stalling the Chief Super for some time already, decided to take the initiative.

'No, it's fine,' she told Vasilico. 'Go. I need to be getting on anyway.'

She saw Vasilico's shoulders untensing. It seemed to her that he was relieved to have had the decision made for him.

'In that case,' he said, 'I shan't detain you further.' He smiled warmly at her. 'Take care, Anna. It's been a pleasure, as always.'

Anna's own smile was rather more strained. 'Goodbye, Detective,' she said, then turned and headed out into the fresh morning air.

9

'Let's turn to the poster we looked at during last week's lecture. What did we make of it? Does anyone have any thoughts?'

There were seven of them squeezed around the table in the cramped, airless tutorial room, their notes open in front of them: Anna plus six second-year students. It was a point of principle for her that, while a number of her contemporaries did everything in their power to delegate all their tutorials to others, she still led a handful herself. Partly it was because she felt it was important to maintain some semblance of a connection with the students and gauge how they were responding to the course, and these smaller group sessions were the ideal forum for doing so. Partly, too, it was because she was only too aware of just how thinly the handful of teaching associates and postgraduate students assigned to her were spread, without adding even more to their workload. They would hardly be going on strike otherwise.

Now, as the students finished turning to their reproductions of a poster circulated by a police force in Yorkshire during the previous Christmas holidays, that familiar awkward silence settled on the room. It was, Anna thought, a holdover from school: an unwillingness to signal oneself as overly keen, a teacher's pet, by volunteering to go first, even though she was sure they must all have *some* opinion on the item in question.

Mind you, maybe it was the content of the poster itself that was giving them pause. 'DON'T BE A VICTIM THIS CHRISTMAS!' it exhorted the young, female party-goers at which it was aimed, followed by a bullet point list of precautions they could take to reduce the odds of their being sexually assaulted. The usual bromides were trotted out: moderate your alcohol intake, always walk in well-lit areas, don't leave your gal pal unattended when she's three sheets to the wind . . .

She smiled encouragingly. 'Who'd like to go first? Come on – there are no wrong answers.'

'I found it offensive,' said Rose Diaz, tossing the words out there with a baleful shrug while the others continued to sit in silence, paying an unhealthy amount of attention to their own cuticles.

'Why's that?'

Rose shrugged, as if it was obvious. 'It's totally victim-blaming. It's all these instructions to women about what not to do if they want to avoid getting jumped, when instead, they should be talking to the men who actually commit these crimes.'

'It's also hella patronising,' one of the other girls, Aisling McGeachin, piped up. 'Like, do they think we don't know this stuff already?'

'Right.' A third student, Beth Wilton, joined in; Rose's indignation appeared to be contagious. 'It's the whole "responsible woman" trope. We're accountable for our own safety, not the police and not the men who might attack us. And if something happens to us, it must mean we weren't vigilant enough or something.'

'That's such bullshit,' retorted Charlotte Copping, the fourth and final female student in the group. 'The ad's not saying women are to blame if they're attacked. It's giving them advice on how to minimise the risks. That's not the same thing.'

'Well, excuse *me* for thinking women shouldn't have to constantly look over their shoulders when they're walking home at night,' Rose snapped, rolling her eyes in disgust.

It was always like this with the two of them – any excuse for a bust-up. Not for the first time, Anna found herself wondering whether it wouldn't have been more prudent to have moved one of them into a different group.

Charlotte scoffed contemptuously. 'Oh, come on. You're acting like you can just magic an ideal world into being if you pretend it's already here. As it happens, I think you're being incredibly irresponsible.'

'And you're absolving men of *their* responsibility.'

'I'm *absolutely* not. But unlike you, I'm being realistic. Who's more likely to listen: women, or the men who target them?'

'Right.' Greg Montgomery, one of only two male students in the group, spoke up tentatively. 'Not taking precautions cos you shouldn't have to and attacking the people who put forward practical suggestions won't result in less women being beaten and raped. Probably the opposite, actually.' He shifted uncomfortably in his seat, then gave an apologetic shrug. 'I mean, I know it's not exactly my place to say, but I just think maybe there's a bit of mixing up of risk and morality going on here.'

'No, Greg,' said Anna firmly, 'it's absolutely fine. You're as welcome to express your views as anyone else here. What do we think?' she asked, opening the question up to the group as a whole. 'Is there a tendency, when we talk about women's safety, to conflate advice with blame?'

No one spoke. Rose and Charlotte were still silently seething at one another, while the others, seemingly feeling they'd done their bit for the day, once more shuffled their notes or picked at their fingernails.

Anna turned to the one member of the group who hadn't spoken yet, and who was currently in the process of shading an entire page of his notebook in black, square by square.

'How about you, Cameron? You've been very quiet this morning.'

And every morning before that since the start of the semester. Back when he was a first-year, Cameron Mitchell had been outgoing and talkative, always an enthusiastic participant in group tutorials. It was as if he'd been replaced by a different person over the summer holidays. Now, he refused to meet anyone's eye, had lost a substantial amount of weight and had taken to dressing entirely in black, his hoodie up over his head even when he was indoors.

'Come on, Cameron,' she said, trying to sound encouraging rather than betraying the exasperation she felt. 'What do *you* think?'

Cameron shrugged. 'Don't see why it has to be one or the other,' he muttered, continuing to colour in his page.

'What do you mean?'

With a sigh, Cameron let his pen fall. He folded his arms sullenly, as if he resented having to explain himself.

'I mean, I just think everyone's afraid to call a spade a spade. Maybe they *should* take some of the blame? Like, if they're irresponsible and don't take sensible steps to protect themselves, then surely it's their own fault if they end up suffering the consequences?' He shrugged. 'Sorry if that's not what anyone wants to hear.'

You could have heard a pin drop. The only sound in the room was the rattling of the ineffective air conditioning unit. Anna gave Cameron a long, hard, appraising look. When she next spoke, her voice was dangerously calm.

'No, go on. Expand on this theory of yours.'

Cameron shrugged again. 'Well, I mean, if I park in a rough part of town and leave my car window open with my big fuck-off new laptop lying on the seat to get lifted, you'd say I'm a complete fucktard – right? But if a female wears a skirt that shows half her arse or gets so blind drunk she doesn't know if she's coming or going and she gets raped or whatever . . . what? Her actions are totally detached from the consequences?'

'You think the two are remotely comparable?'

'I just think it's double standards is all.'

With a final shrug, as if daring anyone to find fault with these views, he fell silent. The air conditioner continued to rattle and groan.

Rose glanced at Charlotte and rolled her eyes. 'For fuck's *sake*,' she muttered. Charlotte merely nodded. Finally, it seemed, they'd found something on which they could agree.

'Well, let me ask you this, Cameron.' Anna's voice continued to be deceptively calm. 'What precisely do you know about rape? Do you, for instance, know anyone who's *been* raped?'

Even as she spoke, the voice at the back of her head was pleading with her to stop, telling her that this line of questioning was completely inappropriate. But it was comprehensively drowned out by the blood pumping angrily in her ears.

Cameron said nothing. He continued to refuse to look at her.

'No? Then let me tell you a little something about it. It's not a consequence of walking through an unlit area or wearing a short skirt or having had too much to drink. It's a *weapon*.'

Her voice was growing louder, increasingly impassioned. At some point, she'd ended up on her feet, her splayed hands resting on the tabletop as she leaned towards Cameron. He remained slumped low in his chair, eyes hidden by the shadow of his overhanging hood. He appeared neither alarmed nor embarrassed nor even angry. He just sat there, silently taking it all in.

'Where do you think the majority of rapes take place?' Anna went on. 'Care to take a guess? No? Conflict zones. And which women end up being raped in conflict zones? It's not the promiscuous ones or the drunk ones or the ones that don't dress sufficiently modestly. It's all of them.'

She counted off on her fingers. 'It's the short ones, the tall ones, the young, the old, the attractive ones, the plain ones – *all* of them. You don't get to opt out by being "sensible". The only way you stop rape from happening is by changing the conditions that lead men to believe they have licence to do what they like to women's bodies because that's what the culture around them tells them from the moment they're born.'

She stopped abruptly, suddenly noticing that the rest of the students were staring at her wide-eyed, not quite able to believe what they'd just witnessed. And, in that instant, reality dawned and she realised she'd gone well past the point of simply challenging a student over an offensive or ill-thought-out remark. She felt hot all over, her skin prickling with electricity. She was sure her face and neck must be bright red.

'So, in future,' she managed to conclude, 'maybe think about that before you say something so bloody stupid.'

She sat down shakily. She felt light-headed, the way you do when you stand up suddenly and all the blood rushes to your feet. Cameron continued to sit in silence, giving no indication that he'd even heard her tirade, far less taken it on board.

An uneasy silence hung over the room, until Anna cleared her throat and once again addressed the group.

'Right, let's turn to Newburn, page 843 . . .'

As soon as the tutorial wrapped up, Anna hurried back to her office, consumed by a mixture of mortification and lingering rage. She knew she'd gone too far – knew, too, that if Cameron made a complaint against her, she wouldn't have a leg to stand on. And yet, if she was being honest with herself, she really couldn't pretend that, given the option to turn back the clock, she wouldn't respond in exactly the same way all over again.

She wondered what had happened to Cameron – how he'd come, seemingly in the space of just a few short months, to hold views that were in such extreme contrast to the ones he'd previously professed. She half-wondered, too, whether she should have mentioned his name to Vasilico in relation to his earlier query about students who'd expressed strong anti-woman sentiments. *Did* these count as anti-woman sentiments? In her view, they at the very least skirted seriously close to it, but she wasn't convinced Vasilico would see it that way. Besides, thinking women bore some responsibility for being raped was hardly proof that he was going round breaking into female students' bedrooms to do just that to them. If it was, there would be grounds to lock up roughly a third of the population – at least according to the latest round of Scottish Government-provided statistics. There was, when all was said and done, no law against being a victim-blaming creep.

Anna's thoughts soon turned, all too inevitably, to Grace Dunphy and the ordeal she'd suffered, and to her own failure to investigate the reasons behind her now six-week-long absence. It wasn't as if she could claim Grace was an unremarkable student who'd simply slipped below her radar. On the contrary, she'd shown considerable promise from day one, and, on at least a couple of occasions in the last year, had expressed to Anna an interest in continuing her studies to postgraduate level after she completed her undergraduate degree. That it had taken being confronted with Grace's mugshot on an evidence board for her to discover the truth spoke volumes as to how badly she'd failed in her duty of pastoral care. She resolved to reach out to Grace personally at the nearest opportunity – if nothing else, then to offer her condolences.

'. . . but of course, the modern, liberated woman wants to have her cake and eat it, flaunting her sexuality while simultaneously recoiling in horror the second she receives even the most benign attention from the opposite sex.'

Anna sat at her desk, eyes glued to her computer screen as the YouTube version of the most recent episode of Leopold's *Hard Truth* podcast played, its host's voice sounding thin and tinny on the cheap, built-in speakers. Leopold sat behind a desk, facing the camera in a suit and tie like some parody of a newsreader, a huge microphone – which reminded Anna somewhat of an oversized phallus – angled towards him. The harsh lighting gave his skin a shiny, oily appearance. The wall behind him was covered with grey noise dampening panels.

'Take lipstick as an example,' Leopold continued. 'Traditionally, used by women to signal their sexual availability. Culturally, the colour red is intended to denote arousal. Has been since before records began, whatever the postmodernists' – he said the word with a contemptuous sneer 'might claim to the contrary with their ongoing efforts to systematically dismantle any semblance of meaning in the world.

'We can extend this, too, to the pervading attitude that we must absolve women of all responsibility for whatever misfortune might befall them in the big, bad world. In the past, if a woman consumed a vast quantity of alcohol and an unscrupulous man took advantage of her while her inhibitions were lowered, we might have said, "It's terrible that that happened, but perhaps she should have considered the consequences of having too much to drink." But now, according to the morality police, you can't even suggest such a thing.

'Like it or not, there are a non-trivial number of bad actors out there. By placing the onus solely on men not to indulge in predatory behaviour – as if telling bad people "Don't do that bad thing" has ever worked – the feminists have created a sense of complacency amongst their fellow women. A culture of irresponsibility, if you will. "Nothing is ever my fault," they tell themselves. "It's not my job to protect myself. The state will do it for me."'

Anna suppressed a shudder. It wasn't hard to guess where the likes of Cameron were getting their views. In fact, she wouldn't have been surprised if he'd listened to this very episode before this morning's tutorial and come armed with these specific talking points. Had Leopold known they'd be discussing victim-blaming? Had he deliberately used his podcast to disrupt her class, making her look unhinged in the process?

She sighed. The idea that Leopold, whose viewing figures were in the hundreds of thousands, would have produced an entire episode with the sole purpose of provoking one of her students into winding her up in a tutorial was so absurd as to be contemptible. Not for the first time, her paranoia was getting out of hand.

She focused on the screen again. For the last several minutes, Leopold had continued to speak, growing increasingly impassioned with each fresh utterance, as if he was working himself up to a crescendo. Now, however, he fell silent and calmly folded his hands on the desk in front of him. When he continued, it was in a far more philosophical tone.

'So, gentle listener, I leave you today with a thought experiment. If a woman's lips say "no" but every other facet of her, including her choice of attire, screams "yes" – which part of her are you going to believe?'

'Closet fan, I see.'

Anna practically jumped out of her skin. She looked up to see Leopold leaning against the doorframe, grinning at her like the cat that had got the proverbial. She hastily fumbled with her mouse, taking what felt like an age to find the little 'X' to close the video.

'You know,' he mused, wandering into the office uninvited, 'much as I'm always delighted to discover I've reached a new listener . . . I'm not sure I should be encouraging you to tune in during office hours.'

He leant one hand on her desk, the other resting on his hip as he gazed down at her. She managed not to physically recoil.

'Would it be reasonable for me to take your newfound interest in my little programme as a sign that you're reconsidering my invitation to you to come on as a guest?'

'I've already made my views on that subject crystal clear,' said Anna tightly. 'I don't intend to repeat myself.'

Leopold shrugged serenely. 'A pity. A fiery exchange between the proponents of two competing ideologies would do wonders for my numbers. Not that I'm exactly struggling in that respect. Number one podcast among males aged 16–24 for six months running.'

He smiled complacently at Anna, inviting her to respond. She said nothing.

'No,' he went on, 'I must admit I'm thinking more about what it might do for *you*. You know – a chance to reach an audience that's not normally exposed to your way of thinking.'

'I don't need you to give me a leg up,' said Anna, through gritted teeth.

'Of course not. Perish the thought!'

Leopold straightened up and began to circle the room, lazily trailing a finger along the spines of the books that lined her shelves. It took all Anna's willpower not to order him to get out.

'Incidentally,' he mused, 'I gather from the grapevine that there was a little contretemps during one of your tutorials earlier today. Apparently you were rather brusque with one of the male students.'

She continued to glower at him, her eyes tracking his every movement.

'The thing about these disaffected young men is that, in my experience, what they need is guidance, not belittlement.'

He reached the doorway and turned to face her.

'All I'm saying is, if you continue to dismiss their concerns out of hand, don't be surprised if they turn to others for direction instead.'

And with that, he sauntered out, leaving the door wide open behind him.

Anna remained in her seat, livid and mortified in equal measure. She couldn't decide what was worse – Leopold's bare-faced insolence or the fact that word of this morning's goings-on had evidently spread like wildfire and she was now the subject of staff room gossip. After a moment, she got up from behind her desk, stormed over to the door and slammed it shut with all her might, then returned to her seat to stew in righteous fury.

10

El Duce invites GodsGift2Women and LifeIsPain to a new chat channel.

GodsGift2Women joins the chat.

El Duce: Someone's early tonight. Your attempt to atone for past transgressions?

GodsGift2Women: Anything to stop u whingeing like an old fish wife
GodsGift2Women: Hey
GodsGift2Women: Wanna see something neat?

El Duce: Define neat.

GodsGift2Women: https://www.youtube.com/watch?v=dQw4w9WgXcQ

El Duce: You expect me to just click that? Knowing you, it's probably a horse getting wanked or something.

GodsGift2Women: Much better than that
GodsGift2Women: Gods honour
GodsGift2Women: Go on, u know u want to

El Duce: Sigh.

El Duce clicks the link.

El Duce: FFS
El Duce: I told you to stop doing this.

GodsGift2Women: What
GodsGift2Women: Just a bit of harmless fun
GodsGift2Women: Its not like Im RAPING them or anything

El Duce: It's drawing unnecessary fucking attention. What happens if one of them calls the cops?

GodsGift2Women: Free country mate
GodsGift2Women: Im not breaking any laws
GodsGift2Women: Just taking a nice wee stroll roon the toon

El Duce: Sticking your camera up a girl's skirt is NOT how I define "taking a nice wee stroll". Are you actively TRYING to fuck us over?
El Duce: Is she even legal?

GodsGift2Women: Thats the thing, harder & harder 2 tell these days
GodsGift2Women: Either way, close enough not to be worth splitting the diffrence

El Duce: You think I haven't looked at the rest of your channel? Your fucking face is in a bunch of these videos.
El Duce: FFS, seriously

LifeIsPain joins the chat.

LifeIsPain: Hey guys
LifeIsPain: Whats happening

GodsGift2Women: Oh nothing
GodsGift2Women: Just the dear leader trying 2 prove hes got the biggest dick here
GodsGift2Women: Which is statisticly improbable seeing as Im in the top 1%

LifeIsPain: LOL
LifeIsPain: Hey Iv been wondring
LifeIsPain: What do u reckon
LifeIsPain: Is Margot Robbie a 6 or a 6.5
LifeIsPain: ?

GodsGift2Women: HAHAHAHAHA

El Duce: Why, you got a hot date with her?
El Duce: Dude, seriously. Who the fuck cares?
El Duce: Your lecturers clearly aren't working you hard enough if you've got time to play Rate My Slut.

LifeIsPain: Sorry
LifeIsPain: Was just asking

*   *   *

GodsGift2Women opens a separate chat channel with El Duce.

El Duce joins the chat.

El Duce: ?

GodsGift2Women posts an animated gif of a nude Margot Robbie from The Wolf of Wall Street.

GodsGift2Women: Hey fellas what dyou reckon? Is Margot Robbie a 6 or a 6.5?

El Duce: Funny.

GodsGift2Women: Seriously
GodsGift2Women: Why the fuck do u keep this dork around

El Duce: I have my reasons.

GodsGift2Women: Reasons
GodsGift2Women: Like what

El Duce: That's for me to know and you to find out.

GodsGift2Women: Wanna know what I think

El Duce: Nothing would thrill me more.

GodsGift2Women: U like having him around cuz he let's u make him ur bitch
GodsGift2Women: Let's u feel like less of a scrub having some one lower down the totem poll

El Duce: You never know, I might be grooming him to replace you.

GodsGift2Women: Yeah right
GodsGift2Women: Love to see u try

El Duce: Just remember who holds the cards here. You don't know jack shit about me. Whereas I know who you are and what you do, shell suit boy.
El Duce: All it takes is one anonymous call to the cops and

you'll be spending the rest of your natural existence caged with the paedos and rapists.

GodsGift2Women: Sure
GodsGift2Women: Then who'd u get to help carry out ur precious "missions". Mr is Margot Robbie out of my league?

El Duce: Not something for you to concern yourself with. But if you think I don't have options, think again.

GodsGift2Women posts a Chewin' the Fat *'Ooooh!' animated gif.*

El Duce: Just fucking watch yourself.
El Duce: And stop posting those fucking videos. I mean it.

El Duce closes the channel.

11

Thursday 31 October

Thursday morning in the Scavolini household played out as something akin to a tragicomic farce. From the moment Anna got up, one calamity after another seemed to transpire, beginning with the boiler cutting out while she was in the middle of her shower and culminating in the realisation that she'd forgotten to look out anything to wear before going to bed the previous evening. Now, as she hurried down the stairs, dressed in trousers and a camisole, she found Zoe on her knees in the hallway, lacing up Jack's shoes.

'Zoe, have you seen my grey top?'

'What grey top?' said Zoe, neither looking up nor sounding sufficiently concerned about what, right now, felt to Anna like the single most important issue on the planet.

'The silk one that goes with these trousers. It should've come through the wash.'

Zoe shrugged, still utterly blasé. 'Well, if it'd came through the wash, I'd've put it over the top banister wi the others.'

'Well, it's not *there*,' Anna insisted. She continued to stand there, half-dressed, waiting for Zoe to treat this situation with the gravity it deserved.

But Zoe, it seemed, was not going to be doing any such thing anytime soon. 'Jackie-boy,' she remonstrated, 'if ye don't keep still, this is only gonnae take ten times as long.' She looked up at Anna again, as if surprised to find her still there, 'Can ye no just wear something else?'

'Forget it,' Anna muttered, before turning and hurrying back up the stairs.

Reaching the first-floor landing, she again rooted through the pile of freshly laundered clothes that had been dumped unceremoniously over the banister, which merely served to confirm that the missing top was not among them. With an angry groan, she stormed through to her bedroom, pausing momentarily to check the display on her phone, charging in the dock atop the nightstand. Still only at 32%. Why did phones insist on charging at a snail's pace whenever you were in a hurry? Come to that, why did the batteries have so little capacity? This one was barely six months old, and already she was lucky if, in the course of a day, she got away with only having to charge it twice.

She crossed to the wardrobe and rifled through the various items of clothing hanging from the rail. No sign of the shirt there either.

'Fuck's sake!'

She knew she was being irrational – that one top was as good as any other. But she'd had her sights set on it, and was determined for at least *one* thing that morning to go as planned.

Heading out into the landing again, she crossed into the bathroom and, in desperation, lifted the lid of the washing basket. There, lying at the top of the pile of dirty clothes, was the elusive grey silk shirt, complete with the stain from the spaghetti bolognese she belatedly remembered having spilled on it last week.

'Anna!' Zoe's caterwauling holler rose from the bottom of the stairs. 'Ye ready tae go?'

'No I am bloody *not*,' Anna muttered under her breath, before responding, with as much good grace as she could muster, 'Coming!'

She ran back to the bedroom, grabbed a shirt from the wardrobe at random, shrugged it on, then snatched up her phone and hurried down the stairs. She was still tucking her shirt into her waistband when she reached the bottom, to find Zoe and Jack waiting side by side, both bundled up in their winter coats.

'See?' said Zoe cheerfully. 'Ye look totally fine in that.'

Anna made a point of not responding. 'How much charge d'you normally get out of your phone?' she asked, as she crossed over to the rack to collect her own coat.

Zoe frowned, puzzled by this question. 'Dunno. Couple days if I go light on the podcasts and Out of Context Human Race videos. Else . . . mibby a day? How come?'

'These days, I'm doing well if I get seven hours out of mine,' said Anna, grabbing her coat from the hook and managing to tear the hanging loop in the process.

'Planned obsolescence, in't it?' said Zoe philosophically, as if she was some sort of expert on the subject. 'They design 'em tae break down after just a few months, so's ye're forced intae buying the latest bells 'n' whistles model. And they suck ye intae their ecosystem so ye cannae just switch over tae the competition. S'how they get their claws intae ye.' She shrugged expectantly. 'So, we gonnae vamoose or what?'

The three of them hurried down the steps to the street, then went their separate ways – Zoe and Jack heading down towards Jack's playgroup, Anna up to Hyndland Road and the fifteen-minute walk to the university.

At the top of Clarence Drive, she stopped and turned to look back at Zoe and Jack as they continued downhill, hand in hand. Since Anna had returned to work following her sabbatical earlier in the year, she'd been sending Jack to playgroup a couple more times a week – chiefly to prepare him for starting school in just over nine months' time. To her, it all seemed to be happening far too quickly. The last three years and ten months had passed in virtually the blink of an eye, and it was hard not to feel she could have made more time for him, if she'd only put in the effort.

It didn't help that, these days, she seemed to have less free time on her hands than at any point she could remember – at least since her postgraduate days, when she'd somehow juggled her PhD and teaching commitments with part-time bar work to make ends meet. And the limited free time she *did* have never seemed to sync up with Jack's. He'd invariably be at playgroup or doing something with Zoe or else would treat Anna's overtures to him with a cool indifference that often took her aback. In her weaker moments, she even found herself feeling just a tiny bit resentful about the relationship Jack had with Zoe, even though she knew perfectly well she had no one to blame but herself for creating the very gap into which Zoe had been only too happy to step, forming a bond with her beloved 'Jacko' that was somehow nanny, big sister and surrogate parent all rolled into one.

At various points over the last three years, Anna had wondered whether it wouldn't have been better if she'd relinquished some of her responsibilities when she'd returned to work after her maternity leave: gone part-time, handed over the reins of running the Criminology programme to someone else. But of course, she would never *seriously* have considered such a course of action. Even entertaining the possibility that she wasn't capable of both being a mother and having a full and successful career would have been an anathema to her. The Anna Scavolini way had always been to pour one hundred percent of her energy into any task she set her mind to, especially in her professional life. Anything less would be an admission of failure.

Ignoring the twang of guilt in her gut, she set her face to the wind and walked on, quickening her pace as she headed up Hyndland Road towards the university.

Shortly after 1 p.m., Anna, sitting on a couch near the back of Offshore, a coffee shop on the corner of Gibson Street and Westbank Quadrant, glanced up from the lecture notes she'd been going over as the bell above the front door rang. A young woman stepped inside, dressed in dungarees and a thick woollen jumper. She walked with her head bowed low, as if she was ashamed to be seen.

It took Anna a moment to recognise Grace Dunphy. So much about her had changed since she'd last seen her: her clothes, her posture, but most of all her face. The bruises had faded, the cuts had almost healed, but it was as if her features had been . . . rearranged. The proportions seemed different, her eyes more sunken, her cheeks more lopsided, her nose no longer as straight as it had once been.

Anna hastily stowed her notes in her satchel and got to her feet.

'Grace,' she said, wishing she'd thought of something more original. *How are you?* seemed inappropriate; *You're looking well* doubly so. What were you *supposed* to say under the circumstances?

Grace gave a small smile. 'Hey, Professor.'

And, somehow, that was enough.

* * *

'. . . and I submitted my final draft a couple of weeks ago,' said Anna. 'That's the end of my involvement till the proofs come back.'

They were both seated on the sofa, facing one another at forty-five degree angles, their knees almost touching. Their orders had been taken and delivered: coffee and a flatbread for Anna, a Diet Coke for Grace. Around them, the noise of conversation ebbed and flowed, the bell above the door periodically tinkling as someone either entered or left the café.

Grace nodded understandingly. 'Must be a weight off your mind, finally having it done and dusted. So when's it coming out?'

'February, all being well,' said Anna, wondering, not for the first time, just where the last twelve months had gone.

'I'll look out for it.'

'Don't be daft – I'll send you a copy.'

Grace smiled and took a sip of her Diet Coke, sucking it gingerly through a straw. From this, plus her newfound tendency to pronounce *s* as *sh*, Anna surmised that she'd suffered damage to her teeth.

'What about Dr Hadid?' Grace asked brightly. 'How's she doing? She been made a permanent member of staff yet?' Grace had been in a couple of Farah's tutorial groups the previous year.

'Not as of yet, no.' Anna's response was guarded.

Grace frowned. 'That's criminal. She's, like, the hardest working out of everyone there.' She realised what she was saying. 'I mean, present company excepted, obviously.'

'No, you're not wrong,' said Anna wearily. 'About any of it. And if I had my way, she'd have made lecturer years ago. But of course,' she went on in a tone of forced levity that belied her actual words, 'it's not up to me, and my opinion seems to count for less and less with the passage of time' – she was aware of her tone growing more resentful – 'while, for others, it's the easiest thing in the world to influence School policy.'

'You're talking about Professor Leopold, aren't you? God, I still can't believe they went ahead and hired that bozo. You know a bunch of us all signed a petition against it?'

Anna nodded. She vaguely remembered the letter that was circulated to everyone's email addresses over the summer. She'd still been on sabbatical, and had had more pressing concerns of her own to deal with at the time, so she hadn't paid it a whole lot of attention. She *had* briefly considered signing it herself, before concluding that to do so would have been seriously impolitic given her own status as a faculty member.

Grace grimaced. 'Not that it did any good. What's a handful of disgruntled feminists in the face of an influx of sweaty little incels all wanting Sensei to teach them how to hate women?'

'Now, now,' said Anna dryly. 'I'm told he brings a great deal of prestige to the university.'

'I think they might be mixing prestige up with notoriety.'

'Well, it's all about engagement, I suppose. Isn't that what they call it?'

Grace smiled, in the process revealing that half of one of her central incisors was missing. 'I think that's what the kids are saying these days, yeah.'

Anna returned the smile. 'So when d'you reckon you'll be coming back?'

Grace's smile faded instantly. They'd both been dancing around it for a while now, but they'd finally come to the real substance of the issue, and one of Anna's primary reasons for asking if they could meet.

'I'm not sure I'm going to,' she said, unable to look Anna in the eye as she spoke. 'I mean, I know I've been handing in sick lines, but lately I've felt like I'm just putting off the inevitable.' She sighed. Shrugged fatalistically. 'I dunno, I just feel like I need a fresh start. Y'know, put some distance between myself and . . . everything.'

There was no need to ask what 'everything' meant. For the first time, Anna wondered whether Grace had known she was pregnant before she had the miscarriage. Probably not, she thought. When you were just about to go into your fourth year of university, you were unlikely to suddenly make a conscious decision to start a family. Or perhaps that was overly presumptuous of her? Maybe that was *precisely* what Grace had been planning to do. Now that it came down to it, Anna realised she really didn't know her all that well.

'I get that,' she said. 'I really do. I just think it'd be such a shame to throw all that hard work away.'

'I've been helping Dad out with the shop,' said Grace, with forced cheerfulness, as if she hadn't heard Anna. 'Mostly in the back room, cos . . .' She gestured vaguely to her face. 'But y'know, it's work. Keeps me from going cuckoo.'

'You could defer for a year instead,' said Anna. 'In twelve months' time, you might feel differently.'

'Or maybe, in twelve months' time, I'll feel exactly the same.'

Anna lowered her eyes, gazing into the dregs of her coffee cup. She supposed it had been a long shot.

Grace managed a strained smile. 'I dunno. We'll see. And now I'd really better . . .' She reached for her shoulder bag.

'Of course,' said Anna quickly. 'I ought to be getting back myself.'

It was a lie – they'd barely arrived, and she'd hardly touched her food – but she had no desire to guilt-trip Grace into staying. So, as Grace got to her feet, she did likewise. Grace shouldered her bag, then turned to face her.

'I'm glad you called,' she said. 'It's nice knowing someone cares.'

'There are *plenty* of people who care about you, Grace,' Anna insisted. 'Whatever you end up deciding, promise you won't lose touch.'

'I, um . . .' Grace twisted one foot round the other leg awkwardly – seemingly reluctant, now that it came to it, to leave things like this. 'D'you know anything about this meeting on Monday night?'

'Meeting?'

'Something I saw on Snapchat. A buncha female students are meeting at the Dewar to talk about their concerns about safety on campus. It's meant to be a sort of support group and . . . well, I'm thinking maybe I'll head along. I know what happened to me didn't happen *on campus*, but I kinda figure I've got some skin in the game.'

'I think that would be a great idea,' said Anna sincerely. At the forefront of her mind was the thought that anything that encouraged Grace to maintain some form of contact with the university could only be a good thing, increasing the chance that she would one day return. She thought, too, that she might well tag along herself, assuming they'd admit a member of staff.

They faced one another awkwardly – neither, it seemed to Anna, sure how to bring this to a close. Eventually, Grace gave a shrug and half-opened her arms. They hugged clumsily – something they'd never done before. Anna couldn't tell which of them found it more awkward.

'You look after yourself, Grace,' she said. 'Hopefully I'll see you again soon.'

Grace gave a small, noncommittal smile, then turned and headed for the exit. Anna remained on her feet, watching her go – a small, forlorn figure in shapeless clothes, her life completely upended in a single, cruel stroke.

12

A couple of minutes before three o'clock, the exodus from the ground-floor lecture theatre in the Rutherford Building began. Anna, waiting in the corridor, pressed herself against the wall to avoid the stream of students that came cascading out of the double doors, conversing animatedly as they hurried to their next classes. She waited till the flow had dried to a trickle before heading in.

Farah was standing behind the desk at the front of the room, gathering up her laptop and notes. She looked up to see Anna approaching, smiling in surprise.

'Anna! What are you doing here?'

Anna shrugged. 'Just passing. Thought I'd look in.' She gestured to the stack of textbooks on the desk. 'Need a hand lugging those back to base?'

They wound their way up through the campus towards the Hutcheson Building, each carrying an armful of textbooks. They took their time, partly because the books were on the heavy side, partly because they hadn't had an opportunity for a proper catch-up since the events at the hospital.

'How's Narinder doing?' Anna asked. 'I take it she's been discharged.'

Farah nodded. 'Yesterday afternoon. She's gone to stay with her parents for a while. She wasn't in love with the idea of going back to the flat. I know how she feels.'

'And you? Are you . . . ?'

'I'm staying with Émile for now. I couldn't face it either, knowing what happened.'

As they began to climb the flight of stone steps behind the student union, Anna's eyes were drawn to a young woman passing in the opposite direction. One of her eyes was swollen shut, her entire face a chequerboard of bruises and scrapes. Anna wondered what had happened to her. Was she one of the other victims whose pictures Vasilico had shown her, rendered unrecognisable by the violence that had been inflicted on her? Could she be someone who'd slipped under the radar; had chosen, for whatever reason, not to report the incident to the police? Or did she have no connection to the attacks whatsoever – just one of the thousands of battered women out there from every walk of life? Perhaps, Anna told herself, there was nothing sinister about it at all. Perhaps she'd just lost her footing on her way home after a night at the pub and ended up face down on the pavement. It was certainly plausible, though Anna suspected it was merely wishful thinking on her part.

Pushing these thoughts from her mind, she turned to Farah again. 'Is Narinder . . . I mean, is she bearing up?'

Farah pulled a typically Gallic facial expression. 'I don't like to say. She won't talk about it at all. But an experience like that . . . it *has* to change you in ways the rest of us can't comprehend.' She was silent for a moment, then added, more brightly, 'But she says she wants to resume her studies as soon as possible. That's good, I think. To focus on something other than the attack . . . ?'

Anna thought of Grace – her life, as it had been, virtually brought to a standstill by her ordeal. 'It *is* good,' she said firmly.

They entered the Hutcheson Building and set off up the stairs, making for the third floor, where most of the criminology staff had their offices.

'Have you heard anything about this event at the Dewar on Monday night?' Anna asked. 'About women's safety on campus . . .'

'Mm. One of the other TAs mentioned something about that. I think a lot of students will go. Some staff too – TAs, mostly.'

'You think so?'

Farah nodded. 'There's a lot of concern. About safety and the general . . .' – she gestured vaguely – '. . . culture.'

'I hadn't realised,' Anna admitted.

Farah let out a small, involuntary chuckle.

'What's so funny?'

'Sorry.' Farah waved her hand in front of her face, as if trying to shoo away her mirth. 'It's not funny – not really. It's just . . . my understanding is that a lot of the girls feel the university doesn't take their concerns seriously. And . . . well, you've been here forever. Most people, they conflate you with the institution and' – she shrugged – 'it's not so surprising if they don't feel comfortable sharing with you.'

Anna wasn't sure how to respond to that. She didn't particularly like the feeling it left her with.

'Are *you* going?' she asked, as they stepped onto the third floor.

Farah wrinkled her nose. 'I'm not so sure. I didn't plan to – not originally. But after what happened to Rindy . . . well, you might say it encouraged me to re-evaluate the situation.'

They turned onto the corridor leading to Anna's office.

'Would Narinder be interested in going, do you think?' she asked.

But before Farah could respond, Fraser suddenly materialised in front of them, stepping out of his office to block their path.

'Ah, Anna,' he said, as if their meeting was one of mere chance and he hadn't been waiting to ambush her, 'I've been hunting high and low for you.'

He glanced briefly – and, to Anna's mind, rather dismissively – in Farah's direction. Farah stood, eyes on the floor, hugging her textbooks to her bosom, a picture of deference.

'I wondered if I might have a word,' Fraser continued, addressing Anna as if Farah wasn't there.

Anna silently bristled. Her conversation with Farah was far from over, and she severely resented Fraser's tendency to treat the TAs as if they were mere dogsbodies, undeserving of basic courtesy.

'It won't take long,' said Fraser, evidently sensing her reticence but too spineless to insist – at least not overtly.

Making a deliberate show of not responding to him, Anna turned to Farah. 'We'll continue this conversation later, yeah?'

'Of course,' Farah nodded.

With some difficulty, they succeeded in combining their respective piles of books into one. Then, as Farah headed off, weighed down by a stack which now reached up to her chin, Anna turned back to Fraser, eyebrows raised expectantly. Giving his familiar wincing smile, he extended his arm, his hand hovering near the vicinity of her shoulder – a none too subtle attempt to chivvy her along.

Anna stepped into Fraser's office. As he shut the door behind them, she stood stiffly in the middle of the room, clutching the strap of her satchel. It was hard to shake the feeling that she'd been summoned to the headmaster's study to account for some indiscretion, real or imagined.

'Please.' Fraser gestured to the vacant plastic chair facing his desk.

Reluctantly, Anna sat down. In these situations, she felt it was generally inadvisable to assume a sedentary position. It tended to merely prolong the agony.

Fraser moved behind his desk and sank into his own considerably more comfortable seat. He thumbed a stack of forms in front of him – a gesture that was clearly intended to appear unconscious but which, to her eyes, seemed altogether too practised to be any such thing.

'As you'll be aware,' he said, 'the six-week feedback forms went out to students earlier this week.'

These were yet another of the pet wheezes he'd implemented when he was installed as Head of School – part of what he referred to as a more granular approach to assessing students' satisfaction levels. In Anna's considered opinion, they were simply yet another opportunity for him to wade into matters that were outwith his field of expertise.

'I've tabulated the data,' he went on, 'and . . . well, there's no nice way of saying this. Your numbers aren't looking great.'

'Oh?' Anna tried to sound unconcerned.

'The students varyingly describe you as didactic; a harsh taskmaster; overly prescriptive in your pronouncements. There appears to be a general feeling that you're aloof and unapproachable.'

Anna attempted to swallow, only to find her mouth unexpectedly dry. Whatever she'd been expecting Fraser to say when he brought her in here, it hadn't been this.

'Also,' Fraser went on, 'I gather there was an incident at one of your tutorials the other day involving you losing your rag with a student.'

'That's . . . that's a mischaracterisation of what happened,' said Anna, finding her voice but tripping over the words in the process. 'The individual in question made a series of inflammatory remarks that caused considerable distress to the other students.'

She was aware she was embellishing things somewhat – *pissed them off royally* might have been more accurate – but she pressed on.

'And I'm sorry to hear the students don't see me as their best friend, but at the end of the day, it's hardly a popularity contest.'

Fraser winced. 'Well, I mean, it kind of *is*.'

She looked at him incredulously.

He gave a strained smile, which made it look like he was in severe pain. That, or trying to squeeze out an impacted turd. 'Whether we like it or not, the university is a business, and businesses live and die by their customer satisfaction. And if said customers feel the product doesn't match their expectations . . . well, they'll take their purchasing power elsewhere.'

Anna knew, though he didn't state it outright, that he was referring primarily to the fee-paying foreign students on whose patronage the university was so reliant to keep its coffers filled.

Fraser fingered a separate stack of forms on the other side of his desk. 'We should all take inspiration from Professor Leopold, I feel. I know he's only been with us a short while, but his satisfaction levels leave everyone else in the shade . . .' – he gave a self-deprecating smile – '. . . yours truly included. He may not be everyone's cup of tea, but he's certainly the toast of the town as far as his students are concerned.'

'That's because he's just telling them what they want to hear,' Anna retorted. 'People love having their biases confirmed, but dishing out easy answers won't equip them to navigate the outside world.'

Fraser gave another of his pained smiles. 'You know, I actually think you and Professor Leopold have more in common than you realise. You're both highly knowledgeable about your respective subject areas, deeply passionate in your desire to transform society . . .' He gave a soft, rueful little laugh. 'And both utterly bloody-minded in your belief that yours is the only way in which that change should be achieved.'

Anna said nothing. She was well aware she could be accused of being thin-skinned, but she couldn't help feeling she was being patronised and mocked, her firmly held convictions reduced to an amusing anecdote.

'It would be really quite something,' Fraser continued, oblivious, 'to have the two of you collaborate on something. Some sort of cross-disciplinary research project, perhaps – the criminologist and the social anthropologist, working together.' His eyes suddenly lit up, an idea coming to him. 'In fact . . .'

He held up an index finger, stalling for time as, with his other hand, he clicked frantically with his mouse, searching for something on his computer. After a few seconds, he gave a little *ah!* of triumph.

'There's an opening on 13 November for an event in the Argyll Hall. A highly respected international speaker was meant to be delivering a lecture on public health policy in emerging democracies, but thanks to the machinations of the Home Office, her visa was denied and she had to pull out.'

He turned to face Anna, an excited light in his eyes. 'What would you say to a debate in front of a packed house? Scavolini versus Leopold, two heavyweights in their respective fields, each setting out their stall for how they'd reshape the world. It could be the event of the year.'

He looked at Anna expectantly, clearly anticipating her sharing his enthusiasm. As she gazed back at him, her expression unchanging, his smile faded, and the light in his eyes went out like a snuffed candle.

'Did *he* put you up to this?' Anna's tone was calm but unmistakably chilly.

Fraser gave an uncomprehending shrug.

'He's been badgering me for days now to come onto his podcast to debate him,' said Anna, unaccountably annoyed at having to spell it out. 'I keep saying no. Now, all of a sudden, along you come with this ruse to get me onto a public stage with him. Seems a bit bloody convenient – for *him*, that is.'

'I can assure you,' said Fraser levelly, 'you're not the subject of any sort of conspiracy cooked up between myself and Professor Leopold. As a matter of fact, I haven't even broached the subject with him yet. I just thought you might welcome the opportunity to amplify your views to a broader audience . . . and to drum up a bit of publicity for the School at the same time.' He shrugged fatalistically. 'But if you're not comfortable with the idea, I'm certainly not going to twist your arm.' He tapped the mouse, closing the window. 'Out of interest, why *are* you so unwilling to debate him?'

'Are you familiar with Brandolini's Law?'

'Refresh my memory.'

'That the amount of effort required to refute bullshit is several orders of magnitude larger than that required to produce it.'

Fraser gave a slight smile.

'Events like these,' Anna went on, 'give the impression that truth is relative. That the ability to perform well on stage is the ultimate arbiter. In reality, they're just willy-waving exercises, both for the well-intentioned debater – who wants to believe that, through the power of her words and intellect alone, she can undo a lifetime of indoctrination and convince someone with an opposing viewpoint that he's been wrong all this time – and for the "reasonable" ideologue who pretends he'd be willing to change his mind if he just heard the right argument. The fact is, these hucksters have built their entire brand on feeding their captive audiences what they want to hear. They'll never admit they're wrong because, the moment they do, their source of revenue will dry up overnight.'

She shook her head firmly. 'I don't debate people like Robert Leopold for the same reason I wouldn't debate a flat-Earther or a Holocaust denier. Because the moment you do, you're lending them a legitimacy they don't deserve. You're telling anyone who listens, "Here are two opposing but equally valid viewpoints".'

She could also have added that she was exhausted fighting what amounted to a rearguard action against reactionaries, constantly bringing proof to the table of systemic sexism and racism, only to be told, 'I don't believe you.' Progressive types, she knew, herself included, lived for the moment when they managed to win an argument against such people – to 'put them in their place' by presenting them with unassailable facts and evidence. But she knew it would never happen. These people weren't attacking from a position of logic. They weren't looking to be convinced. It didn't matter how much proof you brought to the table – they'd just keep sending you back out for more. It was why they were so keen to deny that systemic injustices existed: it was all a ploy to exhaust their opponent, to constantly demand that they produce fresh evidence while never ceding any ground of their own. It meant that people like her had to fight the battle from square one every time. In the meantime, women continued to be raped and murdered, Black people continued to be disproportion-ately criminalised, and the planet continued to burn.

Fraser didn't respond immediately. For several seconds, he simply sat there in silence, folded into the ergonomic curve of his chair, looking slightly dazed. He clearly hadn't anticipated such a vociferous rebuttal.

'Well,' he said eventually, 'like I said, I wouldn't dream of pressuring you to do anything you don't want to.'

But she heard the subtext loud and clear. You're letting the side down. Not being a team player.

Why can't you just fit in?

At various points in her life, Anna had tried genuinely hard to be what other people wanted her to be. Early in her academic career, she'd been deferential to her more established colleagues – to assuage their fragile (usually male) egos; to make it clear she wasn't a threat to them. She'd avoided putting herself forward for gigs she knew she was eminently qualified for to demonstrate her respect for the pecking order and her place within it. None of it had done her a blind bit of good. She wasn't accepted into the boys' club; was still passed over for assignments that were hers by right. So she'd decided to stop playing nicely. To stop caring what people thought of her. If they thought she was awkward, a disruptor, a ball-breaker, then fine – she'd bloody well be all those things and more. Because, when it came down to it, you couldn't win. People made up their minds about you at first glance and, from that moment on, whatever you did merely reinforced their existing opinion of you.

Might as well just be the 'Difficult Woman' everyone already thought you were.

13

'He actually *said* that?' Farah stared at Anna, incredulous.

Anna nodded emphatically. 'Yep. Tried to guilt-trip me into going along with his little wheeze, with a whole side order of "you'll be letting down the whole university if you say no".'

They were sitting bundled up in their coats on deckchairs in Anna's back garden, Anna drinking a bottle of Corona, Farah smoking and using an 'I'll be a post-feminist in a post-patriarchy' mug as an ashtray. It was late, the only light coming from the kitchen window behind them. Zoe was sleeping over at Sal's, and Anna, after putting Jack to bed, had rung Farah and invited her round – partly for some company, partly to continue the conversation Fraser had so rudely interrupted earlier . . . and partly, and most importantly of all, to vent.

Farah snorted. 'In French, we have a name for people like him. We say he's *une pompe à chiasse*.'

'What does that mean?'

Farah looked at Anna, her expression deadpan. 'Diarrhoea pump.'

For a few seconds, they merely stared into each other's eyes in silence. Then, at the exact same moment, they both cracked up in hysterics.

'I'm sorry,' Anna choked through her laughter, waving a hand in front of her face. 'I shouldn't.' With a considerable effort, she succeeded in regaining control of herself. 'I mean, he's *not* – not really.'

Farah appeared unconvinced, but said nothing.

'Actually,' said Anna, turning serious, 'I think he's trying his level best to make things work. He's just' – she shrugged – 'totally out of his depth and trying to manage staff from umpteen different disciplines, half of which he has no understanding of whatsoever.'

Farah nodded soberly. 'A lot has changed recently,' she agreed.

'You got *that* right.' Anna sighed. 'I don't know – there was a time when I loved this job . . . And don't get me wrong,' she added hastily, 'I still do. *Most* of it, anyway. But there's so much bullshit now. All the politicking and the bureaucracy and the endless fights over a smaller and smaller funding pot, all while it feels increasingly like my passion for the teaching and the research side of things is being exploited by a bunch of people who really have no idea what it is I do.'

She glanced sidelong at Farah. 'And don't get me *started* on the way they take advantage of people in *your* shoes. The crappy pay, the term-time-only contracts, the non-existent job security . . .'

Farah shrugged. 'Well, if I'd wanted to become rich, I'd have gone to law school like *Papa* wanted.'

Anna smiled ruefully. The daughter of a French mother and a Palestinian father and the youngest of four girls, Farah had spoken often of being the black sheep of the family – the only one who'd so far failed to bag herself either a job that brought her fame and fortune or, as the next best alternative, a fabulously handsome suitor who'd assist her in begetting her parents a string of photogenic grandchildren. Their experiences weren't exactly identical, but the parallels were sufficient for Anna to have no difficulty empathising with her.

'I'm serious,' Anna said. 'If there was any justice in the world, you'd be a permanent faculty member by now.' *And back-paid for all the uncredited work you've done over the years.* She gestured to Farah with her bottle. 'You really ought to think about applying to other universities.'

'Where would I go?' said Farah. 'Yours is the only dedicated under-graduate criminology programme in the country. I don't want to leave Scotland. I like it here.' She looked at Anna meaningfully. 'And I like working with you.'

Anna smiled, disappointed but grateful. 'You don't think I'm a harsh taskmaster, do you?'

Farah pretended to think about it. Made a non-committal 'mm' noise and waved her hand vaguely, indicating uncertainty.

Anna laughed and gave her a good-natured nudge. 'Careful. I write your yearly appraisals, after all.'

Farah laughed too. She took a last drag on her cigarette, ground the butt into her mug and got to her feet.

'I should go. I have the first-years tomorrow at nine o'clock sharp.'

Anna drained her bottle and stood up too. 'And I should go upstairs and check up on that little boy of mine. Make sure he hasn't woken up and covered the walls in blue crayon again.'

'Oh,' said Farah, suddenly remembering as they made their way back towards the house, 'I spoke to Narinder. The meeting on Monday night? She's interested.'

Anna looked at her. 'Yeah? That's great news.'

'I said I'd go with her. What about you?'

'Sure,' said Anna, glad of the excuse. 'The more the merrier.'

She saw Farah to the front door and stood on the top step, arms folded against the deepening chill, as Farah set off, heading in the direction of the bus stop on Hyndland Road. She waited till Farah was out of sight, then slipped back inside, shutting and locking the door behind her.

She crept up the stairs and along the corridor to Jack's room. There, she slid the door open and peered in. There was no evidence of any crayon incidents having taken place – just Jack, sound asleep and curled up under his duvet, dwarfed by a bed he hadn't yet grown into. Standing there, gazing in at him, she felt the same familiar pang in her chest she always experienced whenever she saw him like this: a reminder of just how tiny and vulnerable he still was – like a twig waiting to be snapped in two. As it so often did, her mind began to wander to all the possible things that could happen to him, and what she'd do if the worst ever was to occur. She shook her head vigorously, forcing herself out of the negative thought loop before it could properly get started.

As she continued to stand there, her phone began to ring in her pocket. Hastily shutting the door to avoid waking him, she hurried to the other end of the corridor and checked the screen. *No caller ID.*

Frowning, she took the call.

'Hello?'

No response.

'Yes? Is someone there?'

A slow, croaky laugh at the other end of the line. Then:

'Anna Scavolini?'

It was a man's voice, heavily distorted and electronic-sounding, is if it had been run through some sort of voice-altering software. No discernible accent.

'Who is this?'

It was what women always said in films and on TV shows when they got a sinister call. It invariably made her roll her eyes over how mind-numbingly predictable it was – but when it came down to it, what else *was* there to say?

The caller gave no response.

'What do you want?'

Again with the clichés.

'For you to stop your anti-male diatribes. If not, you'll face consequences.'

Anna felt her eyes widening in both surprise and alarm.

'How did you get this number?' she demanded.

At the other end of the line, there was a sudden explosion of barely coherent rage. 'ARE YOU LISTENING TO ME YOU DUMB WHORE I'LL STAB YOU IN THE TITS AND FUCK YOUR CORPSE UP THE ARSE TILL IT—'

Anna slammed the 'End Call' button and held the phone at arm's length, as if she expected it to explode or emit a cloud of noxious gas or . . . something. Where the hell did these people get *off*?

She tore down the stairs and checked that the front door was secure, double-bolting it for good measure. Having completed a sweep of the ground floor, making sure that every door and window was locked, she returned to the hallway and leant against the wall, phone clutched to her chest, her breath coming out in short, sharp gasps.

She noticed that her right hand was trembling. Pocketing her phone, she gripped it with her left until the tremor subsided. Slowly, she released the breath she'd been holding in. Then she hurried back up the stairs, gripped by an all-consuming need to be as close to Jack as humanly possible.

14

Friday 1 November

The phone call continued to preoccupy Anna through the rest of the night and well into the following morning. On the surface of it, it was nothing she hadn't experienced before. Indeed, she'd come to regard messages expressing such sentiments as part and parcel of being a feminist with a public profile. Usually, though, these unsolicited tirades came to her in the form of emails which could easily be banished to the Spam folder – out of sight, out of mind. This was, to the best of her recollection, the first time one of these creeps had got hold of her phone number and actually called her to describe what he wanted to do to her.

Several times, she toyed with going to the police, only to come down against the idea. In the past, she'd reported a few of the nastier and more specific email threats, but each time had come away with the sense that the authorities didn't take such communiqués particularly seriously. On one occasion, a particularly obnoxious officer had even implied that she should expect to receive some pushback if she stuck her neck out and made controversial statements. After that, she'd concluded it was a waste of time, and that the police were unlikely to show an interest until one of these nutters actually made good on his threats. At times, an extremely small part of her almost hoped someone *would*, if only so she could turn to them and say, 'I told you so.'

At mid-morning on Friday, any lingering memories of the call were comprehensively upstaged by the news that the School had received

Leopold's written proposal for a Men's Studies course. Until then, Anna had been half-allowing herself to believe he'd simply floated the idea at Monday's meeting in an attempt to get a rise out of her. Now, she was forced to conclude that this was either the most elaborate wind-up in history, or he was deadly serious.

After that, through what remained of the working week and into the weekend, her thoughts returned again and again to the man she was fast coming to regard as her personal nemesis and his presence within the university. Fraser's efforts to pit her against him continued to leave a sour taste in her mouth. It wasn't merely the man himself and the views he held that she resented. It was the hypocrisy of the powers that be dangling an exorbitant salary in front of him to lure him away from his previous posting, while simultaneously pleading poverty when it came to funding research or moving unsung heroes like Farah onto permanent lecturer contracts. She knew only too well that she was doing that familiar, self-destructive thing of fixating on an issue, allowing it to fester in her mind like a weeping sore – but, as with any addiction, it was impossible to break out of the spiral through sheer willpower alone.

She found herself returning to Leopold's YouTube channel again and again, watching one podcast episode after another, tormenting herself with the knowledge that he was dragging her beloved university's reputation into the gutter with his retrograde views and that there wasn't a thing she could do about it. It was the university's unwillingness – or was it inability? – to impose any sort of standards that got to her the most. Had it not crossed their minds that, by allowing him to continue to spew his bile unchecked, they were, in effect, giving tacit approval to every statement his show put out? Or were they perfectly aware but considered it a price worth paying, on the grounds of there being no such thing as bad publicity?

A recurring theme across Leopold's broadcasts was his assertion that society had become 'unbalanced' – that too much ground had been ceded to historically oppressed groups to the point of overcorrection. This, he claimed, upset the 'natural order', and virtually everything wrong with the modern world, from record levels of mental illness to the fact that the trains never arrived on time, could be traced back to this root cause.

Because of *course*, Anna thought, it couldn't *possibly* have anything to do with a decade of austerity, obscene levels of inequality and all the other assorted ills of late-stage capitalism. No – it was all because too many concessions had been made to women and minorities, who now had no idea what to do with all their new-found freedoms and were much happier back when they were slaves and chattel.

Too many men, meanwhile, had swallowed what Leopold called the 'big lie': the notion that they were oppressors who were responsible for all society's ills. They couldn't, he claimed, hope to improve their material conditions until they confronted the falsehoods they'd absorbed and rejected the self-loathing that had been ingrained in them by a female-centric education system. *It's time for men to stop apologising for themselves* was a phrase he was particularly fond of using, and one which, with each repetition, felt increasingly like a barely disguised call to arms.

Anna hit the spacebar, pausing the video she'd been watching on the computer in her home office.

It's time for men to stop apologising for themselves.

Somewhere, in the depths of her subconscious, those words had rung a bell – an echo of something half-remembered. At first, she assumed it was simply the result of having heard Leopold repeat them in so many consecutive videos. But no – she was sure that wasn't it. She'd recently encountered that phrase, or one remarkably similar to it, in another context. But where?

After racking her brains for several minutes, she picked up her phone and called Vasilico.

'Anna!' His voice boomed through the earpiece. 'Always a pleasure to hear your mellifluous tones! How might I avail you of my services?'

'This'll only take a minute,' said Anna, refusing to be moved by his obvious attempt to schmooze her. 'That manifesto The Reckoning published online – is there any chance you could forward me a copy of the text?'

'You've got a theory, haven't you?' He sounded immediately intrigued – so much so that she could practically hear him sitting up straighter. 'Come on – don't keep me in suspenders. What's a brewing in that big old noggin of yours?'

'Quite possibly nothing. But just indulge me anyway.'

'Oh, I'll always have time to indulge *you*, Professor Scavolini.'

Don't push it, she thought, and hung up.

Thirty seconds later, her phone pinged a text alert. She opened it. Vasilico had sent the manifesto in the form of a screenshot of a forum post. She pinched the screen to zoom it in, scrolling up and down as she searched for the passage she had in mind.

It only took her a few seconds to find it.

> We have been conditioned to deny our natural impulses and to be ashamed of our innate, biologically determined superiority. **It is time for men to stop apologising for themselves.** The hour has come for a rebalancing of the scales.

Anna lowered her phone, her heart quickening with a sense of mounting exhilaration. It was just possible that this might be considerably more than 'nothing'.

Working from a print-out and using a highlighter, Anna went through the manifesto line by line, cross-referencing it against episodes of Leopold's podcast. Over the next couple of hours, she identified a further two passages that bore a striking resemblance to statements he'd made on the show.

Manifesto:

> For too long, men have been cowed by the evils of radical feminism, anti-Westernism and postmodern Cultural Marxism.

Leopold:

> *'We are beset by a dark triad of anti-thought: the cod-intellectualism of radical feminism, the scourge of far-left Cultural Marxism and a pernicious, self-loathing anti-Western sentiment, the latter a product of indoctrination about the evils of Empire and a deliberate failure to highlight any of the positives.'*

Manifesto:

> Let it be known that the deviant females who flaunt their sexuality while simultaneously denying it to their male superiors are no longer free to revel in their hypocrisy.

Leopold:

> '. . . but of course, the modern, liberated woman wants to have her cake and eat it, flaunting her sexuality while simultaneously recoiling in horror the second she receives even the most benign attention from the opposite sex.'

In addition, 'the war on men' and 'the war against masculinity' were terms Leopold repeatedly threw around, along with references to the 'social hierarchy' and 'gynocracy' – the latter strikingly evocative of the manifesto's howl of rage against 'gynocratic oppression'.

Anna sank back in her seat, tapping her pen against her teeth as she gazed up at the ceiling pensively. On the face of it, it might be nothing more than a case of the manifesto's authors drawing inspiration from Leopold and repeating his talking points in much the same manner Cameron Mitchell had done in Tuesday's tutorial. It would hardly be surprising, given his popularity and the subject matter of his podcast, if they were regular listeners.

And yet, she felt in her water that she'd alighted on something more significant. To her, it seemed that multiple disparate elements were being inextricably drawn into the same orbit. The manifesto; the women who were its targets; the man whose very presence had upended the cosy consensus of the world she inhabited . . . and the nexus, the focal point at which they all converged, was the university – more specifically, the School of Social and Political Sciences.

For a brief period, Anna contemplated going straight to Vasilico with what she'd discovered, before ultimately deciding against it. After all, when it came down to it, what did she have, really? A handful of similar-sounding quotes? He'd have been well within his rights to laugh her out of the room.

Resolving to keep her own counsel for now, she instead set about educating herself as much as she could about other instances of organised, ideologically motivated attacks on women. She considered herself more knowledgeable than most when it came to misogyny in its various guises, but she was swiftly coming to the realisation that she was entering into uncharted waters. There was a whole other world out there, of forums and chat rooms and the dark web, of which she'd only (mercifully) been dimly aware before – and she knew she was seriously ill-equipped to understand it. She needed to know more about what drove these people – aside from the obvious.

As she'd anticipated, she quickly found that, while such attacks were hardly unheard of, and indeed had become increasingly common over the last decade, the ones being carried out by The Reckoning were virtually in a category of their own, with no obvious direct parallels. Most of the cases she read about took the form of mass shootings, usually in North America, where guns were readily available and those selling them unlikely to ask too many questions about the purchaser's mental state. She counted eleven such events between 1984 and the present day – three of them in the past year alone. Only one incident had been recorded on this side of the Atlantic: an eighteen-year-old who, over the course of several weeks, stabbed three women in the English city of Portsmouth. His motive: a general resentment of women due to his status as a virgin.

'All women need to die and hopefully next time I can gouge their eyes out,' he was quoted as saying. 'Every time I stab someone I like to go home and smell the flesh I have ripped out. Come and arrest me for God's sake before I hunt for my fourth victim.'

That evening, while she, Zoe and Jack were nestled on the living room sofa, Anna continued her grim research on her iPad. Saturday nights had been their designated family movie night for a while now, and tonight's film of choice was *Toy Story*, which held Zoe every bit as rapt as it did Jack – indeed, possibly more so. Anna made sure to glance up from the iPad every now and then, to show that she *was*, in fact, paying attention. In truth, though, her mind was entirely focused on the various newspaper articles she'd sourced about violent attacks on women. She'd discovered that, a couple of years ago, there had been a spate of random assaults in the town of Southend-on-Sea in southeast England, mostly in the university quarter, the victims mainly students. The attacks had taken a variety of forms, from muggings and beatings, to unwanted gropings, to a couple of violent rapes in which the victims, each on their way home from a night out, were dragged into alleyways and assaulted at knifepoint. What *really* caught Anna's attention, though, was that one incident had occurred in the victim's home. Her attacker, wearing an animal mask, had climbed through her open bedroom window while she was sleeping and subjected her to a brutal physical assault that left her with facial fractures and a broken collarbone.

Several of the articles on the Southend attacks were written by Katharine Barnard, a journalist at the *Southend Herald*. She, it seemed, had been the first person to draw a direct link between the various assaults, arguing that, even if they were being committed by different perpetrators, they should be viewed not as isolated incidents but as part of a broader pattern of behaviour. She pointed the finger of blame firmly at one Robert Leopold, then Professor of Social Anthropology at Southend University, whose media star was in the ascendancy. She highlighted his diatribes about the ills of the modern woman sending out 'mixed messages', employing 'the language of seduction' while simultaneously refusing men access to her body, and his assertion that rape was a regrettable but unavoidable consequence of them being denied their basic biological urges. In one particularly incendiary episode of his then fledgling podcast, he suggested that 'sexual conquest' was merely a natural part of human evolution, comparing it to that of the animal kingdom, where it would be laughable to suggest that male animals sought consent from their female counter-parts before copulating with them.

Barnard had lambasted Leopold in an excoriating article, accusing him of inflaming young men's resentment and effectively encouraging them to go out and commit violence against women on a mass scale. For her efforts, she'd been inundated with abuse and death threats, widely covered in the local press at the time, which had led to a mealy-mouthed public statement from Leopold, in which he asked his followers to 'go easy on her', while simultaneously disavowing any responsibility for her harassment. Barnard, as far as Anna could tell, hadn't written anything in the last couple of years, and concluded that the experience had most likely driven her out of the profession. She did, however, find her contact details online on a website advertising her services as a copywriter.

Anna was in the process of opening the email app on her iPad when she became aware that Zoe had just said something to her. She looked up.

'Hmmwhat? Sorry?'

Zoe rolled her eyes theatrically. 'Finally! Ye've had yer nose in that thing for the last hour. I said, if Buzz Lightyear doesnae think he's a toy, then how comes it he follows toy *rules*?'

Anna stared at her blankly. 'Huh?'

'Are you even *watching* this?'

Then, before Anna could even respond, Zoe had rotated herself ninety degrees to face her, clearly intent on having a deep philosophical discussion.

'OK, so Buzz is convinced he's this actual spaceman, right? He doesnae know he's a toy. But when there's people around, he still freezes and acts like an inanimate object, just like all the other toys. What gives? I mean, is this like some sort of unconscious reflex he's got nae control over, or is it more like this learned behaviour thing fae seeing the other toys daein' it?'

'I think you're in grave danger of overthinking a children's cartoon, Zo.'

'It's no just a kiddy movie!' exclaimed Zoe, affronted. 'It's for grown-ups too. And even if it *was*, kiddies are still entitled tae a bit of logical consistency in their fillums.'

Anna smiled with weary forbearance. 'Just settle down and watch the movie, Zoe.'

Clearly far from satisfied, Zoe turned to face the screen again, reaching for a handful of popcorn from the nearby bowl while draping her other arm round Jack, who was too riveted by the action on the screen to have paid any attention to this exchange.

Anna, meanwhile, returned her attention to her iPad and began to type:

Dear Katharine,

We don't know each other, but . . .

15

Sunday 3 November

The following afternoon, Anna was seated at the kitchen table bright and early, her iPad propped open in front of her. All was quiet. Zoe and Jack were out at the park, and the noises of traffic and the general bustle of the West End seemed a million miles away, muffled by the double-glazing.

She adjusted the angle of the tablet so the camera captured her face instead of just her chin and neckline, then pressed the 'Call' button.

The familiar Skype jingle played, before the screen changed to reveal a woman in her late forties with horn-rimmed glasses and long, silver hair which framed a narrow, almost equine face. She was sitting in what appeared to be a home office, gazing down into her low-angled webcam. For a moment, she frowned, the image rattling as she adjusted the camera. Then, seemingly satisfied, she smiled with what looked to be genuine enthusiasm.

'Anna, hi!' said Katharine Barnard. 'Lovely to finally put a face to a name!'

'I wanted to thank you for agreeing to talk to me,' said Anna, once they'd dispensed with the introductory niceties. 'I really appreciate it.'

'Not at all,' said Katharine. 'From what you said in your email, it sounds like you've been having problems up there that aren't too dissimilar to the ones we had in Southend.' She folded her arms on her desktop. 'So, what would you like to know?'

'I wondered if we could start at the beginning. I feel like I was able to piece together the gist from the various articles I read, but—'

'But you'd prefer to hear it straight from the horse's mouth. That's fair.'

Katharine shut her eyes, her nostrils flaring as she breathed in deeply. Anna couldn't tell whether she was delving deep into the recesses of her memory, steeling herself for what lay ahead, or some combination of the two. After a few seconds, she breathed out, opened her eyes and began to speak.

'I suppose *my* involvement started back in . . . oh, it must have been late spring of 2017. At the time, Southend had been experiencing a spate of violent attacks on young women, most of them taking place on weekend nights when the student quarter was heaving. It got so bad the university began issuing guidance to students to avoid certain areas and forms of behaviour. As you can imagine, that went down like a lead balloon.'

Anna gave a small smile of understanding. She couldn't help but remember the similar 'advice' the police in Yorkshire had issued to female partygoers the previous Christmas, and her students' reaction to the poster in question.

'For the longest time,' Katharine went on, 'the media treated these as isolated incidents. Any time any comment was passed on the spike in attacks on young women, it was always in this vague, wishy-washy, "What could be behind this rise?" sort of way – posing an open-ended question but never trying to answer it.'

'And you were the one who linked it all together,' said Anna.

'I'd been interested in the whole "men's rights" phenomenon for a while. I'd spent some time lurking on their message boards. I had a pretty good sense of their ideology and how they perceived women, and I came to regard these attacks as the natural result of the sort of extreme anti-woman worldview that was festering in the chatrooms and on social media sites.'

Anna gave a silent nod of understanding. The toxicity of the online discourse towards women was just one of many reasons why she made a point of avoiding social media like the plague.

'At the time,' Katharine said, 'Robert Leopold was employed at the University of Southend. I gather, from your email, that you're familiar with him.'

'Yes. We recently became colleagues.'

Katharine gave a sympathetic grimace. 'Then I don't need to tell you what he stands for. When the attacks were happening, he was just beginning to break into the mainstream. His name came up again and again in the online spaces inhabited by young misogynist men. I saw how they looked up to him; how they treated his proclamations almost as a ruleset by which to live their lives. You know what their nickname for him is?'

Anna shook her head.

'Daddy.'

'*Daddy?*' Anna almost laughed at the absurdity of it.

Katharine gave a thin smile. 'It started as a pejorative. Someone wrote an article saying his followers were like lost little boys looking to their surrogate daddy for direction. Some of them decided to embrace the moniker, and it stuck. But that really *is* how they see him: this wise, all-knowing patriarch helping them to navigate the world. It seemed—'

At that moment, Katharine stopped abruptly as the door behind her opened and a slight woman with a pixie bob, whom Anna judged to be in her late twenties, stepped into view.

'Just wanted to make sure you were OK, babe,' she said, coming to a rest at Katharine's shoulder.

'I'm fine,' said Katharine, clearly irked by the intrusion.

'D'you want me to get you anything?' the younger woman persisted, either unaware of Katharine's displeasure or choosing to power on regardless. 'Tea? Coffee?'

'Tea would be lovely, thanks,' said Katharine, not entirely uncharitably.

The woman gave Katharine's shoulder a brief, tender squeeze. Then, after treating Anna to a momentary look of marked suspicion, she turned and left the room, shutting the door behind her.

Katharine gave an apologetic wince. 'My partner, Becca. Sorry about that.'

'Don't be,' said Anna. She was glad Katharine had someone in her life – someone who, judging by the look she'd just been treated to, had a seriously protective streak about her. 'You were saying . . .'

'Where was I? Oh, yes – it seemed self-evident to me that there was a direct link between the attacks and the so-called "teachings" of figures like Leopold – telling young men they're victims of feminism; that things have gone too far and women have been accorded more rights than *they* have. He was far from the only person saying these things, but I opted to focus on him due to the local connection. I wrote a couple of articles, accusing him of using irresponsible language – essentially saying, "Is it any wonder some young men feel they have a right to do whatever they like to women when figures like Robert Leopold are validating their grievances?"

'Well, it didn't take long for his followers to find what I'd written. And then the floodgates opened. They bombarded my Twitter account with abuse and death threats. They mass-emailed my employers, accusing me of all manner of things, demanding I be sacked. They also made multiple calls to the emergency services, claiming I was suicidal. I was woken up at four in the morning with police and paramedics trying to break my door down. I also had dog mess posted through my letterbox on more than one occasion, and one time I got sent an envelope with razor blades taped to the inside flap.'

'Christ,' murmured Anna. It was all she could think to say. 'What about your employers? Did they offer you any support?'

Katharine let out a dry chuckle. 'Well, they didn't fire me, so at least there's that. Though that's about the most positive thing I can say about their handling of the situation. Oh, there were a lot of warm words about standing shoulder to shoulder and refusing to kowtow to mob rule, but it was all just hot air. They didn't provide me with any protection, and they *certainly* didn't ban the army of trolls who were posting the vilest messages you can imagine below the line on all my articles. Between you and me, I fancy they were actually rubbing their hands with glee at all that extra traffic to the website.'

Somehow, Anna didn't find this remotely difficult to believe.

'Anyway,' Katharine went on, 'I toughed it out for a couple of months, but those were two months of pure hell. I was barely sleeping, I was constantly waiting for someone to jump me on my way from the office to my car or to break into my house in the middle of the night and do the things they kept posting about doing to me. So, for my own safety, as well as my sanity, I quit journalism altogether.'

As Katharine fell silent, her story having seemingly run its course, Anna found herself thinking back to the threatening call she'd received the other night. So far, she hadn't been subjected to a repeat performance. Indeed, until now, she'd more or less forgotten about it. But now, as the reverberations of Katharine's account continued in the pit of her stomach, she recalled, as acutely as if it was happening again now, how she'd felt when the caller had told her he planned to stab her to death and sodomise her corpse. She wondered again whether she should have contacted the police.

She forced these thoughts from her head. 'You said the harassment' – the word hardly seemed adequate to describe what Katharine had experienced – 'only began when you pointed the finger at Leopold.'

Katharine nodded. 'That was when it really took off. Before that, there was some low level stuff. "Stupid bitch, don't know what you're talking about, go back to the kitchen and make me a sandwich" – that sort of thing.' She briefly affected a note of forced levity. 'You know, just another day in the life of being a woman on the interwebs.'

She sighed. 'But the moment I called Leopold out, the floodgates opened. It was as if someone had loosed the hounds – if you'll excuse the mixed metaphor.'

'By someone,' said Anna, 'you mean Leopold himself?'

'I have no evidence of that,' said Katharine carefully, the former journalist in her asserting itself. 'Leopold's followers are notorious for their fierce loyalty to him. They've been known to trawl the web, looking for perceived slights against him, so they can dish out punishment to the guilty parties. But Leopold himself certainly didn't lift a finger to stop them – besides giving a statement to a rival paper suggesting that I was mentally ill and that people should cut me some slack because of that.'

'I'm sorry,' said Anna. Again, it was the only thing she could think to say.

Katharine's lips briefly flickered in a smile of gratitude. 'I know what you're really wondering, by the way. Don't think it hasn't crossed my mind as well.'

Anna frowned, confused. 'What do you mean?'

'Come, now – a series of violent, misogynist attacks on female students occur in Southend while Leopold is employed at the local university. He decamps to Glasgow, and, as per your email, similar attacks begin taking place up there within a couple of months of his arrival – once again targeting female students. You're asking yourself, is this just coincidence, or does his involvement extend beyond merely providing the perpetrators with an intellectual justification for their hatred of women?'

Anna opened her mouth to respond, then stopped, having no idea what she wanted to say. She recognised now that, at least on a subconscious level, she had indeed been asking herself that very question – at least since she first learned about the Southend attacks, and perhaps even before that.

She realised, belatedly, that Katharine was still speaking.

'I always saw him as a Svengali figure at heart,' the older woman said. 'He pulls his followers' strings, stoking their sense of grievance while hiding behind the cloak of plausible deniability. He might not say, "Go out and commit rape," but what he very much *does* say is, "Well, if men continue to be displaced from their natural place in the pecking order, then it's only to be expected that some will lash out in destructive ways."

'It was the same with his so-called "response" to my harassment. He wasn't *encouraging* young men to tweet me, telling me the order in which they intended to rape me, piss on me and kill me, but he clearly inferred I'd brought it on myself for writing such inflammatory material – which, for his legion of adoring fans, was all the encouragement they needed. He loves to present himself as a neutral third party who's merely documenting social trends, all the while giving his acolytes a tacit nod and a wink to carry on. He's the Pied Piper of Misogyny and they're all dancing to his tune.'

In the silence that followed, the door behind Katharine opened and Becca slipped in, carrying a steaming mug. Anna wondered if she had, in fact, been listening outside, waiting for a break in the conversation. She set the mug down in front of Katharine, who looked up at her with a grateful smile and gave her hand a brief squeeze.

'These people,' said Anna, once she and Katharine were alone again, 'the ones that've been carrying out the attacks in Glasgow – they call themselves "The Reckoning". They have an entire manifesto calling for men to rebel against what they call "gynocratic oppression".'

Katharine grimaced. 'I think what I find most exasperating about these people is the way they've co-opted the language of marginalised groups and recast *themselves* as the victims in order to justify oppressing these groups further. It's really insidious if you stop to think about it. Oh – and, in case you haven't noticed, they *really* don't like universities – especially the arts and humanities. See them as hotbeds of indoctrination, churning out an endless supply of rabid feminists trained to crush the menfolk under their collective boot.'

'I'll be honest,' Anna admitted, 'I'm still trying to get my head round the whole phenomenon. It's new territory for me, this group – this . . . what is it they call themselves? The manoverse?'

'The manosphere,' Katharine corrected her. 'Well, first of all, if you want to make sense of it, you have to understand that it's not a single, unified ideology. It's more of a spectrum – of different categories and subgroups, many of whom hate each other almost as much as they hate women. For instance, you've got your MRAs – that's "men's rights activists" – you've got your Men Going Their Own Way, your pickup artists, your "fathers for justice" types . . . I'm guessing you've probably heard the term "incel" before.'

Anna nodded. 'It stands for "involuntary celibate", right?'

'Right. In the hierarchy into which these groups believe men are divided – and believe me, if there's one thing that unites them, it's that these people are all *obsessed* with hierarchies – they're the lowest of the low. The ones so pathetic and repulsive – in their own minds, at any rate – that no woman will ever voluntarily touch them. Some are content to merely wallow in self-pity and resentment, writing themselves off as lost causes. Others take that resentment to another level, so convinced of their *entitlement* to sex that they'll take up arms to punish the women they view as having denied it to them. Most of the recent examples of mass violence targeted against women were committed by self-described incels.'

'So you think that's what The Reckoning are? Their manifesto specifically mentions women flaunting their sexuality while denying it to men.'

Katharine frowned, considering this. 'Possibly – though, by their nature, incels tend to be extremely isolated, often with no friends to speak of. The ones who carry out violent attacks tend to act alone – which, historically, has given the authorities licence to treat each one as an isolated incident that simply arose in a vacuum. If, as you describe, this "Reckoning" is two or more men working in tandem, then they certainly don't fit the traditional profile.' She took a sip of tea, her brows pursed in thought.

'What I don't really understand,' said Anna, after a pause, 'is why all this seems to have come to a head in the last couple of years. I get that it's been fermenting for a while, but why now? What is it about this particular moment that's given these men the impetus to act on their prejudices?'

Katharine set down her mug. 'Personally, I don't think it can be boiled down to a single unifying factor. Several events in recent years have had a galvanising effect on them. #MeToo was a real watershed moment in that respect. Suddenly, certain types of men who'd been getting away with egregious abuses of power for decades had the spotlight thrown on them and found themselves being held to account for their behaviour. It's like that saying: "every action has an equal and opposite reaction". I'm firmly of the belief that much of what we're currently witnessing is a reactionary pushback against *that* particular "reckoning".' She took another sip from her mug. 'Honestly, though, if you ask me, the single biggest culprit is the internet.'

Anna waited for her to elaborate.

Katharine gave a dry laugh. 'She said, while having a conversation via Skype. But in all seriousness, I don't think it's possible to overstate how massive an impact the rise of social media has had on the radicalisation of these men. Once upon a time, they were alone, isolated in their beliefs, harbouring their bigoted views but with enough self-awareness to know they couldn't get away with expressing them in polite society. Now, all of a sudden, they find themselves being funnelled into these echo chambers, where they're surrounded by other people who hold exactly the same prejudices, constantly having them reinforced. Women *do* get too easy a ride. Men *are* the most oppressed group in society. They *should* be entitled to sex whenever and from whomever they want.'

'And where, in your opinion, does this hatred originate?' asked Anna. 'I get that these men are being radicalised, but presumably they wouldn't be susceptible to this sort of propaganda if it wasn't tapping into something that's already present in them.'

Katharine nodded soberly. 'I agree. And if you want my opinion, it's that, for all their aggression and proclamations of innate superiority, deep down, these men are afraid. Desperately afraid.'

'Afraid of what?'

'Well, of being alone, obviously. But also of being dominated. Of being a victim. Of finding themselves a minority in their own country. All around them, they see evidence that the familiar world they thought they inhabited is evolving; people who were historically oppressed being afforded marginally more opportunities and freedoms. Deep down, I suspect a lot of them are terrified of being treated the same way *they* treat people who aren't like them.' She shrugged. 'Basically, they're afraid of change.'

Anna nodded soberly. She'd never thought of it like that before, but now that she stopped to consider it, it made a great deal of sense.

'It's important to understand,' Katharine went on, 'that there's a real pipeline to this sort of radicalisation. One that begins under the seemingly benevolent guise of supporting one's fellow men – helping them gain confidence, learn how to talk to girls and so on – and ends in full blown Western chauvinism and white supremacy. Funnily enough, misogyny is a lot easier to sell to the uninitiated than racism.'

She gave an exaggerated shrug. 'I know – who knew, right? But once you believe women are a threat to your status as a man, it's just a hop, skip and a jump to believing minorities are a threat to your status as a *white* man. Look at how much of their discourse is steeped in the language of "end times". All this talk of a battle of ideologies, a fight for survival. The wolves are at the gate, and it's incumbent on Western men to step up to defend their way of life – that sort of thing. And my fear is that there are enough of them out there that are sufficiently radicalised that, one day before very much longer, they'll do just that.'

Anna exhaled heavily, blowing a loose strand of hair out of her eyes. 'It just feels so hopeless. And I don't know what the answer is – to Leopold and people like him, to this epidemic of woman-hatred. How are we supposed to respond to people who despise our very existence?'

Katharine was silent for a moment, her lips pursed as she weighed up how to respond.

'Some time ago,' she said eventually, 'I came to the conclusion that the only solution is to treat Leopold and his ilk as hate preachers and deal with them using the same legislation we would employ if, say, a radical Islamist leader was exhorting his followers to blow up planes or buses. This sort of organised anti-woman violence needs to be recognised for what it is. Its aims are ideological, its adherents groomed and radicalised to commit mass violence against a specific demographic to advance that ideology. We shouldn't be afraid to call it by its true name. Terrorism.'

Anna said nothing. The word had had a chilling effect both on her and, it seemed, her surroundings. The very temperature in the room seemed to have plummeted. The sounds from the street outside seemed further away than ever.

She became aware that Katharine was speaking again.

'I know I said earlier that mass attacks targeting women have historically been carried out by lone wolves. But that seems to be changing. If what you've told me about the attacks in Glasgow is accurate, we're seeing something new and altogether more sinister arising – something that shifts the parameters of the game completely.'

Katharine gazed down the lens of her webcam at Anna, her expression one of utter gravity. Anna felt something shifting in her stomach as those cool, grey eyes bore into her.

'They're getting organised, and we need to do the same – and fast. Because they're not going to wait around till we're ready. On the contrary – they've already begun.'

16

'I'm going to be honest,' said Vasilico. 'What you're serving me up, it's – well, it's pretty thin gruel, don't you think?'

He and Anna were standing on the Great Western Bridge, at the top of the steps leading down to the subway station. It was as close as possible to a perfect midpoint between their respective workplaces – the ideal spot for two people, whose time was equally precious, to have a quick council of war during their lunch break. It had started to rain shortly after Anna had set off on foot, and she'd been soaked by the time she arrived. The wind whipped around them, slicing through her winter coat like a sharpened blade.

Vasilico pinched the bridge of his nose and sighed. 'Let's recap the claims you're making. Your colleague, Professor Leopold, was employed at the University of Southend at the time of a series of assaults on female students.'

'Correct.'

'A local journalist wrote that people like him were encouraging young men to harbour reactionary views towards women. She was subsequently the target of a harassment campaign.'

'Right.'

'And Professor Leopold now lives and works in Glasgow, which is also experiencing a series of violent attacks on young women.' He shrugged, hands jammed into the pockets of his overcoat. 'Not a lot to go on, is it?'

'There's the similar nature of the assaults,' Anna pointed out.

'They don't seem too similar from where I'm standing. The Glasgow attacks have all exhibited a consistent modus operandi of assaults committed inside the home, with a strong emphasis on disfiguring the victim's face. From what you've described, the attacks in Southend-on-Sea were considerably more . . .' – he searched for the word – '. . . *diverse* in nature.'

'One woman was assaulted by a man who climbed through her bedroom window,' Anna pointed out.

'Yes – *one* woman, set against how many others?'

'What about the manifesto? There are phrases in there that are lifted practically verbatim from Leopold's podcast. How do you explain away *that*?'

'Coincidence?'

Anna didn't dignify that with any response other than an incredulous glower.

Vasilico sighed. 'So he's a source of inspiration for them.' He arched his shoulders in an exaggerated shrug. 'So what? We've already established he enjoys a healthy following among reactionary young men. Hardly a signed confession, is it?'

With a great effort, Anna managed to resist the urge to grab great clumps of her hair and tear them out at the roots. 'But this is what he *does*. He's a manipulator. He enjoys winding people up and watching from the sidelines. He's all about coded messages and dog whistles.'

She was aware her voice was becoming increasingly shrill and desperate, but she couldn't help that right now. She ploughed on, determined to say her piece.

'Of *course* he's not explicitly telling them to go out and do these things. He's not stupid. He knows he'd have you lot at his door in five seconds flat. What he *does* do is prey on people's existing insecurities to steer them towards what he wants them to do. He's even tried it on me.' She gave a sharp, barking laugh. 'He keeps banging on at me to go onto that show of his and debate him. And then, when I refuse, he needles me about not having the courage of my convictions – *knowing* that that's going to get to me.'

For several seconds, Vasilico didn't respond. He looked at her long and hard, rainwater running from the spikes of his hair, down that infuriatingly chiselled jaw of his and onto the lapels of his coat.

'Tell me something,' he said. 'Is there any possibility that all this is more about you than about him?'

'What's that supposed to mean?'

Vasilico waved a hand dismissively, evidently regretting having broached the subject. 'Look, you've clearly done your research thoroughly. You're to be commended for that. Unfortunately, I rather fancy you've leapt on a handful of minor parallels and vastly overinflated their significance in the grand scheme of things. The simple truth of it is that nothing you've given me is conclusive enough to be actionable.'

Anna pursed her lips tight and said nothing. It wasn't as if Vasilico was telling her anything she hadn't already known deep down. But she wasn't going to give him the satisfaction of admitting it. She stood her ground, head upturned towards him, facing into the worst of the onslaught of wind and rain.

He sighed again. 'Tell me, Anna – all things being equal, what would you actually have me do?'

'Treat him as a person of interest?' It came out sounding more like a question than an answer. 'Intercept his communications. Find out who he associates with. Properly dig into his life. See if he really *is* as squeaky clean as he makes out.'

Vasilico smiled thinly and shook his head. 'Not going to fly, I'm afraid – not without a *lot* more cause than you've given me thus far. Hard as it may be to believe, the top brass tend to get *kind* of antsy about signing off on those sorts of operations without anything concrete to go on – especially when the target is someone with a significant public profile.'

'So you're going to let a fear of negative PR stop you from investigating him.' She knew it sounded petulant the moment she said it.

Vasilico gave her a look of strained forbearance. *'No,'* he said, drawing out the word heavily, 'I'm going to let the fact that you haven't given me *anything* of substance stop me.'

That stung. For a moment, they faced each other, both utterly intractable in their defiance. Then, Vasilico, evidently regretting his harsh words, let his shoulders slump.

'Look,' he said, thumbing over his shoulder, 'I need to be getting back. My in-tray's a mile high.'

'Sorry to have wasted your time,' said Anna glibly.

Vasilico gave her an entreating look. 'Don't do that. You know I'm always happy to see you, and to hear any thoughts you might have on the case. Just . . . keep your expectations in check, OK? I'm not a miracle worker.'

With that, he turned and set off, heading east along Great Western Road, head turned down against the rain. Anna watched him for a minute, quietly seething – more, if she was being honest, at herself than at him. Then she too turned and made her way down the steps, heading back towards the university.

17

That evening, Anna, Farah and Narinder made their way across the university grounds towards the Dewar, the postgraduate club on the ground floor of the main building, where the student meeting was set to take place. The rain had finally stopped a couple of hours ago, but the cobblestones, drenched by the downpour, continued to glisten underfoot, and Farah kept a guiding hand on Narinder's arm in case she missed her footing. Her continuing lack of vision in her damaged eye meant she was far from stable on her feet these days.

They'd collected Narinder from the Khatri family home in Jordanhill half an hour earlier, Farah having warned Anna beforehand not to mention the sexual component of the assault in front of her parents, who were under the impression that their daughter had been the victim of nothing more sinister than a burglary that had turned violent. She'd also warned Anna off raising the matter of Callum and the current status of his and Narinder's relationship. Apparently, they were 'on a break' following his reaction at the hospital and subsequent brush with the law. Anna privately suspected, based on the side of himself he'd shown that day, that this was probably for the best.

The wall of photos Vasilico had shown her of the various victims had given her a sense of what to expect, but even so, when Narinder had opened the front door to them, Anna had been taken aback by her appearance. If anything, her face now looked worse than it had in the immediate aftermath of the assault – swollen, misshapen, the network of bruises rendering the skin a mixture of blues, yellows and purples. Anna hoped her own face hadn't given her away; the last thing Narinder needed right now was to be made to feel self-conscious.

They arrived at the entrance to the Dewar's seminar room to find a dispute unfolding. The doorway was blocked by a severe-looking woman in her early twenties, with shiny, peroxide blonde hair in a ponytail so tight the effect was akin to her having given herself a DIY facelift. Standing in front of her were a woman and a man a couple of years younger than her. As Anna drew nearer, she realised the issue was the presence of the latter.

'You're a piece of work, you are,' said the girl, her arm looped protectively through that of her companion. 'You lot are the ones who had the bright idea to hold this at nine o'clock at night. How's are we expected to come out on a pitch-black night without protection when there's lassies out there getting *jumped*? He's my bloody boyfriend. He's safe, all right?'

The blonde woman raised a single, perfectly sculpted eyebrow. 'And the rest of us are meant to just take your word for it, are we? I think not.'

'So I'm supposed to – what, tie him up at the gate like a dug or send him off to wait in the pub? Get real!'

Her boyfriend, meanwhile – a gangly, awkward-looking individual who seemed to be attempting, unsuccessfully, to cultivate a goatee – merely stared off into the middle distance, determined not to get involved.

At that moment, another woman came striding over from inside. She was in her mid-twenties, with long brown curls cascading from beneath a rainbow beanie, and wore ripped jeans, a black vest top and an unbuttoned red tartan overshirt that was several sizes too big for her.

'We got ourselves a problem?' she demanded briskly. She had the husky voice of a consummate smoker.

The girl jutted her chin as the blonde woman. '*This* one's telling me I have to send my man away.'

'You said it was women only,' the blonde woman said to the one in the beanie. *And you'd better bloody enforce it,* was the unspoken undercurrent.

As the dispute continued to rage on, Anna, taking the initiative, slipped past them, leading the way. Farah and Narinder followed her into the room. It had capacity for around fifty people and had already begun to fill up. A couple of dozen women, ranging from their late teens to early thirties, milled around, conversing and helping themselves to tea and coffee from a table spread at the head of the hall.

'Let's sit over there,' suggested Farah, nodding to an unoccupied table in the corner.

As they headed towards it, they found their way abruptly barred once again – this time by a woman in her late teens with mousy brown hair and a livid complexion backed up by an expression of unbridled fury.

'Hey, hey, hey!' she shouted, jabbing a finger at Anna. 'What's *she* doing here?'

The question appeared to be addressed at no one in particular – certainly not Anna, who'd had to pull back her head sharply to avoid having her eye poked.

'What's the matter?' asked another student, of similar age, making her way over with a concerned frown.

'What's the matter? She's one of *them*, that's what's the matter.' She raised her voice, addressing the entire room. 'No one told me there'd be *staff* here.'

Acutely aware that they'd become the primary focus of attention within the room, Anna, Farah and Narinder all looked around uneasily. Narinder folded her arms about herself defensively, her shoulders drawing in.

'It's OK,' said a voice from nearby. 'She's one of the good ones.'

And then Rose Diaz, from Anna's second-year tutorial group, was drawing alongside them, beaming at Anna as if she'd been fervently hoping she'd turn up.

'Hi, Professor. It's good of you to come. Nice to see at least *someone* at the uni's taking this business seriously.'

Anna smiled gratefully. In truth, a large part of her rationale for coming at all had been to demonstrate just that. That, and to signal that she wasn't quite as aloof and unapproachable as her reputation might suggest.

The girl who'd objected to Anna's presence continued to look distrustful, but she nonetheless backed off. Rose, meanwhile, raised her eyebrows theatrically at Anna before strolling off to join a couple of other Criminology students.

Anna, Farah and Narinder made it to the table and sat down.

'Wow,' Narinder remarked. 'Tough crowd tonight.'

The three of them fell into silence, looking around aimlessly at their surroundings, still not entirely at ease. As the lull in conversation stretched on, Anna's thoughts turned to Jack, and the fact that he was once more missing out on an evening she would otherwise have spent with him. Then she found herself wondering if that was really true, or if she'd merely have found another excuse for being otherwise engaged if this meeting hadn't come along. At the end of the day, why was she *really* here? To support Grace and Narinder? To show that, out of all the university staff, she at least was taking this issue seriously? Was anyone really buying that her presence here was essential – herself included?

The room continued to fill up. Anna was on the verge of ringing Zoe and asking her to put Jack on when her eyes strayed to the doorway and she spotted Grace Dunphy hovering just outside, as if she still hadn't made up her mind whether she was actually going to come in. Anna half stood up from her chair, raising a hand. Seeing her, Grace's face immediately broke into an expression of relief, and she made her way towards them.

Anna pulled out a seat for her. 'Grace. Glad you made it. Come on and sit with us.'

Grace plonked herself down, nodding gratefully.

Anna gestured to Farah. 'You already know Farah, obviously.'

Farah gave a smile and a wave.

'And this is Narinder. Narinder, this is Grace.'

'Hi,' said Narinder.

'Hey,' said Grace.

As they spoke, they both appeared to take in the sight of each other's faces for the first time. Watching them, Anna sensed a mixture of surprise and discomfort from them both. To her, it seemed as if each of them had suddenly found themselves confronted by their mirror image – a sense that, despite not knowing one another, they'd shared something intimate.

At that moment, the bolshy woman in the rainbow beanie approached the table. Dropping to a crouch between Anna and Farah's chairs, she treated them to a crooked but hospitable smile, before addressing Grace and Narinder.

'Guys, thanks for coming out tonight. Listen, it's obvious yous two have been through the mill, and . . . well, I just wanna say there's absolutely no pressure, but if either of yous feels like saying a few words about what happened to you . . . you know, give folk a sense of what we're all up against . . . well, we'd love to hear from you.'

Grace looked at the floor and shook her head almost imperceptibly.

Narinder raised a hand tentatively. 'Um . . . I don't mind saying something, if you think it'd help.'

The woman touched her arm briefly but warmly. 'That's great. I really appreciate it.'

'I mean,' muttered Narinder, with a shrug, 'it's not gonna be a valedictory or anything.'

The woman smiled. 'Well, thank fuck for *that*. We've only got the hall until ten.'

She got up to go, then stopped, turning to face them again.

'Oh – what's your name?'

'Narinder.'

'Narinder,' the woman in the beanie repeated, committing it to memory. 'I'm Kez, by the way.'

She flashed them another smile and moved off into the crowd.

Anna looked around. People were still arriving, though the rate of newcomers had slowed to a trickle. She noticed that the girl and her boyfriend who'd been challenged at the door had been let through, the disagreement apparently resolved to at least one side's satisfaction. There were a couple of other men present too, she saw – both of them in the company of women who appeared to be their significant others. All told, the hall was at close to capacity.

'So does anyone know what format this meeting's supposed to take?' asked Narinder, a note of apprehension in her voice.

'I think we're about to find out,' said Grace.

Anna and the others followed her gaze as Kez strode up to the front of the room, clambered onto the nearest table and, putting her thumb and index finger in her mouth, blew a piercing whistle.

Immediately, the noise of conversation subsided. Everyone turned to give her their full attention.

'All right, everyone,' called Kez, shifting her weight back and forth from one leg to the other like a runner limbering up. 'Thanks for coming out tonight. It's great to see so many faces here. For those of yous who don't know me, my name's Kez Dixon, and I'm in the second year of my Sociology PhD.'

'Aye,' shouted a voice from the back, 'and that doesnae make you better than the rest of us!'

There was some scattered laughter, but the general mood, it seemed, was too serious for banter. Kez smiled, taking the heckle in good humour.

'Some of yous might also know Carys Dean.'

She gestured to a young woman in a bomber jacket with a shaved head *à la* Sinéad O'Connor, standing a little off to the side of the table, feet apart, hands clasped in front of her like a security guard.

'Carys is a Psych undergrad,' said Kez, 'and she's been instrumental in getting the word out about tonight.'

Carys gave a small wave and nodded to the crowd.

Kez spread her hands. 'Look, I'm no gonnae beat about the bush. Yous all know why we're here. We're here cos we, as women, are under ATTACK. In the last few months, there's been a bunch of serious assaults on female students at the university. We don't know for sure how many. The police aren't telling us anything.' She rolled her eyes dramatically. 'I know – big shocker, right? Well, *they* might no be saying it, but *we* know there's a pattern. That the same thing's happening to students all over. There's at least two lassies here the night who've had it done to them . . .'

Well over half of the faces in the room instantly turned towards Anna's table. Narinder and Grace both seemed to shrink into their own bodies.

'. . . plus fuck knows how many more who *aren't* here. And it's no just the stuff yous can see. Every single woman in this room has either experienced or knows someone who's experienced one of the following.'

She began to count off on her fingers. 'The catcalls. The unwanted groping. The threats disguised as banter. The spate of drinks being spiked at the student union. The hordes of drunken fuckheids roaming around Byres Road on a Saturday night, noising up lassies who're just trying to get home . . .'

She let her arms fall in an exaggerated shrug. Her shirt, which had slipped off her shoulders in her exertion, hung around her elbows like a shawl.

'And the university does sod all about it. Why *would* they, when they nailed their colours to the mast earlier this year when they gave a job to Robert fucking Leopold?'

At the mention of his name, a wave of boos and hisses broke out.

'I don't need to tell yous the damage his appointment has done to this place. It's turned the uni into a lightning rod for the worst sort of misogyny. It's led to an influx of his rabid little alt-right troglodytes who've run the culture of this place into the bloody ground. Made the campus completely unsafe for women.'

Nods and murmurs of agreement. Anna could feel the resentment boiling in the room.

'The whole point of this meeting,' Kez went on, 'is for us, collectively, to figure out a way forward. But first, a brave, amazing, *gorgeous* woman who's been through a hell of a lot has kindly agreed to say a few words about what happened to her. I want yous all to give a round of applause, jazz hands, whatever, for Narinder.'

All eyes turned to Anna's table once again. Amid a smattering of polite applause, a decidedly self-conscious Narinder got to her feet. Standing a couple of paces away from the table, she gave a nervous little wave.

'Um . . . so hi, everyone. I'm Narinder . . . or Rindy, if you prefer. Um . . . a week ago, I was on a night out with my friends. I got home and was jumped by this man in a mask. He threw me down on the bed and he . . .' She gestured lightly to her face. 'Well, he did *this* to me . . . among other things.'

Mutters of sympathy and disquiet.

'Another one,' Anna heard someone mutter to her neighbour. 'Same thing happened to my pal Amber.'

Anna glanced at Grace. She saw that she was sitting rigid, the muscles in her face tight, her fingers digging into her thighs.

'It was . . .' Narinder began. 'I mean, I don't even know what to say. It's not something I can make you understand if it's not happened to you. But . . . well, I mean, home is meant to be the place you're safest, right? Only for me it wasn't, and now the doctors are saying they're not sure I'll ever be able to see out of my right eye again.'

More murmurs. People were stunned and horrified, but there was anger there too – an intense, burning rage in desperate need of an outlet.

'And, um . . . that's . . . that's all I've got to say.'

Narinder gave a floppy shrug and slid back into her seat amid more awkward applause. Farah put an arm round her and squeezed her tight.

Kez, who'd been perched on the table for the duration of Narinder's speech, now clambered on top of it again.

'So there ya have it. Women harassed and attacked on the streets and on campus, and now not even safe in their own beds. So the question is, what are we gonnae do about it?' She spread her arms wide. 'I'm opening this up to the floor. C'mon – I want suggestions.'

Immediately, several conversations started up at once as people deliberated within their individual groups. Eventually, the girl who'd got into a standoff at the door over the presence of her boyfriend got to her feet and raised a hand.

'We could organise a protest. Y'know, go on strike, refuse to attend classes till the uni acts.'

Some tentative sounds of agreement.

Another girl piped up. 'Yeah – the TAs are striking. We oughta sync up with them, walk out at the same time.'

More noises of approval.

A third girl, slight and pretty and, to Anna's mind, far too youthful-looking for a university student, stood up.

'Um,' she began, her voice breathy, so softly spoken Anna had to strain to hear her, 'what about organising a SlutWalk? Like they did in Canada after that cop said women should stop dressing like tarts if they didn't wanna get raped?'

She'd barely finished speaking before a tumult of noise broke out – a mixture of support and vehement disagreement.

'So your brainwave is we should repackage women's objectification as female empowerment,' snorted the woman with the peroxide blonde hair who'd objected to the presence of men at the meeting. 'Great idea. Thanks a bunch. Anyone got a sensible suggestion?'

The girl sat down instantly. Watching her sitting there, her back hunched and her expression cowed, Anna felt a wave of sympathy for her. It had clearly taken a lot for her to work up the courage to contribute, only to be shot down in the cruellest possible way.

'Oi!' Kez snapped her fingers. 'Less of that now. Sounded like a perfectly reasonable suggestion to me. I mean,' she went on, pitching to the entire room, 'if nothing else, it's a way to get attention. If the powers that be don't respond to us asking nicely – and we all know they *won't* – maybe they'll respond to an army of women all stripping off en masse?'

The blonde woman sneered. 'So your solution to guys perving on you is to get your tits out for them? Flawless fucking logic there.'

'Hey!' Kez snapped. 'If I'm getting my tits out, I'm getting them out for *me*. You don't get to police my body.'

And then, before anyone could get another word out, her shirt was on the floor and she was gripping the hem of her vest with both hands, about to pull it over her head. As the uproar reached fever pitch, Carys stepped in front of her, raising her hands for calm.

'All right, all right – no one's getting their tits out here tonight. Everyone just cool it.'

The tumult subsided somewhat. Kez lowered her arms, her top still mercifully in place.

'D'you guys not see?' Carys implored the assembled crowd. 'This kind of division's exactly what *they* want. Whatever we end up doing, we've all gotta be on board.'

General murmurs of agreement.

'There's no such thing as a bad idea, all right? We wanna hear from *everyone*.'

The blonde woman huffed contemptuously, but nonetheless said nothing more. Meanwhile, a rather subdued Kez got down from the table and stooped to pick up her shirt.

As an uneasy silence settled on the room, Rose Diaz raised her hand.

'Um . . . so I don't want anyone chewing my head off, but it seems to me that, since a lot of the attacks have taken place off campus, the uni can plausibly claim it's nothing to do with them. But it's pretty obvious it's students that are being targeted, right?'

No one disagreed.

'Perhaps,' Rose continued, 'if we could prove there was coordination going on, that it's Kelvingrove Uni students that are being singled out, then maybe they'd be forced to sit up and take notice. Like, these break-ins – women being attacked in their own homes – in their own *beds* . . . does anyone know someone that's happened to who *isn't* a KU student?'

You're halfway there, thought Anna. The attacks, the identities of the victims, the fact that Robert Leopold floated around the periphery like a ghoulish phantom presence . . . They had all the pieces. They just needed to connect them in the right order. For the umpteenth time, she cursed the thought that these women were being purposefully kept in the dark based on the paternalistic notion that it was for their own good – that a unilateral decision had been made on their behalf that they should remain ignorant as to the threat they were facing. It was all kinds of wrong. No one had the right to make that decision for them – not Paul bloody Vasilico, and not her either.

And then, almost before she was even aware of what she was doing, she was on her feet and addressing the room.

'Excuse me,' she raised her voice above the hubbub, 'but I think I can add something here. The attacks *are* linked and are being carried out by the same group of militant anti-woman activists. They call themselves The Reckoning. All the victims so far have been Kelvingrove University students, the majority of them enrolled in the School of Social and Political Sciences.'

The room was so quiet you could have heard a bluebottle's fart. Everyone was staring at her – including her three companions, who gazed up at her in wide-eyed shock. She hesitated, but if there had ever been a time for having second thoughts, it had long since passed.

'The police think there are two perpetrators,' she went on, 'though there may be more. After each attack, they've posted a manifesto calling on men to rise up and overthrow the gynocracy.' She hesitated. 'In fact, I'm fairly certain they are, at the very least, taking direct inspiration from the words of Robert Leopold.'

Everyone continued to stare at her. There were a few scattered murmurings of disquiet from the crowd, but no one spoke up.

'How do you know all this?' said Kez, taking a few tentative steps towards her.

Anna turned to face her. Again, she hesitated, briefly wondering whether she was doing the right thing.

Fuck it.

'Because the detective leading the investigation told me,' she said.

A moment passed, and then utter pandemonium broke out. The room descended into uproar as fifty-plus women all began to talk at once, a wave of anger and disbelief spreading through the space like a dust storm. Everyone had their own individual way of expressing themselves – and yet, despite the presence of more than fifty different voices, a single, common sentiment nonetheless united them.

How dare they? How fucking dare *they keep this from us?*

18

'Well,' said Farah, 'you certainly put the cat among the pigeons back there.'

'For what good it ultimately did,' grunted Anna.

The meeting had adjourned without any progress having been made on a unified response, and Anna couldn't help but wonder if her revelation might have played some part in that, given that a sense of collective outrage over the police's underhandedness had dominated the remainder of the event. They'd dispersed just after 10 p.m., having resolved to continue the discussion at a future gathering, details to be circulated on social media once they were firmed up.

Now, the four of them made their way down the hill from the university together – Grace and Narinder up front, conversing, Anna and Farah walking a little behind them.

'It was the correct thing to do,' Farah insisted. 'You can't let people remain uninformed about these things – not when even their lives might be at stake.'

Anna nodded uncertainly. She wasn't minded to disagree, though she was beginning to wonder what unintended consequences her actions tonight might have unleashed.

They walked on in silence, Anna tuning into the conversation between Grace and Narinder. It seemed almost perverse to say, but their shared experience seemed to have forged an unexpected bond between the two of them. Anna was secretly glad: the more ties Grace had to other students, she figured, the more likely she'd be to resume her studies.

'. . . the uni never should've hired him,' Grace was saying. 'I mean, what does it say about an institution if they have such low standards that they'll put someone with views like *that* on the payroll?'

'I've got to admit,' said Narinder, 'I really didn't know that much about him till recently. I knew the name, but I thought . . .' She shrugged sheepishly. 'I guess I figured he was just this self-help guru.'

As she walked, Anna slipped her phone out of her pocket and checked the screen for messages. The battery meter, she noticed, was at only 19%, despite her having charged it that afternoon. She sighed. She was going to have to take it back to the shop to get them to look at it, wasn't she? As if she didn't have *enough* on her plate right now . . .

'Well, that's certainly what he *claims*,' said Grace, the contempt in her voice making her views on this only too clear. 'You know a bunch of us signed a petition against them hiring him? 'Course, they totally ignored us. That's why I reckon us protesting won't do a lick of good. Cos it's not got us anywhere until now, right?'

'Oh, I signed that petition too,' said Narinder.

'Oh!' said Grace, surprised. 'I thought—'

'I mean, I wasn't *going* to,' Narinder clarified. 'Like I said, I didn't really know anything about him. But Farah couldn't, on account of she was worried she'd be risking her job if she did. So I said to her, what if *I* sign it? Y'know, sort of like on her behalf.'

They continued to speak, their voices lost beneath the rattle of a passing bus, winding its way down towards Highburgh Road. Anna felt a sudden quickening of her pulse. A prickling of the hairs on her back and arms. A moment later, her brain caught up with what her subconscious had already processed.

'Anna?'

Anna realised she'd stopped moving. The others had come to a halt too and were looking at her in confusion.

'I just remembered,' she said, recovering quickly, 'there's something I need to do. You don't mind if I cut and run, do you?'

And then, almost before they'd finished making their goodbyes, she was off, hurrying across Byres Road during a gap in the traffic. As she alighted on the pavement on the other side, she broke into a run.

* * *

She burst into the house, letting the door slam shut behind her. Heading past the living room door, beyond which Zoe and Sal were probably fingerbanging again for all she knew or cared, she pounded up the stairs to her office. There, she collapsed into her chair, roused her computer from sleep, and, with a shaking hand, clicked through to her email.

It took her a couple of minutes to find the message she was looking for: the copy of the anti-Leopold petition that had been circulated to every university email account back in June. She spun the wheel on her mouse, briefly skimming the lines of text as they scrolled past her – *We, the undersigned, protest, in the strongest possible terms, against the recruitment of Robert Leopold as Professor of Social Anthropology by the School of Social and Political Sciences . . .*

She reached the bottom, and the list of signatories. There were over six hundred names in total, with a roughly 3:1 female to male ratio, many with their subject and year of study appended. Most were enrolled in the School of Social and Political Sciences, though there was the odd mention of Mathematics, English Language, Art History, Scottish Literature . . . Her eyes glanced over Grace's name. A couple of seconds later, she spotted Narinder's . . .

She hit Command-F, bringing up the search box. Typed 'Chloe Mazzaro' and hit Enter.

Your search returned 1 result(s).

Her heart rate ratcheting up again, she called up the search box again, typed 'Jing-Mei Zhao' and hit Enter.

Your search returned 1 result(s).

Gloria Owusu.

Your search returned 1 result(s).

Kimberly Napier.

Your search returned 1 result(s).

Amber Maguire.

Your search returned 1 result(s).

She sat back in her chair, the screen glowing bright in the otherwise darkened room. Her digits were tingling. Sweat curled down her back.

'Holy shit,' she murmured.

19

El Duce invites GodsGift2Women and LifeIsPain to a new chat channel.

LifeIsPain joins the chat.

LifeIsPain: Hey

GodsGift2Women joins the chat.

GodsGift2Women: Sup?

El Duce: Everyone's on time tonight, I see.
El Duce: Good, very good.

GodsGift2Women: Someones in a holly jolly mood
GodsGift2Women: Whats the occasion

El Duce: Fellow freedom fighters, I bring news from inside the enemy camp.
El Duce: The feminazis are in freefall.

LifeIsPain: ???

El Duce: My eyes and ears inside tonight's meeting of the frigid bitches reports that they are, collectively, shitting bricks.

El Duce: There was so much hysteria on display, even the bulldykes were clutching their pearls and screaming to the rafters.

LifeIsPain: LOL!!!!!!!!

GodsGift2Women: ROFLMAO

LifeIsPain: What did they say
LifeIsPain: Do the know any thing

El Duce: Well, it took them so long it'd make a special ed student blush, but they've finally started to put two and two together.
El Duce: Thanks in no small part to that interfering bitch Scavolini, who knows far too much for her own good on account of having the lead detective's dick stuck halfway down her throat.

LifeIsPain: Fucking cunt whore

GodsGift2Women posts 'Triggering Intensifies' gif.

LifeIsPain: It needs a good railing

El Duce: In time. In time. Don't imagine for a minute I don't have plans for her.
El Duce: This all ultimately works to our advantage. She put the fear of God into the rest of them, which at the end of the day is what we want.
El Duce: You could say she's doing our work for us better than WE are.

LifeIsPain: It needs its fucking cunt kicked in
LifeIsPain: The shit it says about Big D

El Duce: Rest assured, Big D is well aware of what she's been saying about Him behind His back.

LifeIsPain: Uv spoken 2 him??
LifeIsPain: When

El Duce: Is that doubt I sense?

GodsGift2Women: LOL
GodsGift2Women: He doesnt like it when you question him
GodsGift2Women: After all El Duce is Gods messenger on earth

LifeIsPain: No
LifeIsPain: Im not douting
LifeIsPain: I just want to know what did he say
LifeIsPain: Tell us
LifeIsPain: Plz

El Duce: He wants us to sit tight for now. To watch, and wait.
El Duce: After all, revenge is a dish best served cold . . .

PART THREE

THE LURE

20

Tuesday 5 November

The following morning, Anna made her way up the hill towards the Hutcheson Building, feeling over-wired and under-slept. As she turned into the courtyard, a tall, suited figure stepped out from behind the bike racks and moved to intercept her. It was Vasilico. She could already tell, from the set of his jaw, that he wasn't pleased.

'About time,' she said, ignoring his look of fury. 'I left half a dozen messages for you—'

'I think you've got some explaining to do, don't you?'

There was an icy coldness to his tone that she wasn't used to.

'Just what the hell were you thinking,' he demanded, 'running your mouth off at that meeting last night?'

She stood her ground, gazing up at him defiantly with her chin outthrust.

'Oh yes,' he went on, 'don't think I haven't heard *all* about it – in spades. Word, it would appear, travels fast. I've already fielded phone calls from two of the victims, wanting to know just why the hell they weren't told the attacks on them were part of a wider pattern, *and* from the Chief Super, who's apoplectic that sensitive information pertaining to an active investigation has been leaked.'

Rather than attempt to interject, Anna kept her lips pursed, waiting patiently for him to exhaust his tirade.

'I thought I told you, *explicitly*, that that information was not to become public knowledge.'

'And I thought I told *you* explicitly how uncomfortable I was with it being withheld from both past and potential future victims,' Anna shot back.

'I told you that information in confidence.'

'Then you should have got me to sign an NDA. I don't owe you my silence, Vasilico.'

She swerved past him and strode on towards the building. Immediately, he fell into step with her.

'Anyway,' she went on, hating that she felt the need to continue justifying herself, 'I didn't tell them anything they couldn't have realistically worked out for themselves. I just connected the dots for them.'

'And left me with the mother of all headaches to deal with.'

'Yeah?' She stopped, swinging round to face him again. 'Well, I might be able to ease that just a tad. You still haven't asked me why I was trying to get hold of you.'

'I've been a *bit* distracted,' he said pointedly.

She continued to meet his gaze, poker-faced. He sighed.

'Fine. I'll bite. What have you found?'

She told him the whole story. Once she'd finished, he made her go through it again. She could tell he still wasn't fully convinced.

'I hope you don't take offence at this,' he said, at length, 'but I still think this all feels somewhat far-fetched. Can you honestly tell me you truly believe, in your heart of hearts, that this colleague of yours is orchestrating these attacks in order to . . . what? Exact revenge against a bunch of students who wanted to get him cancelled?'

Anna sighed. 'You know perfectly well belief has nothing to do with what *either* of us do. It's about weighing up evidence and probability. Look, I've given you the pieces. You're the one who has to make a judgement call here. But let's put it this way – seven different women have been assaulted and you still don't have a single suspect. If I was in your shoes, I'd be crying out for even the most tenuous lead – and I think, in *your* heart of hearts, that you know what I've brought you constitutes considerably more than that.'

For more than a minute, Vasilico said nothing. He stood, massaging the bridge of his nose, his lips a thin, pinched line.

'I agree,' he said eventually, and her heart could have leapt to hear him acknowledge it. 'I think, perhaps, it's time I had a little word with the good professor.' He laughed dryly. 'While I'm at it, perhaps I'll ask him for advice on how to better handle the women in my life.'

Anna flashed her teeth in an insincere smile.

'Just do me a favour,' Vasilico said.

'What's that?'

'Don't go and bloody tip him off like you tipped off those students.'

'I'll forward you links to the videos where he uses similar language to The Reckoning's manifesto,' said Anna, refusing to rise to the bait.

'You do that.'

She turned to go, heading up the footpath towards the entrance to the Hutcheson Building.

'Anna.'

Vasilico's voice halted her in her tracks. She turned to face him.

'You're a pain in the arse, you know that?'

But he said it with a smile.

She responded by turning her back on him and giving him the finger as she walked off. And yet, as she stepped through the doors and felt the familiar blast of warm air from the building's heating system, unbeknownst to him and in spite of herself, she too was smiling.

21

Wednesday 6 November

Robert Leopold was questioned by the police the following morning and released shortly thereafter. He arrived back at the university just after noon, his lugubrious voice booming in the corridor as he called out jovial greetings to colleagues. Anna, working in her office, found herself involuntarily tensing at the sound. It would, she supposed, have been unrealistic to hope for them to have taken him into custody, but she was nonetheless disappointed to find him in such an ebullient mood.

Moments later, he appeared in her doorway, grinning like a cheetah.

'Surprised to see me?'

'Should I be?' said Anna, hearing the flinty edge in her own voice.

Leopold merely smiled knowingly and tutted, shaking his head. He stepped over the threshold and strolled casually towards her.

'I've just returned from a very interesting conversation with two *thoroughly* hospitable police officers. They *seemed* to have got it into their heads that there might be some sort of *connection*' – the way he said the word underscored the very absurdity of it – 'between myself and these *appalling* attacks on girls at the university. Who could have given them that idea, I wonder?'

Anna said nothing. She watched him, jaw tight, as he continued towards her, drawing out every step.

'Needless to say, I comprehensively disabused them of the notion.

Cleared the whole thing up there and then. I doubt I'll be taking up any more of their time.'

He came to a halt in front of her desk and gazed down at her, oozing self-satisfaction.

'Pleased?'

'Ecstatic,' said Anna, through gritted teeth.

Leopold continued to gaze at her. He gave a little chuckle, as if he couldn't quite work her out.

'You're a funny one, aren't you?'

He casually ran an index finger along the surface of her desk, bringing it to rest next to the small, framed photo of Jack she kept beside her computer.

'You know,' he mused, 'if someone has a problem with me, I'd far rather they worked out their differences through open and honest dialogue rather than co-opting the instruments of the state to do their dirty work.'

In the silence that followed, he met Anna's eyes. She stared back at him, every muscle in her body stretched rigid.

'Unless, of course, they're afraid their ideas won't stand up to scrutiny.'

He smiled whimsically, tapping the photo frame a couple of times with his finger. Then, in a surprisingly balletic move, he spun on his heel, pirouetting a hundred and eighty degrees, and strolled out, whistling a merry tune as he went.

'I'm really not sure what you were expecting,' Vasilico said to her later, when she managed to get through to him on the phone. 'It's not as if we had any grounds to hold him, let alone charge him with anything.'

He sounded tired and more than a little exasperated. Anna wondered just how congenial his conversation with Leopold had actually been. To hear Leopold talk, it had been the equivalent of a friendly chat, during which he'd effortlessly set the police straight on the matter of his innocence. Had it, in reality, been a more rancorous affair, with Leopold delighting in putting his interrogators in their place? He'd have been able to do that without much effort, she suspected. She could readily picture him picking apart their – in reality, *her* – allegations, taking considerable delight in painting them in the most absurd light possible, all while subtly conveying that he viewed them as a bunch of incompetent flatfoots desperately scrabbling around in the dark – without ever actually stating it outright, of course.

'Did you ask him about—' she began.

'I questioned him at considerable length on a *range* of different subjects,' interrupted Vasilico, an unyielding edge to his voice. 'I can only conclude that he's either an *extremely* accomplished liar or else genuinely knows nothing. Either way, I have nothing to pin on him.'

'What about anti-terror laws?'

Anna blurted out the question before she'd even had a chance to think about how it would sound.

'What about *what*?' She heard the incredulous laughter in Vasilico's voice.

She knew it made her sound desperate; as if she was clutching at straws – which perhaps she was. Nevertheless, she couldn't now take it back. There was nothing for it but to plough on.

'I'm serious,' she said. 'If he was encouraging his followers to blow up shopping centres or fly planes into skyscrapers, you'd have him in a cell before his feet even touched the ground. He's inciting his followers to commit mass acts of violence against women. What's the difference here? Is it because he's not a Muslim? Because he's *white*?'

'*That* accusation is beneath you,' Vasilico snapped, and this time she heard not only the anger in his voice but also the genuine hurt. 'I watched those links you sent me. I listened to what he said very carefully. At no point does he direct his followers to do anything like what this so-called Reckoning has done. There's a vast difference between what he's putting out there and the sort of incitement that got Abu Hamza banged up.'

Anna bit her lip rather than respond. She was a long way from being as convinced of the distinction as he evidently was.

'Supposing, just supposing I *was* able to arrest him,' Vasilico continued. 'What do you imagine would happen then? Do you think those men's rights cretins would just pack up and go home?'

Again, Anna said nothing. On some level, she recognised that he had a point. It occurred to her, too, that, assuming The Reckoning's actions *were* driven by a desire to avenge Leopold's wounded honour, arresting him might well make things considerably worse.

Vasilico sighed heavily. When he next spoke, his tone was more kindly.

'I know you're not this fella's biggest fan, to put it mildly. And I don't doubt you have good reason to feel that way.' He hesitated. 'But are you sure you don't just *want* him to be guilty because of your personal feelings towards him?'

For the third and final time that call, Anna chose not to respond. She was aware that denying it would only succeed in making her sound like she was protesting too much. Was aware, too, that if she had, then it would have been at least partly a lie.

'Look,' said Vasilico, 'I've got to go. I've recently been informed that the *Tribune* plans to run a story on tomorrow's front page featuring exclusive comments from Amber Maguire and her parents on how they feel about the police deliberately misleading them as to the broader context of her assault.'

It was all Anna could do to stop herself from saying, 'Well, you should have *thought* about that,' before putting the phone down.

She collected her coat and left the office, intending to spend her lunch break pounding the pavement in an effort to work off some of her frustration. As she passed the TAs' office, a noise from behind the door caused her to halt in her tracks. It sounded like a sob, hastily suppressed.

She pushed open the door to find Farah seated alone at the desk by the window, glasses off. Seeing Anna standing in the doorway, she wiped her eyes on the back of her sleeve and hastily composed herself.

'Farah?'

Farah put her glasses back on and managed an unconvincing smile. 'Hey.'

Anna stepped into the room, shutting the door behind her. 'What's wrong?'

'What do you mean? Nothing's wrong. I'm fine.' Farah's voice cracked with barely contained emotion.

Anna gave Farah a disbelieving look, and she folded instantly. She gazed up at Anna, eyes glistening.

'Is it true what they say? That all the victims were signatories to the petition?'

Anna couldn't think how to respond. Her silence, it seemed, was all Farah needed to hear.

'Oh, God . . .'

She buried her head in her hands, her glasses once more landing, discarded, on the table. As her shoulders heaved with sobs, Anna finally managed to snap out of her inertia. Striding over to the table, she dropped to a crouch next to Farah and enveloped her in her arms.

'It's my fault,' Farah wept, 'all mine. I persuaded her to sign that thing. I'm the reason they violated her. I should have been there. It should have been me.'

As words gave way to further sobs, Anna continued to hold her, stroking her hair and murmuring impotent platitudes.

22

El Duce invites GodsGift2Women and LifeIsPain to a new chat channel.

LifeIsPain joins the chat.

GodsGift2Women joins the chat.

El Duce: Ladyboys and gentlemen, I give you COMEDY! I give you DRAMA! I give you HIGH STAKES ACTION!

LifeIsPain: Whats happening
LifeIsPain: Share share

El Duce: At 9 a.m. this morning, our benevolent leader voluntarily surrendered at Maryhill Police Station for interrogation by the Gestapo.

LifeIsPain: OMG

GodsGift2Women: WTF
GodsGift2Women: What grounds

El Duce: Assisting the police with their enquiries. Or some variation on that bullshit.

El Duce: Anyway, this tale has a happy ending. Shortly before midday, He walked out a free man, having run rings round the dim-witted plods.

LifeIsPain: FUCK YES

GodsGift2Women: LOL Total clown show
GodsGift2Women: But seriously what the fucks going on
GodsGift2Women: They dont have anything on him surely
GodsGift2Women: Or they wouldnt have let him go

El Duce: You really have no idea? Neither of you?
El Duce: Tsk tsk. Surely it's obvious.

LifeIsPain: ?????

El Duce: The Scavolini bitch had a word in her detective boyfriend's ear. Persuaded him to turn the screws on Big D. Tried to pin what we've been doing on Him.

LifeIsPain: Fucking cunt shit whore slut
LifeIsPain: Knew it had some thign to do with this

GodsGift2Women: When do we deal with her?
GodsGift2Women: Say the word and I'll give her something 2 fill that big mouth of hers

LifeIsPain: Yeah make it wish it never crossd us

El Duce: All in good time. I know you're both eager to make the sow pay. And I get that, really I do.
El Duce: But don't either of you so much as think about moving without my say so. We'll deal with her when we're good and ready. Until then, we sit tight.
El Duce: Consider this an order from the very highest authority.

LifeIsPain: From big D
LifeIsPain: ?

El Duce: Affirmative.

LifeIsPain: Its so cool he talks to u

El Duce: I'll tell Him you said hi.

LifeIsPain: Oh wow really??

El Duce: No.

GodsGift2Women: :D :D :D :D

El Duce: Be in no doubt, though, He's aware of your passion, and your desire to avenge Him is not unappreciated. But He wants cool heads to prevail.
El Duce: Are we clear?

LifeIsPain: Clear

GodsGift2Women: As a whore's wink

El Duce: Good.
El Duce: Now, to more pleasant matters . . . Who wants details of our next mission?

GodsGift2Women: About fucking time

LifeIsPain: Me me me me me
LifeIsPain: Please I want it

El Duce: Now, now. Perhaps one day, your time will come. This one's for GodsGift.

El Duce: A chance for him to redeem himself for his earlier insubordination.

GodsGift2Women: Im listening . . .

23

Thursday 7 November

Anna came to with a start. For a moment, she just lay there in the darkness, not knowing what had woken her or why every muscle in her body was tense and ready for flight.

She sat up. Turned her head this way and that, even though there was nothing to see, barring the faint glow of the sodium streetlights shining through the fabric of the bedroom curtains. She remained perfectly still, listening.

Then she heard it: the sound she somehow knew had wakened her.

The crunch of footsteps under her window.

She slipped out of bed and, as quietly as possible, padded over to the window. Pulled back the curtain. Peered out, gazing down at the garden below. There was nothing to be seen.

Tugging on her dressing gown, she headed out into the landing and set off down the corridor, treading lightly but quickly. As she passed the door to Zoe's room, it opened and Zoe peered out, bleary-eyed, wearing a knee-length Snoopy T-shirt.

'What is it?' she murmured, evidently still half-asleep.

'I heard a noise,' Anna whispered back.

Zoe frowned. 'What, like a "hoose's foundations settling doon tae sleep" noise or a . . .'

'I mean like a "someone creeping around the garden" noise.'

In an instant, Zoe was wide awake.

'Right. Two ticks.'

She disappeared behind the door. She was back less than ten seconds later, a baseball bat clutched in both hands.

'Let's go,' she said.

As they crept down the stairs, Anna briefly registered the fact that she'd never realised, until now, that Zoe owned a baseball bat. Why *did* she own a baseball bat?

Probably for situations precisely like this one.

They stepped out of the back door into the garden, Zoe leading the way with her bat raised. Anna was just behind her, one hand on Zoe's shoulder, the other holding her phone aloft with the torch mode activated, '999' already pre-emptively entered into the keypad.

Zoe gave an exaggerated shiver. 'Jeez-*o*!' she whispered. 'If I'd known it'd be this bloody parky, I'd've put knickers on.'

Together, they performed a thorough examination of the back garden, Anna swinging the beam of the torch into the various nooks and crannies, before making their way around the side of the house to the front garden. All was quiet. There wasn't even any sound of traffic from nearby Hyndland Road. Even the most dedicated night owls, it seemed, were safely tucked up in their beds.

Zoe lowered the bat and turned to Anna. 'There's naeb'dy here,' she said.

Anna chewed her bottom lip and said nothing.

'Mibby ye just imagined it? Or had a dream or something.'

'I heard something,' said Anna. 'I'm sure of it.'

But she was no longer quite so certain. Already, the precise order of events was starting to feel hazy in her mind. *Could* she have still been asleep when she thought she heard footsteps?

'Well,' said Zoe, trying – but not quite succeeding – to mask the note of scepticism in her voice, 'if ye did, whoever it was, they're long gone now.' She was already turning back towards the house. 'Guess we musta frightened 'em off.'

'Guess so,' said Anna, without much conviction, and followed Zoe back inside.

They returned to their respective rooms, but Anna didn't get back under the covers immediately. She remained sitting on the end of the bed for a good half-hour, tense and unsettled, all her senses still on high alert.

She heard no further disturbances. However, the following morning, after a thoroughly sleepless night, she did a fresh recce in the light of day and discovered, to her dismay, that the flowerbed running along the western side of the house had been trampled, accompanied by a discarded cigarette end, half trodden into the soil.

She debated telling Zoe about what she'd discovered, before ultimately deciding against spooking her. She also briefly considered calling Vasilico and voicing her concerns to *him*, before remembering the decidedly frosty note on which they'd left things following their phone call the previous day. She couldn't face him again so soon – especially as he'd already as good as accused her of crying wolf about Leopold. What, after all, did she actually have to show him? Some trampled flowers and a solitary cigarette butt? She could hear his response already: *Not exactly a smoking gun, is it, Anna?*

Instead, having shooed Zoe – who was joining Sal on a day trip to Largs – out the door, she rang the playgroup to tell them Jack wouldn't be coming this morning, before cancelling her own plans to go into the office. Thankfully, she had no teaching commitments that day, and the one postgrad student with whom she had a tutorial scheduled was only too glad to be gifted an unexpected extra week to work on the chapter they'd been due to discuss.

She made sure all the doors and windows were locked and secure and that the burglar alarm was on, then resolved to make the most of this unexpected free morning and spend it with Jack. She got out the Lego fire station she'd been promising to help him build for ages now, settling on her knees on the living room floor and spreading the bricks out on the rug in front of them.

But the moment, it seemed, had passed. Jack had lost interest, and, over the course of the next half-hour, grew increasingly frustrated by his inability to get the pieces to fit together. He took to getting up and wandering away every couple of minutes, leaving Anna to build the set he'd once pleaded so fervently with her to buy.

In the end, accepting that they were on a hiding to nothing, she abandoned the half-finished building and asked Jack what he'd prefer to do instead.

'Cartoons,' was his emphatic response.

Treating the TV as a babysitting device wasn't exactly the sort of parenting Anna approved of – but, by the same token, she was a firm believer in allowing children to discover their own interests rather than forcing them to do things they didn't enjoy just because they were on some pre-approved list of activities that were supposed to be mentally enriching.

So she settled on the sofa with him and stuck on his *Shaun the Sheep* Blu-ray. While he was engrossed in the colourful escapades on-screen, she almost instinctively reached for her iPad and once more turned her attention to the man who'd consumed so much of her waking life in recent weeks. She wasn't sure what she was looking for – if, indeed, she was even looking for *anything* specific – beyond a distant hope that somehow, somewhere, she'd find something that would be enough to nail Leopold to the wall.

Since her call with Katharine Barnard, Anna had increasingly immersed herself in the online discourse surrounding the man. She'd even, out of a perhaps misplaced sense of morbid curiosity, ventured onto the 'r/Leopold' subreddit – a deeply contradictory space, combining the most extreme misogyny imaginable with starry-eyed hero worship. Scrolling through the page had proved to be an exercise in severe cognitive dissonance. For instance, one extremely popular post took the form of a poll: *Q: Would you rather fuck (a) a dog, (b) a prepubescent child or (c) a femoid?* (At the time of viewing, (a) had over 50% of the vote, with (b) running a close second.) In the post immediately below it, a young man spoke, in genuinely moving terms, about how listening to Leopold's teachings had persuaded him not to end his own life. It seemed almost incomprehensible to her that the same man was capable of provoking such wildly conflicting responses from people. To some, his words gave them licence to indulge in the most disgusting bigotry imaginable. To others, he was a saviour of almost Christ-like proportions.

Now, over the course of the next hour, she watched the latest episode of his podcast, earbud in one ear, the other listening in case Jack needed anything. Leopold touched on his recent experience with the police, decrying the overreach of law enforcement – a subject on which, ironically, he and Anna might, under other circumstances, have found common ground – and offering up his own thoughts on the recent spate of assaults. Much like his response to the crimes in Southend two years ago, he argued that these were the inevitable result of the 'imbalanced' nature of the current state of play between the sexes, and that some men *were* bound to feel that their only recourse was to respond, with force, to the fact that recent advances in the rights and freedoms of women had coincided with – so he claimed – a loss in those same rights and freedoms for men. This outbreak of male violence against women was, he insisted, the inevitable outcome of men no longer feeling able to pursue women in traditional ways thanks to the feminist-initiated discourse of 'toxic masculinity' and 'rape culture'.

'If we go around telling men that they're monsters purely by virtue of their sex,' he mused, with a fatalistic sigh, *'is it any surprise that a minority will decide, "Actually, you know what? We* are *monsters, and we choose to embrace our monstrosity"?'*

What, Anna wondered, could possibly have made him into such a bitter, hate-filled husk of a man? She wasn't a big fan of the whole 'nature versus nurture' binary, believing it to be an overly reductive way of interrogating what was, in fact, a far more symbiotic relationship than proponents of either side of the debate were typically willing to acknowledge. But, in the case of misogyny and other forms of bigotry, she saw little room for equivocation. She refused to believe Leopold had simply been born this way – that he'd emerged from the womb with this seemingly pathological contempt for women. Was there some event in his past – some formative experience that had soured him so comprehensively towards roughly fifty percent of the world's population?

Convinced that the answer to this question must be rooted in the dim and distant past, she set about digging up as much information as she possibly could about Leopold's early life. She began with his childhood in the late 60s and early 70s, following him from his birthplace in North London to his time at the University of Bath, where, like her, he'd studied Sociology and Psychology, before going on to research a PhD in Social Anthropology. His doctoral thesis was titled *An anthropological study of quotidian life among suburban communities in postwar England, 1945–1955* – a subject about which she knew next to nothing – and, from the brief skim she took of it, didn't appear to contain any contentious views. On the contrary, it was incredibly dry and ponderous, embodying all the worst traits she associated with academic prose and which she regularly warned her students to avoid in their own writing. Why use one simple word when you could use half a dozen that required a dictionary for the average person to decipher?

Leopold's preoccupation with gender issues didn't seem to have emerged until his appointment as a lecturer at the University of Southend in 2002. Little of his writing from that period survived, though Anna did succeed in uncovering a paper published by him in the *London Journal of Social Anthropology* in 2006, focusing on his favourite subject: the young men who'd been 'left behind' by the advances of feminism from the latter half of the twentieth century onwards. Tonally, it represented something of a halfway point between the dry, dispassionate academese of his PhD thesis and the tub-thumping sermonising of his present-day work. The ugly, vindictive tone that characterised so much of his later output was almost wholly absent, in its place an earnestness that appeared to manifest from a genuine desire to help these 'lost boys'. One section towards the end of the paper, in which he warned of the dire consequences of continuing to ignore this trend, caught her eye in particular.

There is, I fear, considerable scope for these young men, deprived of either positive affirmation or role models, to be seduced by malign forces seeking to harness their frustrations and sense of unfulfilment for their own nefarious ends. We should all beware the charismatic, unscrupulous 'messiah', offering seductively easy answers to complex problems. These lost boys, so starved of positive reinforcement from mainstream society, will inevitably prove to be 'easy marks' for such snake oil salesmen, who prey on their desire to blame their diminished fortunes on those whose own fortunes have contemporaneously improved; in other words, women, and ethnic and sexual minorities.

Our aim should not be to pretend to have answers to all the challenges they face; nor to encourage a worsening of the already strained relations between the sexes. Rather, we should equip them to live productive, fulfilling lives through positive affirmation, encouraging them to channel their energies into activities which reinforce their self-worth and perceived value to the broader society.

At the same time, we should not shy from difficult conversations. It is vital that we grab the bull by the horns and educate these young men about the reality of their circumstances: that, however it may seem, they are *not* systematically discriminated against by society by virtue of being male; that women and minorities have indeed suffered historic oppression and that it is right that we legislate to correct these injustices, however unfair this may seem in the eyes of those not receiving a 'leg up'. These are difficult conversations, but conversations that must be had, rather than simply playing to young men's pre-existing prejudices and allowing them to grow up consumed by misplaced resentment.

As she read, Anna found herself increasingly struggling to reconcile these words with the Leopold she knew and the bile he regularly spewed to his hundreds of thousands of listeners. What was more, he seemed to have foretold his own descent into shock jock hucksterism. He might as well have been penning a warning to others about his future self. It certainly called into question how much of the ultra-reactionary viewpoint he now espoused was the product of genuine conviction on his part. Had he really undergone such a radical change of heart, or had he merely, having correctly diagnosed the problem, decided that he too could line his pockets by taking up this unsavoury grift?

'Mummy. Mummy.'

Anna stirred to find Jack tugging on her arm. She turned to him.

'What is it, Trouble?'

Jack pointed at the television, which was now displaying the disc's menu screen. 'Cartoon's finished,' he said matter-of-factly. 'Play it again.'

24

Friday 8 November

What was left of Thursday passed without incident, and there were no further sinister noises overnight. Recognising that she couldn't remain holed up at home indefinitely, Anna returned to work the following day. As she approached the Hutcheson Building that morning, she once again found Vasilico waiting for her.

'I'm feeling a slight sense of *déjà vu* here,' she remarked. 'Come to chew me out again?'

'Not as such,' said Vasilico.

She halted. For the first time, she clocked his grave expression. Immediately, her own demeanour changed entirely.

'What's happened?'

Vasilico looked around uneasily at the various students and members of staff in the immediate vicinity, some hurrying to lectures or tutorials, others having stopped to shoot the breeze.

'Can we go somewhere more private?'

With Anna leading the way, they crossed over to the loading bay at the back of the university library and ducked under the awning.

'Well?' she demanded.

Vasilico moved closer to her – so close they were almost touching. Before she could object to this invasion of her personal space, however, he began to speak in a low, urgent voice.

'An eighth woman was attacked last night. Same pattern as the previous four: beaten, penetrated anally with a sex toy and left unconscious. She has a fractured skull.'

'God almighty,' Anna murmured.

She felt a familiar chill running down her spine. A gale of high-pitched laughter from a passing gaggle of students caused her to jackknife involuntarily, the sound as inappropriate to her ears as it would have been in a funeral parlour.

'And, just like clockwork,' Vasilico went on, 'the usual manifesto surfaced on at least a dozen message boards and social media sites in the early hours of the morning. It's been eleven days since Narinder Khatri was assaulted. The shortest gap so far. And not to flog a dead horse, but given that you more or less put the fear of God into the female student body the other night, this has the potential to spiral seriously out of control once word gets out – as it undoubtedly will.'

'What's her name?' said Anna, ignoring the implicit rebuke.

'Sorry?'

'The woman who was attacked last night. What's her name?'

'I hardly think that's—'

'Just tell me.'

Vasilico sighed. 'Jodie. Jodie Kerr. She's eighteen,' he added, rather pointedly.

Anna was already scrolling on her phone. It took her a moment to find what she was looking for – not that she'd ever seriously expected not to.

'There.'

She angled the phone towards Vasilico. Roughly halfway down the list of signatories to the anti-Leopold petition were the words 'Jodie Kerr, Social Policy (1st year)'.

Vasilico exhaled heavily through his nose and said nothing.

'Well?' said Anna. 'Haven't you got anything to say? Aren't you going to tell me it's all just a coincidence?'

'No, I am *not*!' snapped Vasilico. 'I'm thinking.'

She watched, chastened, as he paced back and forth, massaging the bridge of his nose. For the first time, she saw how much of a toll all this was taking on him. His normally smooth jaw was unshaven, and much of the sparkle had gone from his grey eyes. And she knew him well enough to be aware that it wasn't just the stress of leading such an intense, high-profile investigation, or the fact that, in all likelihood, his superiors held him personally responsible for the shitstorm the piece in the *Tribune* had sparked. His empathy for the victims he saw himself as having failed was the real deal. Their trauma would be increasingly weighing on him, and every moment their attackers remained at large was therefore a fresh excuse for him to indulge in self-flagellation.

'Vasilico,' she said quietly.

He didn't appear to hear her. He continued to pace as if she hadn't spoken.

She took a step towards him.

'*Paul.*'

He stopped at the sound of his first name. Turned to face her with a look of surprise.

She moved closer to him and laid a gentle hand on his forearm. It felt odd and uncomfortable – the first physical contact they'd had in a long time – but she kept her hand there till his shoulders became less tense and his arms fell to his sides. He gazed down at her, head low. She met his gaze with a sad, sympathetic smile.

'You OK?' she said softly.

He gave a gruff nod. 'I'm OK.'

She wasn't sure she believed him, but – for now, at any rate – the self-recriminations seemed to have subsided.

'What happens now?'

Vasilico gave a heavy sigh. 'Well, I'd say our options are limited, to put it mildly. Clearly, more of the same's not going to cut it. There was a time when I figured this lot's luck was bound to run out at some point. Eight victims later, I'm not so sure. And while, thanks to you, we now know how they're choosing their targets, the fact they have over six hundred names to pick from means we might as well still be at square one.'

Anna chose not to take this as a personal slight.

'Then consider the Leopold angle,' she implored him. 'Look, I know I can't *prove* he's involved. But surely there can no longer be any doubt that The Reckoning are acting on his behalf – avenging his sullied honour, or whatever it is they think they're doing. And that must mean getting at him is our key to getting at *them.*'

Vasilico opened his mouth, then stopped. Whatever he'd been about to say, he'd evidently changed his mind.

'Go on,' he said, after a moment.

Now that she had the floor, Anna found herself faltering. If Vasilico was expecting her to have a comprehensive, well thought out plan, he was in for a sore disappointment.

'I just think,' she said, 'if there was some way of putting him under pressure – you know, making him appear vulnerable – then maybe it might draw them out. Force them into making some rash decisions . . . to show their hand . .' She dismissed what she'd just said with a wave. 'I dunno. Sorry. I'm not even sure what I'm saying.'

But Vasilico was staring at her intently. There was a light in his eyes once more – a very specific light that she recognised from times gone by. Rather than risk derailing it, she waited, with as much patience as she could dredge up, for him to finish thinking it through.

'You mentioned, the other day, he'd been on at you to debate him,' he said eventually.

'Pretty much every opportunity he gets.'

'Well, supposing – and don't bite my head off here – supposing for a moment you agreed to it . . . A high-profile clash between the two of you, in a public venue . .' He raised an eyebrow, shoulders arching in an expectant shrug. 'Well, it might have the sort of effect you're describing, mightn't it?'

For several seconds, Anna just stared at him, dumbfounded.

'You want to use me as *bait*?' she finally managed to splutter.

'Not as *bait*.' Vasilico was instantly defensive. 'Think of it more as a way of pushing their buttons. Of bringing them out of the shadows.'

'In other words, bait.'

'Think about it. As far as they're concerned, it'd be a showdown between the forces of light and darkness – the figurehead of their woman-hating movement and a feminist criminologist. And, if The Reckoning are as enamoured of the good professor as you make out, there's no way they'd be able to resist the draw of a front row seat at the metaphorical smackdown of the century . .' He clocked Anna's expression. 'I'm not selling you on this, am I?'

'Not exactly.'

She'd listened to his pitch with a mounting horror that grew in inverse proportion to his own apparent enthusiasm for the idea. Her long-standing misgivings about these sorts of debates were one thing. The thought that she'd effectively be acting as a tethered goat was something else entirely.

Vasilico gave her a beseeching look. 'Come on, Anna. As far as I'm concerned, this is pretty much the last throw of the dice. I'm out of other ideas. If we don't manage *some* sort of breakthrough, it's only a matter of time before they do the same thing to some other poor girl. And the way they've been escalating, my fear is that it's not going to be too much longer before we end up with a dead body on our hands.'

Anna didn't respond immediately. She hated the cynical nature of what he was doing, and, right at that moment, she hated *him* too – not least because it was working. Not unlike Leopold himself, Vasilico knew exactly which buttons to push with her. Raising the spectre of a potential fatality because of their – *her* – inaction had effectively been the nuclear option. He knew her too well to imagine she could ever have stood to have that on her conscience.

And, in spite of herself, she realised she was, if not *warming* to his proposal, then at least coming round to the logic underpinning it. It might be a long shot, but she recognised she had the power to use her profile and platform in a way that might just turn the tables in their favour. The alternative was to remain on the sidelines, impotently carping about the shortcomings of the official investigation.

She'd wanted to be involved, hadn't she? No, scratch that – she *was* involved, whether she liked it or not.

She let out a heavy sigh. In her heart of hearts, she already knew her decision.

THE GREAT DEBATE

'DO WOMEN IN TODAY'S SOCIETY
ENJOY MORE ADVANTAGES THAN MEN?'

ROBERT LEOPOLD
PROFESSOR OF SOCIAL ANTHROPOLOGY

VS.

ANNA SCAVOLINI
PROFESSOR OF CRIMINOLOGY

CHAIR:
DR FRASER TAGGART

ARGYLL HALL
WEDNESDAY 13 NOVEMBER, 5.30–7.00 P.M.
TICKETS AVAILABLE ONLINE
OR FROM THE GROUND FLOOR OFFICE

25

Wednesday 13 November

On several occasions over the next few days, Anna came extremely close to pulling out. She was convinced she'd made a colossal mistake; that, if she'd insisted to Vasilico that she be given time to think about it, there was no way she'd have agreed to his madcap scheme. But, each time she came close to picking up the phone and informing Fraser that she was withdrawing, one of two things invariably stopped her.

First was the knowledge that tickets to the event, which had gone online mere hours after she and Leopold had both confirmed their participation on Friday, had sold out in a little over forty-eight hours. If she bailed now, she'd be depriving a significant number of people of a spectacle they clearly had a keen interest in seeing.

Second, and even more potent, was the knowledge that to do so would mean losing face and consigning herself to an eternity of ribbing from Leopold. *What's the matter, Professor Scavolini? Afraid to meet me in the marketplace of ideas?*

And then, of course, there was the possibility, however slim, that Vasilico's ruse might actually work. If this public confrontation did indeed result in flushing out the individuals who, between them, had beaten and/or sexually assaulted eight women and had their sights set on umpteen others, then any personal discomfort she experienced was a price more than worth paying.

* * *

At four o'clock on Wednesday afternoon, she stood in front of her bedroom mirror, disdainfully eyeing up the long-sleeve shirt and trousers combo she'd picked out. She'd tried on at least half a dozen outfits, but, for some reason, none of them had felt right. She'd never been one of those people who spent an hour trying to decide what they were going to wear, but there was, it seemed, a first time for everything.

Unprompted, Leopold's remarks about women's attire in the workplace entered her head.

Fuck it. If she was going to go out on stage and embarrass herself, she might as well make a statement.

She stripped off the shirt and trousers and changed into a black short-sleeved polo-neck top and black tights, before heading through to Zoe's room and pilfering a red vinyl skirt which ended well above the knees. As the *coup de grâce*, she added a swipe of flamenco red lipstick to her lips, again procured from Zoe's repertory. She briefly toyed with borrowing something from Zoe's sizeable shoe collection too, before remembering that Zoe had improbably large feet and that none of her footwear would fit her, even if she stuffed the toes with tissue paper. Instead, she selected a pair of ankle boots from her own shoe drawer – a gift to herself a couple of years ago that she'd worn precisely once, and which gave her a much-needed lift in comparison to her normal flat heels, causing her to appear marginally taller.

Slowly, she made her way downstairs, feeling awkward and ungainly in the heels she wasn't used to wearing. As she entered the living room, Zoe, waiting for her on the sofa, turned and gave a low whistle.

'Oooh! *Someone's* dressed to impress. You look *smokin'*, doll.'

'Shut it, you,' muttered Anna, already regretting her choice. 'I'm self-conscious enough as it is. Anyway, it's all part of my genius plan to show a venal old misogynist he can't bully women into feeling guilty over how they dress.'

'I see,' said Zoe archly. 'And it wouldnae happen tae have *anything* tae do wi a certain Detective Chief Inspector who's gonnae be in the audience, would it?'

Anna jabbed a warning finger in her direction. 'Another word and I'm leaving you at home.'

Zoe just smiled knowingly.

Anna turned to check her lipstick in the mirror. 'You made sure Jack's got everything he needs for his sleepover?' She wiped a trace of excess red from the corner of her mouth with her pinkie.

'Aye,' said Zoe. 'Janice's collecting him and Finlay fae playgroup and she'll run 'em both there the morra afternoon as well. I let the staff know what's what. Said you'd be picking him up at four.'

The invitation from Janice, one of the other mums from the playgroup, for Jack to sleep over with her son Finlay had come out of the blue the other day, but Anna, after initially baulking at the thought of Jack spending the night away from home, had been only too happy to accept. It simplified things considerably, eliminating the need to arrange childcare for the debate, which Zoe had already made clear she planned to attend as moral support.

Zoe inhaled a dramatic breath. 'Right, then, missus – you set?'

'No?' said Anna, managing to make it sound like a question. She felt her shoulders slumping. 'But I'm just going to *have* to be, aren't I?'

Zoe batted away her concern with a breezy wave. 'Ah, ye'll do grand. Old greaseball's no gonnae know what's hit him.' She offered Anna her arm. 'C'mon, Cinders – let's get ye tae the ball.'

The evening continued to draw in as they made their way up the hill towards the university. As they neared the summit, the sound of sustained, angry chanting began to reach their ears, the words indecipherable. Zoe shot Anna a questioning look. Anna merely shrugged, but the knot in her stomach tightened. There had been a febrile atmosphere around the campus for a while now – ever since she blew the lid on the links between the attacks at the meeting in the Dewar. It had been building and building all week, and she sensed that it was approaching some sort of crescendo. She just hoped, however things ended up shaking out tonight, it didn't make things worse.

As they passed through the gates and the main building came into view, the source of the noise became apparent. A group of about a dozen women had gathered at the entrance, two of them holding aloft a huge banner bearing the words 'NO PLATFORM FOR MISOGYNY'. Anna caught a glimpse of a rainbow beanie hat and recognised Kez Dixon as the ringleader. At the same instant, Kez glanced in her direction. Their eyes met briefly, before Kez raised her voice, chanting with renewed ferocity.

'No. Platform. For. Misogyny. NO. PLATFORM. FOR. MISOGYNY. NO . . .'

The other women picked up on her mood and raised their own voices to match. Anna quickened her pace, half-dragging Zoe past them with her head down, feeling every inch a traitor to the cause.

They reached the top of the stairs and stepped out into the West Quadrangle. The chanting below them remained audible but felt less immediate. Less overwhelming.

Anna turned to Zoe with a heavy breath. 'Well, I guess this is where we go our separate ways. You gonna be OK kicking around till it starts?'

'Aye, nae bother,' said Zoe breezily. 'I'll stick around out here; keep an eye out for Sal. Reckoned she'll be here round about five.' She squeezed Anna's arm. 'G'wan. I'll be watching fae the stalls. Ye'll smash it – nae ifs or buts.'

Anna flashed her a grateful look, then turned and hurried towards the cloisters.

She headed straight to the small side room that had been set aside for her. She'd been assured that Leopold would have his own separate green room, and that their paths wouldn't cross ahead of the debate.

Opening the door, she found Farah, Vasilico and Kirk waiting for her. She sensed the tension in the air, though, outwardly, they were all smiles. Putting on a good act for her benefit, she supposed.

'I'll have half a dozen plain-clothes officers in the audience,' said Vasilico, once they'd dispensed with the requisite pleasantries, 'and another four patrolling the grounds outside, ready to lend a hand if anything kicks off. Myself and DS Kirk will be there as well. We've prepared for every eventuality.' He gave a shrug that she assumed was meant to be encouraging. 'Now we just have to wait and see.'

Anna managed a tight smile. 'Simple as that, huh?'

Vasilico winced apologetically. 'Rest assured, no one here is under any illusions as to which of us is putting themselves on the line. And I know it's easy for me to say, seeing as it's not *me* in the spotlight, but you've nothing to worry about. Nothing bad's going to happen to you, I promise.'

Anna met his eyes and managed a grateful smile. She was tempted to tell him not to make promises he was in no position to keep, but she knew it would only sound churlish and ungrateful. By the sounds of it, he'd really pulled out the stops to keep her as safe as humanly possible.

Vasilico continued to face her, a look of genuine warmth in his eyes. As she met his gaze, she felt something stirring inside her that she hadn't felt for a long time – something warm and reassuring that helped blunt the anxiety that was gnawing at her innards.

Vasilico stirred. 'Right. We'll leave the two of you to run your lines.' He flicked his head at Kirk, as if summoning her to heel. 'Come on, you. Let's get a shift on.'

Kirk got to her feet and fell into step with him, flashing Anna a grin and a wink as she went.

More out of a sense of obligation than anything else, Anna saw them out. As he reached the door, Vasilico halted and turned to face her once more.

'I mean it,' he said in a low voice. 'The slightest *sniff* of trouble and I'll be on that stage myself to make sure nothing happens to you.'

'I appreciate it,' said Anna tightly, all the familiar feelings of apprehension instantly returning.

Vasilico dipped his head in acknowledgement. He looked to be on the verge of leaving it at that. Then, having second thoughts, his eyes once more met hers.

'You look incredible, by the way,' he said.

Anna felt the blood rushing to her cheeks. Utterly tongue-tied, she managed a half-smile and lowered her eyes.

Vasilico remained where he was for a moment, as if unsure how to extricate himself from this exchange. Then, stirring, he gave her a last nod and ducked out.

Anna let her breath out slowly. Then, steeling herself, she turned to face Farah, perched on the table at the far end of the room, and whom she suspected had heard Vasilico's final words to her – or at least guessed the sentiment behind them.

'Right, then,' she said brightly, 'shall we do this?'

Over the last week, Anna had met with Farah twice to do dummy runs of the debate. The issue of Farah's guilt over Narinder's attack hadn't come up again since the day Anna had found her crying in the TAs' office, and, as much as Anna would have welcomed the opportunity to further impress on her that what had happened hadn't been her fault, a part of her was privately glad of the excuse to avoid the subject. The last thing she'd have wanted was to prompt a fresh bout of tearful self-recrimination on Farah's part.

With the clock now ticking, they knuckled down and did one more run through the various talking points they anticipated coming up, with Farah playing the role of Leopold. Anna, acutely aware of her own shortcomings under pressure, did her best to resist the urge to respond to each criticism of her positions with a more extreme restatement of what she'd already said – something she knew she tended to do when challenged. Of course, she knew these sorts of prep sessions could only achieve so much. Though Farah could anticipate the sorts of arguments Leopold was likely to make, she was nowhere near ruthless enough to go for the jugular, and, despite Anna urging her to take off the kid gloves, had consistently pulled her punches every time they'd gone into the ring like this.

They were still at it at twenty past five when there was a knock on the door and a floppy-haired young man poked his head in to inform them that this was Anna's ten-minute warning and that he needed to mic her up. Despite fervently wishing she could have had another hour to prepare, Anna dutifully submitted to having the cumbersome wire microphone looped around her ears and the heavy receiver clipped onto the back of her skirt. They were just running through the sound checks when the door opened again and one of the university's secretarial staff – a middle-aged woman with a world-weary air about her – leant in, clutching a cordless phone.

'Are you Anna Scolini?' she said.

'Scavolini,' said Anna irritably.

'There's a call for you. It's a Melanie Walker?'

Anna recognised the name: the senior play leader at Jack's playgroup. What was *she* doing calling her – now, of all times?

'Can you tell her I'm busy?'

The secretary's pinched expression told her exactly what she thought of *that* idea. 'She's quite insistent,' she said, her tone not altering beyond the same flat monotone.

Sighing, Anna took the phone. The floppy-haired technician continued to fuss around her, fiddling with the wires running down her back.

'Hello?'

'Anna, hello. It's Melanie Walker.'

'Yes?' said Anna briskly. She was in no mood for beating about the bush.

'I wanted to talk to you about a rather disturbing incident that occurred at playgroup today,' said Melanie. 'Um . . . well, there's no delicate way of putting this. You see, Jack bit another child.'

He WHAT? thought Anna. This was positively the last thing she needed right now.

She was still trying to work out how to respond when she felt a sharp tug on the hair at the back of her head.

'Oww!'

She turned to glare at the technician, who shot her an apologetic look and continued to fiddle with her headset.

'Anna?' Melanie's voice crackled through the phone. 'Did you hear what I said?'

Already on edge and predisposed towards defensiveness, Anna made a snap decision, then and there, that she was going to brazen this out.

'I heard you,' she said, doing her best to sound like she had the situation under perfect control. 'And what did this other child do?'

There was a pause.

'Wh . . . what do you mean?' said Melanie.

'Well, I doubt Jack just suddenly decided he was going to bite this child out of the blue. He must have had a reason. Therefore, the child presumably provoked him in some way. What did they do?'

Another pause. Melanie, it seemed, was lost for words.

'There's no justification for that sort of behaviour,' she said, when she'd found her voice again.

'I disagree. Until we know exactly what this other child did, I'm not prepared to pass judgement on mine. Perhaps they *deserved* to be bitten.'

This was followed by the lengthiest pause so far.

'We'll talk about this next time you're in,' Melanie finally declared, her tone falling somewhere between confused and appalled.

'I'll look forward to it,' said Anna.

She ended the call and handed the phone back to the wide-eyed secretary, who'd been hovering in the doorway the whole time, listening to every word of Anna's side of the conversation.

As she scuttled off, Anna turned to the technician. 'Are we done?'

'Well,' the technician began, 'I still need to—'

'Good.'

For a brief instant, it looked like he was considering standing his ground. Then, clearly thinking better of it, he too beat a hasty retreat.

As Anna massaged her temples with both hands, Farah made her way over cautiously.

'What was that about?' she asked.

'Oh, nothing,' said Anna, her hands dropping to her sides with a slap. 'Just my life imploding right before I go out on stage to make a tit of myself.'

'You *won't* make a tit of yourself,' said Farah firmly.

With her pronunciation, the word sounded more like 'teat' – which, for some reason, suddenly struck Anna as unaccountably hysterical. She stifled a nervous laugh.

'You're *you*,' Farah insisted, squeezing Anna's forearm. 'You know the subject matter inside out, you look amazing . . . You'll be brilliant, just like always.'

Anna looked at her, feeling a wash of earnest gratitude towards her. She was about to reply when the door opened again. The technician was back.

'Sorry,' he began apprehensively, partially positioning himself behind the door, as if he hoped it might offer some protection, 'but . . . it's time. I need to take you down.'

And just like that, all the feelings of dread, and of regret, came rushing back. *I shouldn't have agreed to this, I shouldn't have agreed to this, I shouldn't—*

Her panicked internal monologue was stopped short as Farah took hold of her and drew her into a hug. She held her for several seconds, so tightly the breath was almost squeezed out of her. But it did the trick. When Farah finally released her, Anna realised she felt a great deal calmer. Or at least felt a sense of inevitability about it all.

'OK,' said Farah, looking her dead in the eyes, her tone brisk and surprisingly authoritative. 'Deep breaths. You can do this. Keep a clear head, and don't forget, whenever you respond to him, choose one or two specific points to address instead of trying to rebut everything he says.'

Anna nodded tightly. Then, sensing the technician hovering just beyond her shoulder, she turned and allowed him to lead her out into the corridor.

'And remember,' Farah called after her, 'his points of attack reveal more about his own weaknesses than they do about you!'

But Anna barely heard her. The door swung shut behind her with a thud that seemed to reverberate in her very marrow. The technician glanced back over his shoulder and gave her a questioning look, as if to ask if she was OK. She managed to nod tightly, then set off after him down the corridor.

26

She followed him down a flight of stairs, then along a narrow corridor. At the other end, Fraser and Leopold were waiting for her. Fraser was in 'smart casual' attire – chinos and an overly tight shirt with rolled-up sleeves. Leopold was in his usual sports jacket and open-collar shirt. Both were mic'd up.

As Anna drew alongside them, Leopold raised an eyebrow. 'Well, well. What have *you* come as tonight?'

Anna met his question with a steely glower. He merely smiled back at her complacently. Before she could formulate a cutting retort, however, the technician was ushering them all through the door in front of them.

And then, before she was even properly aware of what was happening, they'd stepped out onto the stage at the front of the ornate, high-ceilinged Argyll Hall, and were being greeted by thunderous applause, accompanied by the occasional whistle and a couple of borderline rapturous shouts of 'DADDY!'

The lights angled towards the stage were dazzlingly bright, with the result that it was difficult to make out anything of the audience. However, from the volume of the applause, there could be little doubt that the room was full to capacity. Anna briefly raised her hand to shield her eyes, in the hope that it might allow her to see better, before deciding this wasn't a good look and letting it fall to her side.

She felt someone gently touching her upper arm. Turning, she found Fraser by her side, smiling encouragingly as he gestured to one of three low-backed chairs in the middle of the stage, facing a low table with three glasses of water. Leopold was already settled in the one furthest from her, hands folded across his stomach, looking relaxed and contented.

As the applause continued and Anna eased herself into the chair at the opposite end, her eyes drifted to the front row, less ill-defined than the ones further back by virtue of its proximity to the stage. Zoe and Sal were seated together near the middle, both applauding with gusto. Catching her eye, Zoe flashed her a toothy grin and a double thumbs up, then resumed clapping. Anna nodded to her and gave a discreet smile of thanks.

After what seemed like an age, the applause subsided. Fraser, the only one of them still on his feet, beamed at the audience.

'Well, good evening, everyone. Thank you for coming out on this frankly dreary November night.'

He gazed out at the sea of faces before him, nodding contently, as if confirming that the view met with his approval. Now that Anna's eyes had had a chance to adjust to the glare, she was able to make out the assembled throng a little more clearly. What immediately struck her was just how many of the people occupying the stalls were young men – a highly atypical composition for this sort of event.

'It's fantastic to see such a full house,' Fraser went on, 'though it should come as no surprise, given that our two speakers tonight are titans in their respective fields.' He gestured to Anna. 'The speaker to my left graduated from the Sapienza University in Rome with a doctorate in Feminist Criminology. She has been a member of the faculty here for ten years, the last five serving as course director of the only dedicated Criminology MA in Scotland.'

As he spoke, it suddenly struck Anna just how incredibly exposed she was up on this raised platform. For the umpteenth time that evening, she cursed herself for having opted for such a short skirt. She pressed her knees together, and reminded herself that she *was* wearing underwear.

'She is also the author of two books: *Rethinking Justice: New Approaches to Female Offending* and the forthcoming *Untold Stories: A Qualitative Study of Women's Experiences of the Scottish Prison System*. She is Professor Anna Scavolini.'

There was some muted, polite applause from the audience, mingled with an undercurrent of something else. A low rumble of disapproval, of animosity, of something perhaps even more intense than that. Anna, who felt it like a prickling under her skin, glanced at Fraser, saw him falter momentarily, and knew he'd sensed it too. A moment later, though, he carried on, having barely missed a beat.

'The speaker to my right joined us only recently, but in that time has made great waves within our little institution. He graduated from the University of Bath with a PhD in Social Anthropology and had a long and storied career at the University of Southend. He has authored numerous publications but is best known as the host of the successful – and at times controversial – podcast *Hard Truth*. He is, of course, Professor Robert Leopold.'

This time, the room erupted in thunderous applause, accompanied by a succession of shrill whistles, whoops and cheers. Leopold smiled and nodded graciously. Anna realised her fingernails were digging into the arms of her seat. The contrast could not have been more stark. Something was seriously wrong.

Fraser waited for the applause to die out before speaking again.

'The proposition being debated tonight is, "Do women in today's society enjoy more advantages than men?" A deliberately provocative statement that's sure to generate a lively exchange. Each candidate will have five minutes to make his or her opening statement, after which we'll go straight into a freeform discussion. As moderator, I reserve the right to intervene if the speakers wander off topic or their exchanges become overly heated' – he smiled indulgently – 'though I'm sure I'm not alone in anticipating that things could get a *little* spicy.'

A murmur of laughter from the audience.

'I *was* going to start this with a coin-toss, but Professor Leopold has graciously indicated that he's happy for his opposite number to have first bite at the cherry.'

Anna's eyes instinctively shot to Leopold. He glanced sidelong at her, smiled, and silently mouthed two words which, even without a qualification in lip-reading, she understood only too well.

Ladies first.

Fraser gestured to Anna. 'Professor Scavolini, the floor is yours.'

Anna got to her feet, feeling more than a little shaky. She was conscious of her pounding heart, her clammy hands, her heavy breathing amplified and piped back into her own ears by the headset. She swallowed heavily, trying to lubricate her dry throat with non-existent saliva and wishing she'd had the presence of mind to take a sip of water before getting up. She gazed out at the sea of ill-defined faces, imagining hostile intent in each and every one of them. Then her eyes alighted on Zoe, who grinned encouragingly and raised her fist in salute.

Anna began to speak.

'I'd like to start tonight with a point so obvious it almost shouldn't have to be made: to champion the rights of women is not to deny those same rights to men. To argue that women face greater levels of systemic oppression is not to ignore the very real difficulties which men *do* face.'

'Bullshit!' shouted a voice from the audience.

Anna was so taken aback that, for a few seconds, she just stood there, mouth half-open, her train of thought completely derailed. She looked across at Fraser, seated in the chair next to Leopold. She half-expected him to intervene, but he gave no reaction whatsoever. Was she the only one who'd heard the shout? It didn't seem possible.

Somehow, she found the resolve to continue.

'"Do women in today's society enjoy more advantages than men?" On a certain level, I object fundamentally to the framing of the question. It's not a zero-sum game. Many of the issues facing women and men are exactly the same. We should all want every single person on this planet to be able to live the best life they possibly can, not treat it as a competition to establish who has it worse. As such, attempts to portray any progress towards improving the material conditions of women as necessarily requiring a corresponding reduction in those of men is the same pernicious lie spread by reactionary movements the world over, scapegoating and demonising the most vulnerable in order to sow division and blind the masses to the injustices they themselves face.

'With that said, in agreeing to participate in this debate, I tacitly accepted the terms of the proposition – so allow me to lay out just a few of the reasons why I believe the answer to the question should be a resounding "no".'

To begin with, her tone might have been somewhat wavering, and those who didn't know her well might have been tempted to conclude that, much like Leopold had so often intimated, she did indeed lack the courage of her convictions. However, she found, as she continued to speak, that her voice grew louder; developed a more commanding air. She knew this stuff like the back of her hand, and her passion for the subject matter only served to strengthen her resolve to carry on; to state her case with as much confidence and authority as she could muster in this thoroughly intimidating situation.

'Women,' she said, 'are overwhelmingly the victims of sexual violence. The exact numbers fluctuate year by year, but the broad trend is that around 90% of adult rape victims are female.

'They are more likely to be victims of human trafficking, including sexual exploitation and forced labour.

'They are also overwhelmingly more likely to experience sexual harassment such as catcalling, unwanted touching and stalking, to such an extreme extent that many simply regard it as an accepted part of everyday life. How often have we heard stories of women who think nothing of texting the address of their date to their friends before going home with him? How many times are we told of young women and girls regarding the act of receiving unsolicited dick pics as simply the price they must pay for having an online presence?'

There was some scattered laughter from the back of the hall.

Briefly glancing across at Leopold, Anna saw that he had his phone out. He was holding it one-handed, casually scrolling with his thumb, as if he was merely on the train or in a dentist's waiting room. A surge of anger coursed through her – at the laughter *and* at his undisguised disinterest in what she had to say. For an instant, she imagined herself striding over and yanking the damn thing out of his hand. Then, the moment passed, and she somehow found the resolve to face forward and continue.

'Women are still paid, on average, less than men – the gap in 2018 was 17.8%. This discrepancy is especially pronounced at the higher levels of earning, and for women of colour, and becomes larger still when you factor in pre-existing wealth as opposed to just earned income, because income isn't always reflective of the ways in which men are disproportionately the recipients of wealth.

'On an international level, women of all ages are more likely than men to live below the poverty line, and to experience chronic hunger.

'Their voices are marginalised in media, and they have less representation in virtually every system of power that exists, from politics – where less than a third of elected officials are women – to journalism, to the STEM sectors, to the upper echelons of the business world.

'They are severely disadvantaged by hiring practices. Multiple studies have shown that, if a man and woman are equally qualified for a role, the woman is more likely to be passed over. And that's before we get onto the so-called "old boy network", which perpetuates already entrenched inequalities by ensuring that the previous generation of male bosses will always give a leg up to the next at the expense of women.

'Women carry out vast amounts of unacknowledged, unpaid labour – as mothers, as homemakers, as caregivers.

'Essential women's health products, such as tampons, are subject to taxation.

'Socially, women are stigmatised for having sexual desires and for acting on them while men are celebrated for the same behaviours.

'Women's reproductive rights are under renewed attack in multiple supposedly advanced democracies. To suggest that these battles have been won and that women no longer need to worry about them – as many on the political right do while simultaneously working to strip us of our bodily autonomy – is dangerous, disingenuous, and downright malicious.'

She glanced again at Leopold and saw, to no great surprise, that he was still paying more attention to his phone than to her. She swallowed again as she prepared to enter into the final part of her statement.

'If you acknowledge all of the points I've just mentioned, then I put it to you that a reasonable person cannot possibly contend that women enjoy more advantages in today's society than their male counterparts. I reject the motion utterly and invite Professor Leopold to defend it, if he can.'

As she resumed her seat, the audience reacted with a mixture of polite applause and what were unmistakably a series of low boos and hisses. In the front row, Zoe and Sal applauded and whooped loudly – an attempt, Anna sensed, to drown out the boos. Whatever gratitude she felt towards them was overshadowed by the growing sickness in the pit of her stomach. She fumbled for her water glass and gulped down several mouthfuls.

Fraser, judging by his somewhat shellshocked expression, had clearly heard the boos all too clearly. Once again, however, he made no move to take control of the situation. Instead, acting as if he hadn't heard them, he smiled at Anna and nodded graciously in her direction.

'Thank you, Anna.' He turned to Leopold. 'Professor Leopold? You have five minutes.'

Behaving as if he had all the time in the world, Leopold carefully slid his phone into the inside pocket of his jacket, then got to his feet.

'Oh, I'm sure it won't take as long as that,' he said genially.

He folded his arms behind his back, inhaled deeply through his nostrils, then began to speak in his confident baritone.

'Professor Scavolini claims not to care which sex is more disadvantaged – men or women.'

Anna, who was in the process of taking another sip of water, almost choked. It took all her self-control not to angrily shout back that she had, in fact, said no such thing.

'A cynic,' Leopold went on, 'might call that stance mightily convenient. I posit that, in fact, she knows *exactly* which group is really the most disadvantaged in today's world, and is attempting to deflect from this because she knows that objective reality comprehensively demolishes her argument. So, taking a leaf from my opponent's book, allow me to avail you of a few facts.

'Men are routinely discriminated against by the courts in cases of child custody. They are expected to pay for the upkeep of children they've fathered without any corresponding right of access to them or input into how they're raised.

'Men are at a disadvantage when it comes to divorce settlements, with women routinely being awarded half of the former couple's combined assets despite having contributed less than half themselves.

'Men face death or serious injury in combat zones. In virtually every country in the world, it is men, not women, who are conscripted during wartime or compelled to complete military service in times of peace.

'Men suffer from appalling levels of untreated mental health conditions. Nationally, men account for 75% of all suicides. It's the single biggest killer of males under the age of fifty.

'Across the board, men enjoy shorter lifespans than women, thanks in no small part to the gynocentric nature of health policies. Just look, for example, at the gaping chasm between the levels of funding for, say, cervical cancer treatments compared to those for prostate or testicular cancer.'

'That's complete crap!' a woman's voice shouted.

Fraser rose to his feet, a hand raised for calm. 'I'm going to have to ask the audience to refrain from making any further interjections,' he declared, the very picture of the judicious moderator. 'There will be time for questions at the end.'

He turned and nodded to Leopold, indicating to him to continue. Leopold gave an ingratiating smile, while Anna fumed silently. Just where the hell was *this* Fraser when *she'd* been interrupted earlier – to say nothing of all the booing?

Leopold smirked knowingly at the audience. 'So much for the tolerant left – am I right?'

Laughter and applause from the gallery.

'Now, where was I? Oh yes!' He continued, 'Men are subjected to domestic violence at a level comparable to women but are systematically ignored, mocked or instructed to "man up". Male sexual assault is similarly the butt of all manner of distasteful jokes, while, simultaneously, men are vastly more likely to be the victims of false accusations of rape and domestic assault.'

'You're a fucking liar!'

Anna couldn't identify where the voice had come from, and it was drowned out almost immediately by a chorus of angry boos and a solitary 'Shut the fuck up, bitch!', but this time, she was fairly certain the heckler had been Kez Dixon.

Fraser was on his feet in a trice. 'A little courtesy, *please*! This is not a free-for-all. We *will* hear from the speaker.' He turned to Leopold. 'Apologies, Professor Leopold. Please continue.'

Leopold smiled magnanimously. 'That's all right, Dr Taggart. I'm well used to my detractors shouting me down in lieu of any actual rebuttal of my arguments.'

He once again folded his arms behind his back and resumed his treatise.

'Men, on average, receive tougher prison sentences for committing the same crimes as women, many of whom avoid jail time altogether. My opponent, I believe, is a big proponent of reforming the experiences of female prisoners while conveniently having nothing whatsoever to say about the plight of their male counterparts.

'Men face systematic discrimination in the field of education, with learning tailored towards the needs and mental processes of female students, who unsurprisingly achieve better grades and are more likely to go into higher education as a result.'

He was speaking faster and faster, rattling through his points like a marathon runner who, sighting the finishing line, draws on his remaining energy reserves and puts on an extra burst of speed.

'Men are more likely to suffer from workplace injuries or fatalities.

'Men are denied access to equal parental leave.

'Men are almost ten times more likely than women to experience rough sleeping.

'And men are gaslit each and every day of their lives into believing they are the oppressors when it is an inarguable fact that *they*, by any reasonable standard, are the ones who are oppressed.'

He let out a heavy breath, as if winded by this rapid-fire delivery, waited for a few seconds, then continued.

'I could go on to list dozens of other examples of anti-male discrimination, but I feel I've more than adequately made my point. So, instead, I will acknowledge that yes, women were indeed discriminated against in the past, often in the most appalling ways. But those days are over. Female privilege is real, and while feminists who've based their whole careers on professional victimhood may not like hearing it, they enjoy advantages in today's society that men can only dream of. Those who suggest otherwise must surely be lying or, in a more charitable interpretation, frighteningly ill-informed.

'In either event, women now enjoy all the rights and privileges that were previously afforded to men, in addition to several additional forms of special dispensation, stacking the decks in their favour in a way that could only *possibly* be required if you accept the narrative that women are somehow naturally inferior to men . . .' He gazed out at the audience, smiling serenely. 'And if anyone in this room feels brave enough to make *that* argument, I welcome him to step forward and try.'

The applause from the audience, this time, was overwhelming, the noise of feet drumming approvingly on the floor reminiscent of a stampede. A booming chant of 'DA-*DDY*! DA-*DDY*!' went up – and kept going. To Anna, it seemed to be growing louder and more aggressive by the second, building to some inevitable, horrible climax. She felt herself sinking lower in her seat, the very ground seeming to grow unstable beneath her, as if she was perched on top of a piece of flotsam adrift in an endless, angry sea.

'DA-*DDY*! DA-*DDY*!' the chant continued, and, out of the corner of her eye, Anna sensed Leopold watching her. Despite knowing she shouldn't rise to the bait, she found herself turning to look at him. His eyes twinkled, and he shot her a look of such unconcealed glee that it was all she could do to stop herself from being sick.

Instead, she turned away and let her vision go hazy, gazing off into the middle distance as the chant thundered on.

27

Once the noise finally subsided, they moved onto the open discussion. Later, Anna would only remember isolated snatches, like the edited highlights broadcast after the fact.

It seemed to both last forever and pass in a blur. She was aware of constantly feeling like she was on the back foot; of the undisguised hostility cascading down from the audience gallery in waves; of Leopold seeming to anticipate everything she was going to say before she'd even thought of it herself. All her preparation with Farah went straight out of the window, and she was left trying desperately to land some palpable hits on her opponent.

It didn't seem to make any difference. No matter how many statistics she managed to quote, Leopold simply brushed them off as irrelevant, while the audience drowned them out with boos and applauded every utterance he made. She found herself beginning to wish she *had* accepted the invitation to go onto his podcast. At least then she wouldn't have had to contend with a baying mob constantly howling for her blood.

There was, she reflected, another reason not to enter into debates with reactionary provocateurs: because, if they thought they had anything to lose, they wouldn't be half as desperate to persuade you to do it.

'. . . that's what I'm trying to *tell* you,' said Anna; 'that we *know* advancing gender equality benefits the whole of society, not just women.'

A torrent of jeers and boos.

'It creates a stronger economy, it leads to greater levels of productivity and innovation, lower levels of conflict and less overall poverty.'

The jeers were getting louder, threatening to drown her out altogether.

'The irony,' she persisted, a hint of desperation now entering her voice, 'is that greater inclusion of women in the labour force has actually led to an increase in the wages of *men*.'

As the jeers finally subsided, Leopold regarded Anna with a disapproving shake of his head.

'Honestly, Anna, this sort of pandering is beneath you. Do you seriously think anyone still buys the line that the policies you advocate for do anything more than cement the privilege of your fellow travellers? It's called *feminism*. Clue's in the name.'

The audience whooped and applauded, lapping this up like thirsty dogs. Leopold turned to Anna and shrugged as if to say, *I rest my case.*

'Now, Anna,' said Leopold, 'we all know you're fond of reaming off statistics. You'll be aware, then, of a recent survey of young men, aged sixteen to twenty-four, gathering their views on a range of subjects. It found that a whopping fifty percent agreed with the following premise: "Feminism has gone too far and makes it harder for men to succeed." I'd like to invite you to respond to that.'

'Respond to it? How would you expect me to respond? I think it's an utterly depressing state of affairs.'

Laughter and some scattered boos from the audience.

Leopold smiled, as if he'd been hoping that was what she'd say. 'Which was, in fact, the thoroughly predictable response from the feminist establishment at the time of publication. Did any of them, when confronted with these numbers, say, "Hmm, perhaps we should engage with these young men and attempt to understand their concerns"? No. Instead, they collectively threw up their hands in horror and exclaimed, "This is terrible! We must forcibly berate these dreadful woman-haters until they see the error of their ways." Because, at the end of the day, that's the feminist playbook in a nutshell: don't engage, don't empathise, just keep repeating "You're wrong, you're wrong, you're wrong" until you browbeat them into submission.'

'So we're supposed to coddle them, are we?' said Anna. 'Tell them their reactionary views are legitimate? Should we extend that to other forms of bigotry too? Should we say, "A significant proportion of the population believes Black people and Jews are subhuman – gee, I guess they must have a point"?'

A mixture of jeers and loud, angry boos.

'No, but I'd like to believe most reasonable people would at least attempt to *understand* where those views come from. But you're not concerned with that, are you, Anna? You're only interested in claiming the moral high ground – in telling everyone whose views conflict with yours that they're backward, that they're ignorant, reactionary, uncivilised, unrefined – in a word, that they're wrong.'

Thunderous applause ensued.

'Why,' Anna demanded, 'would a woman put herself through the pain and humiliation of having her sexual history dredged up by the gossip rags, of being dragged through the courts, of having her entire life ruined, and risk going to prison for *perjury*, for God's sake, all – what? So she can see the man she accused be acquitted and walk free? Because we both know that's overwhelmingly likely to be the outcome.'

She was shouting. *Why was she shouting?* What happened to 'keep a clear head'?

Leopold scoffed. 'You can't conceive of a single reason why a woman might consider it in her interests to accuse a powerful, wealthy man of a crime he didn't commit? Please don't embarrass us both by pretending to be so naïve. You speak, without a shred of irony, of ruined lives. And yet all one needs to do to end a man's reputation is to put a smell of sexual impropriety on him. It's the oldest trick in the book, and the single greatest weapon in a woman's arsenal. "No smoke without fire."'

I can't believe I have to spell this out, she thought.

She began to speak slowly and deliberately, as if addressing someone unusually slow in the uptake. 'Men in this country are around two hundred and thirty times more likely to *be* raped than to be falsely accused. If you *actually* cared about the men you claim to speak for, you'd be talking about *that*, trying to combat the stigma male victims face, not concocting fantasies about hordes of conniving hussies using fake accusations as a get-rich-quick scheme.'

Leopold snorted. 'You can't possibly know that.'

'Know what?'

Leopold gave a snide, condescending smile. 'You lot are always claiming that the vast majority of rapes go unreported. That there are legions of defiled women who've never come forward but who you somehow intuitively know exist. The reality is you have no idea how many of them there are out there. Same goes for the men. You can't *possibly* claim, with any authority, to know the ratio of raped men versus falsely accused men. It's just not possible.'

'There are *studies*,' Anna began, convinced there was no way he could possibly be this obtuse. 'From them, we extrapolate—'

'Oh, yes,' Leopold chuckled, *'studies.'* He made air quotes. 'Studies conducted by radical ideologues like you, funded by that overpaid, under-qualified rabble in Holyrood with their extremist, anti-male agenda. Studies filled with questions so hopelessly loaded that *everything* counts as rape, including when a man tells a woman she looks nice today. Studies that never see the light of day unless they give you the answers you were looking for. Are *those* the studies you mean, Anna?'

The audience whooped and clapped, practically working itself into an orgiastic frenzy.

This is a circus, thought Anna. It took all her self-control not to put her head in her hands.

'No, but—'

'That's—'

'You're distorting—'

'What I mean is—'

'Yes, please tell us what you *do* mean, Anna,' said Leopold, his words dripping with syrupy sweetness. 'Several of us are very confused.'

And so it went on. With each successive exchange, Anna – beset on one side by a hostile crowd and on the other by an opponent who showed no interest in engaging with the substance of her arguments – found herself flailing, her points invariably drowned out by jeers or brushed aside by a pithy crack from Leopold. By the end of the hour, she was exhausted, both mentally and emotionally. This must be what it felt like to be a boxer in the ring, spending every round desperately trying to land a blow while your opponent danced effortlessly around you, dodging every one of your punches, only to fell you with a solitary sucker punch the moment you stopped to catch your breath.

At around 6.30, once the open discussion had mercifully drawn to a close, Fraser, who had remained a virtual bystander throughout the back-and-forth, angled his chair to face the gallery.

'The time has come,' he said, 'to open things up to the audience. If you have a question, please raise your hand, and someone will be along with a microphone.'

He shielded his eyes, gazing out at the rows of spectators, several of whom already had their hands up.

'Yes, sir – yes, you, in the second row.'

The distinguished-looking middle-aged gentleman whom Fraser had picked out waited patiently while an usher hurried over to him with a microphone.

'We're all gravely concerned about the recent spate of attacks on female students,' he said, his voice booming through the loudspeakers. 'What do you posit is behind this uptick in what some are calling a wave of gendered violence?'

Fraser nodded sagely. 'A sensitive topic, but an important one. Professor Scavolini, have you any thoughts?'

For some reason, Anna found herself feeling unaccountably irked by the fact he'd gone straight to her – as if, by virtue of being the only woman present, it fell to her to make sense of it all.

'Why don't you ask the resident expert on the male psyche?' she suggested, not even trying to hide her sarcasm. 'I'm sure he has plenty of wisdom to impart on the subject.'

Fraser turned to Leopold expectantly. 'Professor Leopold?'

Leopold exhaled heavily, as if the whole subject was one he found profoundly regrettable. 'Well,' he mused, 'as tempting as it is to look for easy answers, I'm afraid the truth is rather complex. While we must obviously deplore the actions of the individuals responsible for these dreadful attacks, the reality – as I attempted to convey earlier during our discussion of attitudes towards feminism – is that we need to at least *attempt* to understand where these men are coming from; to acknowledge the circumstances that give rise to them experiencing these sorts of . . . frustrations.' He glanced across at Anna. 'That is, of course, if my opponent will permit me. We've already established she's not a huge fan of examining the perspectives of those she regards as beneath her.'

Anna didn't even respond. By this point, the jibes and mischaracterisations merely glanced off her; she felt inured to them all.

Leopold continued, growing increasingly impassioned the more he spoke. 'From an early age, boys are taught that they are guilty of the original sin. No, not eating the apple in the Garden of Eden, but rather the sin of being born male.'

Oh God, here we go, she thought. He'd delivered this script before, or variations on it, umpteen times. She could practically recite the words in time with him.

'Boys are told, daily, that they're inherently violent, that they're dangerous, that they enjoy immense, unearned power – that they're "toxic", in the parlance of our times. Is it any surprise, then, that some not only accept this but come to *embrace* it? After all, it's simply in their nature. It's not something over which they have any control. Add to that the barriers that now exist to young men forming normal relationships with women and the constant demand that they bottle up and suppress their natural behaviours, and you have a poisonous cocktail of elements in dire need of an outlet. It was inevitable that they would eventually manifest themselves in such a deeply unpleasant manner. It's really desperately sad, both for the women caught in the crossfire and for the men who feel they have no other way to express their frustrations.'

Fraser turned to Anna. 'Anna? Would you care to weigh in?'

Anna smiled thinly. 'I just love how, any time we discuss women being attacked and victimised, someone inevitably comes riding in on his high horse to claim that it's actually the poor men who are truly suffering.' She twisted in her chair to address Leopold directly. 'You claim it's because these men are being made to suppress their natural urges by the evils of feminism. That's awfully convenient for you. It couldn't *possibly* have anything to do with the plethora of self-styled thought leaders who pollute the airwaves with their reactionary bile, conditioning men to believe they have a right to treat women as punching bags and sex toys!'

'And just why is it that these thought leaders hold so much appeal?' enquired Leopold, a model of reasonability. 'Why do young men listen to them in their millions instead of listening to *you*? I'll tell you why: it's because you don't even *try* to engage with them, far less understand their problems. You accuse men who have nothing of being privileged simply because they're straight, white and male. You write them off while they're still in the womb on the basis of their sex, then have the gall to act surprised when they look at any one of these so-called reactionaries and say, "I like the cut of his jib".'

'You know,' said Anna, 'if you'd *listened* to my opening remarks instead of sitting there with your nose in your phone, you'd know I already acknowledged that there are umpteen ways in which men face genuine hardship. Rejecting the idea that they have it *worse* than women is not the same thing as claiming their lives are all peaches and cream.'

'And yet all you ever talk about are the problems women supposedly face. You feminists never foreground the male experience. You don't offer actual solutions to their loneliness, their depression, their lack of self-worth. You may not *like* what these "thought leaders" are offering, but until you provide a valid alternative, you have no basis for complaint.'

'So, as always, the onus is on women to provide the solutions – to shut ourselves away, to avoid doing anything that might provoke the wrong reaction from these unfortunate, misguided men – these "lost boys", as you call them.' Anna let out an involuntary short, sharp laugh that she *knew* made her sound unhinged. 'But that's you MRAs in a nutshell, isn't it? You're the past masters at diverting attention away from the faults of the system and recasting its victims as the *real* source of those problems. You tell men that nothing's their fault; that it's the women, the feminists, the LGBTQ people that are to blame; that they've been granted too many concessions.

'You know,' she went on, raising her hand to stall Fraser as he opened his mouth to interject, 'if you cared about these young men at all – if you *actually* cared about them – you'd be helping them to navigate and find fulfilment in the real world, not feeding them a pack of lies about it all being the fault of affirmative action and political correctness. Yes, men suffer, but they suffer from the same patriarchal structures as women, not some imaginary, all-powerful matriarchy! But people like you – you don't want to actually improve men's lives. You just want the bragging rights of being able to claim victimhood without experiencing any actual hardship.'

Much of the latter half of this extended rebuke was lost amid a sea of boos and shouts of 'Shame!' from the gallery. Leopold, meanwhile, merely grimaced and massaged his cheek, as if troubled by toothache.

A young, preppy-looking woman in the audience lowered her arm as a microphone was thrust in front of her.

'Thank you both for a very illuminating discussion. My question is, how does one navigate the complexities of modern dating and relationships in a post #MeToo world?'

Fraser nodded sagely, as if this was a quandary he often wrestled with himself. 'Mm. An interesting question.'

He turned to his guests expectantly. Leopold sighed solemnly, as if he found the whole thing a matter of considerable regret.

'With great difficulty, I fear,' he said. 'I hasten to add that my dating years are a considerable distance in the rear-view mirror – and to be honest, I confess to finding that something of a relief. Relationships were fraught enough to begin with, without adding on a whole additional layer of suspicion and uncertainty. I shudder to think how today's youth navigates all the horror stories and assumptions of malign intent.'

'Would you care to elaborate?'

Leopold sighed again. 'I just feel that the . . . well, the *spontaneity* has been lost. The sense of the unexpected. Men nowadays are afraid to even *approach* women in case their intentions are misconstrued.'

'And how do you imagine it must feel to be the woman in that situation?' demanded Anna. 'To constantly worry about your drink being spiked or the guy you decide to hook up with turning out to be a serial date rapist? Those are the concerns young women face every single time they go on a night out.'

'And what about the man in this hypothetical scenario?' Leopold shot back. 'The shy, insecure young man just trying to work up the courage to ask a nice-looking girl if he can dance with her or buy her a drink? How must it feel to know his intentions will automatically be assumed to be impure?'

Anna laughed sarcastically. 'Yes, well, my number one priority happens to be keeping women safe from those who seek to do them harm. We can worry about men's hurt feelings later.'

A chorus of hisses and boos erupted from the audience. She instantly knew she'd just handed Leopold a gift-wrapped cudgel with which to bludgeon her. And sure enough . . .

'So!' cried Leopold, with obvious relish. 'The mask comes off! No question, you certainly sound superficially plausible with your fine words about not dismissing men's struggles. But when push comes to shove, it's "fuck your feelings".'

Cheers and rapturous applause. Anna, with no comeback ready at hand, merely threw up her hands and sank into unhappy silence.

Another audience member – a young man wearing wire-framed spectacles and a conservatively tailored suit – read in a monotone from a scrap of paper while an usher held a microphone in front of him.

'More and more women are choosing to become pregnant out of wedlock. Divorce rates are at an all-time high. What can we say about the impact of these broken families on the wellbeing of children?'

Somewhat unexpectedly, Leopold didn't take the opportunity to dive in and embark on an extended soliloquy on yet another area in which women were to be found morally wanting. As the silence that had settled on the hall extended and grew increasingly awkward, Anna decided to take the initiative.

'Well, first of all,' she began carefully, 'what I'd say is that there are obvious advantages to two-parent households from the perspective of sharing childcare responsibilities. That said, it doesn't automatically follow that two parents are preferable to one in every situation – not if they're having screaming rows all the time and are only staying together for what they perceive to be the sake of their child. I'd be much more concerned about the impact on that child's wellbeing under *those* circumstances.'

The young man remained on his feet, staring at her unblinkingly, saying nothing.

'Um . . . does that answer your question?' she ventured.

'I wasn't asking you,' he snarled.

Anna had already known that a disproportionate number of people in the audience hated her and everything she stood for, but she was nonetheless blindsided by such a blatant display of undisguised hatred. The young man continued to stare at her, his face expressionless and yet still somehow managing to radiate a sense of utter loathing, directed at her with a laser-like focus. She found herself lost for words; was distantly aware of Fraser, clearly somewhat rattled himself, mounting a half-hearted defence of her, explaining that it was his intention to let both speakers weigh in on each question, before inviting Leopold to give his views.

Leopold crossed his legs and leant back in his seat, looking altogether too pleased with how things were going. 'Well,' he declared, rather grandly, 'of course, as a single mother herself, my colleague has what might be deemed a personal stake in being right – and far be it from me to cast any aspersions on her parenting. However, I think we can agree that the numbers are not on her side. It's an incontrovertible fact, for instance, that children of single-parent households are more prone to developmental problems, to psychiatric disorders, to a multitude of behavioural issues . . .'

As Leopold continued to speak, it seemed to Anna that everyone and everything else in the room melted away until it was just the two of them, seated at opposite ends of the stage, a great, dark void surrounding them. She stared across at him, no longer hearing a single word he was saying, just taking in the spectacle of him: the black, oily coif; the tuft of chest hair protruding from the open neck of his shirt; the pudgy hands gesticulating in front of him; the relaxed, complacent posture as he leant back in his chair . . . Perhaps it was because the call regarding Jack's biting of another child remained so fresh in her mind – she couldn't say for sure. In that moment, she just knew she was determined to completely and utterly destroy this repugnant, self-satisfied man; to grind his bones to dust and take a shit on the remains.

Slowly, the rest of the room slid back into focus, as if she'd resurfaced after a lengthy spell underwater. Leopold was still droning on, his supercilious intonation rising and falling as he expounded on the subject of broken homes. She continued not to listen. Instead, stealing a leaf from his playbook, she got out her phone and tapped at the screen until she found what she was looking for. Then and only then did she tune into what he was saying.

'. . . and, of course, research has shown that children whose parents have divorced are significantly more likely to experience instability in their own future relationships. It is, by any reckoning, a vicious and pernicious cycle.'

Leopold finally fell silent, having seemingly exhausted his repertoire. Both he and Fraser looked at Anna expectantly, clearly anticipating some sort of rebuttal. Anna took her time, getting comfortable with one leg crossed over the other, before finally deigning to respond.

'Professor Leopold,' she said, 'I've listened to you pontificate at great length tonight on a range of subjects, and you talk a good game – but I'm not convinced you believe a word of what you're saying. I think the truth is, you've hit on a scheme that makes you money and are shamelessly pandering to your audience of angry little bigots, riding the gravy train as far as it'll take you.'

Leopold regarded Anna with a look that verged on pity. 'You see, Anna, there's your problem right there. You assume everyone who disagrees with you is arguing in bad faith. It's presumptuous and condescending to claim to know someone's mind better than they—'

'I'm going to read some words that I find quite powerful,' said Anna, ignoring him. Holding her phone at arm's length, she began to read from the screen.

'"There is, I fear, considerable scope for these young men, deprived of either positive affirmation or role models, to be seduced by malign forces seeking to harness their frustrations and sense of unfulfilment for their own nefarious ends. These lost boys, so starved of positive reinforcement from mainstream society, will inevitably prove to be 'easy marks' for such snake oil salesmen, who prey on their desire to blame their diminished fortunes on those whose own fortunes have contemporaneously improved.

'"It is vital that we grab the bull by the horns and educate these young men about the reality of their circumstances: that, however it may seem, they are *not* systematically discriminated against by society by virtue of being male; that women and minorities have indeed suffered historic oppression and that it is right that we legislate to correct these injustices, however unfair this may seem in the eyes of those not receiving a 'leg up'."'

She lowered her phone and looked squarely at Leopold. He met her gaze, but she saw from the bob of his Adam's apple that he was having difficulty swallowing.

'Do you recognise those words? You should. You wrote them.'

For a moment, there was complete silence. The whole audience, it seemed, was stunned into inaction. Then, as if responding to some unspoken cue, scattered murmurings began to break out. Leopold's horde of ardent followers, who, earlier, had jubilantly applauded his every pronouncement, evidently had no idea what to make of this.

For the first time Anna had ever seen, Leopold appeared genuinely unsettled. A sheen of sweat glistened on his forehead, and he stared back at Anna with something akin to panic.

Knowing she had him on the back foot, Anna pressed her advantage.

'So I have to ask: what's changed since 2006? That is, other than that you've discovered there's more money to be made by, in your words, "playing to young men's pre-existing prejudices".'

Before Leopold could respond – if, indeed, he even planned on doing so – a sudden crash reverberated in the gallery. Everyone, Anna included, turned to see the conservatively dressed young man who'd asked the question about single-parent households on his feet, his chair lying on the floor behind him. He stood there, staring down at her, eyes and nostrils flaring, then pointed a finger at her.

'You're a lying fucking whore!' he bellowed.

And now Fraser was on his feet, finally galvanised into action, gesticulating emphatically as he attempted to regain some control of the situation. The young man was jabbing his finger at Anna and continuing to shout, while an usher hurried towards him. The hubbub, which had subsided briefly at the man's intervention, now resumed with a vengeance.

This was it, Anna thought. This was the moment the entire ruse had been cooked up to provoke. She looked around wildly. Where was Vasilico? She couldn't see him. *He promised he'd be here,* she thought. *He promised he'd protect me.*

She became aware of Fraser speaking once more.

'. . . have to ask you to leave.'

The young man continued to shout past the usher, who was doing his best to body-block him. 'You should be strung up, you fucking slut! You should be tarred and feathered and hung naked from a lamppost!'

With that, he shoved past the usher and made his way along the row, then turned and stormed up the aisle towards the exit. Anna glimpsed a second figure – another young man, similarly attired – slipping out of his aisle seat and heading after him.

Looking decidedly shaken, Fraser resumed his seat. 'I, uh, I do apologise for that . . . lapse in decorum,' he stammered. He gathered himself, then turned to Leopold. 'Professor Leopold, I'm not sure whether you want to respond to Professor Scavolini's comments?'

But the 'lapse in decorum' had given Leopold time to recover somewhat, and to prepare a response. Looking a good deal less shellshocked now, he gave an open-handed shrug.

'But of course. I have nothing to be ashamed of when it comes to my past.' He turned to face his opponent. 'You've evidently done your homework, Anna. If I'd known you were digging in my closet for embarrassing skeletons, I'd have set aside some time to do the same to you.'

He now addressed the audience. 'As it happens, I *did*, in fact, write the words Professor Scavolini ascribes to me. They accurately portray my thoughts on the subject some thirteen years ago, back when I was a good deal younger and a *great* deal more foolish. Since then, rather a lot has happened. I made an effort to pay closer attention to the views of the people I'd criticised, spent time in their company, and came to understand them better. As a result, I adjusted my views accordingly.'

The sweat was pouring off Anna in torrents, her heart was hammering nineteen to the dozen, and she was far from convinced that the danger – which, just a minute ago, had felt terrifyingly immediate – had passed, but she was determined not to let him off the hook.

'So what you're saying is that you were fallible then,' she said, with as much snark as she could muster, 'but we should just take your pronouncements on trust now.'

Leopold smiled. 'Not at all. I would never expect anyone to take *anything* I say on trust. I've always encouraged my listeners to do their own research.' He gave a little chuckle, as if to suggest Anna was being deliberately dense. 'What I suppose I'm saying is that . . . well, look. I'll level with you all. I'll be fifty-four years old next year.' He held up his hands in response to imaginary exclamations of disbelief. 'I know, I know – I wear it well. The point is, if a man were to spend half a century inhabiting this Earth without his views evolving, I'd call that a surefire sign of a closed, incurious mind.'

He angled his head sideways, giving Anna a beseeching look. 'I listened to the victims of feminism and realised their concerns were valid. I strongly encourage you to do the same . . . Or perhaps the truth is that you won't because you're unwilling to admit that you might just be wrong.'

Anna gritted her teeth and met his gaze, saying nothing. It was a classic catch-22 situation: whatever response she gave would make her look either insecure or dogmatic.

For a moment, they stared back at each other across the expanse of the stage. Then, Fraser clapped his hands together, breaking the tension with forced levity.

'All right, ladies and gentlemen – I think we have time for a couple more questions, and then we'll have to wrap things up . . .'

28

The remaining questions were thoroughly anodyne in nature. No one, it seemed, felt like rocking the boat after what had just happened. Fraser, evidently keen to ensure that there were as few opportunities for further incidents as possible, wrapped things up quickly, thanking his guests and the audience. And then, almost before Anna knew what was happening, they were vacating the stage, sent on their way by a mixture of applause, some scattered boos, and a shout of 'Ye're a fuckin' *queen*, doll!' which could only have come from Zoe.

Anna was the first to reach the back corridor, ripping off her headset and receiver and shoving them into the hands of the bewildered technician. She paced to the far end of the corridor and rested her forehead against the cool wall, willing her pounding heart to settle.

'Anna.'

She spun round to find Leopold facing her. He beamed at her with seemingly genuine bonhomie.

'I wanted to congratulate you on a sterling performance,' he said. 'You're a force to be reckoned with once you get going. I thoroughly enjoyed that . . . even if ambushing me with the more ignominious aspects of my past was a *little* below the belt.'

Still smiling, he extended his hand. When it became clear she wasn't going to accept it, he lowered it, his smile slowly fading.

'You want to talk about below the belt?' she said, her voice low and dangerous. 'You don't use my son against me – *ever*. He's off limits.'

Leopold laughed, but the slight wobble in his voice betrayed his unease. 'Come, now. You know the saying – all's fair in love and war.'

'*Fuck* you,' she snarled.

He stared back at her, his expression somewhere between confused and wounded. 'You really shouldn't take things so personally. It does neither you nor your side of the argument any favours to let yourself be so heavily governed by your emotions.'

Anna stared at him in livid disbelief. She saw now that it really *had* all just been a game as far as he was concerned – a completely consequence-free exercise in tossing around insults, using any means necessary to win an argument that, at the end of the day, meant nothing to him.

And then, before she could respond, Fraser was beside them, all smiles.

'Anna. Robert.' He patted them each on the shoulder in turn. 'I really must thank you for giving us such a thought-provoking exchange. I expected great things, but you surpassed my wildest hopes for the night. A pity about that isolated heckler, but topics like the ones under discussion were always going to raise passions.'

She couldn't do this. She couldn't stand here and pretend to be all nicey-nice after the way things had gone down out there. *Where WERE you?* she wanted to say. *Why the hell did you let things get that far?* But instead, she just murmured something about having somewhere to be and stumbled off, gamely putting one foot in front of the other and hoping she wouldn't trip.

Somehow, she made it back to the side room, where she found Farah, Vasilico and Kirk waiting for her. Before anyone else had a chance to say or do anything, Farah stepped forward and wordlessly folded Anna into a hug. Anna allowed herself to melt into her colleague's arms, and for a few all too brief seconds luxuriated in the feeling of no longer having to be responsible for keeping herself upright. Then, as Farah released her, she turned to Vasilico.

'Well?' she demanded. 'What did you think?'

'I think,' said Vasilico, 'that you coped admirably well under consider-able pressure.'

'That's not what I meant. What did you make of the audience? Did any of them do anything to raise suspicions?'

'Apart from the charmer who stormed out towards the end, you mean?

I put a tail on him, by the way. One of my plain-clothes boys. You probably saw him heading out just behind him. We'll find out who he is and, from there, establish whether he warrants further examination.'

'I thought he was going to try to get onto the stage,' said Farah. 'He was completely furious.'

'He spent most of the debate filming on his phone,' Kirk put in. 'A lot of them did. Par for the course, really. These creepy-crawlies live out their entire lives online.'

Anna sighed. 'So I can expect to be an internet celebrity for all the wrong reasons before morning.'

Vasilico glanced up from his phone; presumably, he'd been checking for updates from his team. 'Other than the aforementioned *Children of the Corn* tribute act, no one else distinguished themselves in any particular way. Though, as I'm sure you're aware, the overall mood was . . . shall we say rather rancorous?'

'Why were there so many of Leopold's followers there?' Anna demanded, asking the question of no one in particular. 'Was it my imagination, or did they make up virtually the entire audience?'

'I'd guesstimate it was between fifty and sixty percent blokes in their early twenties,' said Kirk, 'though it probably felt like more from where you were sitting. They had an outsize impact.'

'And the mood – how bad was it *really*? From up on stage, it felt like practically the whole room wanted my blood . . . but I don't know. Maybe it just seemed that way.' Try as she might, a part of her couldn't let go of the possibility that she was simply blowing things out of all proportion.

'You weren't imagining things,' said Farah, her tone emphatic. 'The mood was very ugly. I'd never experienced anything like it before. And Leopold was a disgrace. Dr Taggart should have stepped in many times.'

Anna flashed her a look of gratitude, as much for the confirmation that she wasn't going crazy as anything. She turned to Vasilico.

'So, other than the guy who thinks I should be hung from a lamppost, we've got nothing?'

Vasilico grimaced. 'I'm afraid it would seem not. I hadn't banked on the place being *quite* so full of paid-up members of the Leopold fan club.'

'Meaning we're no further forward than we were,' she said bitterly. *All that, and for nothing.*

Vasilico raised his shoulders in a helpless, apologetic shrug.

A sense of disappointment and awkwardness hung over the room. No one seemed to know what to say.

It was Kirk who broke the silence.

'Look,' she said, jerking a thumb over her shoulder, 'I'd better head. See if any of the plain-clothes bods've got anything to say for themselves.' She glanced at Vasilico. 'Catch up later, huh, boss?'

Vasilico nodded, still half lost in his own thoughts.

As Kirk left the room, Farah drew close to Anna, laying a soothing hand on her arm. 'Will you be OK?' she asked, her voice low. 'I can stay if you want – you know, if . . .'

Anna smiled gratefully. She shook her head tightly. 'It's fine. You get on. We'll touch base tomorrow, yeah?'

Farah nodded. She gave Anna's forearm one last reassuring squeeze, then turned and headed out, following in Kirk's footsteps.

With just the two of them left, Anna turned to face Vasilico. They both inhaled a breath at the same time, then stopped, Vasilico looking as sheepish as Anna felt.

'You go first,' he said.

'No, go on. I'm not even sure what I was going to say.'

'All right. Well, I was thinking . . . and feel free to say no . . . I mean, I know food might not be the first thing on your mind right now, but . . . d'you reckon I could take you out for something to eat?'

Anna considered what to say. It was true, food was far from her top priority at the moment. In fact, from the constant rolling of her stomach, she wasn't entirely convinced she'd be able to keep anything down. But, on the other hand, now that it came down to it, she wasn't sure she wanted to go home just yet. Plus, right now, the idea of spending a couple more hours in Vasilico's company seemed a long way indeed from the worst prospect on offer.

'All right,' she said.

'All right?' he repeated, surprise mingling with obvious pleasure. He'd evidently been expecting a different response.

'Yeah. Give me a few minutes to get my things together, then let's do it.'

He smiled – a part of him still, it seemed, not quite able to believe she'd said yes. 'OK. In that case, I'll wait for you at the main entrance.'

An awkward moment passed, neither of them seemingly sure how to break things off. Then, Vasilico gave a rueful grimace, as if to say *Aren't we a pair of chumps?*, dipped his head and ducked out, shutting the door behind him.

Alone at last, Anna circled the room, hugging her arms to her chest, savouring the stillness; the quiet. The feeling of being on edge remained, but it was a nice, anticipatory sort of 'on edge' as opposed to the sense of overwhelming panic and doom that had consumed her for the bulk of the debate and its immediate aftermath. She hadn't been out for dinner with a man who wasn't a work colleague in *years*. In fact, the last event that had come even close had been when she went for coffee with Vasilico, around the time she turned down his offer of a job at the anti-corruption unit he was heading up and shortly before he stopped answering her calls. She wondered, having been burnt by him before, whether she *really* wanted to let him back into her life and risk it happening all over again.

She was still pondering this question when there was a knock on the door. She turned as it opened and Zoe slipped in, grinning broadly.

'Hey, you.'

She trotted over and pulled Anna into a hug.

'You. Were. Amazing. Absolutely fabutastic.'

'You really think so?' said Anna, as Zoe released her from her embrace.

Zoe nodded enthusiastically. 'Aye, totes. Ye really socked it to that puffed-up aul' windbag. D'ye hear me clapping fae the front row?'

Anna smiled. 'How could I miss it?'

She filled Zoe in on her dinner plans. Once she was fully appraised of the situation, Zoe's grin extended from ear to ear.

'That's absolutely *belter*. Seriously, doll, I'm made up for ye.'

'It's just a meal,' said Anna gruffly, wondering just which of them she was trying to convince. 'That's all it is. Don't be inflating it into something it's not.'

Zoe nodded sagely. 'Aye, ye say that the noo, but who knows what the night might hold? All's I'm saying is, me 'n' Sal are gonnae get some scran oursels, and Jack's away at his wee slumber party so there's no need tae rush back.'

'Don't be daft. I'll be home by ten, tops.'

'O-*kay*-ee,' said Zoe, a knowing singsong lilt in her voice, 'but just so's ye know, we'll no be waiting up for ye.'

29

Anna and Vasilico made their way down to Dumbarton Road, where Vasilico secured them a table at a small restaurant near the railway station with a classy vibe and a fine line in contemporary cuisine. It was quiet, with only a handful of the other tables occupied, and, in spite of herself, Anna soon relaxed considerably. To her surprise, she turned out to be ravenous, and she attacked her food with gusto, working through her starter of smoked haddock before moving on to a main of Moroccan spiced chicken and rice.

It wasn't until she'd done justice to the latter that she finally compelled herself to engage Vasilico in a conversation consisting of sentences of more than a handful of syllables. She was keen to get his thoughts on Leopold – as much, as anything else, to assuage the lingering worry that she was overreacting to his treatment of her on the stage.

'This was your first time seeing him in action outwith a formal interview setting,' she said. 'What did you make of him?'

Vasilico set down his knife and fork and finished chewing his mouthful of sirloin before responding.

'He certainly cuts a very charismatic figure,' he said carefully. 'You can see why he holds so much appeal for maladjusted young men.'

'Because he's telling them what they want to hear?'

'Well, yes. But also because he's not wrong in *everything* he says. I'm not talking about the misogyny and reductionist views on gender roles,' he added quickly, as Anna felt her eyes narrowing reflexively. 'All that is, of course, beyond the pale. But when he talks about men being bereft of role models and saddled with a sense of collective guilt purely on account of who they are – well, I'm not without sympathy.'

'Oh, really?' Anna heard the edge in her voice.

Vasilico raised his hands in a placatory gesture. 'Don't mistake me. I'm not condoning any of it. But . . . well, take this Reckoning mob. Don't you think there might just be a lack of direction going on there? A lack of positive male role models to show them how women *should* be treated? I mean, I bet a pound to a penny their fathers didn't figure large in their upbringing.'

'Or maybe, just maybe, their fathers – or some other primary male role model – are precisely where they picked up these attitudes from.'

She saw, from his look of scepticism, that he wasn't convinced.

She sighed. 'Hating women isn't some sort of default state into which all men inevitably fall without the appropriate guidance. It's not hard-wired – it's *learned*. They're getting it from somewhere.' She laughed dryly. 'What – you don't think it's their *mothers* that are teaching them those beliefs, do you?'

Vasilico laughed too, albeit half-heartedly. 'I suppose not. But . . .' He spread his hands in front of him, palms down, laying his metaphorical cards on the table. 'Well, look. You know about my upbringing. You know I was mostly raised by a single mum. That I pretty much went off the rails in my teens. That it was my uncle who got me on the straight and narrow.'

'Yeah, and look what sort of a man *he* turned out to be,' said Anna pointedly.

'Hey – you're preaching to the converted. I'm just saying, whatever crimes he committed or allowed to be committed, he did, nonetheless, manage to instil *some* positive qualities in me.'

'Oh yeah?' Anna smiled in wry amusement. 'Tell me more about these positive qualities you see in yourself.'

'Well . . .' Vasilico seemed slightly ruffled. 'I like to think there's a certain dogged determination about me . . . a tenacity, if you like. I'm loyal, I'm self-reliant, I'm self-confident . . . Will those do for starters?'

'Oh, you're *certainly* self-confident,' Anna laughed. 'You'll get no argument from anyone *there*.'

Vasilico smiled. 'Why do I get the feeling you're mocking me?'

'Who, me? Perish the thought!'

Vasilico laughed, then reached for the bottle of red and refilled their glasses. Anna nodded her thanks, and, reaching for hers, sipped contemplatively from it as she mulled over what Vasilico had said. She'd never really bought into the notion that only men could provide the necessary guidance for boys to grow into healthy, well-adjusted men themselves – though, now that she thought about it, she realised Leopold's words on the subject had got under her skin more than she cared to admit. *Could* she be refusing to acknowledge that possibility because she had a personal stake in it being untrue? *Were* boys more naturally inclined to seek out other men as role models – and, if so, where did that leave Jack? Might it even make him more susceptible, before he was very much older, to the honeyed whisperings of self-confessed snake oil salesmen like Leopold?

'It's all a put-up job, you know.' Vasilico's voice cut into her thoughts.

She glanced up. 'What is?'

He shrugged. 'The whole suave, self-assured, man of the world thing? Totally an act. Deep down, I'm still just a wee frightened laddie.'

She studied his face, looking for some clue as to whether he was being facetious or merely using the syntax of flippancy to soften a genuine confession. She found none.

'That right?' she said, slightly incredulous. 'So come on, then – what scares you?'

'Plenty of things. A lot of the same ones that scare *you*, I'd wager.'

'Such as?'

'Oh, you know – rejection, failure, growing old, failing to leave my mark on the world, my bi-annual visit to the dentist. But here's the thing – us men, we like to make out we're brave, that nothing fazes us . . . At the end of the day, though, being a bloke is at least three-quarters "fake it till you make it". There's been a lot of ink spilled lately about how women are afraid – and don't get me wrong, they've got a lot to be afraid *of*. But I don't think those fears are as unique to the female experience as people like you sometimes make out.'

Anna felt herself bristling. 'That's easy for you to say. The fact of the matter is you can't *possibly* understand what you call "the female experience" without having lived it. I'll bet, for example, you've never left a night out early so you don't have to walk home in the dark, or crossed the street to avoid that guy who insists on walking just a *bit* too close behind you.'

Vasilico looked back at her, his expression one of puzzlement. 'Why would you assume that?'

'Well, because . . .' She stopped, finding herself at a loss. 'I mean . . . *look* at you.' She gestured helplessly at him, as if that explained it all.

'What, so because I'm six foot two and go to the gym three times a week, I'm impervious to attack?' There was a trace of wry amusement on his face, though it was quickly replaced by a look of solemnity. 'The fact of the matter is, men are three times more likely to be attacked in the street by a stranger than women. I do this sort of thing for a living. I know the stats.

'And I know it's not deliberate,' he went on, before Anna even had a chance to draw breath, far less respond, 'but when all we hear is "women aren't safe walking the streets", the unspoken inference is that men *are*. Ergo, it's hardly surprising when they start to think that their safety simply isn't a concern for the policymakers . . . particularly when their own experiences are telling them they're just as likely to come a-cropper – in many cases *more* so.

'I'm just saying,' he went on, 'when all you hear is, "you're muddying the waters" or "your concerns aren't a priority" – well, it's not conducive to having a healthy degree of self-worth, or to having a ton of empathy for the people whose concerns you *do* see being taken seriously. No one likes to think of themselves as a statistic.'

He leaned back in his seat, fingering the stem of his glass as he regarded her with a look of solemnity. 'So, in answer to your question, yes, as it happens, I *do* know what it's like to feel unsafe walking home after dark.'

Anna gazed back at him, surprised and touched by this uncharacteristic admission of vulnerability. Until now, the possibility of someone like him fearing for his physical safety had never even crossed her mind. She supposed that could only point to a failure of imagination on her part.

'I guess I've never really thought about it from that angle before,' she admitted.

'Then maybe, just maybe, it's possible Leopold isn't the only one who ignores the data when it conflicts with his own preconceptions,' Vasilico said gently.

Anna nodded soberly. 'I suppose we could all stand to be a bit more empathetic of other people's experiences.'

It took an effort for her to say it. Admitting she could be wrong, or at least suffering from perceptual blindness, wasn't something that had ever come easily to her, particularly when it involved conceding that someone whose worldview was an anathema to her could just have a point.

They fell into silence. Vasilico returned to tackling his sirloin. Anna continued to mull over their conversation.

'I think you're wrong, by the way,' she eventually said. 'All your positive qualities, everything I see in you that's good – you formed those qualities not because of your uncle but in *spite* of him. And that's a credit to *you* – no one else.'

Vasilico lowered his cutlery and looked at her. He seemed so touched that she felt her cheeks reddening and quickly averted her eyes.

'I just . . .' she shrugged awkwardly, 'wanted to say that.'

And then, not trusting herself to say anything more, or even meet Vasilico's eye, she reached for her wine glass and downed a hearty gulp.

'Fancy coming back to mine?' Vasilico asked, as they stepped out into the street. 'I mean,' he added hastily – already, it seemed, wondering if he'd overstepped the mark, 'only for a nightcap . . . and only if you want to.'

Anna turned to face him, a polite but firm refusal already on the tip of her tongue. But then she stopped. Why, she wondered, had her first instinct been to say no? Was it because she didn't want to . . . or was it more because she was conditioned to always turn down such offers? There always seemed to be an implicit need on her part to be responsible; to put duty before pleasure. And yet, what duties did she actually *have* tonight? As Zoe had pointed out, Jack was away at his sleepover, and no one was waiting up for her at home.

She gave an airy shrug. 'Why not? It's not like I've had any better offers.'

Vasilico laughed. 'Well, don't put yourself out on my account! Seriously, if you'd rather not . . .'

'Ah, get a move on before I change my mind.'

She looped her arm through his, attempting to gee him along. In the same split second, she became aware of what she was doing and almost pulled away immediately, until her better judgement prevailed.

'Besides,' she said, quickly turning it into a joke, 'can't have you walking home alone, now, can we? *Anything* could happen.'

'I feel safer already,' he smiled.

As they set off up the pavement, arms linked, a feeling of awkwardness persisted on her part. After a moment or two, however, she allowed herself to acknowledge that she enjoyed the feeling of physical contact between them. By the time they reached the end of the first block, she'd relaxed into his hold.

'I was with the reviews unit for a little over two years.'

Anna, perched on an immaculate leather sofa in the living room of Vasilico's spacious, glass-fronted apartment overlooking the Clyde, continued to listen as his voice travelled through from the adjacent kitchen.

'It was a worthy pursuit, but I wasn't built for desk jockeying . . .'

She glanced up as he appeared in the doorway, a glass of white wine in either hand.

'. . . and when the opportunity to join the SCU came up, I opted to take it.'

He made his way over and sat down next to her on the sofa, handing her a glass.

'I believed in the initiative and . . . well, I was itching to do some old-fashioned shoe-leathering again.' He raised his glass. 'Cheers.'

'Cheers.'

They tapped glasses and drank.

'What about you?' said Vasilico, lowering his glass.

'Me?'

'Yeah – a decade at the same uni, doing the same job. Never feel the urge to spread your wings?'

Anna took another sip of wine to give herself time to think about it. 'Honestly,' she said at last, 'sometimes yes.' She saw his questioning look. 'The job's not what it once was,' she explained. 'There's the constant restructuring, the layers of bureaucracy, the cuts to research funding, the feeling that my boss doesn't value me or even have a clue what it is I do . . .'

'Sounds vaguely familiar.'

'Well, that's the thing. It's the same everywhere, right? I figure I might as well stick with what I know instead of risk it all on striking out into the unknown.'

Vasilico frowned, considering this. 'I get that. Change can be scary. It can even be painful. But sometimes you've got to grab the bull by the horns and take a leap into the unknown.' He grimaced. 'Sorry, I seem to be speaking entirely in clichés tonight.'

'That's OK. I seem to be speaking entirely in self-pity.'

They fell into silence, Anna continuing to nurse her glass as she gazed out at the view from the large floor-to-ceiling window, the reflected lights from the various apartments twinkling in the waters of the Clyde below. Something lingered between them, unresolved, unacknowledged, and she knew they weren't going to be able to move past it till they addressed it.

She set her glass down on the low table facing the sofa.

'Vasilico, why did you break off all contact with me? I know it was a busy time for both of us . . . but you could at least have picked up the phone.'

Vasilico exhaled heavily. He gazed down into his glass, shoulders drawn in, every facet of his body language screaming that this was not a conversation he wanted to have.

'You really want to know, huh?'

'Yeah,' said Anna quietly, 'I really want to know.'

Sighing, he set aside his glass. His eyes remained downcast – unable, it seemed, to meet her gaze.

'Well, if you must know, it was because I was developing feelings for you.'

Not the excuse she'd been expecting.

'O . . . *kay*. Not sure I follow the logic.'

Vasilico lifted his head, craning his neck to look sideways at her. His grey irises shone with such an earnestness that she found herself wanting to look away.

'That's because you don't know me. You don't know what I'm like.'

Forcing herself not to avert her gaze, she continued to stare at him, waiting for him to explain.

He sighed again. This time, he turned to face her properly.

'I don't . . . have a great track record when it comes to women. I've a tendency to let them down whenever things start to get serious.' He gave a wry grimace. 'Ask around. There's no shortage of disgruntled former conquests of mine with stories to tell.'

'What was so different about me, then?' said Anna, nonplussed.

'You seriously don't know?'

She shook her head.

'Then I don't even know where to begin. You're . . . well, honestly, I'm not sure I can even put it into words. I suppose I thought . . .'

He broke off. Barked a short half-laugh, as if he couldn't believe he was about to say this.

'I thought you were too good for me.'

For a long moment, Anna just stared at him. The space between them could be measured in centimetres, the air around them crackling with nervous energy.

'What if I wasn't?' she said, her voice so low and husky she scarcely recognised it as her own.

Vasilico met her eyes, lost for words.

And then, before either of them had time to process what was happening, she leant towards him and, cupping his face in her hands, kissed him.

They broke apart after only a couple of seconds, both staring at one another. Anna brushed the trace of stubble on his cheek with her fingers.

'Is this OK?' she said.

'Yeah,' breathed Vasilico, both surprised by the question and slightly winded. Then, with more conviction, '*God*, yes. But . . . I mean . . . is it OK for *you*? You wouldn't rather take it slow?'

For all of two seconds, Anna genuinely thought about it, then made her decision.

'That's the *last* thing I want to do.'

She moved in again. He stopped her.

'What I mean is . . . I don't know what you're looking for from this. Is this a "one-off" something or a "start of something" something?'

'I'm not sure,' Anna admitted.

A beat.

'But I'd like to find out.'

This time, Vasilico didn't try to stop her as she moved in. They kissed long and deeply, only breaking off to get to their feet and make their fumbling, frantic way through to the bedroom.

30

El Duce invites GodsGift2Women and LifeIsPain to a new chat channel.

El Duce: WHAT THE FUCK WAS THAT SHIT

LifeIsPain joins the chat.

LifeIsPain: U watched it
LifeIsPain: ?

El Duce: course I fucking watched it
El Duce: spiteful fcuking bitch trying to get one over on him

LifeIsPain: What happened i didnt see it
LifeIsPain: Whitenation's stream cut out halfway thru

El Duce: fucking slut dug up shit on Him nd tried to make it look like he was taking us for a ride

GodsGift2Women joins the chat.

GodsGift2Women: Oi oi oi what's all this
GodsGift2Women: Trouble in paradise? Ur hammering that

poor keyboard a little to hard El Duce. All these typos are most un becoming of u

El Duce: don't start with yuor shit boy this is fucking serious
El Duce: bitch found shit Big D wrote years ago and ambushed Him with it
El Duce: shit He prob had to say to get published by the radical left media
El Duce: now 90% of chat on subreddit & forums is "is Leopold a phony?"

LifeIsPain: Fuck fuck fuck
LifeIsPain: This is bad isnt it

GodsGift2Women: You guys need to chill. Seriously
GodsGift2Women: If u 2 scored some pussy once in a while u might not get so wound up

El Duce: Seriously Im not in the mood
El Duce: if you nothing useful to say you can gtf out right now

LifeIsPain: Yeah GodsGift ur not helping

GodsGift2Women: I might just do that
GodsGift2Women: Came on 2 say nice touch block booking the seats & giving out tickets
GodsGift2Women: But if all u wanna do is be a dick and scream into the void dont let me stop u
GodsGift2Women: And dont fucking call me boy ever again

LifeIsPain: Dont
LifeIsPain: Pleas
LifeIsPain: We need work to gether
LifeIsPain: Figure out what 2 do

El Duce: I'll tell you what we do
El Duce: we END her
El Duce: NOW
El Duce: no more pussy footing around. gloves off
El Duce: time to make that foid fucking PAY

PART FOUR

TAKE ME DOWN

31

Thursday 14 November

Anna came to with the sun on her face. She was lying on one side of a low, king-size bed, a crumpled white sheet covering the lower half of her body. Light streamed through the full height window on her left, the blinds raised – or, to be more accurate, never lowered the previous night.

Shielding her vision with the back of her hand, she levered herself up into a sitting position, from where she opened her eyes in stages, letting in just enough light for them to acclimatise. Once she could open them without having to screw them up, she turned and looked across to the other side of the bed. Vasilico was fast asleep, laid out on his back with one arm slung behind his head. Like her, he was naked, his side of the sheet only barely protecting his modesty.

Not that there'd been much of *that* last night.

She sat there for a couple of minutes, gazing down at him with a soft smile, allowing herself to bask in the warm glow of her fragmented memories of what had happened once they'd made it to the bedroom. Then, turning, she reached for her phone, lying on the nightstand beside her. The battery had completely drained overnight. She wasn't surprised. She got precious little juice out of it even when she *did* have the opportunity to charge it. She checked her watch – the only item she was still wearing – instead. Just gone 8.15 a.m.

She eased herself out of bed and, moving on tiptoe, set about looking for her clothes, which had been discarded haphazardly in the mad rush to get to bed several hours earlier. The first item she found was her bra. She was in the process of clipping it on when she sensed that she was being watched. She looked over her shoulder to see Vasilico gazing at her with one eye open, an approving smile on his face.

'What are you doing?' she demanded, wishing she had something to cover her lower half.

Vasilico half-shrugged. 'Nothing. Just admiring the crack of dawn.'

'Well, don't.'

'Why not?'

'Cos.'

'Cos what?'

'Cos I've got a big arse and I'm all doughy round the middle.'

'Haven't you heard? Real men appreciate the aesthetic value of the fuller-figured woman.'

Anna's mouth widened in mock outrage. Vasilico grinned.

She turned to face him, gently mocking. 'And that's how you see yourself, is it? The last bastion of true, rugged masculinity?'

Vasilico pulled a face and shrugged airily, as if to say, *I couldn't possibly comment.*

Laughing, Anna made her way over and perched on his side of the bed, leaning over him so that a loose strand of her hair brushed his cheek.

'Well, I'm sorry to disappoint you, Captain Testosterone, but I'm afraid I'm going to have to cut and run.'

'You're not sticking around?'

She shook her head. ''Fraid not. I've got a lecture at eleven and, hard as it might be to believe, I *don't* fancy giving it in yesterday's clothes.'

'Perish the thought.'

She leant in and kissed him, savouring the sensation of his lips on hers. 'I'll call you, OK?' she said.

'I should bloody *hope* so. I'd hate to think I was only good for a pump and dump.'

She laughed – a high, girlish giggle that sounded most unlike her. They kissed again. Then, straightening up, she got to her feet and resumed the ungainly spectacle of hunting for and gathering up her clothes.

'You're absolutely sure I can't convince you to stay?' said Vasilico, continuing to watch her out of the corner of one eye. 'You could always pull a sickie.'

'You really don't know me at all, do you?' said Anna, picking up her tights, which were still entangled with her underwear.

'Then what am I supposed to do about this?'

She turned to see him gesturing to his lower half, a helpless expression on his face.

Striding over, she whipped the sheet aside, revealing his sizeable erection. He gazed up at her beseechingly, as if it was an unwanted affliction with which he'd been cursed.

She raised an impassive eyebrow. 'Is that supposed to impress me?'

'Impressed you well enough last night,' said Vasilico, with the inklings of a lascivious grin.

She smiled serenely. 'Well, I'm sure you'll figure something out.'

And, with that, she turned and, scooping up the remainder of her clothes, headed out of the room to finish dressing in private.

Anna stepped out of the quayside apartment complex and breathed in the fresh morning air. As she set off, her hair askew and yesterday's clothes feeling decidedly crusty against her skin, it occurred to her that she was currently doing what was colloquially known as the walk of shame.

Well, fuck that. This was no such thing. This was the walk of *triumph*. She'd had a glorious time last night and would do it all again in a heartbeat. Hoped to, in fact – perhaps even this very evening. She still couldn't say for sure whether it was the start of something serious, but she remained as willing this morning as she had been nine hours earlier to go with the flow and see how things panned out.

Before last night, she'd had precisely one sexual encounter since Jack's conception: a one-night stand in a hotel room while she was attending a conference in Cologne. It hadn't been planned, and the only reason she'd allowed it to happen had been the knowledge that she'd never see her hookup, a fellow delegate from the other side of the world, again after that night. So to say she'd been out of practice would have been putting it mildly. But Vasilico had been gentle and considerate, asking her at frequent intervals if what they were doing was OK and devoting as much attention to her pleasure as his own – a rare occurrence, in her experience.

As she made her way up through Thornwood, it occurred to her that the stress and humiliation of yesterday's debate had receded somewhat in the rearview mirror, as had the broader issue of the ongoing attacks on students. It hadn't disappeared completely – far from it. However, for the time being, at any rate, it felt less immediate, less like something she had to personally resolve.

Let the pros handle it. It was what they were paid for, after all.

It took her just under half an hour to walk the mile from the quay back to Clarence Drive. As she stepped into the hallway, she was struck by just how eerily still and quiet the place was for this time of day. Normally, the rush would be on to get Jack ready for playgroup, or else he'd be in the kitchen with Zoe, 'helping' with breakfast. Today, though, there wasn't a sound to be heard.

At that very moment, there was a clang from behind the kitchen door, followed by a muffled exclamation.

'Oh, fudgesicles!'

Anna opened the door to find Sal on her knees on the floor, attempting to scrape spilled coffee grounds back into an overturned tin. Realising she had an audience, she looked up guiltily.

'Oh!' she exclaimed. 'You're home. Um . . . you've caught me at an awkward moment, I'm afraid.'

'Leave that,' said Anna, gesturing to the mess. 'I'll get the hoover.'

Sal scrambled to her feet. 'Oh, no no no, let me. I'm champion klutz, not you. Just point me in the general vicinity and I'll have at it.'

'Just behind you,' said Anna, secretly glad of the offer; getting down on her hands and knees to clean up someone else's mess hadn't been on her list of things to do before she went to work. 'Cupboard under the sink.'

Sal grinned and turned in the direction Anna had pointed. She was wearing an oversized dress shirt, and, as she bent to open the cupboard door, the back of it rode up, giving Anna a perfect, bird's-eye view of her bare backside, adorned with a series of red imprints, made by what looked suspiciously like a spatula.

Well, well, she thought. *So Zoe's been indulging her inner kink.*

'Find it?' she said.

'Yup, got it.'

Sal stood up and turned to face Anna, holding up the handheld vacuum cleaner with a proud grin. As she did so, Anna suddenly noticed something.

'Is that my shirt?'

'Oh, is it?' said Sal, surprised. 'I thought it was one of Zoe's. I just grabbed it out the dryer. You want it back?'

'No, no, it's fine,' Anna said quickly. 'You keep it for now.'

Sal beamed. 'Aw, cheers. Be a bit weird for both of us if you did.'

They stood facing one another awkwardly. Anna had always found Sal to be perfectly pleasant, but the pair of them had next to nothing in common beyond a mutual fondness for Zoe. She never seemed to know what to say to her at the best of times – let alone when she'd just received a front row view of her freshly paddled arse.

'Zoe about?' she enquired, breaking the silence.

'Oh yeah, she's upstairs,' said Sal, seemingly glad to have a question she was in a position to answer. 'I came down to make us breakfast – only I kinda got waylaid by my general butterfingeriness.'

Anna smiled pleasantly. Another awkward silence elapsed as the two of them stood there, neither seemingly knowing how to bring this encounter to a close.

'Well,' said Anna, 'I'd best crack on.'

'Right, yeah.' Sal's relief was palpable. She waggled the vacuum. 'I'll, uh, see if I can figure out how to get this doohickey to work.'

Glad to make her escape, Anna headed up the stairs. By the time she reached the first-floor landing, the hum of the vacuum was in full flow down below.

As she passed Zoe's room, Zoe called out to her from behind the door.

'Anna? That you, doll?'

'It's me,' said Anna, stopping.

''Mon in.'

'You decent?'

'Pff! Never been decent in my life. Get *in* here, wumman.'

Acknowledging to herself that this was indeed an accurate statement, Anna pushed open the door. She found Zoe lying in bed, scrolling on her phone. As Anna stepped into the room, she lowered it and grinned up at her with more than a hint of smug satisfaction.

'Well, well, look what the cat dragged in! Ye don't call, ye don't write . . . what's a girl tae think?'

Anna waved her own phone ruefully. 'Out of juice. As per.'

She perched on the end of the bed. Zoe moved into a sitting position, arms wrapped round her knees.

'So ye took my advice after all, then. How was it?'

'It was . . .' Anna smiled, feeling her cheeks beginning to colour. 'It was really nice. *He* was really nice.'

'*Eeeee!*' Zoe gave a little squeal of delight and clutched Anna's arm. 'So is this the start of something major, then? Cos see if I have tae start picking out wedding dresses and that, I'm gonnae need advance warning.'

'There's not going to be wedding bells anytime soon,' said Anna firmly, 'or, if I have anything to do with it, ever.' She paused. 'But I *did* promise I'd call him.'

Zoe beamed. 'Then that'll do me for now.' She wagged a chiding finger at Anna. ''Bout time ye got yersel back on the bonk bus, missus. Good thing the plumbing still works after all this time.'

Smiling, Anna playfully batted her arm, somehow managing to feel embarrassed and happy in equal measure.

Just then, the door opened behind them. They turned to see Sal entering with a loaded breakfast tray.

'Not interrupting anything, am I?' she said, without rancour.

Anna was on her feet in an instant, clearing her throat briskly. 'No, not at all. I'm gonna hop in the shower, then head into work. She's all yours.'

As she turned to go, Zoe reached out and gave her arm a final squeeze. They made eye contact and shared a brief, loaded look, revelling in their mutual feelings of contentment. Then, the moment passed, and Anna swiftly vacated the premises, leaving Zoe and Sal to their breakfast in bed. Somehow, she doubted her shirt was going to remain on Sal for long.

32

She stuck her phone on to charge, hoping to add at least a *handful* of percentage points to the battery meter before she had to leave, then hopped in the shower. The warm, happy glow from earlier continued to linger. Now that she was alone with her thoughts, however, she realised it was also tinged with a certain . . . well, not exactly *sadness*, but perhaps a sort of melancholic nostalgia for a phase in her life that she now recognised as having at least one foot in the past. For the first time since they'd moved in together nearly four years ago, she and Zoe both had active love lives – or, at any rate, Zoe already did and Anna appeared to be on her way towards one. They were moving in different directions, and, whether she liked it or not, the cosy status quo of those four years now appeared to be coming to an end. Under the circumstances, it would have been odd if she *hadn't* felt at least a passing sense of regret.

She stepped out of the shower and, standing sideways, examined herself in the mirror. Frowning, she pinched her stomach between thumb and forefinger. She wasn't really *that* doughy – not in the grand scheme of things. But she *had* been complacent. Once upon a time, she'd been a dedicated early-morning runner and had regularly done five kilometres before breakfast. All that had fallen by the wayside when she fell pregnant with Jack. She told herself she was going to get back on the wagon again. No ifs or buts. This time, she meant it.

Freshly showered and changed into an outfit more in line with her usual attire, she walked up to the university. Her 11 a.m. lecture was in the Rutherford Building, on the western limits of the campus, so she headed straight there rather than stopping by her office first. As she entered the lecture theatre a few minutes before eleven, her second-years were already beginning to assemble. By the time she'd hooked her laptop up to the projector and got today's slides queued up, the place was close to full.

She allowed herself a few final seconds to savour her memories of the previous night. Then, putting such thoughts to bed, she lifted her head and began to address the class.

'All right – good morning, everyone. We'll make a start. Last time, we talked about quantitative criminology and how it differs from other methods of studying crime. Today, I'd like to drill a little deeper into the specific methodologies employed to collect, analyse and interpret the data . . .'

And on it went. She'd given this particular lecture countless times before now, and it had remained largely unchanged over the last ten years – so much so that she could practically recite the whole thing without reference to her notes. As a result, she was so lost in the flow that, at first, she didn't notice anything untoward.

It happened at about the half-hour mark. One moment, she was expounding on the subject of longitudinal research and the difficulties associated with following the same people across a period of several years or decades. The next, she became aware of another sound competing with her voice on the loudspeaker system – or rather, a *succession* of sounds. At first, it sounded as if someone was in pain – a series of low grunts and groans, punctuated by periods of silence. Then, as she stopped talking and properly listened – and, as she became aware of the expressions of amusement and sounds of stifled laughter coming from the seating area – she recognised, with a flush of embarrassment, that what she was hearing were the sounds of two people having sex.

She put down her clicker and gazed up at her students with an expression of non-amusement.

'Is one of *you* doing this?'

Several students shrugged or shook their heads. Some merely looked confused. Many more were trying, unsuccessfully, to hide their amusement.

'All right,' she went on, raising her voice above the continuing sounds of intimacy, 'well, we appear to have some sort of technical—'

At that moment, she stopped dead as the groans were punctuated by a voice – a voice she recognised, followed by another she knew even more intimately.

Man's voice: *'Is this OK?'*

Woman's voice: *'Yes. God, yes. I'm so wet for you right now.'*

Anna felt the blood draining from her face, her stomach lurching as the realisation of what – and, more to the point, *who* – she was listening to hit her.

More groans followed, accompanied by fresh ripples of laughter from the students. Her eyes darted from one face to another, to yet another, as she tried desperately to work out whether they'd made the connection between the woman's voice on the recording and the one currently standing in front of them.

'There seems to be—' she began.

But even as she spoke, she experienced a sickening premonition of what was coming next. And then, with the slow-motion inevitability of a train derailing, came the moment when, mid-coitus, she'd farted, followed by:

'Oh God. Sorry.'

'Hey – better out than in, I always say.'

By now, the students weren't even *trying* to suppress their laughter. Great gales of it came rolling down from the benches above her. To their credit, a handful – most of them girls – had the good grace to look embarrassed, if only because they were probably imagining what it would be like to find themselves in a similar situation.

As the laughter continued, Anna fumbled with the overly convoluted set of controls in front of her. Why the hell did a projection system need so many different buttons? With clammy fingers, she jabbed at them semi-randomly, hoping one would do what she needed. Finally, more by luck than anything else, she found the button that shut down the entire apparatus, causing both the sound and the slide projected on the screen behind her to cut out.

As the laughter continued at a more muted level, mingling with chatter as the students gossiped about what they'd just witnessed, Anna managed to find her voice.

'Right, well, it's obvious some prankster's found a way to muck around with the sound system, so we're not going to be able to continue today.

We'll pick this up again next week. Congratulations. You've got an unexpected early lunch.'

She was quite impressed she'd managed to keep it together sufficiently to string these sentences together, and to make them sound halfway authoritative.

As the benches emptied, she began to gather up her things, all the while studiously keeping her eyes downcast to avoid meeting the gaze of any of the students trooping past her on their way to the doors on either side of the podium. The conversation and sounds of amusement both continued unabated.

Please, let none of them have recognised my voice.

The room had almost emptied now – just a few remaining stragglers making their way to the doors. As she zipped up her laptop bag, she lifted her head and found herself face to face with Cameron Mitchell, the boy she'd chewed out in a tutorial a couple of weeks ago. He was standing oppressively close to her, with a look of sly satisfaction that deeply unnerved her.

'Can I do something for you, Cameron?'

'Depends. You offering?'

'Excuse me?'

'I'm fairly sure I didn't stutter.'

Anna glanced around. A solitary female student bounced down the steps and headed out the left-hand door without a backward glance. She looked in the other direction. Another male student, whose name she couldn't currently call to mind, hovered in the doorway, watching her and Cameron with what might have been a look of apprehension. But then, it could just as easily have been something else.

She turned back to face Cameron.

'What is it you want?'

Cameron's smile didn't falter. 'Like I said, depends what's on offer. D'you take requests, or do blokes just have to take what they get?'

'I've no idea what you're talking about.'

Cameron's smiled broadened. 'Oh, I think you do.'

He took another step towards her, so close now that their noses were nearly touching. She stared back into his eyes, unnerved and outraged in equal measure.

'So listen,' he said, 'is it strictly missionary for you, or d'you like taking it up the arse?'

She wasn't sure who the slap caught more off guard – him, the recipient, or her, the one who dealt it out. As she withdrew her stinging hand, for a moment he just stared at her, a look of shock on his face, the side of his cheek already turning red from the blow. Then, the sly smile returned – the look of someone who'd got exactly what he wanted.

'Cam, c'mon. Let's go.'

At some point, the other student had arrived by Cameron's side, and was now tugging urgently at his arm, trying to get him to move.

For a moment, Cameron ignored him, refusing to budge. Then, relenting, he allowed himself to be led away, walking backwards to keep Anna in his sights until the last possible moment, the wicked smile not leaving his lips for a second.

As soon as she was sure she was alone, Anna whipped out her phone and rang Vasilico's number. As she held the phone to her ear, her hand clammy and trembling, she heard his familiar honeyed tones soliciting her to leave a message – the same tones which she'd found so arousing last night when he'd whispered tender nothings into her ear, but which now enraged her beyond all measure.

'Vasilico, when you get this, call me *immediately*. Your . . . I dunno, your flat must have been bugged or something. My . . .' She dropped her voice to a barely audible hiss. 'My entire second year just heard us *doing* it.'

She paused long enough to pace over to the door and peer out into the corridor to make sure no one was there, before continuing.

'Look, I don't know if this is The Reckoning or what, but I think it's safe to say whoever did this is organised and means business. I mean it. Call me.'

She hung up. Took several deep, deliberate breaths, attempting the futile task of calming her frayed nerves.

Fuck, fuck, FUCK.

Ten minutes later, she was on the third floor of the Hutcheson Building, striding along the corridor towards the sanctuary of her office.

Just keep walking. Don't make eye contact with anyone. Don't think about it at all.

Easier said than done.

She was within sight of her destination when the door to Fraser Taggart's office abruptly swung open. Before she'd even had time to slam on the brakes, Fraser himself was standing in front of her, barring the way. She brought herself to an undignified halt, coming within a hair's breadth of colliding with him.

'I need a word,' he said.

She didn't have time for this.

'Can it wait? I'm actually in the middle of dealing with—'

'No, Anna,' said Fraser. 'I'm afraid it *can't* wait.'

For the first time, she properly clocked the severity of his expression. Whatever he wanted her for, it most assuredly wasn't a friendly chat.

33

Shoulders tensed, Anna stepped into Fraser's office. He shut the door behind them and gestured to the chair facing his desk.

'Have a seat.'

'I'm all right, thanks,' she said stiffly.

For a second or two, he looked like he was going to argue with her. Then, he shrugged, as if to say, *Well, I tried,* before stepping behind the desk and settling into his own chair. For several long, excruciating seconds, he just sat there, one hand on his chin, the other drumming the tabletop, as if he was trying to figure out where to start.

Eventually, he sighed.

'There's no easy way to say this. This morning, I received an email. Well, actually, considerably more people than just me received an email.'

'From who? What about?' *Just get to the bloody point, Taggart.*

Fraser gazed back at her. For a brief moment, his eyes flashed in what looked suspiciously like anger. Then he sighed again.

'You know, there's an easy way and a hard way of doing this. I hoped, for both our sakes, you'd opt for the former. But if you insist on making this difficult . . .'

'Fraser,' said Anna, with as much patience as she could muster, 'I really, honestly, sincerely have no idea what you're talking about. Would you just stop playing games and tell me?'

Fraser's eyes were like cold steel. 'What I'm *talking* about, *Anna,* are the photographs sent from your university email address at 10.41 this morning to every staff and student account on the system. Photographs I now wish to God I hadn't seen because, quite frankly, *no* one should see one of their work colleagues in that context.'

'*Which* photographs?' Anna demanded in exasperation. '*What* email?'

But even as she said it, something shifted in her bowels as an awful, sickening thought occurred to her. She realised she knew *exactly* which photographs Fraser must be referring to – photographs that had never been intended for public consumption, far less circulated around the entire campus.

'Oh, God,' she murmured.

She'd taken them about six months ago, on a spring morning when the sun was shining and the world felt new and hopeful. Jack was at playgroup and Zoe was in town, catching up with friends, and, at a loose end and with the house to herself, she'd decided she might as well try out the camera on her then brand new smartphone.

She's started off by taking pictures of inanimate objects: a pair of shoes, the bowl of fruit on the kitchen table. Soon, she'd moved on to what she gathered were known in the trade as 'selfies'. The first few were nothing to write home about: just her looking into the lens, trying out a variety of different facial expressions, from serious to smiles. Then, she'd added a couple of pouty ones to the mix; the kind she'd seen teenagers make on social media, and which had always struck her as faintly ridiculous – but then, who was she to judge? One thing had led to another and, before she knew it, she was undoing first one button, then another, then another still. Then, she was slipping her left breast out of her bra, tracing the nipple with an index finger . . . all while the phone continued, at regular intervals, to make its artificial shutter sound effect as she snapped picture after picture after picture.

By the time she was done, she'd amassed close to sixty photos in total, several of which left absolutely nothing to the imagination. Her clothes, which she'd shed in stages, lay in a pile on the bedroom floor while she sat with her back propped against the foot of the bed, hair tousled, legs wide open, the fingers she'd used to play with herself still glistening as her breathing slowly settled.

Half an hour later, changed into fresh clothes and with not a single hair out of place, she'd headed out the door to pick Jack up from playgroup, and hadn't given what she'd done more than a second's thought . . .

Until now.

Dimly, she became aware that Fraser was speaking again.

'. . . I assume I don't need to tell you about the university's policy on the distribution of explicit images. As soon as I saw them, I deleted them, of course, and alerted Computing Services. The email has now been recalled, though I shudder to imagine how many people will have already opened it . . .'

Anna now slid shakily into the chair that, just moments earlier, she'd rejected. The entire centre of gravity seemed to be shifting beneath her.

'Just what the hell, Anna?' Fraser stared at her in exasperation, as if he was the aggrieved party here. 'What were you *thinking*?'

Anna stared at him in disbelief. 'What, you think . . . you think it was *me* who sent them?'

'They were sent from *your* email address. They're pictures *of* you – pictures that were clearly taken *by* you.'

When your back is up against the wall, fight like hell.

Anna's expression hardened. 'Get a good look, huh? Study them in detail, did you? Of *course* I didn't send them. In all the years you've known me, have I ever struck you as the sort of person who'd do something like that? How stupid do you think I *am*? Someone's obviously gained access to my account.'

Fraser looked unconvinced.

'Did you ask Computing Services when they last reviewed the robustness of their systems?' she went on. 'Because I don't know about you, but this sounds to me like a pretty bloody egregious breach of security.'

She knew she was overdoing it somewhat, trying to bury her shame and mortification with big, expansive hand gestures and self-righteous indignation. But sometimes, attack really *was* the best form of defence.

And now Fraser had his thinking face on, drumming his fingers on the tabletop as he mulled this over.

'*Could* you have sent the pictures without realising it?' he said, not sounding like he really believed in his own proposition.

Anna snorted, incredulous. 'What, just accidentally attached them to an email and just accidentally bulk-mailed them to the entire university? Don't be ridiculous.'

'I'm not talking about an accidental misclick. I mean . . .' He grimaced, as if he hated to even suggest this, but . . .

He sighed. Sat up a little straighter, hands folded on the desktop, like a physician preparing to deliver an unwelcome diagnosis.

'Look,' he said, 'I'm aware you were diagnosed with bipolar disorder some years back. That you're not currently medicating. Is there *any* possibility that you're . . . you know . . . ?'

He gazed at her expectantly, as if pleading with her to make this easy for him.

Anna stared at him in disbelief. 'Am I currently in the grip of a manic episode, you mean? Have I gone cuckoo bananas and taken to mailing out pictures of my twat to random people because, oh, hey, folk with bipolar are all pants-on-head crazy? Is *that* what you mean?'

Fraser at least had the good grace to look embarrassed. 'I mean . . . I just can't help but think it makes a degree of sense. I think we can both agree you've not been quite yourself for a while now. There was your outburst in that tutorial the other week . . . your decidedly . . . *uncharacteristic* choice of attire last night . . . Taken together, it all screams "cry for attention", frankly.'

She said nothing. She couldn't believe what she was hearing.

Fraser gazed at her beseechingly. 'Why, in God's name, did you even *take* those pictures in the first place? Why *keep* them?'

Realising they'd now moved on to the victim-blaming phase of the interrogation, Anna once more opted to retreat into unrepentant defiance.

'Why? Let's see. Maybe it's because I like how I look in them. Maybe it's because I took them in the privacy of my own home using my own camera and it's therefore *none of your God damn business.*'

'It becomes my business,' snapped Fraser, 'and that of the university, when its email servers are used to distribute *pornography*. Surely you can see that?'

He exhaled heavily and leaned back in his chair, as if he found this all incredibly draining.

'Obviously, this is an extremely delicate situation. We have to tread incredibly carefully to make sure things don't get any more out of hand than they already have. Under the circumstances, I think you should go home until the matter is resolved one way or another.'

Anna stared at him in disbelief. 'You can't be serious,' she spluttered. 'I have classes. Admin. Supervision meetings.'

'Yes. Well.' His tone strongly implied, *You should have* thought *of that, shouldn't you?* 'Be that as it may, it's my considered judgement that your continued presence here will prove a distraction at best and, at worst, actively undermine the university's ability to uphold the ethics and integrity for which it is rightly known. I'm asking – no, *instructing* you to leave the campus immediately and return home to await further direction.'

He folded his hands on the desk and treated her to a wincing half-smile. 'I know it probably doesn't feel like it, but it's for your own good as much as anyone's. The last thing I want is to give anyone any ammo to use against you. I *am* on your side here, Anna.'

She held his gaze for several long, uncomfortable seconds. To give him *some* credit, he managed not to look away.

'You're right,' she said. 'It *doesn't* feel like it.'

With that, and with as much dignity as she could muster, she got to her feet and walked out.

34

Anna strode across the campus, moving quickly and keeping her head low. As much as she told herself, over and over, that it was only her imagination, she couldn't shake the feeling that everyone she passed was looking at her, silently judging her, condemning her with their eyes. On a couple of occasions, she caught a gale of laughter from a passing group of students, causing her to jackknife.

They're not laughing at you, *they're not laughing at* you . . .

And yet, how could she possibly be sure of that? How many of the thirty-two thousand odd students and nearly ten thousand members of staff at the university would have checked their email accounts between 10.40 this morning and however long it took Computing Services to recall the offending message? She wagered it was a significant proportion of them. Everyone had their email on their phones these days, and were conditioned to looking the moment they heard the chime announcing the arrival of a new message. Because every communication demanded an instant response, and everyone craved instant gratification.

She let herself into the house, leaving the door to slam shut behind her. Just like when she'd returned from Vasilico's apartment a few short hours earlier, back when she was still walking on air, the house seemed unusually quiet, as if she'd stepped into a soundproofed booth.

'Hello? Zoe?'

No response.

Looking around, she spotted a scrap of paper lying on the hallway console table bearing a message in Zoe's loopy, girlish handwriting:

Out to lunch w Sal. Back late a'noon.

She crumpled the page in her hand and let it fall to the floor. At that precise moment, there was nothing she wanted more in all the world than to pour everything out to Zoe, who wouldn't judge her, wouldn't condemn her, wouldn't say anything to her except *There, there, doll. It's all right.* She knew, of course, that it *wasn't* all right, that it was never going to *be* all right, but she desperately needed someone who'd say it to her all the same.

She was still standing there in the hallway when her phone began to ring. She retrieved it from her pocket, checked the caller ID, and suppressed a sigh. It was Hugh MacLeish, her old boss and quasi-mentor.

More out of a sense of obligation than anything, she took the call.

'Hugh?'

'Anna. I've, ah, just heard what's happened. It's . . . well, are you all right?'

Anna felt herself forcing a tight smile, even though there was no one around to see it. 'Well, Hugh, to be honest, I've had better days.'

'Yes, yes, of course. Can't imagine. It really is a . . . well, it's just not good at all, is it?'

Hugh was tripping over his words, clearly finding this whole conversation decidedly uncomfortable. *Well, Hugh, that makes two of us.*

'Um . . . is there . . . What I mean is, is there anything I can do for you?'

'Have you got a magic wand?'

'Ah. Well, now . . . no, I'm afraid not.' He hesitated. 'I . . . I just want you to know, I, uh, didn't see the offending message. You know what I'm like with technology. Check my emails once in a blue moon. You, ah, you've nothing to fear on that . . . on that account.'

Somehow, the fact that it clearly mattered so much to him that she knew this struck her as overwhelmingly lovely.

'Thanks, Hugh,' she said wearily. 'That's . . . that's good to know.'

'I'd, ah, I'd offer to talk to Fraser – see if he can be persuaded to reconsider his, well, his course of action, but I . . .'

He trailed off, leaving the thread dangling unceremoniously. Anna, however, knew only too well what he was getting at, and had no desire to force him to suffer the indignity of having to admit what they both knew: that his word no longer carried any weight whatsoever.

'That's OK,' she said. 'I'd rather just let this play out – not be seen to be calling upon friends in high places.'

Hugh laughed bashfully. 'Oh, well, I don't know that I'm deserving of *that* accolade . . .'

As he spoke, something occurred to Anna. It came at her out of the blue, but it was something she'd been mulling over, at the back of her mind, ever since her confrontation with Fraser. From the moment he'd brought it up, she'd been wondering how it was that he knew about her diagnosis. She could count the number of people she'd shared that information with on one hand, and one of them was . . .

'Hugh,' she said, a newfound steeliness in her voice, 'be level with me. Did you tell Fraser I'd been diagnosed as bipolar?'

The lengthy silence that elapsed at the other end of the line told her all she needed to know. She shut her eyes, pressing her fingers to her forehead.

Oh, Hugh . . .

'I . . . I didn't feel there was any harm,' Hugh stammered, more flustered than ever now. 'You were so very open about it with me, and with the changing of the guard, I felt . . . well, that is to say, I assumed, if Fraser knew, that he'd make whatever accommodations you, er . . .'

Again, he trailed off into unhappy, regretful silence.

And yet, try as she might, Anna couldn't find it within herself to be angry with the silly old man. She saw that, in his own naïve, patrician sort of way, he'd thought he was helping her, and she couldn't bring herself to hold that against him. What he'd done was an egregious breach of confidence, but one made with the best intentions.

Deep breaths, Anna.

'It's OK, Hugh,' she said, with as much magnanimity as she could dredge up. 'You weren't to know.'

Hugh continued his befuddled waffling for a while longer, offering up endless apologies, each one more fulsome and grovelling than the last. After a while, Anna, having realised that the roles had now been firmly reversed and *she* was the one consoling *him*, let him down as gently as she could and rang off, silently cursing the day she'd ever let him into her confidence about something so deeply personal.

That was the trouble with opening up to people, she told herself; with making yourself vulnerable to them. Whether they meant to or not, they always ended up using it to hurt you.

With neither Jack nor Zoe due home for some time, Anna was left facing the prospect of a long, miserable afternoon with nothing but her own thoughts for company. She alternated between stewing on the sofa and pacing around the living room, her mind racing as she sought desperately for ways to convince herself that things weren't as bad as she thought they were – only to conclude, each time, that, in actual fact, they were worse.

In an effort to distract herself with practicalities, she rang Farah to let her know that either she or someone else would need to cover her tutorial group at three o'clock, and quite possibly her commitments tomorrow as well. When Farah asked her how long she thought she'd be off for, Anna was forced to level with her and say she didn't know, but that it could be some time.

'It's completely disgusting,' said Farah vehemently, 'this way he's treating you. He should be lending you his full support now, not . . .' – she cast around for the appropriate analogy – '. . . throwing you out like yesterday's leftovers.'

'He says he's doing it for my own good,' said Anna, deadpan.

At this, Farah practically had a spluttering fit. *'Espèce de merde!'* she swore. 'He's just covering up his own asshole.'

Anna remained on the line for a few minutes longer, but somehow, she found Farah's righteous indignation even harder to endure than either Cameron's sly mockery or Fraser's fussy indifference to her feelings, and she ended up ringing off prematurely, claiming she had another call.

She sank onto the sofa, leaning forward, her fists pressed to her temples, clutching great clumps of hair. How had this happened? How the *fuck* could this possibly have happened?

It came to her in a sudden burst of clarity.

Her phone.

Of course – it had to be her phone. There was no other possible explanation. She'd used it to take the pictures, and, in her madness, had left them on it instead of deleting them when she came to her senses. And – *and* – the phone had been lying on the nightstand next to the bed the whole time she and Vasilico had been at it last night. That, she now recognised, was a far more credible explanation for how they – whoever *they* were – had managed to produce a recording of them than her initial assumption that the apartment itself had been bugged. Somehow, someone had got inside her phone and used it to access her most private moments.

They were probably still inside it now.

Snatching up the phone, she fumbled with the touchscreen, hitting icons semi-randomly until she finally found the option to reset her login details. Having changed both her password and pin number, she then began to systematically work her way down the dizzying list of accounts whose details were stored on the device, resetting the password for each one in turn, all the while racking her brains as to how her security might have been compromised. Had she ever left her phone unattended or her password written down somewhere? She didn't *think* so. She'd had it drilled into her so many times at the university's mandatory IT security training sessions that that was the one thing you never, *ever* did.

She was still working through her passwords when the phone rang again. This time, it was Vasilico. To her surprise, and no small amount of irritation, his reaction, when she told him everything that had happened, was far more blasé than she felt the situation warranted.

'It'll be fine, I'm sure,' he said, his silky-smooth purr setting her teeth on edge. 'OK, so it's going to be a tad awkward for a while, but we just have to weather the storm. Nothing else for it! At any rate, we can safely conclude that last night's debate succeeded in putting the wind up them.'

'That's easy for you to say,' Anna snapped. 'I'm the one with the reputation that's being torn to bits before my eyes.'

'Whereas I have none to speak of, presumably.'

'Oh, don't give me that,' she retorted. 'You know as well as I do that we're held to different standards. For you, I'm just another notch on the old bedpost. I'm the sex-crazed slut who's had her private business spread all over the entire university.'

There was silence at the other end of the line. When Vasilico next spoke, his tone was gentle but unequivocal.

'I've *never* thought of you as a notch on my bedpost, Anna.'

She considered explaining to him that she'd meant it in the sense of how others would view them, not how *he* viewed her, but had neither the energy nor the patience to coddle him, so she said nothing.

'I'll drop by this evening once I've finished chasing up some leads,' he said, his tone betraying neither irritation nor injury. 'In the meantime, stay safe.'

She ended the call without saying goodbye.

Reluctant to leave the house in case Fraser called with an update or she ended up running into someone who'd seen the pictures, Anna phoned Zoe and asked her if she could pick up Jack from playgroup at four, saying she didn't feel up to it, then ringing off before Zoe had a chance to ask her why.

She'd barely hung up when the phone rang again. For a brief moment, she thought it was Zoe calling back to give her the third degree, but when she checked the caller ID, she saw that, in fact, it was Marion Angus, a former student of hers who was now a lecturer at Glasgow Caledonian University, and with whom she'd remained in touch over the years. Marion suffered from severe and chronic verbal diarrhoea, and their sporadic phone conversations always ended up lasting for far longer than was justified by their content. Why on earth was *she* calling, at mid-afternoon on a work day?

Anna was all set to let it go to voicemail – but then, she thought, perhaps an hour-long waffling session with a woman who was capable of delivering an entire soliloquy about her own trials and tribulations without once asking the other party how they were doing might be just what she needed right now. And, if her phone was engaged, it would also put paid to her having to field any further calls from concerned colleagues.

Reluctantly, she accepted the call.

'Marion. Hi.'

A pregnant pause.

'Anna,' said Marion stiffly, followed by another pause. 'How are you?'

'I'm . . . well,' said Anna, surprised by this uncharacteristically terse opening gambit. 'And you?'

'I'm hale and hearty, yes.'

Another lengthy pause. Then:

'Anna, the reason I'm calling is to make sure you're all right.'

Anna wondered whether it was possible that news of the email business had made it as far as Cali already. The very thought made her shudder.

'Shouldn't I be?' she said, a little more curtly than she'd intended.

'Well, it's just . . . Look, I don't mean to be a nosy Nellie – I mean, feel free to tell me to go and boil my bananas if you like – but . . .' She exhaled a heavy breath. 'Well, I'm just not sure it's the best idea to be quite so . . . *unfiltered*. From a career standpoint, I mean.'

'Is this about the debate last night?' said Anna, her mind alighting on the only possible explanation she could think of for what Marion was saying. She sighed. 'God, tell me you haven't watched any of the videos. I know it wasn't my finest hour, but—'

'What debate? No, of course not. I'm talking about the things you're saying on Twitter. About the university.'

'*What* things?' Anna's head was throbbing with the effort of trying to make sense of this. 'I don't even *have* a Twitter.'

'We-ell . . .' a note of doubt had now entered Marion's voice, '*someone* claiming to be you is posting on there, and they're being *pretty* specific about what they think.'

Silence. For what seemed like the thousandth time that day, Anna felt her heart sinking into the pit of her stomach.

'Are you *sure* you've not been on Twitter?' Marion continued, with infuriating obliviousness. 'Cos, I mean, it does sound a *lot* like you . . .'

'Marion,' said Anna, 'I'm going to have to go.'

'Anna, have you—'

Anna stabbed the End Call button, silencing her.

After some difficulty, technology having never been her strong suit, Anna managed to successfully install the Twitter app on her phone. From there, it didn't take her long to find the posts Marion had been referring to. An account in the name of Anna Scavolini, declaring her to be 'Criminology Professor at Kelvingrove University' and with a picture lifted from her profile page on the university website, had been tweeting fairly incessantly for the last few days, posting a seemingly endless stream of pithy remarks about the university as a whole and certain members of its staff in particular.

Anna Scavolini @AnnaScavoliniGlasgow · 12m
Ever get the feeling your just a cog in a machine? I love
teaching but some days it feels like my passion is being
squeezed out of me by people who just see me as a
resource to be #exploited

Anna Scavolini @AnnaScavoliniGlasgow · 43m
Kelvingrove University fails to value it's hardest working
staff, preferring to pay senior managers obscene salaries
and spend money on pointless vanity-projects....UAE
campus anyone? #SackThemAll

Anna Scavolini @AnnaScavoliniGlasgow · 2h
Fraser Taggart is a clueless Idiot and should have never
have been put in charge of the school of Social and Political
Science, he is out of his depth and needs replacing
immediately, preferably by a woman #Feminism #Patriarchy
#ReplaceFraserTaggert

Anna Scavolini @AnnaScavoliniGlasgow · Nov 13
What self respecting University would employ a man like
Robert Leopold? Every day he brings #Kelvingrove further
into disrepute with his #misogyny and #MRA bullshit.
Embarrassed to work for them #EndPatriarchy
#SackLeopoldNow

From a brief glance, it certainly *sounded* like a vague approximation of
her, and some of the views on display were eerily close to ones she'd
expressed herself in real life, albeit in private. But still, Anna's immediate,
instinctual response was to feel insulted that Marion had ever thought any
of these tweets had come from her. The punctuation, the grammar, and
quite frankly everything about them just screamed 'imposter' – to say
nothing of the fact that there was simply no way she would ever be so
foolhardy as to go onto the internet and publicly traduce her employer in
anything close to this fashion.

She saw that a number of the tweets had had comments posted to them.

She clicked through to a few to get a flavour of the discourse. It was about as highbrow as she'd anticipated.

'PREACH it sister!!! #workersrevolt'

'LOL someones getting fired tomorrow.'

An animated gif of a woman with glasses shaking with rage, accompanied by the words *'TRIGGERING INTENSIFIES'.*

A link to join the Socialist Workers Party.

'Drunk at midday are we professor? #ginoclock'

'Shut the fuck up you stupid whore.'

She returned to the account's profile page. According to it, she'd joined Twitter in September this year, and had already racked up thirty-two followers, including a couple of colleagues who'd evidently assumed it was really her. She read the most recent posts again. Even though it was obvious to her that they were fake, the fact Marion had been taken in suggested that others might well end up having a similar response. At any rate, having someone out there pretending to be her was unlikely to do her any favours in the long run. She assumed there must be some way of reporting accounts for impersonation. She was trying to find the relevant button when the page refreshed with a new tweet.

Anna Scavolini @AnnaScavoliniGlasgow · 7s
Come see me in all my glory ;) https://tinyurl.com/y54893re

Anna's mouth went dry. She knew what the link was going to contain even before she tapped it.

The site it took her to went by the moniker of 'Carnal College', and if the name didn't already make it clear that it was a porn site, the neon, nightclub-esque colour design and animation of a gyrating striptease artist certainly got the message across. As she scrolled down, her worst fears were confirmed as, one after another, the naked selfies she'd taken earlier in the year slid into view, arranged in chronological order so that each one was more revealing, more explicit, more *detailed* than the last.

Mercifully reaching the end of the string of images, she continued to scroll, but what followed provided her with no comfort. Several of the site's members had chimed in with their views on the photos. *Don't read them, don't read them, don't read them,* she told herself – but she couldn't help it. She had to know what they said.

They were every bit as disgusting as she'd anticipated, ranging from the appreciative to the deeply disparaging; references to her C-section scar and stretch marks cropped up frequently, along with some incredibly detailed descriptions of what the users in question would have liked to do to her. Apparently, she was a 'filthy whore' who was 'begging for it', and various other refrains on the same general sentiment. Several of the comments were ratings out of 10, with 4 and 5 the most frequently recurring numbers. At the bottom of the page, posted in the last couple of minutes, was a comment by user CreamPie23:

i wouldn't even rape that

Anna lurched to her feet. Her legs were like rubber. She made it as far as the hallway before collapsing onto her knees and vomiting up the contents of her stomach onto the hardwood floor. She hadn't eaten anything since the quick slice of toast she'd wolfed down before heading out to work that morning, so what came up was mostly liquid, but the compulsion to retch didn't subside.

She was still dry-heaving on all fours when she heard the front door opening. She looked up to see Zoe and Jack standing in the doorway, hand in hand, both staring at her.

'What's wrong with Mummy?' said Jack, a note of apprehension in his voice.

Immediately, Zoe snapped out of it. 'Jack, away up the stair and play wi yer toys.'

Jack didn't take his eyes off Anna. 'But—'

'I'll see tae Mummy. On up the stair.'

As Jack reluctantly climbed the stairs, casting one last uncertain glance at his mother before disappearing from view, Zoe hurried over to Anna and dropped to a crouch next to her.

'Aw, hunnybun,' she said, gently rubbing Anna's back in circles. 'What's happened tae *you*?'

Anna gazed up at Zoe, her face streaked with tears, her breath coming out in ragged gasps. She saw Zoe registering the look in her eyes and knew she understood implicitly that this wasn't just an untimely case of food poisoning.

'Did something happen?' There was an almost accusatory note in Zoe's voice. 'What's wrong?'

And so Anna told her everything.

35

Anna perched on the sofa, a heavy blanket around her shoulders, the steaming mug of tea Zoe had made for her within easy reach. She normally didn't touch the stuff – she'd often thought there couldn't possibly be a more insipid beverage on the planet – but, at the moment, she reckoned it was about all she'd be able to keep down.

She was still working herself up towards actually putting that theory to the test.

In the background, one of her Max Richter CDs was playing on the music system at a low volume – her go-to refuge whenever she was feeling stressed or anxious. There was a melancholic air about it, but it always seemed to have a calming effect on her, Tilda Swinton's languid voice drifting in and out of her consciousness.

For the last couple of hours, Zoe had been keeping Jack entertained and out of the way. However, she'd popped downstairs to check on Anna on multiple occasions, repeatedly asking her how she was bearing up and whether there was anything she could get for her. Anna felt like telling her there was absolutely nothing she could possibly get for her that would make the situation any better, but managed to refrain from doing so, simply responding each time with a polite, 'No thanks, I'm fine.'

'Fine' was, of course, the very *last* thing she was. Less than twelve hours earlier, she'd been basking in the afterglow of her night with Vasilico and full of giddy optimism for the future. In retrospect, all that now seemed like someone's idea of a sick joke. Now, when she thought back to that night, all she was left with was an ashen taste in her mouth, as if the very thing that had given her so much pleasure had been rendered somehow squalid and disgusting by the act of public exposure.

It was a common misconception that, following a major trauma, you became a completely different person. According to prevailing thought, there was the old you – the one that existed on the 'before' side of a tangible dividing line – and then there was the new you – the one on the other side that you now embodied exclusively. In reality, it was nothing like as clear-cut. You unquestionably changed as a person, but the person you were before didn't simply cease to exist. Two different versions of you now inhabited the same mind and body, trying to find some way to reconcile themselves with one another. So, on the one hand, there was Anna the unrepentant sexual being, fully capable of taking pleasure in her own body and in the act of making love with another person. On the other was the Anna who'd come into existence that morning, consumed by shame and self-loathing; by the belief that her body, and her desires, were disgusting and obscene. That *she* was disgusting and obscene.

Unlike many of her feminist fellow travellers, Anna wasn't against pornography as a matter of principle. True, a huge amount of it was unquestionably degrading and produced under the most exploitative conditions. But then, the same could be said of a great many industries, particularly those that sourced their labour from parts of the world where workers' rights were lax to non-existent. However, it had always been merely an abstract concept for her, to be debated from the position of an outside observer and occasional consumer rather than someone with a personal stake in any of it. Now, her own private sexual pleasure had been repackaged and re-contextualised into something obscene for the gratification of a bunch of strangers – not one of whom, she was convinced, would ever give a second thought as to how the images they were perving over had been obtained or how she, the person who featured in them, felt about it. As far as she was concerned, sites such as the one to which her photos had been posted – where people got their jollies from viewing private images of strangers, uploaded without their knowledge or consent – represented the absolute sewer of the internet. Never in a million years had she ever dreamed she'd find herself featuring in a starring role on one of them. For the thousandth time, she cursed the day she ever took those pictures – an act so massively out of character for her, it was hard to reconcile herself to the fact that it had been her *doing* it. She wondered what on earth had possessed her – because 'possessed' really *did* seem the most apposite word for it.

Because she'd been alone, she supposed. Because she'd had a new bit of kit to try out. Because she'd been at a loose end. Because of the thrill of the forbidden. Because, ever since the changes wrought by pregnancy and childbirth, she'd been unaccustomed to thinking about her body in anything approaching a sexual light, and to be suddenly struck by the realisation that yes, it still *was* attractive, stretch-marks and all, had been a moment of profound self-actualisation.

And now she was reaping the whirlwind sown in that moment of madness.

On a purely philosophical level, she knew she had nothing to feel guilty about – that the people glorying in her exposure and making disgusting remarks about her were the ones who should be consumed by shame. She remembered her words when Narinder had asked her if there was anything she could have done to avoid what had happened to her.

This is not on you, all right? You didn't do anything wrong.

How easy it had been for her to say those words, secure in the knowledge that she wasn't the one who had to live with the consequences of the decisions she'd made. And what cold comfort they now provided, when it was pictures of *her* intimate parts that were plastered all over the internet and the inboxes of her colleagues and students. How many of the people viewing them had already downloaded them and shared them with their friends, or posted them to other websites? Because that was how it worked, wasn't it? People made copies. They passed them around. They traded them for other, similar images obtained under equally immoral circumstances. It was an unavoidable fact that her naked body was now out there for public consumption, and would remain so, dogging her for the rest of time. Those images would be discovered and rediscovered again and again, including by people who knew her in real life. The worst part was that she wouldn't even necessarily know when she was having a conversation with someone who'd seen graphic close-ups of her at her most vulnerable.

And then there was Jack. What would happen when he was just a few years older, when his friends and classmates came across the pictures and he was forced to endure a barrage of taunts about how they'd seen his mum's snatch?

It didn't bear thinking about.

Vasilico arrived shortly after nightfall, looking irritatingly sleek and well-groomed in his tailored suit. Seeing the state Anna was in, he immediately offered up a profuse and fulsome apology for his offhanded manner earlier and asked if there was anything he could do – a question Anna found herself resenting more each time she heard it. It was like when you suffered a bereavement and people kept coming up to you to say, 'Let me know if you need anything', neatly absolving themselves of the need to actually put any thought into the matter and tossing the ball firmly into *your* court.

'Not that I'm trying to compare it to what you're going through right now,' said Vasilico, 'but I feel like absolute unholy shit for my part in this. *I* was the one who strong-armed you into doing that debate. *I* put a target on your back.'

Anna lifted her head and looked up at him from the sofa with weary eyes. 'Yeah? Well, it's not like anyone forced me to go along with it. I knew they were bound to respond in some fashion. That was the whole *point*. I just didn't think it would be anything like *this*.'

Vasilico gave a strained, unhappy smile. 'Doesn't mean I wouldn't do anything to make it up to you if I could.'

'Just tell me you got something useful out of it, at least.'

Slowly, Vasilico lowered himself into a vacant chair. 'I wish I could. The handful of audience members we've been looking into all came up clean – relatively speaking. That troll who called for you to be strung up? We pulled him in for questioning. He's just some terminally online little scrote with an interest in men's rights issues. He has solid alibis for all bar one of the assaults. He's not connected to any of it – of that I'm only too confident.'

'You should look into Cameron Mitchell too,' said Anna. 'He's the second-year who taunted me at this morning's lecture. He's been going off the rails for a while now – retreating more and more into MRA talking points.'

Her voice sounded distant and impassive in her own ears. She was going through the motions, forcing herself to focus on the practicalities to avoid thinking about . . .

'Cameron . . . Mitchell.' Vasilico wrote the name in his notebook. 'I'll look into it. Anyone else you can think of?'

'No,' said Anna, then suddenly remembered something. 'But there *is* something else. A while back, I got an anonymous phone call from some bloke saying he'd kill me and fuck my corpse if I didn't stop my anti-male diatribes.'

Vasilico looked up sharply. He stared at her, shocked by her offhandedness. 'When was this?'

Anna shrugged disinterestedly. 'I dunno. Couple of weeks ago, maybe? I didn't make a note in my diary.'

'You should have mentioned this to me before.'

'Yes, I should have,' Anna snapped, stung by the implicit rebuke. 'Hindsight's a bloody wonderful thing.' She sighed, relenting. 'Sorry. There's a lot I'm wishing I'd done differently right now.'

Vasilico shook his head. 'No, *I'm* sorry.' He made another note in his notebook. 'We'll pull your phone records, see if we can trace who it came from. Hopefully whoever it is wasn't smart enough to use a burner phone.'

'There's one other thing,' said Anna. 'About a week later, I woke up in the middle of the night hearing someone creeping around the garden. I didn't see anyone, but the flowerbed was all trampled and I found a cigarette end as well.'

'And you didn't report this to the police?'

'I take it that's a rhetorical question.'

Vasilico shut his eyes and sighed. 'Oh, Anna, for God's sake . . .'

'Yeah, all right,' she retorted. 'If wishes were horses, beggars would ride. Anyway, what about Leopold?'

'What about him?'

'Well, are you going to arrest him?' Anna shrugged belligerently. 'How many more coincidences is it going to take? How many more crimes have to take place against people who've spoken out against him before you admit he has something to do with this? Pull him in. Go through all *his* devices. Strip away every last vestige of *his* privacy.' Her eyes narrowed. 'Do to him what they've done to me,' she said with vehemence.

The look of genuine compassion on Vasilico's face suggested he'd like nothing more than to do just that. And yet, before he even spoke, she knew what he was going to say.

'The moment I have conclusive proof that he's the one pulling the strings, believe me, I'll have him in a cell so fast his feet won't touch the ground. But we both know we're a long way from that. Until we've got some sort of smoking gun, I've no more grounds to arrest him than I did yesterday. I'm sorry.'

Anna said nothing. She knew he was right, of course, but she couldn't bring herself to acknowledge it. She just lowered her eyes and drew her arms more tightly about herself.

Vasilico got to his feet. 'For the time being, let's see how we get on with those phone records. And I'm going to have Cybercrime pull that website to pieces – see if they can establish the identity of whoever uploaded those pictures.'

'Thank you,' muttered Anna, more out of obligation than anything.

'On a semi-related note, I'm also going to need you to let me have your phone.'

'What for?' said Anna. On some level, of course, she knew the answer to this already, but her brain was so frazzled, it was no longer making the obvious connections.

'It'll only be for a short while, I hope, but I want the techies to take a look at it too; see if they can figure out how The Reckoning gained access to it – assuming, that is, they're the ones behind this. With any luck, they'll have left some breadcrumbs leading back to them.'

'I already did a factory reset,' said Anna.

Strictly speaking, it had been Zoe who'd actually done the deed. Indeed, it had been her suggestion to begin with; such advanced technological functions were beyond Anna's means. At the time, she'd been only too happy to go along with it, even if it had seemed an awful lot like shutting the stable door after an entire pack of horses had already bolted. Now, though, she saw, from the tightening of Vasilico's jaw, that it had been the wrong thing to do.

'No matter,' he eventually said, clearly making a considerable effort to hide his exasperation. 'Let me have it anyway. You never know – there might still be a trace on there. All being well, you'll have it back before noon tomorrow.'

With some reluctance, Anna handed it over. Despite the thing having brought her nothing but misery, so much of her life was tied up with it, and she relied on it for everything from checking her emails to maintaining her weekly shopping list, that not having it on her person at all times left her feeling almost naked.

Do NOT think about being naked.

Vasilico slid the phone into the inside pocket of his coat and gazed down at her with a sad, sympathetic smile. 'I know it feels hopeless. Like your whole life's been upended. But you'll get through this.'

'You don't know that.'

'Oh, but I do. You're stronger than these people, Anna. Remember that.'

Anna lifted her head. She returned his smile without enthusiasm.

'I'm going to make sure there's a constant police presence here,' he went on, now briskly businesslike. 'There'll be a car parked outside 24/7.'

Anna nodded a silent acknowledgement.

'If you want, I can also have an officer stay with you in the house.'

Anna shook her head. 'That won't be necessary.'

'If you're sure . . . ?'

'I'm sure.'

She just wanted to withdraw from the outside world as much as humanly possible. Having to put up with a stranger in the house, constantly getting in her way and just generally making a nuisance of themselves, was *not* on her agenda right now.

'All right,' said Vasilico, 'but if at any point you change your mind . . .'

'You'll be the first to know.'

He nodded, a part of him clearly unhappy with her refusal. He remained standing before her, seemingly reluctant to leave. For a moment, it occurred to her that he might be considering bending down to kiss or embrace her. She knew that was the last thing she wanted right now. And he seemed to sense it too. A moment later, he gave a brief dip of his head.

'Right. Well. I'll crack on, then.'

As he turned to go, Zoe appeared in the doorway. He acknowledged her with a nod.

'You offski?' Her question sounded vaguely accusatory.

'I think,' he said, 'right now, I'm more use out there than I am here.'

Zoe glanced briefly in Anna's direction, then turned to face Vasilico again. 'Gie her time,' she said, more gently. 'Sure it's only been a hot minute.'

They were speaking in whispers, presumably labouring under the impression that Anna wouldn't be able to make them out from the sofa. But she heard every word.

Having seen Vasilico out, Zoe returned to the living room, sliding into the chair he'd recently vacated.

'Got everything ye need?' she asked, for twenty-fourth time.

Anna smiled wanly. 'Unless you've got the power to alter reality, then yes, I reckon I've got pretty much everything that can possibly be of use to me.'

Zoe managed to return the smile. She was silent for a moment, before piping up again.

'Um, I'm gonnae get Jacko ready for beddy-byes in a bit. 'S it OK if I bring him down tae say n'night?'

At the mention of Jack's name, Anna felt her stomach lurching afresh. She'd been putting this off for some time, but the moment had now come.

'Actually,' she said, 'there's something I want you to do. I need you to call Mandy and ask if she can take him for a few days.'

Mandy was the mother of Zoe's nine-year-old niece. In her younger years, her life had been far from a bed of roses, with stints in both the red light district and as a petty shoplifter to her name. Since then, though, she'd proved remarkably successful at turning her life around, and was one of the few people Anna would trust in a pinch to protect Jack with as much ferocity as she would herself.

Zoe looked a little taken back, though she recovered quickly.

'Sure,' she began, 'I'll ring her in the morning and—'

'No, not in the morning. Now. I want him gone tonight.'

This time, Zoe didn't even try to hide her disbelief. She stared at Anna, mouth agape.

As levelly as she could, Anna laid out the situation as she saw it.

'I don't know for sure what's coming down the pike, but these people are targeting me, and I don't want to risk them deciding to go after Jack too. Leopold mentioned my having a son at the debate last night. For all I know, that was a dog whistle to his followers to consider him fair game

– or else they'll choose to interpret it as one. Until this all blows over, I want him as far away from all this – and from *me* – as possible.'

Zoe clearly wasn't at all happy about the idea – though, to her credit, she didn't put up more than a token resistance. With a look on her face that made her feelings abundantly clear, she rang Mandy, who agreed to come and collect Jack straight away.

Which meant the only person left for Anna to sell the idea to was Jack himself. He was considerably less than thrilled, clenching his fists and stamping his foot when Anna, crouching down on her knees on his bedroom floor, explained to him that he was going to be staying with his Auntie Mandy for a while.

'No!!!' he squealed, features contorted in pure rage. 'Don't wanna.'

'You *like* it there, darling,' said Anna, mentally pleading with him not to make this any harder for her than it already was. 'Think of all the fun you'll have playing with Ruby.'

'Don't like Ruby,' said Jack sullenly. 'She's a stupid bitch. Girls are stupid.'

It was all Anna could do not to recoil like she'd been slapped in the face. While the two things weren't really comparable, it was hard, under the present circumstances, not to see Jack's naïve expression of casual sexism as sitting at one end of the same continuum on which men like the ones who, right now, were systematically destroying her life existed.

Her resolve hardened. She took hold of Jack's arm, forcing him to look at her.

'Now, you listen to me, Jack. I don't want you saying things like that, you hear me? If girls are stupid . . . well, then, that must mean I'm stupid as well, mustn't it?'

Jack merely shrugged and lowered his eyes.

'And another thing,' said Anna, suddenly remembering. 'What's this I hear about you biting another child at playgroup?'

Jack shrugged again, refusing to look at her.

'Well? Answer me.'

'Didn't,' said Jack, still not meeting her eyes.

'You're lying, Jack. And you *know* how I feel about lying.'

She tried to lift his chin to make him look at her, but he shook her off and barged past her, heading for the door.

'Fine,' he muttered. 'I'll go.'

As his angry footsteps thumped down the stairs, Anna continued to kneel on the floor, chin resting on her chest. As if she didn't already have enough to contend with, she now had a child who resented her and was prepared to tell blatant untruths to her face.

And to bite people. Mustn't forget about the biting.

Mandy arrived twenty minutes later from her flat in the East End.

'Honestly, it's nae bother,' she breezed, standing on the doorstep with one arm on Jack's shoulder, while Jack stood with his rucksack at his feet, scowling down at his shoes. 'Ye know he's welcome for as long as it takes. You just gie's a holler when ye're ready tae have him back.'

Anna wasn't sure how much Zoe had told Mandy about the circumstances behind her needing to take Jack – whether she'd spun her a yarn or given her something approximating the truth – but she was grateful to Mandy for not asking questions. She kissed a fiercely resistant Jack goodbye, then watched as Mandy led him by the hand down the steps to her car, where tiny, red-haired Ruby, in so many respects the spit of Zoe, was waiting in the passenger seat, fiddling with the knobs on the radio.

Her relief at knowing he was out of harm's way was tempered by a deep, aching sense of guilt that nonetheless now devoured her. Here she was, once again effectively outsourcing her duties as his mother – to say nothing of the responsibility she bore for having brought this threat to their door in the first place. No *wonder* he resented her. She promised herself to make it up to him once all this was over, then asked herself how many times she'd told herself that, and for how many different reasons. Better times, it seemed, were perennially just around the corner.

With Jack safely out of the picture, Anna sloped through to the living room and finally allowed herself to give in to total despair. She sank into the sofa, shut her eyes and let out a low moan of anguish. She'd been in some tight scrapes in her time, but she doubted she'd ever felt such a sense of utter, soul-crushing hopelessness – of life as she knew it being as good as over.

She opened her eyes again as Zoe, fresh from exchanging a few words with Mandy outside, made her way into the room, wearing a sympathetic smile that, somehow, only served to make Anna feel even worse.

'How ya doin', love?'

Anna could only manage a dry laugh.

Zoe eased herself onto the sofa next to her. 'All this *is* gonnae blow over sooner or later, y'know. Seriously, doll, there's that many dirty pictures out there on the internet, yours'll soon get lost in the wash.' A thought came to her. 'Heh, I bet ye a pound tae a penny there's ones of *me* out there somewhere. I wasnae exactly circumspect in ma younger days.'

Anna made no response, though she was privately of the view that the two scenarios weren't remotely comparable. Zoe's attitude to public embarrassment had always been to take it on the chin. Back in high school, she'd once been the subject of a smear campaign by a boy in their year, Barry Elliott, who'd told everyone she'd sucked him off behind the bike sheds. Rather than denying it, Zoe had embraced the lie and embellished it, proudly telling anyone who would listen how his penis looked like a malformed Nik Nak and how, when he'd climaxed, he'd called out for his mum. Barry Elliott never tried to spread rumours about her again.

The point was, Zoe had never really had a reputation of professional respectability to uphold, or a career that could potentially be scuppered by something like this, whereas Anna—

She realised what that said about how she viewed Zoe and hated herself for even thinking it.

'Hey.' Zoe nudged Anna's shoulder. 'I got one for ye. What dae incels use for lube?'

Anna shrugged.

'Extra virgin olive oil.'

With a great effort, Anna forced a wan smile. 'That's pretty good.'

'Best ye're gonnae get at nine o'clock on a Thursday night.'

They sat in companionable silence for a while. At length, Anna concluded that the time had come to raise a subject she'd been dreading having to confront.

'You know . . .' she began.

Zoe glanced across at her. 'Hmm?'

Anna launched into the speech she'd been rehearsing in her head. 'You should really clear out too. You're as much of a potential target as Jack, and—'

'Anna.' Zoe gave her a severe, no-nonsense look. 'Shut the fuck up.'

Anna dutifully snapped her mouth shut.

'How many times is it now you've been there for me when I've been in a jam? Huh? Tell me, cos I've lost track.'

Anna continued to say nothing.

'Well . . . it's lots. And now you're in deep doody, and it's my turn tae be there for *you*. So I don't wannae hear another word about me clearing out. Got it?'

'Got it,' said Anna.

In truth, she'd never truly believed Zoe *would* agree to leave, but she was relieved, all the same, to have had the idea so comprehensively thrown back in her face. Relieved and profoundly grateful.

The feeling didn't last long, however. The sense of overwhelming despair came back only too quickly, and she slumped forward, pressing her hand to her face in a vain attempt to prevent the emotions churning inside her from spilling out.

Zoe stroked her back. 'Hey. Hey. It's gonnae be all right.'

Anna groaned in despair. 'You all keep saying that, but you're wrong. How *can* it be? Everything I've worked for, everything I've built – it's all gone. Flushed down the toilet. It's over.'

She lifted her head to look at Zoe, her vision blurry through tear-filled eyes.

'Tell me, without my reputation . . . without my career . . . who *am* I?'

Wordlessly, Zoe reached over and wiped first one eye, then the other, with her index finger.

'You're Anna Scavolini,' she said gently. 'And I reckon that's enough.'

36

El Duce invites GodsGift2Women and LifeIsPain to a new chat channel.

LifeIsPain joins the chat.

GodsGift2Women joins the chat.

LifeIsPain: That was fuckign EPIC!!!!
LifeIsPain: Incedible work El duce

GodsGift2Women: Yeah nice going man. Specially with the audio

El Duce: (Takes bow) Why thank you, thank you very much.
El Duce: Truth be told, I just took advantage of a most fortuitous situation. None of us could have predicted she'd be riding the cock carousel last night.

LifeIsPain: Lol hope detecitve Chad made teh most of it
LifeIsPain: Doesnt sound like hell be getitng any more nooky for awhile

GodsGift2Women: :D :D :D

El Duce: Serves him right for simping on her like a complete cuck.

GodsGift2Women: Btw like what I did with the twitter account?

El Duce: Not bad, though you need to work on your punctuation. No one who looks at it twice is going to think it was written by a university professor.

GodsGift2Women: Whats wrong with my punctuaiton
GodsGift2Women: ???

El Duce: Nothing at all. You crack on, my son.

GodsGift2Women: Any way the tweets were just a little side project
GodsGift2Women: The snaps of her whoring herself out are the real gold dust
GodsGift2Women: Any luck thatll sink her for good

El Duce: Computing Services were faster off the mark in getting the email pulled than I expected.
El Duce: Still, no matter. Damage done.

LifeIsPain: LOL serve's it right dirty fucking slut

El Duce: Precisely. If you can't handle the heat, get out of the kitchen.
El Duce: Or, if you don't want pictures of your gash plastered all over cyberspace, don't take pictures of your fucking gash.
El Duce: Radical idea, I know.

GodsGift2Women: Exactly, cant have it both ways

El Duce: And we can be sure plenty who did see it will have passed it around to their friends.
El Duce: That's the joy of this sort of business. You get to sit back and let others do the legwork for you.

LifeIsPain: Liek chinese whispers

El Duce: Oh, meant to say.
El Duce: Big D is very pleased with the roles you've both played in today's high jinks. Asked me to personally pass on His gratitude.

LifeIsPain: AMAAAAAAAZING
LifeIsPain: (die's and gos to heaven)

GodsGift2Women: Vengeance is sweet

El Duce: Believe me, we've a long way yet to go before He's fully avenged. But rest assured, there's plenty more planned for tomorrow.
El Duce: Strap yourselves in boys, the fun's just beginning . . .

37

The morning brought with it no reprieve – just more of the same hopelessness and impending doom as the previous day. It didn't help that Anna had had a largely sleepless night, lying awake well into the wee hours fixating on her situation while being spooned by a snoring Zoe, who'd insisted on spending the night with her – a gesture of support which, however much Anna appreciated it, she suspected hadn't been conducive to her getting any meaningful shut-eye. She rose just before six, gingerly extricating herself from Zoe's limbs and creeping downstairs to begin going through the motions of her morning routine.

Shortly after eight, Fraser rang on the landline with an update. Computing Services had managed to establish that there'd been a suspicious login to Anna's email account at 10.34 a.m. the previous day, just minutes before the message containing the pictures of her was sent out – from an IP address in Shanghai that they were reasonably certain was spoofed.

'So there you go,' said Anna, with more than a touch of well-deserved self-righteousness. 'I wasn't the one who sent it. Like I *told* you.'

'That much is true, yes,' Fraser agreed. 'But there's a further dimension to all this.'

She waited for him to continue.

'Computing Services *also* established that the reason the intruder was able to access the pictures in question is because they were saved to the cloud storage account linked to your email – an account provided to you by the university. What that means is that, regardless of whether or not you sent the offending message, you nonetheless committed a serious breach of your terms of employment by using an account provided *by the university* to store pornographic imagery.'

Anna couldn't think of a single thing to say in response to this. She simply stood there, phone to her ear, listening to the blood pounding in her ears. It didn't seem possible – and yet, now that she thought about it, it *did* make a certain amount of sense. Linking her phone to her university account was one of the first things she'd done when she bought it, on the grounds that it would be convenient to be able to access all her files on the go. Of course, she'd been presented with a multitude of disclaimers, and somewhere within those reams of text were no doubt all manner of stark warnings about the potential consequences – like giving the account's provider access to your entire camera roll. But she'd clicked OK on all of them without even reading them – because of *course* that was what you were conditioned to do when presented with a dense wall of legalese. *Just agree to everything. It'll never come back to bite you.*

Fraser sighed heavily. 'I wish I had better news for you, but I'm afraid a decision has been made to formally suspend you, on full pay, pending an investigation into your conduct. A letter will be posted out to you informing you of the specifics. You are, of course, welcome to consult with your trade union representative.'

He sounded like he was reading from a script.

'A hearing will be scheduled to take place in due course, at which you'll be invited to set out your side of the story. Until then, I request that you don't set foot on university grounds and refrain from any contact with your students or colleagues.' He hesitated. 'I also need to make you aware that, should the hearing find against you, the university will consider the full range of available disciplinary measures at its disposal, up to and including your dismissal.'

She'd known this was always a possibility, of course. But still, to actually hear it stated was like a blow to the solar plexus.

Fraser sighed again. 'I'm sorry, Anna. I wish I hadn't been forced into this position.'

By you was the unspoken postscript.

'And another thing. What's this I hear about you using your Twitter account to cast aspersions about the university and its staff – myself included?'

She groaned in exasperation. 'Serious question, Fraser: have you actually looked at this account yourself, or are you just going by what you've heard from the rumour mill?'

'Well,' Fraser huffed, clearly somewhat rattled, 'to be precise, I haven't yet had the opportunity to *personally* inspect—'

'Well, when you *do* get round to it, you might consider taking a moment to ask yourself whether it's credible that someone with a PhD from the Sapienza doesn't know the difference between "your" Y-O-U-R and "you're" Y-O-U-apostrophe-R-E.'

You absolute fucking tool, she almost added. But she didn't. Instead, she slammed down the phone, leaving him to reflect on her words.

Zoe was up and about soon afterwards. She had a routine medical appointment scheduled and would be gone for most of the morning. She'd offered multiple times to have it rescheduled, but Anna had put her foot down and insisted she go. She ended up practically having to shoo her out the door, remaining on the doorstep until she'd rounded the corner to make sure she actually went. As she stood there, hands jammed into the pockets of her dressing gown, her eye was drawn to the police car parked across the road. She didn't envy the officers inside, tasked with keeping vigil on the house all through the night. She briefly considered inviting them in to get some respite from the cold, before deciding she *really* wasn't up for entertaining.

Barely half an hour later, the phone rang again. This time, it was Farah. Word, it seemed, had spread like wildfire around the university about her suspension, and her colleagues had been making their views on the matter clear.

'Everybody is up in arms,' Farah said, her voice quavering with the strength of her feeling. 'None of us can believe it, how they're treating you. Sophie Hennessy is circulating a petition, saying we'll all walk out unless you're immediately reinstated.'

As much as Anna was genuinely touched by this news, to the extent that she felt her eyes pricking, her immediate thought was just how precarious Farah's teaching contract actually was.

'Farah, *please* don't do anything to jeopardise your own position,' she said. 'Not on my account. Besides' – and she hated having to admit this – 'the matter's out of their hands. I've breached the terms of my employment. They have to follow the rules.'

Farah let out an angry, wordless exclamation. 'Urrrrgh! Well, they should find some way to bend them, then. You've given so much to them over all these years, and . . . and . . . and you're the one who's been wronged here!' she all but spluttered. 'It's completely disgusting.'

'I'm just sorry to have to leave you and the others to carry the can,' said Anna. 'The timing's hardly ideal, especially with the upcoming strike action.'

'Oh, that,' said Farah. 'With everything else happening, I'd forgotten all about it. I wonder, perhaps, whether it would be for the best if it was called off . . .'

'Bloody well better not be,' said Anna vehemently. 'And don't let anyone guilt trip you into thinking you're letting the students down or any other bollocks like that. This is entirely on the heads of management. They made their bed. They can lie in it.'

They rang off shortly afterwards, and silence once more returned to the house, accompanied by the familiar feelings of loneliness and isolation. As much as Anna had been buoyed by the news that her colleagues were kicking up a stink about her suspension, it hadn't escaped her notice that, barring Farah and Hugh, none of them had got in touch to lend their support to her directly. True enough, they were probably under strict orders not to contact her, but it was hard not to feel abandoned – contaminated, even, as if they feared to get too close to her, lest some of the poison rub off on them. But then, she supposed, if anyone *had* called, she'd probably only have resented the intrusion, and the need to keep up appearances by pretending to them that she was OK when she really, *really* wasn't.

She spent much of the morning curled up on the living room sofa, scrolling on her iPad, which, in the absence of her phone, was her primary link to the outside world. The @AnnaScavoliniGlasgow Twitter account had given up posting diatribes about her employers and had instead taken to reposting the link to the pictures of her on the porn site every hour on the hour. Her attempts to get the account suspended had yet to meet with any success. She'd finally worked out that she couldn't actually report it without first creating an account herself. Having duly done so, in the name of @TheRealAnnaScavolini, she patiently clicked through the various steps of the unexpectedly dense complaints form, only to be informed that her complaint would be considered in due course and that, in the meantime, she was welcome to block the account if it was causing her offence.

Out of morbid curiosity, she visited the *Hard Truth* YouTube channel, where she discovered that Leopold had not been resting on his laurels. Within the last twelve hours, he'd rushed out an episode which, on paper, focused on mental health but, in reality, was just an excuse for him to weigh in on her recent 'difficulties'. He sat, facing the camera, hands folded, a suitably concerned frown etched into his brows as he purred into the giant metal cock angled towards him on his desk.

'*A colleague of mine,*' he mused, '*was recently suspended following an incident in which she . . . well, I'm almost not sure whether I can actually say it on this platform.*'

He made a big deal of humming and hawing, grimacing theatrically as he pretended to consider the potential pitfalls of elaborating.

'*She . . . let's just say that several of us were exposed to considerably more of her than we felt comfortable seeing.*'

Of *course* he had to be one of the ones who saw the email before it was recalled, Anna thought.

'*This colleague . . . Out of respect for her privacy, I shall simply refer to her as "Anna S".*' He flashed the camera a knowing smirk. '*Anna recently suffered a somewhat bruising encounter with yours truly in a public debate. I knew, at the time, that she was . . . well, let's say in a delicate place mentally . . . and I can't help but wonder whether, had I gone just a little easier on her, she wouldn't have felt compelled to try to claw back the initiative by making such a spectacle of herself.*'

He gazed down the lens of his camera, his expression grave. '*Because make no mistake, that's what this behaviour ultimately is, whether Anna realises it or not: a cry for attention. You'll hear no end of rationalisation from the third-wave feminists about this sort of thing being "empowering" or "sex-positive", but, at the end of the day, when a woman photographs herself in a state of undress, or allows* others *to photograph her, it's because she wants people to see her – for them to respond in some way, whether with outrage or arousal, or . . .'*

He trailed off, as if reluctant to follow that line of thought to its conclusion.

'But it's like I always say: you simply can't debate radical feminists in a logical manner. They're too driven by their emotions; by their sense of resentment. And you see the results – when they don't get what they want, they lash out in ways that are destructive to those around them and, most tragically of all, to themselves.

'With all that said, I wish to make clear to anyone watching that I don't condone harassment or the sharing of these images with others. What Anna needs, at this point in time, is to be left alone, and to hopefully receive the help and support she needs . . .'

Listening to him, Anna felt her anger rising to fever pitch. She knew, just as surely as *he* undoubtedly did, that, for his followers, such words would be like a red rag to a bull. It was the Katharine Barnard situation all over again. The dog whistle was as loud as a clarion.

Vasilico dropped by the house shortly afterwards to return her phone. As they'd feared, the factory reset Zoe had performed had done its job only too well, removing any trace the hackers might have left behind. Anna tried to ignore the implicit rebuke behind his superficially conciliatory tone as he conveyed this information to her; she could tell he was itching to let rip with the I-told-you-sos.

He also informed her that the caller who'd threatened her a couple of weeks earlier had already been ruled out from having any involvement in either the attacks on female students or the leaking of her photos.

'He's nobody,' Vasilico said, with a regretful shrug. 'He lives in Middlesbrough and has never so much as set *foot* in Glasgow. Just another angry troglodyte who heard you talking about feminism on some radio programme and decided you needed taking down a peg or two.'

Somehow, to Anna, that was almost worse than the alternative. To engender so much hatred in people who didn't even know you that they were willing to call you up and tell you, in graphic detail, how they planned to kill you – it was almost beyond comprehension. But she didn't say any of that to Vasilico. She just thanked him distantly for letting her know and ushered him back out the door before he had a chance to put down roots.

Late in the morning, the phone calls started. The first one came while she was in the kitchen, waiting for the kettle to boil. One minute, she was standing there, gazing off into space. The next, her mobile, which she'd stuffed into her pocket without a second thought after Vasilico handed it over, was trilling merrily. She fished it out and inspected the screen. The number showed as unknown.

'Hello?'

'Um . . . is that Anna?'

The voice was low, male and awkward, with an undercurrent of nervous amusement, almost as if he was doing this on a dare.

'Yes?' she said, the question *Who's this?* implicit in her rising inflection.

'Um . . . so, I'm wondering . . . what are your rates?'

'Rates?'

'Yeah . . . like, how much for a BJ, how much for a hand-job, how much for the whole shebang, that sorta thing?'

'*Excuse* me?'

'Well, I mean' – the caller sounded decidedly irked now – 'you're either open for business or you're not.'

'I'm *not*,' she said emphatically. 'Don't call this number again.'

She stabbed the 'End Call' button with an angry thumb.

A couple of minutes later, it rang again. This time, she was already half-anticipating something similar. And sure enough . . .

'Aye, so, I've got an hour at one o'clock,' said the voice – also male, but this one brisk and businesslike. 'Reckon that's enough time for a massage and the full service. You're near Hyndland Road, right?'

'Just who do you think it is you're *calling*?' she managed to splutter.

'Thought that'd be obvious. You're Anna Scavolini, right?'

'Ri— I mean, what's it to you? Where the hell did you get this number?'

'Where d'you *think*? Companionable. You know, the website?' he said, as if it was common knowledge. 'Look, are you some sort of prick-tease? Cos I've got a busy schedule. I haven't got time to—'

She ended the call.

And so it continued. Every few minutes, her phone would ring, heralding yet another voice describing, in gratuitous detail, the services he expected her to render unto him. Some of the accents were local, others English or American. A couple sounded vaguely Eastern European. Before long, the landline became involved too, bleating away in the hallway almost as often as her mobile. Wherever her 'services' were being advertised, it was clear the now-infamous leaked pictures were part of the package: judging by a number of the comments made to her, the callers were as familiar with her body as she was.

At first, she answered every single call, spurred by a degree of morbid curiosity coupled with what she could only assume was a desire for self-flagellation – an act as compulsive as picking at an open wound rather than allowing it to heal.

'You're, like, a 36D, right? Cos I do like a good handful.'

'To be honest, I normally only do blondes, but in your case I'm prepared to make an exception.'

'Nice landing strip, by the way. And there I thought you feminazis were all about the bush.'

'So do you, like, do golden showers?'

Some of the callers didn't talk but merely listened in silence to her increasingly shrill demands for them to say something. One made a series of unintelligible noises that she didn't realise, until she'd been listening to him for nearly a minute, were the sounds of him rubbing one out.

In the midst of it all, her mobile pinged an email alert. It was from the John Lewis department store, telling her that her order for a £1,399 flatscreen television had been received and would be dispatched within twenty-four hours.

'The *fuck* . . . ?'

She was trying to dredge up the login details for her John Lewis account – which she belatedly remembered having been among the ones she'd changed yesterday – when she got another email alert. This one was from an agricultural supplies website she hadn't even *heard* of, far less registered an account with, informing her that her order for thirty 5-litre bottles of liquid fertiliser would be delivered on Monday.

Her phone began to ring again. Torn every which way, she took the call.

'What?' she almost yelled.

'*This is an automated message from Halifax. We recently noticed a suspicious transaction of – one – thousand – one – hundred – and – forty – two – pounds – and – ninety – seven – pence – on your credit card ending – seven – seven – zero – four – and have placed a temporary block on your account. If this transaction was genuine, please press one. If you do not recognise the transaction, press . . .*'

Was this message even the genuine article, she wondered, or was it too part of some ploy to extort her? Normally, she was reasonably quick off the mark when it came to spotting scams of this sort. Right now, though, her brain was so frazzled and she was being pulled in so many different directions at once, she could barely understand the words being recited.

As she continued to listen to the dizzying range of options presented by the pre-recorded voice, her phone pinged yet another alert in her ear. This time, it was a text message from the provider of one of her other credit cards, again stating that a block had been placed on the card in question following an unusually large transaction.

In the hallway, the landline phone began its incessant trilling once again.

Beset by pings and ringtones on all sides, Anna sank to the floor in the living room doorway and put her head in her hands.

She wasn't sure how long she remained there, but the next thing she was aware of was the sound of the front door being unlocked. She lifted her head and turned to look as it opened and Zoe entered, laden with shopping bags. She took in the sight of Anna, sitting on the floor with her back against the doorframe, and gave a bemused smile.

'Whatcha doing down there?' She nodded to the house phone. 'How come ye're no getting that? Could be some'dy important.'

Anna distantly took in the fact that the phone was still ringing. She didn't move – just stared back up at Zoe wordlessly.

Deducing something was seriously amiss, Zoe hastily set down the shopping bags and headed over to answer the phone herself.

'Hello?'

As she listened to the voice at the other end, her expression changed, first into one of disbelief, then of rage.

'The fuck is *this*?' she snapped. 'Naw, I dinnae gie a *fuck* whit ye thought.

Call this number again and ye'll be pickin' yer teeth aff the flair. Away an' shite, ye wee fud!'

She slammed down the phone and turned to Anna, silently beseeching her for an explanation. Anna continued to gaze up at her, not moving.

In that instant, Zoe seemed to read the situation with remarkable speed and accuracy.

'This been going on all morning?'

Anna nodded. 'They got my credit cards too,' she said helplessly.

Zoe's expression hardened. 'Right,' she muttered.

Then, as Anna's mobile started to ring again, Zoe whipped it out of her hand and cancelled the call.

'Give that back,' Anna spluttered, surprised and semi-outraged.

Zoe responded by hiding it behind her back like a child. 'Naw,' she said flatly.

'But I need to cancel my cards!'

'They'll wait. Let's just concentrate on *you* the now.'

She switched off the phone and pocketed it, then extended her hand to Anna. Reluctantly, Anna accepted it, allowing Zoe to help her to her feet.

They were just turning to head back through to the living room when the hallway phone started to ring again. Anna automatically tensed, as if expecting a physical blow. Zoe's eyes flared.

'Fuck this,' she muttered.

She stormed back out to the hallway and snatched up the phone.

'Now you listen tae me, ya durty fuckin' pervert. Whitever it is ye're after, she's no offerin', awright? So get aff this phone right now or I'll come over there, cut aff yer tiny dick, staple it tae yer forehead and—'

She stopped abruptly, her expression changing instantly to one of surprise and uncertainty.

'Right,' she said, much more quietly.

Still wearing the same vaguely chastened expression, she offered the phone to Anna.

'Um, it's for you.'

Mystified, Anna took the phone. She put it to her ear gingerly, a part of her still expecting to be hit with yet another obscene set of demands.

'Hello. Am I speaking to Anna Scavolini?'

The voice at the other end belonged to a woman. That alone caused Anna to relax considerably.

'Yes,' she confirmed, albeit still with more than just a hint of suspicion. 'Who's this?'

'Oh, good,' said the woman. 'I tried calling your department, but they said you were taking a leave of absence – which I'm *guessing* isn't by choice.'

There was an arch, knowing ring to her voice that Anna immediately found intensely irritating. Whoever this woman was, she sounded altogether too familiar with her business.

'I seem to remember asking who you were,' she said.

'You did indeed, yes. Sorry. My name's Callie Benson. I'm a lecturer at Abertay University. Your, er, recent difficulties have caused quite a stir here, I'm sorry to say. News travels fast, particularly on the academic circuit, and—'

'I'm sorry – you're calling to tell me this *why*?'

She was annoyed beyond all measure, and still couldn't believe that this woman, whom she didn't know from Adam, would think it necessary to call her up to *tell* her that her 'difficulties' had become the subject of salacious gossip as far afield as Dundee.

There was a pause at the other end of the line, during which Anna briefly wondered whether Callie was still there. But just as she was about to repeat her question, Callie spoke again.

'Because something remarkably similar happened to me a few years ago.'

This time, it was Anna's turn to be reduced to silence. She was aware of Zoe hovering nearby, shooting her a questioning frown, but ignored her.

'Are you still there?' said Callie.

'I'm still here,' said Anna quietly.

'I wondered if we might be able to meet. There are things I can tell you that could be of help to you . . .' She hesitated. 'But what I have to say, I'd much rather say face to face.'

38

They set off for Dundee shortly after ten o'clock the following morning, Anna driving. As they cruised up the hill towards Hyndland Road, Zoe waved cheery-bye from the passenger seat to the two officers on house-watching duty. For a moment, Anna wondered if they would give chase, but the panda car remained resolutely stationary and was soon lost to view.

Anna wasn't due to meet Callie until two o'clock, but Zoe had encouraged her to make a day of it, reasoning that it would do her good to spend some time away from the house and from Glasgow, and, after some initial, half-hearted resistance, Anna had grudgingly come round to the idea. She'd even allowed Zoe to talk her into leaving her phone behind, switched off and stowed safely in the desk drawer in her office.

At least the morning had brought with it a sliver of positive news. The previous afternoon, Zoe, doing some detective work of her own, had succeeded in locating and reporting the page featuring Anna's photos and contact details on Companionable, an 'adult work' website that boasted 'over 200,000 *very* satisfied customers'. Overnight, the site's administrators had acted with surprising – and commendable – speed and taken the listing down. The fact that the house phone was no longer ringing off the hook suggested that this arm of the harassment campaign had, at least for now, been neutralised.

No such luck with the Twitter profile. Anna, surreptitiously checking her emails on her iPad while Zoe was in the shower earlier that morning, had received what read suspiciously like an AI-generated response to her complaint, claiming to have reviewed the @AnnaScavoliniGlasgow account and concluded that it did not violate the platform's terms and conditions. She'd briefly toyed with firing off an angry response, before concluding, with a certain weary fatalism, that it was almost certainly futile.

The drive through to Dundee took them just under two hours. They could have done it in less time if they'd chosen a more direct route, but Zoe had insisted on going through Grangemouth so they could see the Kelpies. As they passed by the massive steel horse-head sculptures looming above them by the side of the M9, Anna tried her best to muster a suitably enthusiastic response to Zoe's excited gesticulations. She knew Zoe was trying to lift her spirits, and it wasn't that she didn't appreciate the gesture, but when you really just wanted to be left alone, it was difficult not to privately resent the effort required to avoid hurting the other person's feelings. But she dutifully smiled and nodded, playing along for Zoe's benefit.

'Yes, Zoe, I see them,' she said, not taking her eyes off the road in front of her.

They arrived in Dundee shortly before midday. It wasn't a part of the country either of them had ever had cause to visit before, and, for a while, Anna's focus was exclusively on making sure she didn't take a wrong turn.

Zoe, it transpired, had a clear plan of action, stating a desire to climb to the top of Dundee Law and look out over the city and surrounding countryside. And so, having bought sandwiches at a nearby deli (Anna let Zoe choose for them both), they set off on foot, following the winding path as it circled the hill, periodically passing picnic tables and park benches – which, after a while, began to look more enticing with each step – as they made their way to the summit.

Gradually, the trees flanking them on either side gave way to open air and the ground levelled off. Up ahead, the tall stone war memorial loomed against the overcast sky, and the view of the city and the Firth of Tay opened up before them. Putting on a burst of speed, Zoe ran to the railings and, filling her lungs with air, let out a full-throated whoop of pure joy.

Anna followed at a more sedate pace and joined her at the rail.

Zoe turned to her with a grin. 'Whoo-ee! I'm no much of a sightseer, but that's a mighty fine view if I ever saw wan.'

Anna smiled, saying nothing. The view before them was indeed spectacular, both the sprawl of the city and the magnitude of untamed nature encompassed in a single panorama. There was something undeniably freeing about being up so high, as if all her troubles had been left far below and out of sight. From here, it didn't all look quite so hopeless. For the first time in more than forty-eight hours, she felt able to properly breathe again.

They headed over to one of the benches to eat their sandwiches, sitting shoulder to shoulder, coats buttoned up to their chins to ward off the eddying November wind.

'So you and Sal seem to be getting pretty serious,' Anna remarked, more for something to say than anything else.

Serious enough for her to let you lather her arse with my spatula, she could have added but didn't.

Zoe nodded contentedly. 'Aye, she's a diamond, so she is. Nearly as big a dafty as me, and that's sayin' somethin'. No gonnae pretend I didnae luck out there.' She paused, then added, 'How about you and *il Commissario*? Still reckon that's got legs?'

Anna sighed heavily. She'd been hoping Zoe wouldn't ask this question, but she supposed it had been unavoidable. Besides, she could hardly object. She was the one who'd brought up the topic of relationships.

'I dunno,' she said. 'A couple of days ago, I thought maybe, but now . . .' She shook her head. 'I don't know,' she said again. 'Frankly, with everything else that's happening, a relationship's pretty well the *last* thing on my mind.'

Zoe looked sidelong at Anna and gave her a kindly smile. 'He cares about ye. Ye'd have tae be blind as a bat no tae see it.'

'I know that.'

For a while, they sat there, saying nothing as they gazed out at the view in front of them. Then, as the silence between them deepened, Anna spoke again, more to herself than to Zoe.

'I'm just not sure it's enough.'

With their two o'clock appointment now rapidly approaching, they headed back down to the car and drove into the city. The place Callie had recommended they meet was Sloane's, a coffee house on Commercial Street, less than half a mile from the University.

They stepped into the warmth of the small, dimly lit establishment, a handful of its tables occupied but not exactly doing a roaring trade. As Anna looked around, wondering how she and Callie were meant to recognise each other, a voice called out from near the back.

'Anna?'

Anna turned and looked as a tall woman in her late twenties with golden-brown hair reaching almost to her waist rose from a table and raised her hand in a discreet greeting. Feeling something akin to relief, Anna returned the wave and headed over, Zoe bringing up the rear.

'Callie, right?' she said, coming to a halt at the table.

Callie nodded. 'I recognised you from your uni profile page,' she said, answering the question Anna hadn't asked but which had nonetheless been on her mind. 'I mean,' she added hastily, 'I haven't *looked* or anything.'

Anna, who'd almost succeeded in forgetting that there were nudes of her plastered all over the internet and in her colleagues' inboxes, felt an instant pang in the pit of her stomach at this unwelcome reminder as to why she was here.

In the silence that followed, Callie noticed Zoe for the first time. Her eyes narrowed in suspicion.

'I thought it was just going to be you,' she said to Anna, her tone verging on accusatory.

'Zoe's my friend,' said Anna, immediately defensive. 'Anything you can say to me, you can say to her.'

From the expression on Callie's face, it was clear these words had failed to assuage her.

''S OK,' said Zoe, seemingly sensing that now was not the time for a protracted stand-off. 'I'll just go for a daunder – see the sights and sounds of braw Dundee.' She turned to Anna. 'We'll catch up later, aye?'

'OK,' said Anna, privately thinking that whatever Callie had to say to her, she'd undoubtedly end up sharing with Zoe anyway.

Callie waited till Zoe had safely left the premises before inviting Anna to take a seat. Once the waiter had taken their order and retreated behind the bar, Anna turned to her expectantly.

'I hope you'll excuse me skipping over the pleasantries and getting straight to the point,' she said, 'but I've travelled a long way, and I still have no real idea what I'm actually doing here. You said yesterday you had information that might be of use to me. Well, I'm all ears.'

Callie glanced briefly over Anna's shoulder, presumably making sure there was no one within earshot. To Anna, it all seemed slightly excessive – but then, she reminded herself how *she* would feel if they were discussing *her* 'recent difficulties' in a public place.

'OK,' said Callie, 'so six years ago, I was in the third year of my Computing Science BSc. I was at a different university then, not Abertay. It had a great reputation – a "put it on your CV and doors'll open for you" sort of deal. I'd fought really hard to get in and from time to time I still tell myself it was worth it in the long run, but . . . well.'

Anna fought back the urge to ask her to elaborate. She sensed now was not the time to disrupt the flow of the narrative.

'One night,' Callie continued, 'I went along to this house party. Friend of a friend sort of thing. I didn't really know a whole lot of the folk there, and I spent the first hour or so feeling like a total spare part, basically counting down the minutes till I could make a dignified exit.

'One of the few people there that I *did* know was this guy from my Quantum Computing class. Well, when I say I knew him, I didn't "*know* him" know him. I'm not sure many people *did*. He was sort of quiet, kept to himself, wasn't really in my orbit, know what I mean? But this night, he comes over and he's like, "Fancy meeting *you* here," and I'm all like, "What were the odds?" You know, like we were in some wacky sitcom or something.

'Anyway, we get talking over drinks and find we've got a bit more in common than I initially thought – at least when it comes to which of our lecturers we reckon are top tier and which ones are a waste of space. At this point, I'm already starting to feel a bit woozy, but I figure it's just cos I haven't had anything to eat, and when he offers to get me another drink, I don't say no.'

She paused as the waiter returned with their coffees. Again, she waited till he'd retreated to the bar before continuing.

'Next thing I know, I come to and I'm lying on a stranger's bed, on top of a pile of coats, and he's . . . you know . . . *doing* me. Like, he's on top of me and my pants are around my knees and he's inside me. And at first I find it more weird than anything else – like, how did we both end up in this situation? And then I'm like, *Oh, he must have got the wrong end of the stick,* cos there's no way I'd have agreed to this. I was seeing someone at the time, and . . .' She gave a vague gesture with her hand. 'So I says to him, "What are you doing?" and he's like, "Shh, I'll be done in a minute." So I just sort of lay back and let him get on with it.'

She gave a fatalistic shrug. 'Maybe that was the wrong thing to do. Maybe I should've spoken up again or fought him off or something, but . . .'

She was silent for several seconds before continuing.

'It took me at least a couple of days to realise what had happened was rape. Like, it's so obvious in retrospect, but at the time, I think . . . I dunno, I guess maybe my subconscious was trying to spare me the trauma or something. I dunno – I'm not a psychologist.'

'It's not uncommon,' said Anna quietly.

She found herself thinking back, unavoidably, to her own rape, under remarkably similar circumstances, by a university student when she was sixteen. It was his indifference that had stuck with her the most about that night – the sense that, in his eyes, she wasn't a person at all, but rather a hole to be filled. She doubted he'd ever given what he'd done a second thought. To this day, he probably still didn't realise he'd done anything wrong – if he even remembered it at all.

Callie looked at her long and hard. 'You understand. I know you do.'

Anna said nothing. She was left with the uncomfortable feeling that Callie could see right through her – that, right now, she was every bit as exposed as in the pictures of her that were currently doing the rounds on the internet. She took a sip of coffee to avoid having to fill the silence.

Eventually, realising that Anna wasn't going to elaborate any further, Callie continued.

'As soon as I was clear in my mind about what'd happened, I went and complained to the uni. The, um, event took place in halls of residence, so I figured they were my first port of call.'

She gave a wry grimace. 'Big mistake. They carried out this whole investigation thing, then passed it on to the Student Disciplinary Committee. Whole thing took nearly twelve months, during which I missed a bunch of my classes on account of stress and anxiety. I ended up having to delay graduating by a year. Meanwhile, during all this, he's free to continue attending his classes like nothing's happened. Innocent until proven guilty, right?'

Anna gave a small nod of understanding. 'Did you ever consider going to the police?'

'Early on, I thought about it, but the disciplinary people talked me out of it. Told me it would be traumatic and that there was an extremely low likelihood of a charge. Plus, they claimed it'd only hold up the uni's own investigation.' She sniffed disdainfully. 'Basically, they were just covering their arses.

'So I put my trust in them instead of the police. Only, after a year's faffing around, they called me up and told me they were dismissing my case due to lack of evidence.'

'Fucking hell,' said Anna, though she'd have been lying if she claimed to be particularly surprised.

Callie gave a dry smile. 'Those were more or less the first words out of *my* mouth too. 'Course,' she went on, 'I asked to file an appeal, but that's when they hit me with the *real* kicker. Apparently, the right of appeal is only open to the accused, not the complainant.'

This time, Anna just stared at her in open-mouthed disbelief.

'So I was out of options. Only thing I could do was try to put it behind me and get on with my life.' Callie snorted. 'I should've been so lucky. A couple of days later, nudes of me got emailed to the entire uni – from *my* email account.'

Anna, who'd been in the process of raising her cup to her lips, froze instantly. Slowly, she returned it to the saucer.

Callie gave a grim smile. 'Thought that might strike a chord. At first, they accused me of doing it deliberately – some mad stunt to get back at them for their handling of the case. But eventually they admitted some unknown user had gained access to my account. Never traced the culprit, of course, but I knew it was him.

'The pics were on my phone,' she explained. 'When I . . . after he'd finished, y'know, doing me, I found it lying on the bed. I always figured he must've got into it while I was out for the count and transferred them to his own device.

'Afterwards, I did some asking around, and I found out a bunch of other girls had had bad experiences with him as well. They said he was always dead creepy; that he didn't understand the meaning of the word "no". Then I found out from a guy friend of mine that he was pretty notorious among the male students too. That he'd bragged about having a "rape list" of girls at the uni he wanted to do.'

Anna suppressed a shudder.

'He ended up dropping out in his final year,' said Callie. 'Told everyone I'd ruined his life with my "false rape accusations".' She laughed humourlessly. '*Me* ruin *his* life. But it became his thing for a while: going around, telling anyone who'd listen that all women were conniving harridans out to destroy men with their lies. According to what I heard, he genuinely saw himself as some sort of moral crusader out to shine a light on this great wrong being perpetrated against mankind. Then, by all accounts, he simply disappeared off the map.'

There were quite a few of them out there, Anna thought. Men who were convinced that they really *were* under grave threat from an army of vindictive women and that any attempts to hold them accountable for their own bad behaviour were merely lies dreamed up to crush them under the boot of the wicked, all-powerful gynocracy. Because *they* couldn't possibly have done anything wrong – oh, no.

'Another fun fact I found out afterwards,' Callie added: 'that particular uni has the highest number of sexual violence reports in the whole of Scotland.'

'This university,' said Anna, 'which one is it?'

Callie told her its name. One of the most prestigious in the country, it frequently featured in rankings of the top ten universities in Europe.

Anna nodded soberly. 'I thought so. I've heard similar stories.'

'They can't publicly acknowledge it,' said Callie, 'because that would mean an end to their precious reputation as an international centre of excellence. So instead, they treat it as this embarrassment to be brushed under the rug. Upper management sets the tone and the rest follow their lead. They're all complicit.'

She took a long, shuddering breath. 'Thing is, I know my story's not unique. And I know it's not the only uni whose procedures for handling complaints aren't fit for purpose. Honestly, if one of my students came to me to say they'd been raped and asked me if they should take it to the official complaints system, I'm not sure I could, in good conscience, say yes. Not after what I went through.'

On more than one occasion, Anna had pondered what she would do if she ever ended up in that situation herself, and each time had reached the same conclusion as Callie. Of course, you were supposed to encourage women to speak up; to 'not let them get away with it'. But she herself had never reported what had happened to her at sixteen, and she knew only too well the typical experience of the justice system for women who did.

They sat in silence for a couple of minutes, sipping their respective drinks with little enthusiasm, each lost in their own thoughts. At length, Callie set down her cup and lifted her head to face Anna once again.

'I want to be clear about one thing. I'm not interested in telling any of this to the police. I've kept this to myself for the last five years. I don't normally talk about it to *anyone*. So if you're going to ask me to go on the record, then I'm sorry, but no. I can't put myself through all that again.'

'That's OK,' said Anna softly. 'I wouldn't ask that of you.'

Callie gave a small, grateful smile. 'I just hope some of what I've told you will help in some way – even if it's just knowing you're not the only woman who's been through this. But it's not *just* that. See, I think there's a decent chance the person who did this to me is the same one who leaked those pictures of *you*. The moment I heard your story, the first thought that entered my mind was, "He's done it again."

'A couple of years ago, he tried, unsuccessfully, to get onto the Computing Science MSc at Abertay. I know, from the grapevine, that he's applied to other unis. You should try to find out if he ever got onto the programme at Glasgow. If he did . . . well, I know it doesn't *prove* anything, but still – it'd be pretty big coincidence, right?'

'Right,' Anna agreed. She knew it would merely be one more coincidence on top of a pile that had been steadily accumulating over the last several weeks, and that her efforts to persuade Vasilico to act on them had had limited success to date. Still, surely there had to come a point when the pile got so high that it became impossible to ignore.

'Is there anything more you can tell me about him?' she asked. 'Anything that could help narrow it down. A physical description, maybe?'

Callie grimaced. 'Honestly, I'm not sure I can. This probably isn't going to come as a shock, but, since it happened, I've done pretty much all I can to forget everything about him. But I remember him being a pretty skinny little thing. Like, I'm not sure he'd have had the strength to hold me down if I hadn't been roofied.'

Anna thought back to the descriptions several of The Reckoning's victims had given of a slight but muscular assailant. 'Compact' was the word Narinder had used. Was it possible he'd bulked up in the intervening years?

'What about his name?'

For a moment, Callie hesitated, almost as if, like summoning Cthulu, saying it out loud would invite dire repercussions. Then, having reached a decision, she leant across the table towards Anna and met her eyes.

'James,' she said in a low voice. 'James Venable.'

The drive back to Glasgow took place in near-total silence. This time, Zoe took the wheel and, seemingly sensing that Anna was in no mood for conversation, refrained from probing her about her conversation with Callie. Anna sat curled up in the passenger seat, her forehead pressed against the window, gazing listlessly at the barren fields passing by in the fading light.

Katharine Barnard. Grace Dunphy. Callie Benson. All of these women had, to one extent or another, been irrevocably broken by their experiences at the hands of the men who sought to subjugate them, and had retreated behind the cloak of anonymity, shutting off a part of themselves as they attempted to insulate themselves from the horrors they'd endured.

The reason men like these kept winning was that, time and time again, women decided it simply wasn't worth standing up for themselves. Better to slip away into the shadows and lead a life half-lived in the hope that they'd be left alone.

And she resolved, then and there, that these men were not going to do the same to her. No fucking way.

PART FIVE

THE TURNING TIDE

39

Excerpt from a private chat between El Duce and GodsGift2Women.

El Duce: What the fuck do you mean you don't know where they went?
El Duce: Were you or were you not told to keep an eye on them??

GodsGift2Women: And if I had wheels I wouldve. Not my fault they took the car
GodsGift2Women: What was I suppose to do follow them on foot?

El Duce: Yeah yeah, alright smartarse.

GodsGift2Women: Hard enough keeping the place under survailence with the pigs camped outside 24/7

El Duce: Poor you. Life's so hard.

GodsGift2Women: Fucks she playing at any way?
GodsGift2Women: Ud think she had enough on her plate without taking time out for a day trip

El Duce: Sod's law her leaving her phone switched off.

El Duce: Actually, I wonder if we might have overplayed our hand.

El Duce: The audio, the photos, the escort site, the flatscreen telly orders etc. Perhaps she's gotten wise.

GodsGift2Women: Nah she's a typical broad totally clueless about tech

El Duce: Well if she HAS wised up, it's on you.

El Duce: That shit with the Twitter account, the porn site, the escort service? All your handiwork.

GodsGift2Women: Half of that was ur idea dickflap

GodsGift2Women: And the biz w the audio was that cockless incel faggots handy work

GodsGift2Women: Just the other day u were congratulating us on a job well done

GodsGift2Women: Any way Im just the dogs body u made that perfectly clear

GodsGift2Women: Not gona pin any of this shite on me

One minute passes.

GodsGift2Women: U there
GodsGift2Women: ??

El Duce closes the channel.

40

Sunday 17 November

When Anna had got home on Saturday evening, her first port of call had been to the Kelvingrove University staff portal to check whether a James Venable appeared on any of the class lists. It was at this point that she'd discovered that access to her account – including her email, the library catalogue and class lists – had been unceremoniously withdrawn. Clearly, her employers were determined that the terms of her suspension should include her ability to even do basic admin.

Reluctant though she was to rope anyone else into what she was doing, thereby opening them up to the possibility of disciplinary action themselves, she'd ultimately been forced to accept that she wasn't going to get anywhere on her own and, relenting, had rung Farah. As a mere TA, Farah's access to the portal was heavily restricted, and class lists were one of the features that were out of bounds. However, she'd agreed to ask a lecturer colleague who owed her a favour to take a look for her on Monday. Until then, all Anna could do was wait.

In the meantime, she spent much of Sunday morning cancelling her various credit and debit cards – of which she turned out to own far more than she'd ever realised, let alone had any use for – and contacting various shops to ensure that the multiple extravagant orders she'd received confirmation messages for had been cancelled. Then, in the afternoon, she rang Mandy to find out how Jack was doing. She'd been calling daily since Thursday, each time dreading being told that Jack had either spent the last twenty-four hours bawling his eyes out or smashing plates and drawing on the walls as an act of protest against his present circumstances. But so far, and to her unending relief, it sounded as if he was neither homesick nor making trouble for his host.

'Och, he's grand, so he is,' said Mandy. 'Him and Rubes've been playin' dress-up. Tell ye, he wears my heels better'n *I* do.'

But when Anna asked her to put Jack on, he once again refused to come to the phone, leaving an apologetic Mandy to relay to her that he was 'still a wee bit sore 'bout bein' sent away.' Anna rang off, consumed by renewed feelings of guilt and shame that refused to subside, no matter how many times she told herself she'd done the right thing.

Later, she got a call from a decidedly tetchy Vasilico, demanding to know where she'd driven off to on Saturday without informing him.

'Out,' was her monosyllabic response.

'Out?' Vasilico echoed, incredulous. 'That's all you've got to say? Just out? Where? Why?'

'Because I fancied a change of scenery, all right?' said Anna, deliberately responding to the second question rather than the first. 'I don't know if you're aware of this, but it's not much fun being stuck at home under virtual house arrest while someone's busy pulling your life to pieces.'

Until she had confirmation that Venable was studying at the university, she'd decided against saying anything to Vasilico about her conversation with Callie Benson. She hadn't forgotten his reluctance to even *consider* interviewing Leopold until he had solid grounds to suspect his involvement, and the case against Venable was even more tenuous than that – for now, at any rate. While she suspected everything that had happened since Thursday would probably make him more amenable toward bending the rules on her behalf than he had been previously, she was determined to investigate the matter as thoroughly as possible herself first – if for no other reason than to avoid the embarrassment of once again being seen to have jumped the gun if it all turned out to be a big, fat nothing.

'Well, in future, I'd prefer if you keep me abreast of your movements,' said Vasilico irritably. 'The people we're up against here have seriously assaulted eight women already.'

'I'll do my best to remember that,' Anna snapped. *You patronising knobhead,* she might well have added.

'Another thing: DS Kirk and myself paid a visit to Cameron Mitchell at his parents' digs out in Barnhill yesterday. Spoke to him at some length. He denies having anything to do with either the leaked audio or the photos, *or* the attacks on female students.'

'And you believed him?'

'He didn't strike me as an especially skilled liar. He also claims never to have *heard* of The Reckoning, though he did profess to being a staunch admirer of Professor Leopold and his teachings. Told me he was thinking of dropping out of Criminology and switching to Social Anthropology next semester.'

'Oh yeah? Well, they're welcome to him.'

'He also claimed you hit him.'

'Technically, it was a slap,' muttered Anna. For some reason, the distinction struck her as important.

'Oh, for Christ's sake,' Vasilico sighed. He seemed to count to five before speaking again. 'You know I went to bat for you in there? Accused him of making shit up to deflect from the trouble he was in? How does that make *me* look?'

'So . . . what?' Anna retorted, unrepentant. 'You're going to charge me with assault?'

Vasilico laughed humourlessly. 'I doubt very much that it would be in the public interest to pursue a conviction. Just do me a favour: if you take it on yourself to wallop any of your other students, don't leave it for me to find out from *them*, OK?'

Anna put down the phone, a part of her wondering why she'd ever allowed herself to fuck him.

Monday's post brought with it two deliveries for Anna, neither of which she was particularly overjoyed to receive. The first, a bouquet of flowers from her colleagues at the university, at least fell into the 'kindly gesture' category, though Anna privately found it more impractical than touching. She'd never seen the point of flowers. They required constant care – a delicate balance of just the right amount of hydration and sunlight – and invariably ended up dying on her anyway. Still, to show willing, she put them in a vase and plonked it on the kitchen table. Hopefully, by placing them somewhere where they were likely to get in the way, either she or Zoe would be compelled to check their water once in a blue moon.

The second item was the promised letter from the university stating the terms of her suspension and setting a date and time of Thursday 28 November at 10.30 a.m. for her disciplinary hearing. It reminded her that she was entitled to be accompanied by either a trade union representative or a colleague, and once again stressed that the possible penalties, should the hearing find against her, included her dismissal.

To occupy herself while she waited for word from Farah, she loaded up the @AnnaScavoliniGlasgow Twitter account on her iPad to see what it was up to. It was still merrily tweeting away, interspersing links to the pictures of her with reposts of its diatribes against the university and its staff, though the former now carried a prominent disclaimer warning that the site in question featured explicit content. She was of two minds as to whether this made the situation better or worse. A part of her suspected it would just make those with prurient tastes even more likely to click it.

'So I just had a thought.'

Glancing up from her iPad, Anna turned to face Zoe, who was curled up at the other end of the sofa with her phone.

'Hmm?'

'That site that posted they pics of you. It's like some kind of a message board, right?'

'I guess,' Anna shrugged, wondering where this was going.

'So here's what I'm thinking: what if we have a nosey around, see what else the account's been posting on there? Might find some clues tae who he is.'

'Knock yourself out.'

She didn't mean to sound uncharitable, but the thought of wading through that site and being bombarded by pictures of tens of thousands of women, unaware that their private images were being shared for the sexual gratification of strangers, made her stomach churn.

But if Zoe was in any way offended by Anna's tone, she didn't let it show. She began tapping on her phone, brows furrowed in concentration, the tilt of her neck giving her a pronounced double chin.

A few seconds later, she wrinkled her nose. 'Carnal College. Classy.'

She tapped some more, scrolled a bit, then lifted her head and looked across at Anna.

'I know it prob'ly doesnae make it better, but ye look hot as fuck in they pictures.'

Anna gazed back at her and saw that, far from attempting to bring some levity to the situation, Zoe meant this as a sincere compliment. And, as hard as it might be to explain why, Anna found it genuinely touching.

She gave a watery smile. 'Actually, it does make it better. Thanks, pal.'

Zoe returned her attention to her phone, continuing to scroll, pinch and tap, lost in her task. Anna, meanwhile, attempted to distract herself by reading the news on her iPad. A high-ranking member of the Royal Family, notorious for his long-standing friendship with a billionaire paedophile, was denying accusations of having had sex with a trafficked teenager, while, on the other side of the world, violence between protesters and police was escalating in Hong Kong. She knew, in an abstract sense, that this stuff mattered, but, try as she might, she couldn't bring herself to care about any of it.

After ten minutes, Zoe lowered her phone and piped up again.

'OK, I think I'm getting the hang of this. The way the site works, it's sorta like a credit system. Every pic costs a certain number of points. Ye get points either by buying 'em or by getting likes on pics ye've uploaded yersel.'

'If you have to pay to see pictures, how come I could see the ones of me?' said Anna.

'I was *getting* tae that,' said Zoe. Her tone was one of amusement, but she was clearly irked at having had her flow interrupted. 'So not every pic's behind the paywall. Some of 'em are public – y'know, tae reel in prospective buyers. Yours've been put up in the freebie category.'

'To ensure they'd be seen by as many people as possible,' said Anna glumly. 'Got it.'

'Right. The guy who put 'em on the site goes by the username of Zambolo93. Most of what he posts is candids of lassies out on the razz – y'know, upskirts 'n' the like. They've no had many likes. But he does post a helluva lot of comments on other people's pics – the usual pervy shite. Ye can prob'ly imagine.'

Anna could, only too well.

'I reckon that means he must be paying a pretty penny for the privilege,' said Zoe. She gave a wry grimace. 'Wouldnae like tae see *his* credit card bill.'

'Right,' said Anna, 'but I don't see how this actually *helps* us. I mean, presumably the site doesn't publish its users' actual *names*.' Once again, she didn't mean to sound ungrateful, but she wasn't really feeling the notion that any of this counted as a breakthrough.

'Aye,' said Zoe, a tad defensively. 'Don't think many perverts'd be signing up tae Carnal College if it meant their details going on a public roster. But here's the thing. That username, Zambo1093. Well, mibby we can figure something out tae that. I mean, "93" might be his birth year, right?'

'Could be,' Anna acknowledged.

'So we could be looking for some'dy in his mid-twenties, thereabouts. And if this bloke's as much of a horn-dog as he seems tae be, I'd be willing tae lay my last Malteser on him being active on other wank sites. And ye know how it goes: the mair liberally ye sow yer oats . . .'

'. . . the greater the risk of leaving a trail of jizz leading back to you?' Anna suggested, following the metaphor to its logical conclusion.

Zoe beamed. 'Couldnae've put it better masel, doll.' She picked up her phone again. 'Right, then – back tae the grindstone.'

41

It was nearly half an hour later when Zoe finally announced, 'Think I've found something.'

Anna lifted her head. She watched as Zoe continued to tap on her phone. Slowly, a grin spread across her face.

'Oh my God. Ca-*ringe!*'

'What is it?' Anna demanded. 'Let me see.'

She got to her feet and headed over to behind Zoe's end of the sofa, leaning over her shoulder to look at her phone.

On the screen was the homepage of a YouTube channel going by the name 'ZAMBO'S WORLD'. On the banner at the top of the page, surrounding the large, all-caps logo, was a poorly cut out collage of glamour models in skimpy attire, pouting for the camera with their swollen lips. The statistics below the banner showed that it was home to a grand total of 147 videos and 36 subscribers.

Zoe craned her head to look up at Anna expectantly. 'Whatcha reckon? Zambo? Zambolo? Coincydink, or . . . ?'

'Not exactly going to hold up in a court of law, is it?'

'I know, but . . .'

She tapped the 'Videos' tab. The screen changed to show a list of thumbnails and titles. Most of the former consisted of candid photos of young women in short skirts. As far as the latter were concerned, 'BURDZ IN DA WILD', 'Glasgow HOT Night Life' and 'City Centre After Dark – TOTAL SCENES!' ably conveyed the overall tone.

Zoe tapped the first one. The screen changed to shaky, handheld footage of a busy street. It was dark, and the pavements were occupied almost exclusively by people in their late teens or early twenties, all enjoying a night of merriment. Several were clearly the worse for wear, sitting on the kerb or staggering unsteadily in one direction or another, leaning on their equally legless friends for support. There was a roughly even mix of male and female revellers, but the camera focused exclusively on the latter as its owner weaved through the crowds, the low angle ensuring that the viewer was treated to a front row view of their bare legs and miniskirts.

'Oh, for God's sake,' muttered Anna, grimacing in disgust.

'I know,' said Zoe. 'Restraining order waiting tae happen, right?'

'That's Sauchiehall Street, isn't it?'

'Think so.'

They continued to watch. The video continued for several more minutes, offering up more of the same content. The *pièce de résistance* came near the end, when the footage slowed down to a crawl and advanced, one frame at a time, to show the upskirt view of one particularly inebriated girl, who had either mislaid her underwear at some point during the night's festivities or else hadn't bothered to wear any in the first place, her shaven vulva on full display for several seconds.

At last, the video ended. Zoe turned to look at Anna. 'I mean,' she said, 'it's of a piece wi the stuff Zambolo93's posted on Carnal College.'

'Mm,' said Anna.

It was neither an 'mm' of scepticism nor an 'mm' of agreement – more of an 'mm, let's keep digging'.

Zoe, who was evidently thinking along similar lines, continued to scroll through the list of videos. After a few screens' worth of thumbnails, she came to one that was different from the rest. The thumbnail was a picture of an overweight South Asian man in a red baseball cap and shell suit, posing in an exaggerated shrug with a cheesy grin on his pudgy features. The title was 'ZAMBO'S PICK UP TIP'S'.

'Let's see if we can learn a thing or two fae lover-boy,' said Zoe, and tapped the thumbnail.

The screen cut to a shot of the whitewashed wall of what appeared to be a residential property, canted at a slight angle. Off-screen, the operator fumbled with the camera, adjusting its position, which only served to make the matter worse. Seemingly satisfied, however, he stepped into frame and walked over to the wall before turning to face the camera. It was the man from the thumbnail. He was dressed from head to foot in Kappa, giving him the appearance of an unusually large teenager, even though he was clearly in his mid-twenties.

'Snazzy dresser,' chuckled Zoe.

The man clapped his hands together and addressed the camera.

'Awright, boys! It's yer main man Zambo here.'

He spoke in a broad Glaswegian accent, his words vying with the crackle of the wind whipping at the camera's built-in microphone.

'So a lot of yese have been saying tae me, "Zambo, howzit ye manage tae score with so many chicks?" Well, I'm here tae tell yese that it isnae rocket science. I mean, it is *a science, but yese don't need a PhD in babe-ology tae up yer game.'*

Zoe looked up at Anna. Her face, contorted into a grimace of pure cringe, said it all.

'So buckle in, boys, cos I'm gonnae give yese all a crash course in the art of the score. By the time yese're done here, you too will have no difficulty in negotiating the sexual marketplace and finding a high quality woman.'

Zoe involuntarily let out an amused snort.

Zambo started to count off on his fingers. *'Number one: all women are hypergamous. If ye havnae heard that word before, first of all, where've ye been? But basically what it means is, all burds are looking tae marry up. They'll no look at ye twice if they think ye're lower than them in the social order. So if ye wannae land one with high sexual market value, ye've gottae look the part. That means dressing sharp, having good hair, shaving off that bum-fluff. If ye can afford it, ye wannae get some bling like yer man Zambo here.'* He held up his arm, showing off an expensive-looking gold watch.

'Reckon he knows how tae tell time wi that?' said Zoe.

'Which leads me intae point number two: it's all about the upsell. For females, men are just a resource tae be exploited.'

Zoe snorted. 'And women *aren't* tae they creeps?'

'It all comes down tae biology. Historically, men offered resources tae women – like food, shelter, protection fae rival tribes, et cetera. And over time, women evolved tae seek that out. So see if ye're on the dole or working back shifts at Maccy D's? She disnae need tae know that. 'Member the three

"I's: imbellish, imbiggen, improvise! But see if ye're gonnae do that, for the love of God, do yer homework first. Don't just say, "I work in medicine," then when she says, "Oh, really? What's that like?", just stand there looking glaikit. Ye need tae know at least something 'bout what ye're selling – cos otherwise, who's gonnae buy it?'

Zoe, who'd been fighting hard not to laugh for some time now, let out a massive, snorting guffaw. 'Oh. My. God. This guy's a *chode*! An absolute *chode*!'

Anna wasn't minded to disagree with this assessment. She watched, with a mixture of disgust and amused disbelief, as Zambo continued his lecture.

'Number . . . now, where were we? Number four, I think. Point number four: women are emotional, not logical. Which means ye've gottae use reverse psychology on them. Case in point: nice never works. Ever hear the phrase "Treat 'em mean, keep 'em keen"? That's how ye gottae handle 'em. So what yese wannae do is employ this technique called "negging". . .'

Anna, who'd watched in silence so far, could keep quiet no longer. 'Just so we're clear,' she said, her voice rising in disbelief, 'we reckon *this* is the guy who's ruined my life? *Him?*'

'I know. What is it wi these bawheids overcomplicating everything? Dunno if ye've noticed, but most women urny that picky.'

'D'you know, I'm actually *offended*? I always knew these people didn't remotely understand women, but I didn't realise they were *this* fucking imbecilic.'

'Well, Anna,' replied Zoe, with mock severity, 'in that case, it's obvious you're just not a high quality woman. I mean, what lassie wi blood pumping in her veins could possibly resist *that*?'

She gestured to the screen, where Zambo, still gesticulating with one hand as he continued to address the camera, casually used the other to reach inside his tracksuit bottoms to adjust himself.

''Least now we know what he looks like,' said Zoe. 'And it's pretty obvious he's a Weegie.'

'Mm,' said Anna noncommittally. 'Safe to say he's not the brains of the operation, though.'

'Aye. It's a start, though, right?'

Anna belatedly remembered her manners. 'It's *absolutely* a start.' She patted Zoe on the shoulder. 'Nice one, Zo. Unlike me, you, clearly, are a high quality woman.'

Zoe grinned – to Anna's mind, both amused and genuinely pleased by the compliment.

They watched a few more videos together. Zambo's on-camera appearances turned out to be fairly sporadic. For the most part, he preferred to film his subjects from a first-person perspective, sometimes giving live commentary on them, like some sort of perverted ornithologist out studying the local wildlife. In some, he directly approached and addressed the women he was videoing, usually to deliver pickup lines of the most clichéd variety. Many were merely cringe-inducing, the women in question invariably giving him short shrift. Some, however, were far more unsettling.

In one, titled 'AN INTIMATE ENCOUNTER', taken on a crowded train, the passengers packed together like sardines, he could be seen rubbing himself up against the hindquarters of the woman in front of him, who was either none the wiser or – perhaps more likely – ignoring him on the grounds that responding in any way would only make the situation worse.

In another, 'PLAYING HARD 2 GET', shot late at night in an otherwise deserted part of the city, he approached and sat down next to a painfully young-looking woman waiting alone at a bus stop, and, after surreptitiously filming her in silence for a couple of minutes, during which she tried her best to pretend not to have noticed him, began to speak to her.

'Awright there? How ya doin'?'

The girl glanced at him briefly, gave a flicker of a smile, then instantly looked away again. Anna immediately recognised that smile as the universal reaction of a woman who was receiving attention she didn't want, but dare not risk doing anything to anger the person giving it to her.

'Been waiting here long?'

She shrugged. Shook her head.

''Bouts ye headed?'

She shrugged again, eyes steadfastly staring ahead.

'Just home.'

'Home, aye? Whereabouts ye stay?'

No response. She folded her arms more tightly about herself.

'D'ye not wannae talk tae me?'

Another slight, flickering smile from her – one which barely masked the anxiety burning inside her.

'What's yer name?'

'Sophie.'

It seemed to Anna that it slipped out involuntarily . . . or perhaps it was more that she was desperately trying to convince herself that, if she gave him *something*, he'd leave her alone.

'Sophie, aye? That's a nice name. Pleasure to meet ye, Sophie.'

He extended his hand towards her. She glanced in his direction, gave it the briefest of shakes, then continued to hug her arms about herself.

'Ye got a boyfriend, Sophie?'

Sophie made a noncommittal sound.

'That a yes or a no?'

No response. She reached into her handbag for her phone.

'Gonnae say that's a no, then. I'm pure shocked, so I am. Lovely-looking lassie like you.'

Continuing to do her best to ignore him, Sophie tapped her phone into life and began to text.

'Who's that ye're messaging?'

'My pal,' she said, still not looking at him. 'She's meeting me here.'

'That right, is it?'

From his amused tone, it was clear he didn't believe her.

'Uh-huh. She'll be here any minute.'

Her thumbs continued to dance on the screen. Anna couldn't tell whether she was genuinely texting someone or just tapping randomly in the hope that it would persuade him to leave her alone.

'So how long've ye been single for, then?'

No response.

'Would ye like me tae be yer boyfriend?'

Sophie finished texting and got abruptly to her feet.

'Y'know,' she said, her voice high with fear, 'I think I'll go and meet her, actually.'

'Hey, hey, what's brought this on? Where ye goin'?'

But Sophie was already moving off, feet pounding the pavement, determined to get away from him as quickly as possible.

'*To meet my friend,*' she muttered, not looking back.

The view on screen lurched as Zambo got to his feet.

'*Well, hold up. I'll walk with ye. Lotsa weirdos about this time of the night. Ye never know who ye might run intae.*'

He set off in pursuit, the camera vibrating violently as he hurried after her. Sophie quickened her pace.

'*Aw, c'mon!*' he called. '*Come back and chat! What's wrong? Was it the boyfriend question? I WAS ONLY PAYIN' YE A COMPLIMENT!*'

Sophie was practically running now, her handbag bouncing against her hip as she struggled to increase the distance between them.

The video cut to what appeared to be a few minutes later. Sophie was considerably further up the street now, still maintaining her desperate half-walk, half-run. Zambo continued after her at a far more sedate pace, like a beast of prey playing with its next meal.

The footage continued for another minute or so. Then, almost as if he'd grown bored of the chase, Zambo came to a halt. He continued to film Sophie from a distance for a few more seconds. Then, mercifully, the video ended.

A heavy silence hung over the living room.

'I feel sick,' said Anna.

Zoe said nothing. She merely lowered her phone and let her breath out in a long sigh through her nostrils.

They sat together in unhappy silence, their earlier amusement long forgotten. Men like this 'Zambo' might be pathetic, but they were also dangerous, and that video had served as a stark reminder of the wafer-thin line that existed between behaviour that was merely tasteless or cringy and that which tipped over into something that was outright terrifying.

42

By the early afternoon, they'd spent a good couple of hours watching videos on Zambo's YouTube channel, hoping to come across further clues as to his identity or whereabouts. So far, they'd been unsuccessful on both counts, though, based on the architecture that appeared in his sporadic direct addresses, Anna reckoned he might live somewhere on the Southside.

They were still hard at it when the doorbell rang. Zoe got up to answer it, and, moments later, Anna heard her giving a delighted little squeal from the hallway. Shortly thereafter, she appeared in the living room with Sal in tow. Sal's hair colour had changed to lime green since Anna had last seen her. She had one arm looped through Zoe's, while, in her free hand, she held a carrier bag branded with the logo of one of the local delis.

'Figured you'd be going a bit stir crazy cooped up in here,' she said. 'So I brought lunchie munchies.'

In stark contrast to the flowers, Anna was decidedly grateful for this gesture – doubly so given that Sal, who barely knew her, had no real reason to go out of her way like this for her.

They were all sitting round the table, tucking into the impressive spread Sal had produced from her bag, when the house phone began to ring in the hallway. Leaving Zoe and Sal giggling as they fed each other bits of pastrami, Anna headed out to answer it. It was Farah, calling to say she hadn't had a chance to talk to her colleague yet, but that she'd be seeing him later and would press him on the matter of the student lists. She offered to drop by on her way home to fill Anna in on the outcome.

'Sure you want to risk consorting with a *persona non grata*?' Anna joked. 'What would the powers that be have to say about that?'

She was in a more positive frame of mind because she had a belly full of sourdough bread and assorted deli meats. In times of great stress, life's small pleasures often had a disproportionate effect on lifting your mood.

'Fuck them,' said Farah emphatically, her accent becoming stronger than usual, as it invariably did when she was angry. 'They can try to stop me. Ah!' She gave an exclamation as she remembered something. 'While I have you, perhaps you can look up something for me? I've emailed all your students you had one-to-ones with in the next two weeks to say they've been postponed, but I haven't yet had a response from Mila Zelenska.'

'She never checks her university email,' said Anna, who'd had her share of trouble in the past attempting to establish contact with the elusive PhD student.

'Do you have an alternative address I can try?'

'I do. It's on my mobile. Two secs.'

Setting down the house phone, Anna went up to her office and retrieved her mobile. She switched it on and headed back downstairs, glancing at the screen as she went. About a hundred missed call alerts scrolled past in rapid succession, followed by a low battery warning. Hoping it would at least last long enough for her to look up Mila's contact details and relay them to Farah, she quickened her pace.

No such luck. Even as she lifted the receiver again, the screen went blank. Her attempts to coax any further life out of it proved futile.

'Sorry, Farah,' she said, still thumbing the power button to no avail. 'My useless phone's given up the ghost. Try asking at the secretaries' office. They should have her details on file.'

She rang off and stomped back through to the kitchen, much of her earlier positive mood gone. Just as life's small pleasures had the power to lift one's spirits, all it took was an equally small irritant to bring them crashing back down to earth. She tossed the dead phone on the table and slumped into her chair.

'Remind me to never buy one of those again.'

Sal reached for it and examined it. 'Ooh, that's a snazzy bit of kit. What's the matter with it?'

'Absolutely nothing,' said Anna irritably, 'other than that the battery lasts about as long as my three-year-old's attention span.'

Sal frowned, still examining the phone. 'That's not right. These things are supposed to last for donkey's years. How long've you had it?'

'About six months,' said Anna, failing to see why this mattered or why they were even still talking about it.

Sal continued to turn it this way and that. 'And when'd it start acting up?'

Anna forced herself to think. 'Couple of months ago, I think. Zo, when did I start moaning to you about it?'

'Aye, 'bout two months sounds right,' Zoe confirmed. 'Seriously,' she said to Sal, 'ye should hear her when she gets going properly. 'S all "fuck" this and "piece o' shit" that.'

'Uh-huh.' Sal held down the power button, trying to get it to boot up. 'And was this like a gradual thing, or did it come on *suddenly*?'

Again, Anna delved the recesses of her memory. 'It was pretty sudden. One day it was fine. The next, it was like this. Why? D'you think it got damaged or something?'

Sal glanced at Zoe. A look passed between them that Anna, feeling infuriatingly slow on the uptake, couldn't read.

Sal turned to Anna again. 'I *think*,' she said carefully, 'maybe we should take this to my sister.'

43

The flat Sal shared with her older sister, Jen, overlooked Dowanhill Park, a mere ten-minute walk from Clarence Drive. The three of them had been greeted, upon their arrival, by Jen's twin three-year-olds, Ewan and Maisie, who both flung themselves on Zoe, tackling her to the floor and crawling all over her. Watching Zoe rolling around, shrieking and pretending to resist as they tried to tickle her, Anna couldn't help but smile, her heart warmed by this display of pure, uninhibited joy.

The two Brinkley sisters could not have looked more different. Where Sal was short, pale and slightly dumpy, Jen was tall, tanned and slender. Where Sal's hair changed from one outrageous primary hue to another as frequently as the weather, Jen's was a natural-looking dark brown, though it *was* shaved on one side, with a long, floppy fringe combed down over the other. She also had a philtrum piercing and wore a leather jacket with big pointy studs even when she was indoors. Clearly, a desire to buck conventional fashion trends ran in the family.

Having introduced Anna and Jen to one another, Sal took Jen aside and explained the situation to her – too quietly for Anna, who still felt she had next to no idea what was going on, to hear. In short order, Jen had relieved Anna of her phone and disappeared with it into what she called 'the Dungeon of Pain' – in reality, the home office from which she did her top secret IT security work. Anna, left on the living room sofa like a patient waiting for the doctor to come out with her test results, watched as Zoe continued to play with the twins, who clearly regarded her as part of the family.

'She's dead good with the hell spawn,' said Sal, joining her on the sofa. 'I used to be favourite auntie, but she's totally stolen my thunder.' She spoke cheerfully and without rancour.

Anna nodded but said nothing. She was struck by the realisation that Zoe, who spent a considerable chunk of her time here these days, had a whole other life about which she knew next to nothing. Perhaps unavoidably, she also found herself thinking about her *own* child, banished from her side for his own safety because she'd once again brought trouble to their door. When would it be safe for him to come home? Would it *ever* be truly safe?

Jen emerged from the Dungeon half an hour later with Anna's phone in her hand, looking grave and preoccupied. Anna found herself automatically rising to her feet, as if bracing for an unwelcome diagnosis. Zoe untangled herself from the twins and got to her feet too.

'Well,' said Jen, 'it took some doing, but I think I've got to the bottom of what's going on.'

'What?' said Anna. 'What *is* going on?' She was sick of being kept in the dark – of people talking in whispers about her problems in a language she barely seemed to comprehend.

'There's a Trojan implanted on your phone,' said Jen, once Sal had taken the twins out to get ice cream. 'A highly sophisticated exploit that infects the device at a firmware level, making it extremely difficult to detect or remove. Basically, it's allowing a third party to access everything on it. That's your apps, your passwords, your docs, your photos – the works.'

'Jesus,' Anna murmured. The technical jargon might have been alien to her, but she understood the gist of what Jen was saying well enough.

'That's not all. The most pernicious part of it – the main reason your battery's been draining so quickly – is that the perps have effectively turned it into a remote listening device. The mic's active 24/7, sending them a live broadcast of whatever it picks up. You know how you get those wackjobs who think the government's using their TV to snoop on everything they say? This thing's doing it for real – only it ain't the government that's listening.'

With sickening clarity, Anna realised it all made perfect sense. The leaking of her photos, the comments on the Twitter account that seemed eerily close to sentiments she'd expressed in private, and – oh God, of *course* – the audio of her and Vasilico having sex . . . The root cause of all of it was this tiny, indispensable device – a device which, like everyone in this day and age, she carried with her at all times and kept permanently switched on.

'I . . . I changed my pin and reset all my passwords the other day,' she stammered. 'We even did a factory reset. Are you saying that wasn't enough?'

Jen shook her head. 'Uh-uh. That might do the trick for your classic buffer overflow exploit or SQL injection, but this is multiple orders of magnitude nastier than one of those.'

'Right,' said Anna, as if she had the first clue what Jen was talking about. 'But how come the police didn't pick up on this? They already had their tech people go through it, and they came up with nothing.'

Jen gave a small, almost sympathetic smile. 'I don't doubt they did their best, what with the time and resources at their disposal. But this thing here is about a gazillion times more sophisticated than what those nine-to-fivers are used to dealing with. Not to toot my own horn, but I fancy there's only a handful of people in the whole country with the wherewithal to ferret out something this spicy.'

Anna shook her head, lost for words. She felt more overwhelmed by what she was hearing with each passing second.

'Right,' Zoe put in, filling the silence on her behalf, 'but, now we know what's going on, shouldnae be too tough tae figure out who's listening in, I'm guessing?'

Jen looked pensive. 'Doubtful.' She turned to Anna. 'I'm not gonna make you go all googly-eyed trying to explain the specifics to you, but take it from someone who knows a thing or two about these things: this whole apparatus is cloaked behind multiple layers of obfuscation. It's gonna be nigh-on impossible to establish, with any certainty, the location of the server it's broadcasting to. And even if we did, we'd *still* have to trace who's listening in at the other end. If they're sophisticated enough to implant a custom rootkit on your device, you can bet your bottom dollar they're not your garden variety amateur hour schmucks who pirate movies off the net without even turning on a VPN.' She clocked Anna's glazed expression. 'Just take my word for it – these charmers've covered their arses.'

'But how did this . . . this *thing* even get on my phone in the first place?'

Jen shrugged. 'Any number of ways. Even the most secure device in the world isn't impenetrable to someone who knows what they're doing. My best guess is you got sent an email with an exploit buried somewhere in it. You opened it, and *kablam!* It set to work in the background, worming its way deep into your phone's tender nether regions. Suffice to say, the people behind this were probably planning it all for months, carefully laying the groundwork before they hit the "detonate" button last week.'

Anna swallowed a mouthful of saliva. The knowledge that The Reckoning had already had her in their crosshairs, long before she'd even heard of *them*, chilled her to the bone.

'So what do we dae now?' asked Zoe, her voice cutting through Anna's thoughts.

Jen looked at Anna. 'That's really up to Anna.'

Anna blinked in surprise. 'Me?'

'It's your phone. You're the one who's directly affected by all this. I'm reasonably confident that, with a wee bit of elbow grease, I can remove the exploit. But there's a fairly obvious disadvantage to doing that – namely, you'd be letting whoever's behind this know you're onto them.'

Anna pondered this. Could she really keep up the pretence of being none the wiser? It would effectively require her to be acting 24/7, and she knew, better than anyone, that lying was far from her forte. But, on the other hand, she could immediately see the advantages to leaving this direct connection to her tormenters open – the ability to feed them false information being top of the list.

'Is there any chance,' she said, 'when you were poking around in there, that you could have inadvertently tipped them off? Um, what I mean,' she added quickly, as Jen's brows knotted into a frown, 'is, given how adept these people seem to be when it comes to . . .' – she searched for the word – '. . . *hacking* or whatever . . . is it possible they already know they've been found out?'

'Well,' said Jen, mock-affronted, 'if you're no happy with the service, madam, you're welcome to shop elsewhere.' She gave a kindly, understanding smile. 'No, you're absolutely right to ask. But I've been around the block more than a coupla times, and believe me, I took every precaution before I dove on in there. I'm as sure as sure can be that they're none the wiser.'

Anna nodded slowly as she once again considered her options. Every path seemed fraught with pitfalls.

Eventually, she reached a decision.

'I think,' she said carefully, 'we should do nothing for the time being. I don't want this . . . this *thing* spying on me for a moment longer . . . but I also don't want to give up what could be a useful weapon to have in my arsenal – and right now, I've got precious few of those.'

'So you're saying . . .'

'I'm saying leave it the way it is, but, for the time being, I'm going to keep my powder dry and not use it. If whoever's behind this has been listening to every word I've said, they'll have heard me going off on one about the battery before now. With any luck, they'll think I've abandoned it for that very reason.' She attempted a laugh. 'It's not as if I've not been tempted before now.'

Jen handed her the phone. 'In that case, you'd best hang onto it for now. If you change your mind and want me to disinfect it, you let me know, any time, day or night. In the meantime, you can have one of my old pay-as-you-go jobbies for essential calls and such.'

Anna managed a strained smile. 'Thanks, Jen. I really appreciate this.'

Jen dismissed her gratitude with a wave. '*De nada*. Any pal of Zoe's, blah-de-blah. I'll go dig out that spare phone for you.'

She turned towards her office.

'There's one other thing,' said Anna.

Jen stopped. Turned to face her.

'The person who posted those pictures of me online – we're fairly certain he's a YouTuber who calls himself Zambo or Zambolo. Beyond that, we have no idea who he is. I don't suppose there's anything you can do to trace him?'

Jen nodded, furrowing her chin. 'Sure. I'm aye up for a challenge. Lemme have the particulars and I'll see what I can rustle up.'

Leaving Jen to her work, Anna and Zoe headed back to Clarence Drive. Anna had left Jen with links to the Twitter account, porn site and YouTube channel. It meant, of course, that yet another person she'd somehow have to find a way to look in the eye in future would be getting a front row view of her private parts. At least Jen didn't seem like the judgemental sort.

Besides, she'd grown so used to the idea of her privacy having been obliterated that she was beginning to think she'd become inured to it. What difference did it ultimately make if the whole world knew about her personal grooming habits or that she had a mole on her left inner thigh? At the end of the day, she was just flesh and blood, same as everyone else.

It was late afternoon and the light was fading by the time they got home. They set about preparing dinner and were just sitting down at the kitchen table when the heavens opened. It had been threatening to rain all day and the sky had been growing progressively more overcast since early afternoon. To Anna, possibly the *least* superstitious person on the planet, it couldn't help but feel like a harbinger – though of what, she had no idea.

A little after 6 p.m., Farah arrived in a state of breathless excitement.

'There *is* a James Venable at the university,' she gabbled, as Anna relieved her of her sodden umbrella in the hallway. 'He's studying part-time for a Masters in Computing Science. He enrolled last year.'

Anna set the umbrella to one side and attempted to help Farah out of her equally drenched coat. 'That's amazing work, Farah. Really well done. There's no doubt about it – you,' she said, 'are a high quality woman.'

Farah grinned, bemused but evidently pleased. 'Oh,' she said. 'Well, thank you. But that's not everything. I have some more information as well.'

She retrieved a damp scrap of paper from her trouser pocket and consulted it.

'A date of birth – 4 April 1992 – and a home address: Flat 0/2, 9 Douglas Street, Laurieston.'

Farah was still towelling her hair dry in front of the fire in the living room when the pay-as-you-go phone Jen had lent to Anna started to ring.

'This is your friendly neighbourhood technological super-genius,' said the voice at the other end of the line. 'It's Jen,' she added, after a pause, 'in case that wasn't obvious. So listen – turns out the delightfully named Carnal College is a somewhat tougher nut to crack than I was hoping. No obvious back door to their user database.'

'Oh,' said Anna, unable to hide her disappointment. 'Well, thanks for trying—'

'Slow down, buttercup! I hadn't finished. I was going to say – luckily, our friend Zambo, a.k.a. Zambolo, is a tad less security-conscious than the lovely guys and gals at Carnal College. So we've got his username, right?'

'Right,' agreed Anna. She glanced at Zoe and Farah, who were both watching her expectantly from the sofa. She put the phone onto speaker for their benefit.

'So next step is to try and log into his account. I put in his username and click "Forgot Password". Up pops a message: "A password reset link has been sent to za * * * * * * *@h * * * * * *. * * *." Z plus A plus seven asterisks is the exact same number of characters as "Zambolo93". Ergo, I surmise that the big dumdum uses the same name for his email addy as he does for his late-night one-handed browsing sessions. And "H, six asterisks, dot, three asterisks" – a thousand to one that's gotta be "Hotmail. com". With me so far?'

'Almost,' said Anna, who was beginning to feel slightly breathless herself in the face of Jen's rapid-fire delivery.

'Next thing I do is head onto the more popular corners of the web. Amazon, Skype, Google, Facebook – y'know, the ones so widely used, odds are everyone's gonna be signed up to at *least* one. And wouldn't ya know it, boy genius here's on a bunch of 'em, all tied to the same email. Takes me a hot minute, but eventually I find one that's a tad less secure than Carnal Knowledge, and, a hop, skip and a jump later, I'm in. And wouldn't ya know it? It's only got his full credit card details on file there, along with the corresponding name and postal address. Got 'em here for ya, if you're ready.'

Heart pounding with anticipation, Anna glanced at Zoe, who whipped out her own phone, ready to take the details down.

'Fire away,' she said.

'He's one Sohail Zamir,' said Jen. She spelled out both names. 'I know – Zambo, Zamir. Creative, huh? The address is 29 Rosedene Crescent, Cardonald G52. I cross-referenced it with the electoral register,' she added, before Anna could voice her doubts. 'It's legit. Safe to say he ain't the sharpest tool in the shed. So whaddaya think? Did your girl come good or did she come good?'

'Jen,' said Anna, with utter sincerity, 'I don't think I have enough superlatives in my vocabulary to do you justice.' She managed to resist the temptation to tell *her* that she was a high quality woman.

'Oh, pshaw. 'S what I do. 'Sides, having seen how these specimens get their kicks, I'm gonna enjoy watching 'em get their balls squeezed good and proper.'

Once she'd thanked Jen profusely once again and – having promised to keep her updated – rung off, Anna turned to Zoe and Farah.

'So what happens now?' asked Zoe.

Anna didn't respond immediately. Things had moved so fast in the space of the last few hours that a part of her would have preferred to catch her breath and take stock rather than rush headlong into anything else. But she was also firmly of the view that this campaign of intimidation and humiliation – not just against her but against *all* the women who'd been targeted by The Reckoning for the crime of daring to stand up for their rights and for common decency – had gone on for long enough. And she'd reached the point where she'd taken things as far as she realistically could with the help of her friends.

It was time to call in the professionals.

44

Vasilico made Anna go through the whole story twice. He kept getting her to backtrack, making her repeat herself or fill in additional details. She held very little back, giving him what amounted to a blow by blow account of everything that had happened since Friday morning, the last time they'd seen each other face to face. For good measure, she also showed him some of the videos of Zamir from his YouTube channel, including the one of him harassing and stalking the young girl at the bus stop.

She could tell Vasilico was far from happy that she'd carried out her own investigation without informing or involving him – though, to his credit, he refrained from treating her to a lecture on the subject. He probably knew her too well by now to imagine it would have any effect. Nor, for that matter, was he in a position to deny that her actions had produced significant results. Uncovering Zamir's identity was a case in point, and she would have been lying if she'd pretended she didn't derive a certain amount of satisfaction from pointing out that Jen Brinkley had managed, in a couple of hours, to accomplish what the police had singularly failed to.

Vasilico stood in the centre of the living room, brows pinched as he mulled over what he'd heard while Anna faced him, arms folded, waiting for his judgement. Out of the corner of her eye, she was aware that Zoe and Farah, too, were watching him expectantly. Kirk, who'd arrived with Vasilico, leant against the mantelpiece, casually examining the state of her chewed-down fingernails, but Anna sensed that she too was eagerly awaiting her boss's verdict.

At length, Vasilico stirred.

'Right. Here's the lie of the land as I see it. As it currently stands, I'm reluctant to move on Venable. It's all still too circumstantial – especially given that Callie Benson is unwilling to go on the record about what happened to her.

'*However*,' he raised a finger as Anna, Zoe and Farah all simultaneously opened their mouths to protest, 'what I *am* going to do is have him watched from dawn to dusk. I want to know where he goes, who he associates with, when he takes a shit and whether he washes his hands afterwards. To tell the truth, I've been giving serious thought to embedding an undercover officer at the university for a while now.'

'That's my cue,' said Kirk, launching herself off the mantelpiece with a grin. She adopted a theatrical whisper. 'I loves me an excuse to play dress-up.'

That could actually work, Anna thought. Kirk looked just about youthful enough to pass for a student – at any rate, one who'd delayed going to university by a couple of years. And it was surprisingly easy to inveigle your way into classes you weren't enrolled in – especially the ones with a sizeable number of students. For the most part, you just turned up to the lecture theatre on time and found a seat. Provided you didn't draw any undue attention to yourself, it was unlikely anyone – lecturer and students alike – would notice there was an extra body present.

'What about Zamir?' she said, a good deal more hopeful now that it sounded as if things were finally starting to move in a productive direction.

'That one's a bit more clear-cut,' said Vasilico. 'I really don't want to know how this ... *accomplice* of yours came by his credit card information, but be that as it may, there's plenty we can pin on him that's actionable – the persistent stalking and harassment of young women, for a start. His face is out there, and there are any number of ways we could have put a name to it.

'So here's what we're going to do. We're going to head over to Cardon-ald, DS Kirk and I, and have a nice, friendly chat with Mr Zamir. Let him know we're aware of what he gets up to in the city centre on a Saturday night. See if the threat of half a dozen sexual harassment charges loosens his tongue. And, if we can get him to cop to knowing Venable ...'

'Right,' said Anna, already moving towards the hallway to collect her coat. 'In that case, I'm coming with you.'

'You most assuredly are *not*,' said Vasilico.

'I bloody well am. This piece of shit robbed me of every last vestige of my privacy. If you're going to take him down, I want to be there to see it happen.'

'Eh, she's got a point, boss,' said Kirk, sidling over. 'Sure it'll not do any harm.'

'Quiet, you,' snapped Vasilico. He turned back to Anna, who glared up at him, refusing to back down.

'Look,' she said, 'the other day, you told me you'd do anything to make it up to me for putting me in harm's way. Well, right now, I'm asking you to do this for me.'

Vasilico continued to meet her gaze. He said nothing, but she sensed, from the almost imperceptible flinch in his eyes, that her words had hit their mark. It was a low blow, she knew, but right now, she didn't care.

He sighed wearily. 'All right. You stay in the car. You say and do nothing. Clear?'

Anna, still meeting his gaze defiantly, jerked her head in a terse nod of acknowledgement, then turned and headed to fetch her coat.

45

Vasilico brought his Porsche to a halt at the kerb on Rosedene Crescent, Anna in the passenger seat next to him. In the rearview mirror, she saw Kirk pulling to a halt behind them in her considerably less ostentatious coupé.

Anna turned and gazed up at the property where, according to his credit card details, Sohail Zamir lived. The houses on the street were all fairly upmarket, and this one – a detached, two-storey affair with a well-tended garden – didn't exactly gel with the image still seared into her mind of a tracksuit-clad twentysomething male offering spurious pickup tips to his handful of followers.

'Lights are on,' said Vasilico, who, like her, was eyeing up the house. 'Looks like we're in business.' He turned to Anna. 'I'll be back shortly. Sit tight.'

He got out of the car and, joined by Kirk, headed up the garden path. Anna watched, waiting with as much patience as she could muster until she saw Vasilico ring the doorbell. Then, springing into action, she quickly unbuckled her seatbelt, got out of the car and strode up the path to join them.

As Anna appeared by his side, Vasilico turned to her with a look of abject fury. She met his gaze brazenly. He opened his mouth, no doubt to order her back to the car, but at that moment, a shadow appeared behind the frosted glass of the door. Vasilico glanced at it, then at Anna, who shrugged and said nothing. Kirk offered no comment, but was clearly expending considerable effort into trying not to smile.

Vasilico sighed and turned to face the door as it opened.

In terms of build and facial features, the man standing in the hallway bore an unmistakable resemblance to the one who appeared in the YouTube videos, but something didn't seem to add up. He looked older, his hairline prematurely receding, and he was dressed in expensive-looking suit trousers and a silk shirt, the top two buttons undone. He looked for all the world like a man unwinding after a gruelling day at the office.

He gazed back at the three of them pleasantly.

'Can I help you?'

'Mr Zamir?' said Vasilico.

'Yes?'

'*Sohail* Zamir?'

'Yes?' he said again, more warily this time. 'What's this about?'

Vasilico produced his police ID. 'DCI Vasilico, Specialist Crime Unit. This is my colleague, DS Kirk.'

He didn't deign to introduce Anna.

'I wonder if we might have a word inside, sir?'

From his strained expression, Zamir was clearly unnerved. Nonetheless, he managed to rearrange his face into an obliging smile.

'Well, yes, of course. But I really don't—'

But Vasilico was already stepping across the threshold. 'Very hospitable of you, sir. Don't mind if we do.'

Kirk headed in after him. Anna followed quickly, shooting another uncertain glance at Zamir as she passed him, helpfully holding the door open for his unexpected guests and doing his best to mask his unease. He shut it behind him and turned to face the three of them, clustered together in the narrow hallway.

'Now,' he said, folding his hands together in front of him, 'perhaps you wouldn't mind telling me what this is about. You say you're with the Specialist *Crime* Unit?'

'That's right,' said Vasilico brusquely. 'Anything you'd like to share with us, Mr Zamir?'

There seemed to Anna to be little doubt that he'd chosen to interpret Zamir's discomfort as a sign of guilt. As she watched, he took a couple of steps closer to their host, invading his space in a way that made her feel a sharp twinge of anxiety on his behalf.

'Um . . . No . . . ?' Zamir slowly inched away from Vasilico. 'I don't believe there is. Are . . . are you sure you've got the right address?'

'Quite sure,' said Vasilico. He gestured to Anna. 'Happen to recognise this woman?'

Zamir glanced briefly at her, then shook his head. 'No, I've never seen her in my life.'

'Please take a closer look, sir.' A dangerous edge now entered Vasilico's voice. 'I'd like you to be absolutely, one *hundred* percent certain before you say anything you might wish to take back at a later date. Say, in a police interview room or a court of law.'

At this, Zamir rallied somewhat. With a show of defiance that wasn't quite matched by the tremor in his voice, he folded his arms and glared back at Vasilico.

'Now look, just what exactly is going on here? You can't just barge into my house, making veiled insinuations without telling me anything. What are you *really* here for?'

'We'd like to talk to you about your various extracurricular activities. Seems you've got quite the little sideline in the production and distribution of online movies.'

'Online . . . movies?' Zamir repeated the words, utterly incredulous. 'I run a chain of hotels. I'm not in *film production*.' He gave a nervous laugh. 'Is this some sort of a wind-up?'

Vasilico shot Kirk a brief look. It was almost imperceptible, but Anna spotted it. Surely it must be dawning on him that there was a distinct possibility they'd made a mistake?

Zamir took a tentative step forward in what Anna suspected was an attempt to reassert his status as the man of the house.

'You said "movies", didn't you?'

'That's right,' Vasilico confirmed. 'To be precise, a series of amateur videos hosted on a YouTube channel.'

'In that case, are you sure it's not *Asif* you're looking for?'

They all looked at him blankly.

'He's my little brother,' he explained. 'He lives with me.'

'Your . . . brother.' Vasilico repeated the words slowly, in the tone of someone gradually realising he'd made himself look like a fool. 'He doesn't, by any chance, have access to your credit card, does he?'

'Sometimes.' Sohail Zamir now sounded significantly more confident. 'He doesn't have his own, so I let him use mine when he needs it. He always pays me back in cash,' he added, as if this served as evidence of his good character.

'And do you know if he ever calls himself Zambo or Zambolo online?'

'You can ask him yourself. Here he comes now.'

They all turned as, as if on cue, the front door opened and the familiar figure of the heavyset, baseball cap-wearing man from the Zambo's World channel stepped into the house, slipping a pack of cigarettes into the pocket of his tracksuit bottoms. Seeing the visitors, he froze mid-step. His eyes darted from the two detectives to Anna, then back to the detectives. Several unbearably tense seconds passed, during which not one of the five people crammed into the hallway moved or breathed.

Then, Asif Zamir turned and ran.

'Stop him!' Vasilico roared.

He was out of the door immediately, pelting after the fleeing figure. Kirk was mere moments behind him. Anna hurried after them, emerging from the house in time to see the two detectives sprinting up the pavement after Asif, who, for all his bulk, was managing to move with considerable speed.

Anna glanced back at Sohail Zamir, who stood helplessly in the hallway, looking bewildered, frightened and more than a little incensed. She offered him a helpless shrug, then took off after Kirk and Vasilico, wishing she'd worn trainers rather than flats and that she wasn't so out of practice at running.

By the time she reached the street, she'd lost sight of them. In the distance, she heard the continued slap of shoes on concrete, followed by a shout from a voice she recognised as Vasilico's.

'Give it up, Zamir!'

Struggling gamely on in her inflexible flats, Anna set after them once more. The pavement was slick underfoot with rainwater and dead leaves, and, on a couple of occasions, she narrowly avoided missing her footing.

She'd got as far as the end of Rosedene Crescent when she heard the sudden blaring of a horn and a screech of tyres, coming from the direction of Paisley Road West, the main thoroughfare linking Cardonald to the city centre. For a moment, she heard nothing but the distant purr of traffic. Then, a woman's scream rent the still air.

Filling her lungs, Anna put on another burst of speed and hurried in the direction of the commotion.

She reached the main road to find a crowd of a dozen or more gathered on the pavement. People were murmuring to one another, some shaking their heads in dismay or disapproval, several with their phones either pressed to their ears or raised aloft, filming the scene in front of them.

A large Eddie Stobart lorry was parked diagonally across both sides of the road. Up ahead, Kirk stood near the kerb, phone to her ear. As Anna approached her, she lowered it and, covering the mouthpiece, shook her head.

'This is a massive fuck-up,' she said in a low voice.

Anna advanced past her towards the lorry, where she spotted Vasilico crouching, one arm extended towards a crumpled, man-sized shape wedged behind one of the front wheels. Anna's pace slowed as she took in the sight of Asif Zamir's familiar red baseball cap, lying on the road a few feet away.

Her gaze racked back to Vasilico, who looked up at her, met her eyes and gave a discreet shake of his head.

46

Tuesday 19 November

Asif Zamir was pronounced dead at the scene. By the time the emergency services arrived, the crowd had swelled considerably and a news van had pulled up, presumably alerted by one or more of the onlookers – thus putting paid to Vasilico's initial plan to keep the death under wraps for as long as possible, in order to avoid tipping off his co-conspirators. If there had been any suggestion of there still being even an outside chance of this happening, it was definitely quashed several hours later back at Specialist Crime Unit headquarters, when a grim-faced Kirk presented Anna and Vasilico with her phone, playing footage of an angry, tearful Sohail Zamir being interviewed by the media on his doorstep, accusing the police of being directly responsible for his brother's death.

Shortly thereafter, they were dealt a further blow when the Cybercrime team reported their initial findings from their examination of Asif's electronic devices, seized in the aftermath of the accident. Neither his laptop nor his mobile phone appeared to contain a record of any communications pointing to his involvement in the attacks on female students. They were still looking, but the technician who briefed them said she was confident that, if there was anything damning to be retrieved, they'd have found it by now.

On a more positive note, if you could call it that, they'd successfully established, from his browser history, that he was indeed the person who'd uploaded the pictures of Anna to the Carnal College website and, until his death, had been operating the @AnnaScavoliniGlasgow Twitter account. The technician also reported that his hard drive contained significant quantities of photos of a similar nature to the ones of Anna, plus what she described as terabytes and terabytes of raw video footage of women filmed in a variety of settings, most of them unawares.

One other potentially juicy discovery was that Zamir's phone was installed with a program no one on the Cybercrime team had encountered before called 'X-CHAT', which appeared to be a proprietary, end-to-end-encrypted messaging app with one particularly noteworthy feature: the moment a chat session ended, all records of it were immediately and permanently erased.

'Now, I'm not going to say, "If you've got nothing to hide, you've got nothing to fear", said the technician, 'but . . .'

Vasilico nodded. '. . . but if you've got nothing to hide, why are you using a home-made messaging app programmed to scrub every trace of your conversation history?'

'Precisely. I mean, it could be this is just something he uses to trade upskirting vids with his dodgy mates . . .'

'. . . but it seems like overkill for someone who happily uploaded videos of himself harassing girls in which he's readily identifiable.'

Kirk drove Anna home shortly before 6 a.m., and shortly after they'd both witnessed the arrival of the Chief Super – a thin, raven-haired woman in her early fifties who promptly collared Vasilico and escorted him to her office for a one-to-one briefing cum bollocking.

'*Not* a good look, Mr Vasilico,' she was heard to remark as she shut the door.

Upon entering the house, Anna treated Zoe and Farah, who'd both stayed up all night waiting for news, to a précis of events, before heading upstairs and promptly collapsing, fully dressed, into bed.

47

El Duce invites LifeIsPain to a new chat channel.

LifeIsPain joins the chat.

El Duce: You'll have heard the news I take it?

LifeIsPain: No what news
LifeIsPain: ?

El Duce: FFS. Stop jerking yourself off for one second and turn on any news channel.

LifeIsPain: ?????

El Duce: That fuckwit pickup artist only went and got himself killed.

LifeIsPain: What pick up artist
LifeIsPain: Whats hapening

El Duce: Does being this retarded come naturally to you or do yuo have to work hard at it?
El Duce: Asif Zamir

El Duce: AKA GodsGift2Women
El Duce: Am I getting through your thick skull?

LifeIsPain: OMG
LifeIsPain: Taht guy who went under the lorry
LifeIsPain: That was Godgift?

El Duce: Sigh. He shoots he scores.

LifeIsPain: Fuck man
LifeIsPain: This is horible

El Duce: He was a soldier in a war. He knew the risks.
El Duce: Besides, he brought it on himself.

LifeIsPain: I dont uderstand

El Duce: He was running from the pigs when he went down.
They were after him for something.
El Duce: Plain clothes detectives. You don't send THOSE
round if your in arrears on your council tax.
El Duce: Wouldn't be surprised if this had something to do
with that POS Youtube channel of his. I lost count how
many times I told him to taek it down.

LifeIsPain: U dont think
LifeIsPain: It cud have sth to do with
LifeIsPain: U know . . . . the mission
LifeIsPain: ?

El Duce: Can't rule it out I suppose.
El Duce: But either way there's nothing that leads back to us.
We never met IRL, he didn't know our names.

LifeIsPain: But u knew
LifeIsPain: His I mean

El Duce: Of course I did. You think I don't take precautions?
El Duce: Besides it wasn't hard to work out. "Zambo" = not exactly subtle.

LifeIsPain: Waht about me

El Duce: What about you?

LifeIsPain: Do u know who **I** am

El Duce: Perhaps. Perhaps not.
El Duce: That's not something you need concern yourself about. Besides, you've got more important matters to worry about.

LifeIsPain: Liek what

El Duce: When a soldier falls in battle, he has to be replaced.
El Duce: Zamir might have had shit for brains, but he carried out his missions with a certain finesse. I'm going to need someone with a similar level of dedication to the task.
El Duce: So here's my question for you.
El Duce: Are you ready to prove you're worthy?

48

Anna was woken while it was still dark by the ringing of her temporary pay-as-you-go phone. Fumbling for the light-switch next to her bed, she blinked sleep from her eyes before reaching for it.

It was Vasilico.

'I'm sending a car for you,' he said. 'Be ready to leave in twenty minutes.'

'Where . . . ?' Anna stifled a yawn. 'What time is it?'

'I'll explain everything when you get here.'

He rang off without another word.

Shortly afterwards, Anna was heading down the front steps and into the icy, pre-dawn chill. A police car idled at the kerb. Still not fully awake, she slid into the back seat. The driver acknowledged her with a nod.

'Where are we going?' Anna asked, as they set off.

'Shettleston Police Station,' replied the driver, without looking back at her. 'Boss's orders.'

Sensing that this was all she was going to get out of him, and not yet feeling sufficiently awake to attempt a proper interrogation, Anna accepted this information at face value and sank into the seat, shutting her eyes in the vain hope of getting a few extra minutes of sleep.

Vasilico was waiting for her in the foyer of the two-storey, brown-brick police station on Shettleston Road. It was the first time Anna had seen him since the death of Asif Zamir, though he'd rung her yesterday evening to give her a brief update. Apparently, the Chief Super was satisfied that he and Kirk had not been at fault, and had agreed – albeit grudgingly – that he could remain in charge of the investigation . . . for now, at any rate. The police, meanwhile, would batten down the hatches and prepare to ride out yet another public scandal.

Remaining infuriatingly cryptic, Vasilico escorted Anna through the reception area and down a long, narrow corridor leading to the back of the station, before ushering her through a door and into a small, dimly lit observation room with a couple of chairs facing a television mounted on an otherwise empty desk. On the screen, in a comparatively over-lit interview room, a young man with a pockmarked face and floppy, curly hair sat hunched over a table, wearing a white, police-issue boiler suit. Facing him on the other side of the table was Kirk, leaning back in her seat with her legs crossed, watching him.

Vasilico nodded towards the screen. 'Recognise him?'

It took a moment for Anna to realise that she, in fact, did.

'Yes,' she said, her own surprise audible in her voice. 'He's one of my second-years. Eddie something. Eddie McCallum?'

'McAllister,' Vasilico corrected her. 'Nice, quiet lad, by all accounts. Lives with his parents through in Dalmarnock. He was caught in the wee hours trying to break into the bedroom of a third-year Philosophy student who stays just down the road from here. Georgia McKay.'

Anna opened her mouth, a question on the tip of her tongue, but before she could get it out, Vasilico beat her to it.

'I checked. Her name's on the anti-Leopold petition too.'

She'd known it would be, but she was glad to get the confirmation all the same.

'She stays in a fourth-floor tenement flat,' Vasilico went on. 'A passerby saw him climbing up the drainpipe.' An amused note entered his voice. 'By the time we got there, he'd managed to get himself stuck. Took the combined might of the local bobbies and the Fire Service to get him down.'

Anna's eyes returned to the TV. Eddie continued to slump on the table, chin resting on his folded arms, practically horizontal.

At that moment, Kirk stirred to life. 'Right, Eddie,' she said, a buoyant note in her voice, as if she was geeing him up for one last push, 'that's you had a good long time to think about how you want to play this. Seeing as you've waived your right to a lawyer, I don't see any reason why we should delay any longer. So let's start at the beginning. When did you first become involved with The Reckoning?'

Eddie gave no response.

'D'you hear me, Eddie?'

Nothing.

'Look, I get that the strong, silent approach normally works wonders with the ladies, but I hate to break it to ya: I'm not like other girls. So why don't we cut the act and make some headway?'

Eddie muttered something inaudible.

Kirk leant forward. 'What's that? Didn't quite make ya out.'

Eddie lifted his head long enough to give her a glare of pure contempt. 'I said, I don't answer to foids.'

With that, he lowered his head and said nothing more.

Kirk turned towards the camera and spread her arms wide in an exasperated shrug.

Anna continued to study Eddie, who remained in his supine position, so still he almost didn't appear to be breathing. *Of course* – she remembered him now. He was the student who'd witnessed her altercation with Cameron Mitchell in the lecture theatre. The one who'd dragged Cameron away after she slapped him. She liked to pride herself on knowing the names of all her students and at least *something* about them, but he wasn't someone who'd ever made an impression on her. He'd neither excelled himself academically nor made a name for himself by expressing unusual or controversial positions. He'd always just been . . . *there*, quiet and anonymous, never once giving any indication as to the extremist tendencies he apparently harboured.

Like a sleeper agent.

With Kirk's attempts to get Eddie to talk having hit a brick wall, Vasilico headed into the interview room to join her, leaving Anna to watch on the screen. Initially, Eddie seemed no more inclined to cooperate with Vasilico than with Kirk. Gradually, however, worn down by the DCI's calm but persistent questioning, he began to open up.

It began about eight months ago, he said. The instigator and leader of the group was an individual calling himself 'El Duce'. At the time, Eddie was an active member of the 'r/Leopold' subreddit, and one night, El Duce reached out to him by direct message, saying he recognised him as a kindred spirit – one who, like him, was awake to the injustices faced by men and the urgent need to correct society's current trajectory. Shortly thereafter, they took their conversation off Reddit to X-Chat, the encrypted messaging service El Duce had built himself. There, Eddie was introduced to 'GodsGift2Women', with whom El Duce had been communicating for even longer. None of them ever met in real life, or were meant to know the real identities of the others. Eddie only learned that GodsGift2Women was Asif Zamir twenty-four hours ago. He still had no idea who El Duce was.

'No names, no personal details,' he said. 'That's a big rule. But I always figured he knew more about us than we knew about him. He knew who GodsGift was, and he made out he knew who I was too.'

They'd been communicating on X-Chat for a while, talking in general terms about the plight of men and what practical steps they might take to overthrow the yoke of feminist tyranny. When the anti-Leopold letter went out, it was as if they'd found their calling.

'El Duce called it a launchpad,' said Eddie, his eyes practically shining with idealistic fervour. 'He said it was just the start – punishing the bitches who'd spoken out against Big D. That we'd move onto bigger and better things. And he was convinced that, once they saw they didn't have to be cowed, other men would soon rise up and take back their proper place in the social order. He called us "the harbinger of the return of Man".'

Kirk, lazily drawing swirl patterns in her notebook, let out an amused – and seemingly involuntary – chortle. For several seconds, Eddie gave her a long, seething stare, before continuing.

The group had a clear hierarchy, with El Duce at the top, Zamir in the middle and Eddie at the bottom. The 'missions', as Eddie called them, were all carried out by either El Duce or Zamir, until Zamir's death, at which point El Duce called on Eddie to 'step up'. At this, Eddie became self-pitying and borderline weepy for a spell, claiming to have blown his big chance to prove his value as a soldier in the 'war', and, in the process, let down mankind as a whole – but, most of all, 'Big D'.

Once he'd recovered, he continued his account, explaining that El Duce always chose the targets, based on a number of factors, including their accessibility and living arrangements, as well as what seemed to have been his own individual whims. A picture quickly emerged of El Duce as someone not keen on his decisions being questioned.

'And why should he have to explain anything?' Eddie demanded, responding to a question no one had asked. 'He's the leader. The commander-in-chief. He brought us together. Gave us a sense of purpose. Gave us back our self-respect. And he did all the heavy lifting – identifying the targets, watching them, establishing their routines and such. GodsGift used to test him all the time, seeing how far he could push him before he snapped. But even *he* knew we'd have been nowhere without him. He was the only one of us with a line to Big D.'

'So let me get this right,' said Kirk, sitting up a little straighter. 'Are you saying El Duce is in direct communication with Leopold?'

At this, Eddie, seemingly realising he'd said too much, abruptly clammed up. Despite gentle, followed by not-so-gentle, prodding from Vasilico, they got nothing further out of him on the subject, other than that the name 'James Venable' meant nothing to him.

'I dunno anyone called that,' he shrugged. 'Not IRL, and not . . .' His expression hardened. 'Anyway, it doesn't matter. We're soldiers in a war. Names are meaningless. All individuality is secondary to the objective.'

He also, rather more enthusiastically, confirmed that he and his co-conspirators were behind the leaking of the photos of Anna and the various other attacks on her reputation and privacy. That was punishment, he claimed, for her efforts to embarrass Leopold during their debate.

He grinned, savouring the memory. 'Worked too, didn't it? We fucked that slut up good and proper. See how easy it is? We've all got our dirty little secrets.'

Anna watched Vasilico's jaw pulsating in anger, and, for a moment, was worried self-restraint was going to fall by the wayside and that he was about to leap over the table and begin laying into Eddie. After a moment, however, he simply shook his head. When he next spoke, it was with something approaching pity, or at least disappointment.

'What led you down this route, Eddie? You're an articulate lad. And you're obviously bright. You must have done well at school to get into a big, prestigious uni. You could have made something of yourself. Why chuck it all away for all this bitterness and hatred?'

Eddie scoffed, as if he couldn't believe Vasilico was being so dense. 'It's all right for you, with your looks and your muscles and your big dick – everything handed to you on a plate; all the foids throwing themselves at you. Some of us aren't so lucky. We have to make do with the cards we're dealt. But I guess the status quo looks pretty sweet if you're an alpha.'

'Oh, *stop!*' Kirk practically guffawed. 'His ego's big enough as it is without you inflating it any more.'

'There's two types of people in the world,' Eddie went on, once again pointedly ignoring her. 'Winners and losers. And I'm not gonna be a loser.' He thumped his chest, glaring defiantly at Vasilico. 'I refuse.'

'And your idea of proving that is to climb into girls' bedrooms to sexually assault and beat them so badly that they lose their eyesight? That they *miscarry*?' This time, Vasilico struggled to hide his disgust.

Eddie gave an unrepentant chuckle. 'I wouldn't expect you to understand. You still think the world is fair to men. That it's possible for males and females to co-exist without one side dominating the other. But I've seen the truth. And the truth is it's us or them, and I'm fucked if I'm going to lie down meekly and let them stamp on my throat. You need to put them in their place, and you can't do it by asking them nicely. You've got to make them AFRAID.'

Kirk snorted. 'Oh yeah. Positively shaking in my boots here, bub.'

This time, Eddie deigned to look at Kirk for an extended spell. When he next spoke, the tone of his voice chilled Anna's very marrow.

'Some MRAs make out they don't hate females. Claim they actually want what's best for them. That what we're trying to achieve will be as good for them in the long run as it'll be for men. Not me. I despise every one of your rancid kind with every ounce of my being. You creatures are lower than cattle and I'll not sleep till you're treated like them.'

And, with that, he once again slumped on the desk with his head in his arms and said nothing more.

Once Eddie had been escorted back to his cell, Anna, Vasilico and Kirk gathered in the viewing room for an impromptu council of war.

'If nothing else,' said Vasilico, 'we can agree, with some degree of certainty, that two of the three conspirators are now accounted for – one dead, the other awaiting his first court appearance. That just leaves the elusive El Duce to be unmasked and apprehended. Unfortunately, I'd imagine the odds of him going to ground are pretty high. I doubt it'll take him long to realise last night's "mission" didn't go to plan.'

'So what happens now?' said Anna, who was keen that they didn't lose the momentum that seemed to have developed.

'We'll redouble the watch on James Venable; be on the alert for any sign he's getting ready to clear out. And I want a tail put on Leopold too. If they really *are* in cahoots, I doubt they'd be stupid enough to meet face to face, but I want to know if there's any change in his routine. If McAllister's telling the truth, his whole carefully orchestrated plan is currently crashing and burning before his eyes.'

Anna was sorely tempted to point out that, if he'd just listened to her in the first place when she came to him with her suspicions about Leopold, so much of what had subsequently unfolded could have been avoided. But she sensed now was not the time for self-righteousness.

With nothing further to keep them there, they prepared to head their separate ways – Kirk to the university, to relieve the plain-clothes officer watching Venable; Vasilico to headquarters to brief the Chief Super, who, ever since Asif Zamir's death, had been demanding daily, in-person updates.

'Can I give you a lift back?' Vasilico said to Anna, as they stood together at the top of the steps outside the station.

'It's OK – I'll make my own way.'

'Are you sure? It's on my route.'

'I'm sure,' said Anna firmly.

Vasilico looked at her uncertainly. She could imagine what he was thinking; even had a sense of what he wanted to ask her. *Have I done something wrong?* She hoped he wouldn't. She wasn't sure she could explain it to him – not least because she wasn't sure she herself even fully understood.

'I . . .' Vasilico began, then stopped. He regarded her with a sympathetic, almost cringing smile. 'How are you doing?' he asked instead.

'I'm getting by,' said Anna – which was as much as she was prepared to say to anyone on the subject right now.

For a moment, Vasilico appeared to be on the verge of saying something else. But then, the opportunity seemed to pass.

'Well,' he said gruffly, 'best get on,' before heading down the steps to his car.

49

Over the next couple of days, Anna continued to exist in something approaching a state of limbo. With no work to go to, and nothing she could meaningfully contribute to the investigation, she had nothing to do except sit in the house, waiting for something to happen.

At the forefront of her mind was the question of Jack and when she was going to bring him home. She knew she'd need to make a decision soon. Indeed, Mandy had tentatively broached the subject on Wednesday night when Anna once again phoned to check in with her. The threat felt like it had receded somewhat, with two of her tormenters having been neutralised, one way or the other, and no fresh instances of harassment against her, but she nonetheless remained convinced that the matter couldn't possibly be considered settled while the third man – and not merely a lackey but, by all accounts, the ringleader – was still at large.

On Friday afternoon, Vasilico swung by to update Anna on the progress of the investigation over the last couple of days. Kirk, posing as a Computing Science student, had been tailing Venable since Tuesday, but reported that, so far, he'd shown no signs of having been spooked by the downfall of his two supposed co-conspirators or behaved in any way as to arouse suspicion.

'According to her,' Vasilico said, 'our boy's not much of a people person. Keeps himself to himself for the most part. When he's not at lectures, he's most likely to be found in the uni library or home at his flat in Laurieston. Either he's one seriously cool cucumber . . . or he's not El Duce after all.'

Anna could have added that one of the few proactive things she *had* managed to do over the last forty-eight hours was to investigate Venable's social media presence – or, more accurately, lack thereof. He didn't appear to be active on any of the usual places – highly unusual, she knew, for someone his age. But she wasn't ready for yet another lecture about leaving the detecting to the detectives, so she kept those thoughts to herself.

Vasilico showed her a photo Kirk had managed to surreptitiously snap of Venable during a lecture. In his mid-to-late twenties, with jet black hair arranged in a severe, almost Hitler-esque side parting and a compact but sinewy build, Anna could readily believe he was the slim yet muscular attacker described by several of the victims – but was forced to concede that she could just as readily believe the opposite.

Vasilico rubbed the back of his neck and sighed. 'I hate to say it, but if he doesn't give us a good reason to suspect him soon, I'm not sure how much longer the Chief Super's going to sanction this op for. We've got two perfectly good officers getting what amounts to an adult education and naff all to show for it.'

'So what you're saying is we have nothing.'

Vasilico frowned. 'I wouldn't put it like that. We've accounted for two out of three members of The Reckoning.'

'And you're going to chalk that up as a victory, are you? One idiot crushed under a lorry, another in custody. Meanwhile, the ones that are *actually* responsible get to melt away into the shadows without facing any consequences for what they've done?'

She knew she was taking her frustrations out on the wrong person. But, for better or worse, he was her only real point of contact with the police. If *he* didn't get to hear how she felt about the matter, no one else was going to.

Vasilico glared back at her, jaw tight, hands on his hips. She knew he was having to fight hard not to give into the temptation to respond in kind to her tirade.

'I can assure you,' he said at last, 'the investigation is still very much an ongoing concern.'

He spoke with conviction, and yet, to Anna's ears, it sounded unbelievably hollow.

After Vasilico left, Anna took herself for a long, solitary walk, bundled up against both the increasingly bitter cold as winter tightened its grip and any possibility of being recognised as 'that woman who got her bits out on the internet'.

As she stalked across the city, she thought long and hard about what she was going to do – if, indeed, there was anything she *could* do. If Venable *was* El Duce and was allowed to get away with what he'd done, she'd never be able to live with herself. The same went for Leopold – doubly so, if she was being honest. If he *had* been directing The Reckoning's actions behind the scenes and successfully evaded punishment . . . well, it would simply be the 'plausible deniability' schtick at which he was so adept taken to its most extreme conclusion. He would have got to mastermind a campaign of terror against the women of the university, but because he'd kept his head down and pulled his puppets' strings from behind the curtain, because he'd never actually struck a single physical blow himself, he would never have to face any consequences.

Just another hate preacher . . .

It wasn't until she'd been walking for nearly two hours that an idea began to take shape. It was vaguely formed – more of an abstraction than an actual, concrete plan. By the end of the third hour, though, it had begun to solidify. And, by the time she made it back to Hyndland and turned off Crow Road onto Clarence Drive, she was no longer in any doubt as to what she had to do.

50

Transcript of a telephone call between Anna Scavolini and Farah Hadid, 8.16 p.m., Friday 22 November 2019.

Call begins.

Farah: Hello? Anna? What's wrong? Is everything OK?

Anna: *(laughs dryly)* Well, I mean, define 'OK', under the circumstances.

Farah: Of course. Sorry. What I mean is . . . nothing's happened?

Anna: *(sighs)* No, nothing's happened. And that's sort of the point. I feel . . . well, I suppose I just feel helpless, powerless, not knowing when the next attack's going to happen or when I'm going to wake up to find more of my private life plastered all over the web for everyone to see.

(clears throat) Anyway, I called because I wanted to tell you I've made a decision.

Farah: You have?

Anna: It's Leopold. Right from the beginning, it's all led back to him. Whether or not he's been personally directing these creeps, it's *his* retrograde philosophy that's been driving them. *He's* the one who provided them with the blueprint. And I know . . . *(sighs)* I know that's not enough in the eyes of the law, but if the last few weeks have shown me anything, it's that the law just isn't equipped to deal with people like him. At least, not through the official channels.

The point is, I can't let him get away with it. Not after all the lives he and his acolytes have ruined – mine included. And the way things are headed, that's exactly what's going to happen. Vasilico says the investigation's still an active concern, but I can read the tea leaves as well as the next person. They're on the verge of winding it up. They've got the low hanging fruit. For them, that's enough. Even my friendly neighbourhood guards have packed up and gone home. Can't justify the manpower, they say.

(deep breath)

So here's what I've decided. Tomorrow, I'm going to go to the police and tell them Leopold tried to sexually assault me.

A lengthy silence. Then:

Farah: Anna. I . . . I don't . . . know what to say.

Anna: Say you agree with me. Say you understand why this is the only option left to me.

Farah: Anna . . .

Anna: I know it's the nuclear option. And believe me, I wouldn't even be considering it if I wasn't desperate. Think about it – there are precious few ways more guaranteed to destroy a man's reputation. It doesn't even have to result in a charge, let alone a conviction. All it takes is an allegation, and for the rest of his life, he'll be followed around by rumour and innuendo wherever he goes. He'll be tied up in employee tribunals and internal investigations for years. It's like the man said himself: there's no smoke without fire.

Farah: I . . . Anna, this is . . . I mean, God knows I understand why you would consider this. But you need to think so hard about what you're saying.

Anna: *(a note of exasperation)* I already told you, I *have*. I've thought about practically nothing else all afternoon. This is not some spur of the moment thing.

Farah says nothing.

Anna: *(sighs heavily)* Everything that's gone wrong with my life – the smears, the humiliation, the fact I might soon not have a job – it's all because of him. How can it be right that his reputation remains intact while mine is in tatters?

More silence.

Anna: Please say something, Farah. I need to know you're on board with this.

Farah: There really is nothing I can say that will make you change your mind, is there?

Anna: There's not.

Farah: *(sighs)* In that case, I won't try. But I don't like this.

Anna: I don't like it either. But it's what has to be done.

Farah: Where's Zoe? Is she with you? You've spoken to *her* about this?

Anna: She's sleeping over at Sal's tonight. It's just me. And no, I haven't told her. She'd never go along with this. Not in a million years. She's too . . . honourable.

Farah: Then let me come to you. You shouldn't be alone just now.

Anna: Thanks, but I think I'm going to have an early night. *(attempting levity)* Big day ahead of me tomorrow, after all! *(pause)* There's just one other thing.

Farah: What?

Anna: Will you go with me? To the police. I . . . I don't think I can do it on my own.

A pause, then:

Farah: Of course I will. You know that.

Anna: *(sighs with relief)* Thank you.

An awkward silence elapses, as if neither of them knows how to end the call.

Anna: Farah.

Farah: Yes?

Anna: You're a true friend.

Farah: Hey, we women must stick together, yes?

Anna: *(wearily)* Got that right. Us against the patriarchy.

Farah: Get some rest, Anna. I'll see you tomorrow. Sleep well.

Anna: And you.

Call ends at 8:23 p.m.

51

Saturday 23 November

A little after 3.15 a.m., the silence that lay upon both the house on Clarence Drive and the street outside was momentarily broken by the sound of glass shattering. A few seconds later, a lithe figure dressed from head to foot in black, barely visible in the darkness, clambered through the broken window above the kitchen sink. Barely making a sound, he dropped to the floor. Then, straightening up, he crossed to the downstairs hallway and began to climb the stairs.

Alighting on the first-floor landing, he paused to get his bearings, before setting off down the long corridor leading to the bedrooms. Upon reaching the door to Anna's room, he stopped again. Pressing an ear to the door, he listened to the sound of regular, steady breathing coming from within. He waited a couple of minutes. Then, satisfied that the occupant was indeed asleep, he turned the handle and slid the door open.

The shape of a woman lay in the bed, curled up in a near-foetal position beneath a thick duvet, her back to the door. She made a soft, snuffling sound, unconsciously drawing the duvet tighter about herself, and continued to slumber. The figure in black waited another minute before advancing.

As he crept forward on the balls of his rubber-soled shoes, he reached into his pocket and drew out a long, thin knife with a sharpened tip. He moved carefully, alert to the danger that he might trip on something unseen in the dark and give himself away.

A few steps later, he reached the bed. The woman continued to sleep on, unaware. Blade at the ready in one hand, he reached out with the other, ready to pull back the duvet.

At that very instant, the woman in the bed sprang to life. She flicked the switch hidden beneath the duvet, causing the bedside lamp at the other end of the electric cord to burst into dazzling light. In the same movement, she threw back the covers and rolled over to reveal her grinning face.

'Hello, lover!' said DS Alex Kirk. 'Fancy seeing *you* here!'

Even as the black-clad figure recoiled in surprise, the main room light went on. The figure spun round to find Paul Vasilico standing in the doorway, blocking his escape. His breathing ragged, he turned his head this way and that, eyes wide and frantic through the slit of his balaclava.

Seeing no other option available to him, he barrelled towards Vasilico, slashing the air wildly with his knife, trying to brute force his way out. Vasilico deftly sidestepped, knocking the knife out of his attacker's hand with a blow to his wrist. As the figure staggered backwards, Vasilico moved aside to allow three well-built uniformed officers to enter. They grabbed hold of the flailing figure and forced him to his knees, pinning his arms behind his back.

Vasilico advanced and whipped off the balaclava, revealing the intruder's face.

'Well, well,' he said grimly, 'if it isn't the one and only James Venable, otherwise known as El Duce. Such a pleasure to finally put a face to a name!'

Still struggling against the combined strength of the three officers holding him down, Venable glowered up at Vasilico, his jet black fringe plastered to his glistening forehead. As he continued to breathe noisily through flared nostrils, Anna stepped through the door and gazed down at the man who'd wreaked so much untold destruction, both on her and on so many other women throughout the city, over the past few weeks.

'James Venable,' Vasilico recited, his tone expressionless, 'I am arresting you on suspicion of the assault of Chloe Mazzaro and Gloria Owusu, the assault and sexual assault of Grace Dunphy and Narinder Khatri, and the attempted murder of Anna Scavolini. I believe that keeping you in custody is necessary and proportionate for the purposes of bringing you before a court or otherwise dealing with you in accordance with the law. You are not obliged to say anything but anything you do say will be noted and may be used in evidence. Do you understand?'

'Fuck you,' Venable snarled.

Vasilico raised a solitary, unimpressed eyebrow. 'You have the right to have a solicitor informed of your arrest, and to have access to a solicitor. These rights will be explained to you further at a police station.' He addressed the officers holding Venable down. 'Careful. He may have other weapons concealed on him.'

Kirk, having emerged from the bed, bounced alongside Vasilico, positively buzzing with pent-up energy.

'Ooh, do I get to frisk him? Please say I can frisk him.'

Together, the three officers hauled Venable to his feet, their grip on him not letting up. As he stood there, seething, Kirk advanced, crackling her knuckles theatrically in preparation. But even as she reached out to begin patting him down, Venable made a sharp, jerking movement, extending his right arm outwards. His captors, caught unawares by the suddenness of the action, had no time to stop him.

For a few seconds, it seemed as if nothing had happened. Then, from the doorway, Anna spotted the small plastic button pinched between Venable's thumb and forefinger, and the thin length of wire extending from it into the sleeve of his pullover.

Vasilico seemed to notice it at more or less the exact same moment. Striding forward, he ripped out the wire, revealing the small transmitter at the end of it, the tape Venable had used to secure it in place bearing several black, wiry chest hairs.

'Shit,' said Vasilico.

Venable met his eyes and gave a thin, triumphant smile.

Within an instant, Kirk had her phone to her ear.

'Kirk here. Get in there and yank the plug on any electronic devices you see. Do it *now!*'

She turned to Venable, barely able to disguise her desire to do serious violence to him.

'And you, ya little shit, if you've just done what I think you've done, you can add destruction of evidence to your rap sheet.'

With a scowl of disgust, Vasilico jerked his head at the uniforms. 'Get him out of here.'

The three officers frogmarched Venable towards the door. There, he slammed on the brakes, bringing himself to a standstill facing Anna. The look in his eyes was one of utter, animalistic hatred. Determined not to shrink away, she forced herself to meet his gaze, unblinking.

A couple of seconds passed, then the officers moved him on, bundling him past her and out into the corridor. As their footsteps clomped down the stairs, Vasilico made his way over and touched Anna lightly on her forearm.

'You OK?'

Still too shaken to formulate a verbal response, Anna managed a tight nod.

'I take back what I said earlier,' said Vasilico. 'This was absolutely the right thing to do.'

When Anna had gone to him that evening with the plan she'd concocted during her long walk, to say he'd been sceptical would have been the understatement of the millennium. And she could understand why. There was no guarantee that her attempt to provoke Venable into trying to take her out – using the one threat that, more than any other, she'd calculated would draw a reckless response from him – was going to work. Nor was it without considerable personal risk. There wasn't even any guarantee that he was still listening to the feed from her hacked phone. After all, it had been days since she'd last switched it on. It had been a last, desperate throw of the dice, and a part of her still couldn't quite believe it had paid off.

And now? Now, she felt a desperate need to shower; to wash away the filth that seemed to cling to her skin. The things she'd said to Farah in that call, about planning to use a false accusation of attempted rape to slander an opponent . . . Even though she'd merely been weaponising the misogynists' own rhetoric against them, it still left her with the feeling that she'd crossed some invisible moral line.

In fact, of the two of them, and in stark contrast to the roles they'd played in their call, rehearsed multiple times before they carried it out for real, Farah had been the more readily accepting of the moral virtue of the plan. Even as Anna had admitted her own reservations, Farah had urged her to put doubt aside and follow through with it, insisting that it didn't mean she was a traitor to the cause or guilty of giving truth to the worst lies men's rights activists told about women.

On a rational level, of course, Anna knew all this. But she still needed that shower.

52

By the time they'd completed the short drive to the SCU building on Napiershall Street, Kirk had received an update from the officers who'd been stationed outside Venable's flat in Laurieston. Upon entering the premises at her command, they'd discovered his desktop PC switched on and in the process of performing a remotely activated deep wipe of its hard drive. The nearest officer had succeeded in disconnecting it from the mains, halting the procedure mid-flow, but it remained to be seen how much, if any, of the drive's data would be recoverable.

Shortly afterwards, and for the second time that week, Anna found herself in a police observation room, watching on a television screen as Vasilico and Kirk interviewed a member of The Reckoning. Like Eddie McAllister, Venable waived his right to legal representation. Unlike Eddie, however, he had no qualms about answering his interrogators' questions. He proudly copped to everything, confirming that he was indeed the elusive 'El Duce' and that he was the ringleader of the group responsible for the attacks on female students across the city.

He also admitted to being behind the hacking of Anna's phone and the leaking of her personal photos. The group had had her in their sights for some time, he said, seeing her as just the sort of ranting misandrist they ought to make an example of.

As he spoke, Venable smiled at the memory. 'Oh, yes, Detective Chief Inspector – we all very much enjoyed listening to you railing her. I'm not going to lie, she's got a cracking set of lungs on her. And I gather that mouth of hers is good for other things besides spewing anti-male hate. I can see why you would, given the chance.'

Vasilico didn't respond – something Anna imagined must have required considerable effort on his part.

'There were others too,' Venable went on, a glint in his eye. 'Others we spent time laying the groundwork for. Others with embarrassing secrets that'd destroy them if they got out. Your little girlfriend was lucky. In her case, it was just some cringy snaps of her slutting it up. Bit demeaning for her, yeah, but it's not like she committed any crimes. There's people out there with *real* skeletons in their closets.

'And for all you know, perhaps we put systems in place so they'll leak automatically at a certain point, without someone needing to hit the detonate button.' He smiled. 'You'll just have to wait and see.'

Vasilico returned the smile humourlessly. 'Such a pity, then, that you're not going to be around to enjoy the fruits of your labours. You're going to prison for a very long time, sunshine. You lost. It's over.'

'You think so? I'm not so sure.'

Vasilico said nothing. He sat, arms folded, waiting for Venable to elaborate.

Venable sniffed loudly and exaggeratedly. 'Smell that? Know what that is?'

Vasilico didn't humour him with a response.

'It's *fear*.' Venable's smile extended from ear to ear. 'We've made women afraid again. Afraid of us, and of our raw, God-given power. Afraid of what we can and will do to them. Thanks to us, they're double-locking their doors. They're carrying rape alarms. They're avoiding walking home alone at night, or, in some cases, going out at all. We've reminded them just how weak and defenceless they actually *are*. I call that a victory.'

He barked out an incredulous laugh. 'What – you think it was just the three of us? That you can kill us or lock us up and the problem will just conveniently go away?'

He leaned forward towards Vasilico, his eyes shining with the zeal of a true believer.

'There's *thousands* of us. Hundreds of thousands. Maybe even millions of us out there. And you never know where and when we'll spring up next. Cos we've given men a taste of what they can do, what they can *be*. And once you've tasted freedom, you're not going to settle for servitude again. The liberation of men is more than just words and deeds – it's an idea, and you can't kill an idea.'

Vasilico said nothing. He just regarded Venable with a look of disgust.

'Is she here, by the way? Your slut girlfriend. Is she listening to us?'

Still, Vasilico didn't react.

Venable's smile deepened. 'She is, isn't she?' Lifting his head high, he faced the wall-mounted camera directly and spoke in a loud, commanding voice. 'Well, you listen, Anna Scavolini. You might think you're hot stuff. You might think you got the better of us. But know this: you haven't won *shit*. Any time you get ideas above your station – hell, any time we feel like it – we can destroy you all over again, just like *that*.' He slapped his hand down hard on the table.

'It doesn't take much. The click of a button, a word in the right ear . . . Just remember, there are countless other men just like us – men who'll be more than happy to finish what we started. You'll never be safe from us, not as long as you draw breath.'

Anna couldn't listen to any more of this. The observation room felt tiny and airless, Venable's mocking words, thin and tinny though they sounded on the TV's speakers, seemed to come at her from every direction. Fumbling with the door handle with clammy hands, she stumbled out of the room and headed down the corridor towards fresh air.

Vasilico caught up with her half an hour later outside the building's entrance, trying to simultaneously savour and ward off the bitter early morning cold after the oppressive heat in the observation room.

He drew alongside her. 'You OK?'

'Uh-huh,' said Anna, with a brightness of tone that was unlikely to convince anyone.

'Don't listen to a word he says.' Vasilico nodded towards the building's interior. 'He's just a pathetic little shit-stirrer who knows his goose is cooked.'

'*I* know that,' said Anna, still trying to sound blithe and unconcerned. She hesitated for a moment. 'He say anything of actual value?'

'Other than that him being in cahoots with Leopold was just a story he spun to impress his lackeys and keep them in line, then nope, not a sausage.'

Anna turned to look at him. 'And you believe him?'

Vasilico considered the question. 'On the balance of probabilities, yes. We'll keep sweating him, obviously, and we'll continue to keep Leopold under surveillance, but if you want my honest opinion, I fancy our man in there is telling the whole truth and nothing but the truth. I don't think he feels he has anything to lose at this stage.'

They remained standing side by side for a couple of minutes, both lost in their own thoughts. Eventually, Vasilico stirred.

'Well, better get back to it.' He paused, then added uncertainly, 'You coming back in?'

Anna shook herself out of her reverie. 'No, I think I'm going to head home. See if I can catch up on some of the sleep I *didn't* get last night.' She paused. Met Vasilico's eyes. 'You'll let me know if there's any news? About . . . anything?'

Vasilico dipped his head in acknowledgement. 'I'll do that. And Anna?'

'Yes?'

He hesitated. She sensed he was on the verge of saying something potentially profound. But in the end, all he said was:

'You look after yourself.'

She smiled tightly, then turned and headed across the car park towards the street.

53

MinassianFan4Ever invites El Duce to a new chat channel.

MinassianFan4Ever: Hey
MinassianFan4Ever: You there?

Two minutes pass.

MinassianFan4Ever: All ok?

One minute passes.

MinassianFan4Ever: How come you arnt answering?

Three minutes pass.

MinassianFan4Ever closes the channel.

PART SIX

THE RECKONING

54

The following morning, Vasilico briefly swung by the house to inform Anna of the Cybercrime team's progress on recovering data from Venable's hard drive. While much of it was either lost altogether or severely compromised, they were slowly but surely piecing the remnants together and had managed to decrypt fragments of the direct messages between Venable, Zamir and McAllister – or El Duce, GodsGift2Women and LifeIsPain. As it turned out, while the X-Chat app was designed to delete all correspondence the moment the channel in question was closed, Venable had, in fact, been backing up complete logs of their conversations to his computer, seemingly from the very beginning – presumably so he'd have something he could use against them should the need ever arise.

Much of the conversation history was badly corrupted, and it was going to take time to unpick and sift through everything, but, as Vasilico put it, 'Our boy's not going anywhere anytime soon.' The police were as confident as it was possible to be that he would be denied bail at tomorrow's court hearing. 'Then,' said Vasilico, 'he can join his wee pal McAllister in the big hoose.'

Anna suggested that, should the police need any assistance with combing through the drive's contents, they could do considerably worse than to call on the services of Jen Brinkley, who was the best there was. Vasilico, who evidently hadn't forgotten about the circumstances under which Anna came by Sohail Zamir's credit card details, got a rather peculiar look in his eyes for a moment, before nodding and saying he'd bear that in mind.

In the early afternoon, Anna headed through to the East End to pick up Jack from Mandy. A part of her still wasn't quite ready to believe it was all over. In particular, she continued to harbour doubts as to Leopold's innocence, and was more than prepared to believe Venable had lied in a last effort to shield 'Big D' from the fallout.

But she knew she couldn't go on behaving as if disaster was just around the corner indefinitely. More to the point, she missed Jack something rotten, and was sure he must feel the same way about her – or, at least, she hoped he did. That ache had only grown stronger with each passing day, and she knew she was approaching the point where it would become utterly unbearable, so she'd decided to take a calculated risk and bring him home.

'Aye,' said Mandy, leaning against the wall of the narrow hallway corridor in her fourth-floor tenement flat, ''part fae one or two wee upsets, he was brand new. Hardly even knew he was here half the time. And ye know we're happy tae have him anytime.'

'Seriously, Mandy, I don't know how to thank you enough,' said Anna, sincerely hoping it would be a long time indeed before she was forced to call upon her services like this again. 'You know if I can ever return the favour, you only need to ask.' She hesitated. 'You said there were one or two upsets . . . ?'

'Och, it's nothin', really. Jist, coupla times when I was puttin' him doon for his nap and he wisnae havin' it. Y'know whit like weans are – the mair they need their forty winks, the mair adamant they are they're no for havin' it.'

'Mandy, if something happened . . .'

'Like I say, it's nothin'. Jist . . .' Mandy drew closer to Anna, lowering her voice. 'OK, so I've gottae ask – has he ever tried tae bite ye?'

Anna suppressed a groan.

'Only we had a coupla near misses, so we did. Got quite a set o' gnashers on him, that wan. I mean, see me, I'm tough as auld boots. I kin take it. But jist if he ever tries tae dae it tae another wee yin? Dunno, might find yersel wi a lawsuit affa wan o' they hoity-toity West End mums.

'Specially if he manages tae dae an injury tae their precious wee Cecily or Percy.'

'I promise I'll have a word with him,' said Anna, remembering, with a sinking heart, how her previous attempt had gone. 'And I am so, *so* sorry.'

Mandy dismissed her with a wave. 'Ach, it's nae bother, God's honest.' She held up a scrawny arm, pinching the skin to demonstrate. 'See? Hide like a bloody rhino.'

Anna thanked Mandy profusely one last time. Then, having collected Jack and his rucksack from the living room, she took him by the hand and led him down to the car.

Jack said nothing during the long trudge down the four flights of steps, but his grip on Anna's hand was like a vice. She waited till she had him safely buckled into the back seat before turning to address him from the driver's seat.

'Did you have a nice time with Mandy and Ruby?'

Keep things nice and light to start with. Then *we can get into the small matter of the biting.*

Jack merely shrugged.

'Well, *Mandy* says you had a nice time. That you and Ruby got up to all sorts of games together. Why don't you tell me about some of the things you did?'

'Don't want to,' Jack muttered.

'Why not?'

'Cos.'

'Cos what?'

No response. Instead, Jack deliberately turned his head to gaze out of the window, as if he hadn't heard Anna.

'Jack. Please look at me when I'm talking to you.'

Slowly, Jack turned his head to face Anna, his brows pursed together into a furious glare that almost caused her heart to skip a beat.

'What's wrong, Jack? I thought you'd be pleased to see me.'

. . . which was at least half a lie, and she knew it.

'Well, I'm not,' muttered Jack.

Anna's head jerked back sharply. She'd anticipated Jack might be difficult following his period of enforced exile, but she hadn't expected such burning animosity from him.

'Oh,' she snapped, her annoyance getting the better of her. 'Well, in that case, shall we go back up the stairs and you can stay with Mandy for another week, then?'

'Fine,' Jack growled.

Anna stared at him with a mixture of exasperation and disbelief. She knew children were capable of extreme mood swings, but it was always something she'd associated with teenagers rather than toddlers. Right at that particular moment, she felt as if she barely recognised him.

'You know something, Jack?' she said, her tone icy. 'You're turning into a not very nice little boy. You're rude to me, you said really nasty things about Ruby, and . . . and Mandy tells me you tried to bite her . . . *twice*!'

Jack folded his arms and stared at the floor.

'Are you listening to me?' She reached back and gripped his arm. 'You don't do that, *ever*, you hear me?' She shook her head in disbelief. 'Why, Jack? Why would you do something like that? What's wrong with you?'

'So you'd give me into trouble,' Jack mumbled.

Anna wondered whether she'd heard him correctly.

'*Excuse* me?'

Jack lifted his head to look at her, his bottom lip protruding sullenly. 'You only pay me 'tention to give me into trouble.'

'That's just not true,' said Anna.

But even as she said it, she found herself wondering. It was certainly true that her interactions with Jack weren't limited to reading him the Riot Act, but she remembered being that age clearly enough to know that, when you were a child, a single negative interaction with a parent was enough to immediately make you forget about all the positive ones. And, if she was being completely honest with herself, she had to admit she'd been a lot more cranky than usual for a while now. Not just since the business with The Reckoning, but going back a lot earlier than that – ever since she'd returned to work following her sabbatical to find the university riven by change and uncertainty. Some of the associated tension had inevitably bled into her home life, and Jack couldn't have failed to pick up on it. Children were awfully perceptive when it came to these things.

'Oh, Jack.'

She reached back and put a hand under his chin, gently lifting his head to make him look at her.

'Listen to me. You are the most important thing in my life, OK? No ifs, no buts. And if I've given you any reason to think otherwise, then I'm sorry. Things have been a bit . . . fraught lately, but I want you to know there are going to be some big changes going forward, and that includes me making a whole lot more time for you.'

As she spoke, she knew that, this time, she meant it; that, come hell or high water, she was going to make whatever changes she had to in order to give herself a less stressful existence and Jack the sort of relationship with his mother that he deserved.

'No ifs, no buts,' she said again.

Jack continued to say nothing, but his expression softened somewhat, his facial features returning to a more innocent, childlike state. Anna felt her muscles untensing.

'Now,' she went on, keeping her tone as breezy as possible, 'it's the weekend, and we've got the whole rest of the day to ourselves. Is there anything special you'd like to do?'

For a moment, Jack thought about it.

'Go to the Lego shop?' he asked in a small voice, a tentative smile edging across his lips.

Anna allowed herself her first full, unguarded smile in she didn't know how long.

'We can absolutely do that,' she said.

55

Monday 25 November

True to her word, Anna spent the rest of the day giving Jack her undivided attention. They went to the Lego shop in Buchanan Galleries, then returned to the house to build bricks together and make chocolate chip cookies, getting flour all over the kitchen counter and each other. Later in the evening, as they snuggled together on the sofa, watching cartoons, Anna realised she'd craved and needed this sort of mother/son bonding every bit as much as Jack had.

The following morning, Anna wrapped up warm against the cold and headed up to the university. It was the start of the TAs' three-day walkout over their pay and working conditions, and she was determined to show her support, ban from the premises be damned. As she made her way up the hill, the noise from what appeared to be a sizeable turnout came rolling down to greet her. As she neared the summit, she saw that the protestors had gathered on both sides of the road, waving placards and chanting.

They seemed to have self-organised into two distinct groups. On the right, outside the main gate, were the TAs – a motley assortment, mostly in their twenties or early thirties, bundled up in coats and scarves, their placards touching on the usual points of contention: 'FAIR PAY FOR TAs', 'NO TO TERM TIME ONLY CONTRACTS', 'END FAT CAT SALARIES'.

On the left, at the foot of the slope leading up to the university library, was a slightly younger crowd, mostly female, their banners devoted to the matter of women's safety on campus. Most were dressed similarly to the TAs, though around half a dozen had braved the November cold and turned up in their bras, a variety of heartfelt and provocative slogans written on their exposed flesh. Kez Dixon, instantly recognisable in her rainbow beanie, even from a distance, had gone one step further, the words 'THIS IS NOT AN INVITATION TO RAPE ME' daubed across her bare breasts and stomach. She strode up and down the line like a general marshalling her troops, bellowing into a bullhorn as she led an angry chant:

'NO TO VIOLENCE! NO TO MISOGYNY! NO TO VIOLENCE! NO TO MISOGYNY! NO TO . . .'

What struck Anna more than anything was the relative youth of both crowds. Though the average age of the TA camp was naturally higher than that of the students, she doubted there were more than half a dozen people there over the age of thirty-five. She was left with the unshakeable sense that what she was witnessing was a youthful revolt against an old, out-of-touch establishment whose days were numbered. Her heart stirred with a newfound feeling of hope, spurred by a conviction that the forces of revanchism couldn't stand in the way of progress indefinitely. *One way or another,* she thought, *we're going to beat you.*

She spotted Farah among the crowd of TAs, clutching the pole at one end of a placard declaring 'ON STRIKE FOR FAIR PAY'. Farah caught sight of her at the same moment and greeted her with a cheery wave of her free hand. Anna quickened her pace up the hill.

What happened next seemed to unfold in slow motion, the sight of it so incongruous that, at first, neither Anna nor, seemingly, anyone else registered what they were actually seeing. One moment, a young man in a dark jacket and trousers was walking towards the crowd from the direction of the library. The next, he was taking aim with the hunting rifle in his hands.

BANG!

A shot went off. Screams. Shouts of panic.

BANG! Another.

People began to flee in every direction. Banners and placards fell to the ground, abandoned in the mad dash to take cover. Neither looking nor knowing where they were going, people collided with each other, shoving their fellow protesters out of the way, no thought in their minds other than their own self-preservation.

BANG! BANG!

The gunman fired indiscriminately into the fleeing scrum, seemingly intent on causing as much carnage in as short a time as possible.

Anna, who'd ducked behind a car parked at the nearest kerb when the shooting started, raised her head cautiously, searching in vain for a glimpse of Farah. People continued to scatter, many of them hurrying through the gates towards the main building, others fleeing downhill in the direction of Byres Road. Up ahead, just twenty-five metres away from her, the gunman continued to let off a shot every now and then, though the initial flurry of activity had subsided, and he now seemed content merely to fire the occasional reminder as to his presence. From her vantage point, Anna couldn't see any bodies on the ground, which was a relief. If he *had* managed to hit anyone, it evidently hadn't been fatal. Not immediately, at any rate.

As she continued to shelter behind the car, a hand suddenly landed on her shoulder. Stifling a scream, she turned to find none other than Robert Leopold crouching behind her, his normally complacent features drawn into a mask of panic.

'What are you—' she whispered.

'Shh!' He put a finger to his mouth. 'Not a sound!'

She watched as he half-crawled towards the row of university-owned townhouses behind them and scrambled up the steps leading to the entrance to Number 4, using the low wall as cover. Reaching behind him, he opened the door, then beckoned insistently to her.

She didn't move.

'Get in here, you idiot!' he hissed.

Anna hesitated for a moment. She glanced back at the gunman, now standing in the middle of the deserted road, looking this way and that. Then, as his head turned in the direction of the main building, she seized her chance and, crouching low, scuttled over to join Leopold. He ushered her inside, shutting the door behind them as quietly as possible.

An eerie silence hung over the lobby of the one-time townhouse, with its ornate, tiled flooring, wood-panelled walls and blocked-off fireplace. As Leopold paced up and down, opening the doors to various rooms and peering inside each in turn, Anna sank to the ground with her back against the wall, trying to control her staccato breathing.

'Fuck, fuck, fuck,' she whispered to herself, head in her hands.

From the end of the hallway, Leopold turned to look at her.

'Did you see who it was?'

Anna, unable to make head or tail of the question in her panic-stricken state, just stared at him blankly.

'The gunman,' he snapped impatiently. 'Did you recognise him?'

Anna shook her head. 'I've no idea. I didn't get a clear look at his face.'

'Well, whoever he is, he's evidently psychotic.' There was more than a hint of disgust in Leopold's voice.

Having completed his recce of the various rooms, he headed back down the hallway towards her.

'Come on. We'll hide in here till it's safe.'

She stared up at him helplessly, unable to make her muscles do her mind's bidding.

Grunting in exasperation, he hauled her roughly to her feet, then half-dragged her through to the classroom at the back of the building. He steered her inside and shut the door behind them. Then, as she stood helplessly in the centre of the room, the orderly desks and chairs that surrounded her in stark contrast to the chaos that had unfolded outside just moments earlier, he strode over to the window and began to tug the heavy drapes shut.

Anna watched him warily, still far from ready to wholeheartedly trust him, in spite of what her eyes were telling her. Having finished closing the drapes, he crossed to the nearest desk and leant against it, winded from the effort. He caught her looking at him and met her eyes. For a moment, they just faced each other in silence. Then . . .

'What the hell are you even *doing* here?' Leopold snapped.

She was so taken aback by the question, she didn't know what to say.

'You're supposed to be on suspension. Why are you here, at this of all times?'

'As it *happens*,' said Anna, bridling, 'I came to lend my striking colleagues some support.'

Leopold snorted, showing just what he thought of *that* justification.

'I might ask the same of you,' Anna went on. 'What were *you* doing out and about at eleven in the morning? Come to film some visual material for your upcoming exposé on radical, far-left saboteurs, did you?'

Leopold scoffed loudly. 'Suppose I should have known better than to expect rationality from a woman in a crisis!'

She noticed he hadn't actually answered her question, then wondered why the hell they were arguing about this.

Seemingly concluding that there was no hope of their having a sensible conversation, Leopold threw up his hands and moved over to the other side of the room, as if intent on putting as much distance between them as possible, lest her feminine irrationality rub off on him.

As silence once more descended, Anna slipped her phone out of her pocket and began to tap the screen. She desperately wanted to contact Farah to make sure she was all right. She was halfway through composing a text when it occurred to her that Farah might not have silenced her phone. If she was hiding somewhere nearby, the last thing Anna wanted was to lead the shooter right to her.

Should she call the police instead? On one level, it hardly seemed worth the effort. They'd probably been so inundated by calls about the incident by now that all she'd be achieving was to clog the lines with redundant information. Unless, that was, everyone else was making the same assumption as her.

She should probably call them.

She was on the verge of doing just that when she heard something that caused her to stop dead, her heart lurching into her chest.

The sound of the front door groaning open.

She and Leopold both remained stock still, listening. Then, a few seconds later, the sound that followed caused the very marrow in Anna's bones to freeze: slow, heavy footsteps, advancing across the tiled foyer towards them.

She looked at Leopold. Their eyes met. He began a half-hearted, helpless shrug.

Then, the classroom door swung open.

56

The first thing they both saw was the muzzle of the rifle, slowly extending through the doorway. It was followed by the gun-barrel and then finally the gunman himself, training his weapon on them as he stepped into the room. Taking one hand off the gun, he leant behind himself and pushed the door shut.

He looked to be in his late teens or early twenties; thin and sallow-skinned, with drawn-in cheeks and hollow eye-sockets. He was wearing a few days' worth of beard growth, as dark and stringy as the stuff on his head. His most striking feature were his black, piercing eyes, which shone with an almost feral light.

Strangely enough, the first thought to enter Anna's head was that this was a set-up – that Leopold had deliberately brought her here to ensure she'd be a sitting duck. Those thoughts didn't last long, though. One swift glance in Leopold's direction told her that he was as terror-stricken as her.

The gunman came to a standstill a couple of metres away from them, continuing to train his rifle on them. For several seconds, the only sound was that of his breathing as he slowly and deliberately inhaled and exhaled through his nostrils. Then, he lowered the rifle and smiled.

'Well, well. The famous Professor Leopold, in person. It's an honour, sir.'

He took a couple of steps towards Leopold, his hand outstretched. Leopold merely stared at it.

Seeing that Leopold wasn't going to shake it, the shooter lowered his hand again. He gave another smile, accompanied by a soft chuckle, as if he'd fully expected such a response. He turned his attention to Anna and smirked.

'And you. The man-hating slut whore. Thought you were supposed to have been fired.'

Anna said nothing. She sensed that saying *anything* right now would be a seriously bad idea.

'I suppose there's a certain . . . serendipity to you both being here.'

He had a slight lisp, Anna noticed, giving him an almost serpentine diction. *Ssserendipity.*

'What's your name, son?' Leopold asked tentatively.

The gunman gave him a knowing look, as if Leopold should have known better than to ask.

'Well, we're going to have to call you *something*.'

The gunman shrugged, seemingly accepting this as a valid point. 'In that case, call me . . .' He thought for a moment. 'Elliot.' He smiled to himself again, as if this was some sort of private joke.

Leopold attempted a smile of his own. 'Elliot, then. What do you want from us, Elliot?'

'From her?' Elliot nodded dismissively at Anna. 'Nothing – other than for her to die in a suitably entertaining way.'

Anna clenched her fists by her sides in an attempt to stop her hands from shaking.

'But you, my revered guide and teacher,' Elliot continued, 'for you, I have a task of the utmost importance. But first.' He held out a hand, palm upward. 'Phones.'

Neither of them moved.

'GIMME YOUR PHONES!'

His yell was so sudden, so ear-splitting, that they instantly complied, obediently handing their devices over, then watching as he laid them on the floor, one by one, and smashed them with the butt of his rifle. Then, once more training the weapon on them, he used his hip to shove the nearest table against the door, before perching on it, facing them, rifle laid across his lap.

'There. Now we aren't going to be interrupted.' He smirked at Anna. 'Betcha thought you were clever, didn't you? You and your chad boyfriend, taking down the forces of darkness. 'Cept you didn't know about me, did you? Didn't know about the fourth man.'

He gave a high-pitched giggle that, to Anna, seemed more than slightly involuntary. Far more so than with Eddie McAllister or even James Venable, she was left with the distinct sense that she was dealing with a true lunatic – and one, at that, who'd already shown himself to be utterly indiscriminate when it came to firing on innocent bystanders.

Elliot now turned his attention to Leopold again. 'So here's what's going to happen,' he said breezily, as if they were discussing nothing more consequential than the weather. 'You and me are going to do a little broadcast together.' He affected a mock-whisper. 'I know I'm totally fanboying at the moment, but I've always dreamed of being a guest on your show, and finally I've got my chance.'

'What kind of broadcast?' asked Leopold. He looked and sounded stricken.

'The most important one you'll ever make. You see, I've prepared a list of demands.'

Taking one hand off his rifle, Elliot started to rummage in the inner pocket of his coat.

'I think you'll be fairly amenable to most of them,' he went on. 'After all, you were my single greatest source of inspiration.'

He drew out a crumpled, folded scrap of notepaper and held it out to Leopold.

'Here.' He smiled. 'I won't bite.'

Tentatively, Leopold shuffled forwards. Extending his entire arm and body to avoid getting any closer to Elliot than he absolutely had to, he took the piece of paper, then retreated back to join Anna.

He unfolded the paper and examined the words scrawled on it, lips fluttering slightly as he murmured them aloud. Then he lowered the paper and looked at Elliot, his face ashen.

'I can't read this,' he said.

Elliot shrugged. 'I admit it doesn't quite have your usual eloquence, but I did my best, with all my limitations. We can work on the wording together if you like.'

'No . . . I mean . . . what you're asking for . . . Repealing the laws against rape and sexual assault . . . No education for girls after the age of fifteen . . .

All single females beyond the age of eighteen to be assigned to a male partner . . . It's . . . well, it's monstrous. It'll ruin me.'

Despite the icy terror that consumed her, Anna nonetheless registered the utter absurdity of this statement. Even now, he was thinking of his reputation.

Elliot scoffed. 'Oh, come on. It's what you've always advocated for. Maybe you haven't been *quite* so upfront about it until now, but it's not as if your *true* followers haven't been able to understand the subtext. You'll just be spelling it out a bit more clearly for the hard-of-thinking.'

'Listen to me.' Leopold was practically pleading now. If he'd got down on his hands and knees, he could hardly have cut a more pitiful specimen. 'Whatever you've read into my remarks; whatever hidden meaning you think you've detected – you're wrong. This . . . proclamation you've written – it goes against everything I stand for.'

If the circumstances had been different, Anna would have laughed at this statement. As it was, mirth was the furthest thing from her mind.

'All right, yes,' Leopold continued, 'I may have said some things that were a little on the incendiary side . . . but that was just my attempt to be provocative! All I've ever wanted is to spark healthy, forthright debate. They were just . . . thought experiments, if you like.'

Elliot's expression was one of stony indifference. He didn't seem disappointed to have discovered that his idol was not the ideologue he'd thought – merely irritated by his continuing refusal to cooperate.

'In that case,' he said, 'if you're so devoid of integrity that you'll willingly broadcast lies to your loyal fans, you should have no scruples whatsoever about reading the words I've prepared.'

Leopold continued to stare at him, his skin a sickly grey. 'Wh-what if I don't?' he stammered.

'Then I'll shoot you in the kneecaps,' said Elliot calmly.

Leopold swallowed heavily.

'That'll do for starters. Don't worry – I'll make sure you're still able to *speak*.'

Leopold shook his head in horrified disbelief. 'You're insane,' he murmured.

Elliot raised an eyebrow. 'Am I? Maybe. Or maybe I just see the world more clearly than the sheeple. People like us . . . "radicals", you might say

. . . they love to mock us and dismiss us, but we're the ones who understand what has to be done in order for change to happen . . . and we're willing to *do* it too. Gotta break a few eggs to make an omelette, am I right?' He barked out another sharp, hysterical laugh, rocking back on the table and kicking up his legs.

Anna glanced at Leopold. He met her gaze out of the corner of his eye and gave a tiny, helpless shrug, as if to indicate that he had no choice but to comply.

Anna thought desperately. She'd only had a brief opportunity to glance at the statement over Leopold's shoulder, skimming the first few lines, but she could imagine, only too clearly, how the rest of it would play out. It would be the usual predictable stuff. There would be the demands for laws allowing abortion, divorce, *anything* approaching bodily autonomy for women, to be repealed. Women would be ordered to return barefoot to the kitchens, to be willing and pliant homemakers and baby-incubators, under threat of retributive violence. And she knew there'd be men who, having heard the clarion call, would be more than happy to respond. Men who'd been waiting for a figure of Leopold's standing to say, out loud, the very things they'd whispered in pubs and on message boards for years. This broadcast, if it went out, would be the spark that set off the powder keg of toxic male resentment that had been fermenting for decades, resulting in a wave of anti-woman violence the likes of which had never been seen.

This broadcast could not be allowed to go out. Anna knew the only hope of preventing it was if the police, who must surely be on their way by now, were able to intervene before Leopold made it. That meant she had to play for time, in whatever way she could.

Somehow, against the odds, she managed to find her voice.

'You called yourself the fourth man earlier. Does that mean you and Venable were in cahoots? Did *he* put you up to this?'

Elliot gave a slight shrug, as if it was immaterial. 'He knew about the plan in the vaguest sense. The details were all mine, though. Besides, went and got himself arrested, didn't he? And that was all his own fault. Couldn't keep a clear head.' He tutted softly.

'And do you think, if he hadn't been arrested, that he'd have been standing here alongside you today?'

Elliot glowered. 'What's your point?'

'My point is that, when push came to shove, Venable was happy to dish out orders from behind his keyboard, but he wasn't so keen on leading from the front. And I'll tell you something for nothing: even if he wasn't currently sitting in a prison cell awaiting trial, you'd still be standing up there on your own today.'

'Anna . . .' Leopold whined softly, his voice tight with fear.

Ignoring him, Anna continued to address Elliot. 'Why? Because he sees you as expendable. He *used* you, just like he used McAllister and Zamir. He doesn't care whether you live or die. He sent you out here to do this, knowing it would never bounce back on him.'

'That's *bullshit!*' Elliot roared.

Anna flinched involuntarily, while Leopold jackknifed like he'd just been pistol whipped.

Elliot jumped down off the table. With a couple of quick strides, he was facing Anna, the muzzle of the rifle pushing into her cheek. She felt the residual heat from the recently fired shots stinging her flesh. Stifling a whimper, she shut her eyes and tried to stop herself from trembling.

'Venable was a clown,' Elliot snarled. 'He didn't have the first clue, and whatever he thought, he sure as fuck wasn't using *me.*'

He took a step back, lowering the gun slightly. Anna could feel the indentation it had left on her cheek, as well as the flecks of spittle clinging to her hair.

Elliot smirked. 'He was happy playing in the minor leagues, roughing up random tarts and posting his bullshit manifestos on message boards. He'd *never* have had the vision or the balls to pull off something like this. In a couple of weeks, no one'll remember who he even was. But after today, every cunt on earth's gonna remember *my* name.' He swung round to face Leopold. 'Now record the fucking statement!'

Shaking all over, Leopold clutched the piece of paper, now dog-eared and moist with the sweat from his palms. 'Wh-what am I supposed to record it on?' he stammered. 'You smashed my phone.'

Elliot rolled his eyes. He took his own phone from his pocket and held it out to Leopold.

Leopold stared at it helplessly. 'That . . . that's no good to me. It doesn't have any of my details. The URLs and passwords . . . for my channel and whatnot. They were all stored on there.' He gestured to the shattered remnants of his phone, lying on the floor a few feet away.

Elliot bit his bottom lip, eyes lowering to the floor as he processed what Leopold had told him. This was clearly something he hadn't accounted for. After a long, nerve-racking pause, he raised his eyes to Leopold again.

'Where *do* you have the details?'

'On my computer,' said Leopold. 'At my flat on Bank Street.'

Elliot thought for a moment, then made a snap decision.

'We'll go there, then. We'll get better production values broadcasting from your studio anyway.'

57

They emerged from the classroom and stepped out into the foyer: Leopold first, followed by Anna. Elliot was just behind her, clutching her by the scruff of the neck, the rifle once more pressing into the side of her face. Slowly, they made their way across the floor until they came to the front door. There, they halted.

'All right!' Elliot bellowed. 'We're coming out! If anyone tries to get in our way, I'll shoot this cunt bitch in the throat!'

There was no response.

Leopold looked to Elliot for instruction. He gave a curt nod. Leopold reached for the door handle.

They stepped out into the daylight, moving as a single, multi-limbed entity, shuffling a few centimetres at a time, Leopold with his arms raised. At first, Anna, blinking against the harsh sunlight after so long spent in the gloom of the classroom, could see nobody. However, as they slowly made their way down the steps to the pavement, she noticed that the mouth of the terrace had been cordoned off with a strip of police tape. A couple of stricken-looking uniformed officers were half-crouching behind the large corner pillar around which the tape had been wound. She spotted a couple more stationed behind a car on the other side of the main road.

Where are they all? she wondered. Surely they'd have called in the big guns – the armed response unit, anti-terror officers and the like. They'd have had time to get here by *now*, wouldn't they?

'Which way?' Elliot said to Leopold.

'Left,' said Leopold.

'Get a move on, then.'

They set off, slowly shuffling up the pavement towards the main road. The uniformed officers watched their every move, but, to Anna's relief, made no attempt to intervene. The outside world was as eerily silent as the classroom had been.

They reached the main road and began to make their way up the last forty metres or so before the top of the hill, after which it would be a straight run downhill to Bank Street. They'd just passed the set of traffic lights outside the university's main gate when a woman stepped into view barely ten metres in front of them.

'Going somewhere, ya piece of shit?' she roared.

Kez Dixon had put her top back on since Anna had last seen her, but the effect of coming face to face with her on the otherwise deserted pavement would have been no less incongruous had she been stark naked. She stood facing them, feet planted wide apart, hands on hips.

Elliot, who'd brought all three of them to an unceremonious halt the moment Kez stepped in front of them, jabbed the muzzle of his rifle hard into Anna's neck, making her wince. She stared at Kez in panicked disbelief. *Please,* she thought, *don't do this.*

'Get the fuck out of my way, slut!' Elliot yelled.

'Or what?' Kez bellowed back. 'Gonnae shoot me? Huh? Big, brave man, hiding behind a woman with yer pop-gun.'

'Kez,' Anna stammered, trying to project her voice as much as she could, 'just do as he says.'

'Oh yeah, you'd like that, wouldn't you?' Kez's response was directed at Elliot rather than Anna. 'For me to cower in terror in the face of your incredible manliness; this . . .' – she gestured to him – '. . . awe-inspiring display of testosterone! Well, I ain't scared of you, ya wee turd.'

Elliot was growing increasingly frantic. His grip on Anna's collar tightened. 'I'll do it!' he ranted. 'I'll fucking kill her!'

'Yeah, and that'd really show the world what a brave boy you are, wouldn't it? Shooting a defenceless hostage who can't even fight back. Tell ya what.' Kez thumped her chest and spread both hands in a come-hither gesture. 'Ya wannae shoot someone? Shoot me. I'm right here for the taking. Come on, big man!'

The pressure on Anna's neck eased somewhat. She sensed that Elliot was giving serious consideration to Kez's invitation.

'Crazy bitch . . .' Leopold muttered. 'Going to get us all killed . . .'

'What are you waiting for?' Kez demanded. 'Too feart, are ya?'

Elliot made a snap decision. In what felt like a split second, the muzzle left Anna's cheek, and he wrapped his free arm round her throat and angled his rifle at Kez, balancing it on Anna's shoulder.

Just then, another shout went up, this one from the main gate.

'What're ya picking on *her* for?'

It was one of the other women from the meeting at the Dewar – the one with the peroxide blonde hair who'd objected to the idea of a SlutWalk. She stood in the middle of the gateway, arms folded, legs apart like Kez's.

'I'm a fucking rad fem lesbo dyke who thinks men like you should be castrated at birth. Surely I'm a *way* juicier target?'

Elliot swung Anna round towards the gatehouse, now pointing his rifle at this fresh target. Anna felt his hot, rapid breath in her ear, and the tremble of his hand on her collar.

Another voice rang out.

'Or you could shoot me!'

Elliot swung Anna round again, this time towards the slope up to the library, where the young woman from the meeting at the Dewar with the Sinéad O'Connor haircut now stood.

'I'm a rabid skank whore who'll fuck anything that moves. Don't *I* need to be punished?'

'Jesus *Christ*!' Leopold wailed, clearly convinced he was going to die here.

'Oi!'

It was Kez again, still blocking their route to Bank Street.

'Eyes on the prize, wee knob. I'm the one you want. Take yer best pop at me.'

Anna glanced at the two nearest police officers, both of whom looked like they were on the verge of shitting themselves.

'Shoot *me*!'

'No, *me*!'

Another shout went up, then another. On all four sides, women from Kez's group were emerging from cover to challenge the gunman. There were at least eight of them now, all shouting at him, belittling him, daring him to shoot. Elliot shook uncontrollably, not knowing where to look or point his gun. Among the faces, Anna spotted Grace Dunphy, her hair tied back to reveal her battle-scarred features, yelling with as much fervour as anyone else.

As the cacophony of voices continued to bombard them, Kez's voice rose above the fray, a rich, full-throated roar:

'Are we gonnae stand here all day, ya worm-dicked little beta cuck, or are ye gonnae do me?' She paused for a moment, then added, in a softer, more intimate voice, 'Or can ye no get it up?'

With a sudden bellow of rage, Elliot flung Anna to the ground. Gripping the rifle in both hands, he took aim and fired off a shot. Anna, lying on the tarmac, hands shielding her head, saw Kez go down. At the same instant, Leopold let out a howl of terror and took off in an ungainly, waddling run, fleeing down the hill.

As Kez lay groaning on the ground, clutching her shoulder, Elliot stopped to reload his rifle. But before he could do so, there came a great trampling of feet, and then, a second later, what seemed like an entire army of women was upon him, dragging him to the ground, punching, kicking and otherwise pummelling him. One of them threw the rifle out of reach before joining in the collective assault. As Anna crawled away from the fracas on her elbows, the four police officers, who, collectively, had been about as useful as a chocolate fireguard until now, finally sprang into action, hurrying forward to seize Elliot, probably as much to prevent the women from beating him to death as anything else.

Anna, still on the ground, looked across to Kez, now being tended to by the Sinéad O'Connor lookalike. She raised her uninjured arm and gave Anna a weak but defiant thumbs-up. Anna managed to acknowledge it with a dazed nod.

As the officers hauled a severely bruised and bloodied Elliot to his feet and began to march him towards the gatehouse, while simultaneously attempting to shield him from the mob of vengeful women, Anna heard the sound of hurried, approaching footsteps. She turned to see Vasilico sprinting up the hill towards her, the tails of his coat flying behind him. She dragged herself to her feet as he reached the top and faced her, breathless.

'I got here as soon as I heard,' he said, between gasps. 'A bomb threat . . . in the city centre. Armed . . . response unit . . . Oh, Jesus, Anna. Thank fuck you're OK.'

And with that, he enveloped her in his arms, clutching her tight, pressing her face to his chest.

At first, her natural instinct was to try to break free. But it only lasted for a moment before she surrendered and allowed him to hold her.

A CHANGE IS GONNA COME

58

Later, after the hue and cry had died down, Anna got a more detailed explanation from Vasilico as to why the police had been so slow to respond to the shootings. Apparently, less than twenty minutes before the gunman had opened fire outside the university gates, they'd received a credible terrorist threat targeting a hotel in the centre of Glasgow. The armed response unit and a sizeable percentage of the city's police force were immediately deployed to the location, where an explosive device was indeed discovered. It was disarmed without incident, but the diversion did its job, allowing the gunman free rein to wreak havoc on the university campus.

All told, the damage would have been a lot worse had he not been such a lousy shot. His weapon – established to have been stolen from his cousin, a farm labourer – ultimately put six people in hospital, more by luck than by any skill on his part. Of these, only one was kept in for more than twenty-four hours. The rest were discharged the same day – among them Kez Dixon, who suffered nothing worse than a grazed shoulder. Farah, whom Anna caught up with later that day, was unharmed, though, like everyone else involved, seriously shaken up. She and several of the other protesters had made it to the Dewar Postgraduate Club and barricaded themselves inside the seminar room while the gunman continued his rampage outside.

His real name, it turned out, was Denis Walsh, a former sociology student at the university who'd dropped out the previous year after growing disillusioned by what he described to his advisor of studies as the course's 'far-left, anti-male agenda'. The name 'Elliot', presumably, was a reference to the terrorist responsible for the murders of several people in a misogyny-fuelled attack in California in 2014. Remnants of more than two dozen X-Chat conversations between El Duce and an individual calling himself 'MinassianFan4Ever', recovered by the Cybercrime team in cooperation with Jen Brinkley, confirmed Walsh's account to Anna that Venable had cultivated him separately from his other two lackeys, effectively treating him as a side project to be deployed in the event that things with Zamir and McAllister fell apart. So far, no evidence had been uncovered that Venable had groomed any further 'sleeper agents' – but then, so much data had been destroyed before the plug was pulled on his computer that it was impossible to know with any certainty. Venable himself remained tight-lipped on the subject. Vasilico, mindful of how they'd allowed themselves to believe the matter was fully resolved once before, only to be proven disastrously wrong, vowed that the Specialist Crime Unit would most assuredly not be relaxing its guard *this* time.

Anna chose not to attend Walsh's interview. Vasilico did offer her the opportunity to sit in, but she turned it down. She never wanted to see him again.

A week later, Anna and Zoe sat side by side on a bench overlooking the children's play area in Thornwood Park, watching Jack tearing around with a handful of other children. It was perishing cold, the temperature having plummeted over the last few days, but Jack didn't seem to mind. Bundled up in his mittens and duffle coat, his cheeks aglow with a combination of the cold and his own enthusiasm, he slid down to the bottom of the slide, then turned to grin proudly at his two minders.

Zoe clapped enthusiastically, while Anna gave a more reserved smile and a nod. They watched him for another minute or so, before Anna broke the silence.

'D'you reckon he's doing OK?'

Zoe pondered the question, then gave an unconcerned shrug.

'I reckon he's doing just grand,' she said.

She paused for a moment, then turned to look at Anna.

'And you? How are *you* doing?'

Anna considered long and hard how to respond. It wasn't a question that came with a nice, easy, ready-made answer. She'd only had two nightmares since the shootings, and she was managing to venture out of the house without constantly fearing being recognised for the wrong reasons. Both of these, on balance, she'd decided to chalk up as wins. They were still getting the odd dirty phone call to the landline – once every couple of days on average – but they now seemed more pathetic than threatening.

On the other hand, she'd always fiercely guarded her privacy, and it was impossible to ignore the fact that that had been unceremoniously wrenched away from her and that, now that the proverbial genie was out of the bottle, there was no longer any way of putting it back in. She also had no way of knowing just how wide-reaching the consequences of her 'exposure' would be. What, for example, might it mean for her future job prospects, regardless of the outcome of the hearing? Would any prospective employer want to bring themselves into disrepute by association?

Perhaps most destructively of all, however, were the overpowering feelings of shame that now consumed her attitude towards her own body. Since the pictures had leaked, she'd had to actively avoid catching sight of herself in the mirror when she stepped out of the shower each morning. For someone who'd always been reasonably comfortable in her own skin (the wish that she was half a head taller notwithstanding), this was an unfamiliar and deeply unpleasant sensation, and it was difficult to see any light at the end of the tunnel, or to shake the fear that, as in so many other respects, things would never be the same again.

'I'm managing,' she said eventually.

They fell into silence again. Jack and his friends had now made it over to the climbing frame and were having a competition to see how high they could climb.

'So listen,' Zoe piped up, as Anna continued to watch him, 'there's something I need tae tell ye.'

Something about the tone of her voice caused Anna's senses to prick up. She turned to look at Zoe, twisting round on the bench to give her her full attention.

'Me 'n' Sal have decided, we're gonnae get a place the gether.'

It came out in a rush, as if she'd been holding it in for a while – which, it occurred to Anna, was, in all likelihood, exactly what she *had* been doing.

'I know we've no known each other all that long,' Zoe went on, only marginally less breathlessly, 'and I know it's too soon tae say I'm definitely gonnae spend the rest of ma days wi her, but . . .' She shrugged almost sheepishly. 'But I feel like I need tae make a proper go of this – no just treat it like some teenage fling where we see each other the odd evening and on weekends. I . . . well, I've no felt this way about someone. No since Carol.'

Anna smiled gently. In truth, she'd been half-anticipating some sort of announcement along these lines for a while – in fact, ever since Zoe had first brought Sal home with her, their hands in each other's back pockets like it was the most normal thing in the world to be doing. But it still came as a shock all the same. No matter how much you prepared yourself for these massive, life-altering changes, you were never *truly* ready.

'I don't mean I'm packing my bags right away or anything,' Zoe added quickly. 'It's still early doors. We need tae find a flat first, for one thing. But I figured I oughta say something now 'stead of dropping it in yer lap once it's a done deal, cos, obviously, I know it's gonnae mean changes.'

She twisted uncomfortably, clearly racked by guilt over her decision.

'Zoe . . .' Anna began.

'I mean, I'm no gonnae disappear or anything. I'll make sure, wherever we end up, it's somewhere close by, and I'll be round all the time, and whenever ye want me tae babysit Jacko, ye know all's ye have tae do is pick up the phone and—'

Anna took Zoe's hand in hers, cutting her off.

'I think that's amazing news. I'm so pleased for you.'

'Really?' Zoe's response was one of relief tinged with lingering disbelief. 'Ye're sure?' She exhaled an exaggerated breath. 'Aw, thank fuck, cos see, it's been chewing me up for *weeks* now. I was gonnae say earlier, only ye had all sorts of stuff of yer own going on and it didnae seem right, and . . .'

She stopped, finally running out of breath, and gazed at Anna, a wild, almost desperate look in her eyes.

'Ye're sure it's OK?'

'I'm sure,' said Anna firmly.

'Good, cos I think . . .' Zoe hesitated, then added tentatively, 'I think mibby I love her.'

Anna drank this in. She knew how badly Zoe had been hurt in the past – that to let another person into her life like this, for anything more than a consequence-free fling, was a seriously massive deal for her.

'Plus,' Zoe added, with the inklings of a sheepish smile, 'she's got *the* most fantastic arse.'

I know, Anna almost replied, *I've seen it.* Instead, she simply said, 'She's certainly a high quality woman.'

Then, to spare her own blushes, she turned back to the climbing frame, where Jack and his pals were still in full flow with their competition.

'Careful, Jack!' she called, her voice catching with the emotion of it all. 'Not so high now!'

'There's something else,' said Zoe, after they'd settled into silence again for a couple of minutes. 'I'm gonnae go back tae uni.'

'You?!' exclaimed Anna in disbelief, before she could stop herself.

'I know, I know,' said Zoe, unoffended by Anna's reaction, 'prob'ly no whit ye had on yer bingo card for me. But it's something I've been thinking about for a while as well. I'm . . .' She gave an exaggerated grimace. 'Well, we both know neither of us is getting any younger. I fancy I'm a *wee* bit too old tae still be trying tae figure oot whit I wannae be when I grow up. Point is, I'm gonnae be thirty-eight in a coupla weeks. I'm closer tae seventy than I am tae zero. And let's face it, I'm no exactly daein' anything productive wi that Media Studies degree.'

'So what are you going to do?' Anna asked, still struggling to overcome her surprise.

'Something wi kids.' Zoe's answer was unequivocal. 'I dunno if that's nursery or daycare or teaching or whit have ye . . . but definitely something wi kids.'

Anna considered this. It wasn't at all what she'd anticipated, but, in so many respects, it made total sense.

'I get that,' she said. 'I mean, I've seen the way you are with Jack – and with Jen's two. No one can say you aren't a natural.'

Zoe waved a hand, mock-bashful. 'Ah, g'wan. That's only cos ma ain mental age is, like, five.'

Anna smiled. As much of an inevitable blow as all this was, she nonetheless found that her own mood had lifted considerably by virtue of sharing in her friend's happiness.

Zoe glanced over at Jack, who, having tired of the climbing frame, was now standing on the roundabout, loudly entreating the other children to give him a push. She looked back at Anna.

'Only bit I'm no looking forward tae is how's I'm gonnae break it tae Jack.'

Anna took Zoe's hand in hers and squeezed it. 'We'll tell him together. 'Sides, like you said, it's not like you'll be moving to the other side of the world.'

'Seriously, doll,' said Zoe, her deep eyes gazing into Anna's, 'thanks. For, like, *everything*. All the stuff ye've done for me . . . I'm no sure I'll ever be able tae pay it back.'

Anna snorted. 'Come off it, Zo. We both know it's not exactly been a one-way street.'

'I mean it,' Zoe insisted. 'You were there for me when I was in my worst place. You pulled me back outta that . . . pit.' Her eyes crinkled, tears threatening. 'You're the best pal a lassie could ask for.'

Anna felt tears of her own beginning to well. 'I know you are,' she managed to say, 'but what am *I*?'

Zoe choked a laugh. 'Cheeky cow!' she said, batting Anna's arm playfully.

Their eyes met. For a moment, they said nothing. Then, Anna gave a squeal of pure joy and enveloped Zoe in a hug. They remained like that for over a minute before releasing one another.

'I'm made up for you, pal,' Anna said, as they faced each other once more. 'You deserve every happiness.'

'I know,' said Zoe earnestly. 'And so do *you*. Don't forget that.'

I'm trying, Anna thought.

59

Vasilico was waiting for her at the top of the steps by the Great Western Bridge. It seemed, by unspoken consensus, to have become their designated meeting place – the closest thing to neutral territory for either of them.

'Hi,' he said, as she drew level with him.

'Hey,' replied Anna.

They stood there, facing one another awkwardly, hands jammed into the pockets of their coats.

It was Vasilico who finally broke the silence.

'So I thought you'd want to know, we've finished combing through Venable and Walsh's electronic devices.'

'And?' said Anna.

'Nothing further to report in the case of the former, but the latter turned up some unexpected gems.'

'Such as?'

'Well, for a start, he was far less conscientious than Venable about covering his tracks. His chat logs made for some *very* interesting reading. Turns out he was in contact with a whole cavalcade of similarly-minded reprobates from various countries. There was a lot of trading tactics with one another, along with hints about similar operations being planned in New York and Madrid, to name just a couple. Naturally, that info has been passed on to the relevant authorities in their respective jurisdictions. Arrests should be imminent, if not already underway.'

He smiled encouragingly, having evidently noticed Anna's palpable lack of an attempt to even feign enthusiasm. 'It's a good result. Far better than we had any right to hope for. We took out one terrorist cell, and several others are on their way to being dismantled. Thanks, in no small part, to you.'

Anna managed a stiff smile, though she couldn't help but be reminded of a multi-headed hydra: cut off one, and another dozen would pop up in its place. But she kept her thoughts to herself. Frankly, it was exhausting always being the designated killjoy.

'You know,' she said, 'you could have told me this over the phone.'

'I know,' said Vasilico. 'But I wanted to see you.' He paused, then added hopefully, 'And I'd thought, perhaps, the feeling might be mutual?' He smiled at her encouragingly.

'Of course,' she said. But it sounded hollow and unconvincing.

Vasilico's smile faded. They remained standing there, each lost in their own thoughts. After a few moments, Vasilico broke the silence again.

'Can we . . . ?'

Anna stirred. 'Hmm?'

Vasilico rubbed the back of his neck awkwardly. 'What I mean is . . .' He let his arms fall heavily to his sides. Sighed.

'Where do we stand – you and me? I need to know, one way or another. That night we spent together was . . . incredible . . . and I'd hate to think it was destined to forever be a one-off. I mean, I like you, and I *think* you like *me*. At least, you seemed to, that night. What I'm trying to say is, I'd really like to give this a go, if it's what *you* want as well.'

He fell silent, gazing at her hopefully, the remnants of an encouraging smile on his face.

She didn't respond immediately, though her heart had sunk as she listened to him. She'd been both anticipating and dreading this conversation for some time – anticipating because she knew they had unfinished business, dreading because . . .

'It's difficult,' she said finally.

'It doesn't have to be,' said Vasilico. 'I mean, I know we don't exactly share the same interests – and yes, the height difference is . . . absurd, to put it mildly. But whatever differences we have, we can compromise or work around them or . . .' He raised his hands in an open-palmed shrug. 'What I'm saying is, it's only difficult if we choose to make it so.'

'But it *is*.'

Anna's voice cracked with emotion as she spoke. Vasilico looked at her with a questioning frown. When she next spoke, she managed, with some difficulty, to make her voice sound more controlled.

'And not because it's something I'm choosing or because we don't vote for the same political parties or share the same views on criminal justice or any of those other things.'

She sighed unhappily and decided to lay her cards on the table.

'Any time I think about the two of us making love, I'm immediately taken back to that recording of us.'

Vasilico's expression softened into one of profound sympathy. She saw it, and knew he got it.

'For me,' she went on, 'the prospect of . . . intimacy with another person anytime soon is fraught, to say the least. With you and me, it takes on a whole other level of complication.' Her voice fractured once again. 'And I hate that they've taken that from us. I do. I hate it. But I can't divorce myself from how it makes me feel.'

She gazed up at him sadly. 'I can't be your lover, Paul. At least,' she added, 'not now. Not yet. In time, maybe . . .' She trailed off.

Vasilico nodded sadly. 'I understand. I mean, it's different for me and . . . and I'm not going to pretend I like it. But I understand.'

'Thank you.' Anna's voice was almost a whisper.

She doubted he had any idea how much this meant to her – that he was willing to accept what she was telling him without embarking on a protracted campaign to change her mind. She felt her insides unclenching as the tension dissipated.

'And whatever you need,' Vasilico went on – 'time, space, whatever – you can have it. And hopefully, at some point . . .'

He trailed off. He was silent for a moment, then continued, 'But whatever you decide . . . and however long it takes . . .' He looked down at her with a gentle smile. 'Promise me we won't lose touch again.'

She gazed back up at him, returning the smile.

'I promise.'

She let the moment pass, then added, a touch slyly, 'Besides, I seem to remember it being *you* who wouldn't return *my* calls.'

'Oh!' exclaimed Vasilico, with exaggerated indignation. 'So that's how it's going to be, is it? Didn't think you'd be *this* adept at holding a grudge!'

'Haven't you heard?' Anna was smiling now. 'Hell hath no fury like a woman scorned.'

Vasilico threw back his head and laughed long and deeply. And then Anna laughed too – partly with relief, yes, but also with genuine pleasure, for the first time in as long as she could remember. They drew a few odd looks from the pedestrians passing them by in either direction, but if either of them noticed, they didn't let it stop them.

60

That afternoon, Anna headed into the university. This time, it was at the invitation of Fraser Taggart, who'd called that morning to summon her to his office for 3 p.m. As she headed through the Hutcheson Building, she acknowledged the greetings from the handful of colleagues she passed, her steps buoyed by their hushed declarations of support.

She'd attended her disciplinary hearing the previous Thursday. Still deeply shaken by her near-death experience just days earlier, her mind had only been half there, and she'd let her union rep do all the talking. She didn't have much of a feel for what had been said by either party, what defence – if any – had been mounted on her behalf, and a part of her still didn't especially care.

The hearing itself had taken place in the comparatively grander environs of the main building. As such, this was her first time setting foot in her own building since Fraser had unceremoniously ordered her home three weeks ago, and the effect was oddly surreal – like stepping into another reality. She felt unexpectedly light of head and of step as she headed down the corridor to Fraser's office and knocked.

'Come in!'

She opened the door and stepped inside. Fraser rose from behind his desk, a genial smile on his lips.

'Anna. Welcome, welcome. Have a seat.'

She did so, less because she particularly wanted to than because she suspected things would go a lot quicker this way.

'It may interest you to know,' said Fraser, once he'd resumed his seat, 'that Professor Leopold is no longer employed by the university.'

'Oh,' said Anna, not sure what else to say to this news.

'Yes. Something about taking time out to focus on his self-care. In truth, I didn't particularly understand his reasoning, but . . .' He shrugged. 'Needless to say, I'm sorely disappointed by his decision, though I doubt you're of a similar mind yourself.'

Anna said nothing. In truth, she didn't really know *how* to feel. A few weeks ago, she'd have regarded this as a sizeable victory. Now, though . . .

She'd noticed, the other day, that Leopold had deactivated his YouTube channel and taken down his podcast. Perhaps his own culpability in radicalising and engendering resentment in a generation of young men had finally caught up with him. To Anna, though, it couldn't help but feel as if, confronted by the monster he himself had created, he'd preferred to cover his tracks, evading all responsibility for the damage he'd caused.

Plus ça change.

'Well,' said Fraser, when it became clear Anna wasn't going to say anything, 'I suppose we should turn to the matter at hand. That, er, unfortunate business with the, um, pictures.'

He cleared his throat noisily, attempting to cover his embarrassment.

'I'm pleased to report that the investigation has concluded satisfactorily and both myself and the Head of College are on the same page as to the way forward. Ahem . . . in light of everything that's transpired . . . the unfortunate business to which you've been subjected and whatnot . . . we've taken the decision to issue you with a written warning, to remain on your employment record for the next nine months, and to take no further action beyond that. You're free to resume your duties with immediate effect.'

He smiled hopefully, clearly anticipating a positive response from Anna. Instead, she said nothing. She simply sat there, hands folded on top of her satchel, lying in her lap, gazing at the crack in the wall behind him. She felt . . . nothing. Neither relieved nor vindicated. Just . . . nothing.

Eventually, realising he was going to get nothing from her other than silence, Fraser opted to plough on as if he hadn't noticed. Opening one of his desk drawers, he took out an envelope and slid it across to her.

'Erm, this letter sets out the decision in writing, and you are, of course, free to peruse it at your leisure – though I don't expect you'll find it contains anything much beyond what I've already told you.'

Anna took the envelope wordlessly and slipped it into her satchel without even looking at it.

His discomfort evidently growing, Fraser cleared his throat again. 'Yes, well, I'm glad this could all be resolved with a minimum of drama and acrimony. You're a much-valued colleague and there's absolutely nothing worse, for all of us, than to have this . . . unpleasantness hanging over us like a cloud.'

He'd now taken to rearranging the stationery on his desk to give his hands something to do.

'Of course, I'm not suggesting the discomfort *you* experienced wasn't an order of magnitude more severe than that to which the rest of us were subjected. But still, we're . . . well, we're like a family, really, I suppose. And families are there for each other through thick and thin. An attack on one of us is an attack on us all and . . . well, what I'm saying is we're *here* for you, Anna,' he insisted forcefully. 'Whatever you need. Any time. Any way.'

He fell into awkward silence, gazing across the desk at her hopefully, his rictus smile and wincing eyes all but pleading with her to dig him out of this hole.

Anna inhaled deeply through her nostrils and out through her mouth, taking her time before she spoke.

'Fraser,' she said, 'I've heard a lot of hot air in my time, but this absolutely takes the biscuit. You speak of families. Of people being there for each other. Well, I didn't feel like anyone was there for *me* when I needed them most.

'I'm not talking about my colleagues,' she quickly clarified; 'the lecturers, the teaching associates, the clerical staff – all the people who strive every day to go the extra mile with limited time and resources and are paid a pittance for the work they do. I never doubted they were on my side. I'm talking about the university itself: the senior management, the Principal, the Head of College – and *you*, Fraser.'

Fraser's Adam's apple bobbed as he swallowed heavily, his expression like that of a deer staring down the barrel of a rifle.

'You tried to make out that I was mentally ill – that I'd done the things I was accused of in a fit of mania. You weaponised my own mind against me. You treated me like a criminal and an embarrassment and left me to fend for myself when what I needed, more than anything, was for my employer to have my back. So no, I *don't* feel supported, and I most assuredly don't feel valued.'

Throughout this speech, Fraser's features had grown progressively more ashen. He stared back at her, shocked into silence. He watched her helplessly as she got to her feet, lifting her satchel with her.

'I suppose I ought to thank you for one thing: for making this easy for me. If you'd actually expressed any remorse for your part in all of this, I might have had second thoughts. But instead, you've helped me clarify that this is the right thing to do.'

As she finished speaking, she produced an envelope of her own and placed it on the desk. Fraser gazed down at it, at the words 'DR FRASER TAGGART – HEAD OF SCHOOL', then lifted his head and looked up at her.

'What . . . what is this?' he said, even though the answer was obvious.

'My resignation,' said Anna.

Acknowledgements

This book went from an idea to a completed manuscript so quickly a part of me still can't quite believe it's really done and dusted. Compared to some of the 'difficult births' I've experienced in the past, the whole journey, from beginning to end, was remarkably trouble-free, and the version you've just read remains shockingly close to the first draft. But any good book requires an editor to turn it into a great one, and this one wouldn't be what it is without Suze Clarke-Morris's eagle eye and sharp narrative instincts. It's also, in no small part, thanks to her that Anna continues to strive to be a better mother, even if her efforts have, so far, had mixed success at best.

Thanks also to Neil Snowden, who helped me figure out some of the knottier issues at the plotting stage, and Tim Barber for once again delivering a stunning, eye-catching cover.

Researching the various male supremacist movements was something of a grim eye-opener for me, and I spent far more time than I care to dwell on immersing myself in the Manosphere and the minds of its adherents. Be in no doubt, what's depicted in this novel is merely the tip of a decidedly ugly iceberg. As such, I'm grateful to the various journalists, academics and content creators who've dedicated themselves to exposing and debunking the views of the poisonous individuals on whom Robert Leopold and his acolytes are modelled. I want to give a particular shout-out to Münecat (youtube.com/@munecat) and Emma Thorne (youtube.com/ @EmmaThorneVideos), whose videos tackled this thoroughly grim subject with both insight and humour, making my task just a little more palatable.

It was through Emma's videos on the pickup artist industry that I encountered and promptly became obsessed with the phrase 'high quality woman' – one which I intend to insert into as many conversations as possible from hereon out.

A massive, super-sized thank you to my ARC team for their considered feedback and for helping me to squelch those last remaining typos: Anne Simpson, Bev Dodds, Caroline Whitson, Catherine Mackenzie, Charlie Brigden, Daniel Sardella, Luiz Asp, Sarah Kelley and Susan Burns.

Finally, thank you to YOU – yes, YOU – for reading my ramblings and giving Anna a home on your e-reader or bookshelf. It means more to us than you can imagine.

Printed in Great Britain
by Amazon